EMP RESURRECTION

Dark New World: Book 5

JJ HOLDEN
&
HENRY GENE FOSTER

www.jjholdenbooks.com

ISBN: 1546501746
ISBN-13: 978-1546501749

EMP RESURRECTION

- 1 -

0700 HOURS - ZERO DAY +186

CASSY STOOD OUTSIDE her home and once again considered whether to patch the many bullet marks on her walls, scars of several battles since EMPs destroyed the America she had known. First had come Peter and his refugees from White Stag Farms, but despite enslaving Cassy's group of EMP refugees—the Clan, as they now called themselves—Peter had been overthrown with help from some of his own people. Then came raids by cannibals, other survivor groups, and even another enclave, or survivor settlement. All that fighting occurred before she had led the local survivor groups into a confederation of allies, and the area had become safer. For now, anyway. Maybe it really was time to patch the holes. They served as an ugly reminder of even uglier conflicts.

Frank stood beside her quietly, gazing at the wall, too. Finally he said, "Good thing you built our HQ out of sandbags. Other than the windows, it's a tank against small arms. Thinking again about patching the walls?"

Cassy nodded, and fiddled with the rawhide thong that tied her long hair into a ponytail. "It might be time. And they're called earthbags, not sandbags. They'll stop a fifty-caliber round, you know. I think that maybe with the Empire looming to our west and ISNA and their North Korean overlords to our east, we should enjoy this time. It's the first real peace we've had since the lights went out six months ago."

Frank said, "You do know it's an illusion, right? Peace. Safety. Even if you don't count all the wars we fought in other countries, that two hundred years of peace we had at home was a historical anomaly. And if you count our wars in other countries, we've never been at peace for longer than a decade or two."

Cassy pursed her lips, jaw clenched. "It never was two hundred years of peace at home. The Indian wars, the Mexican-American War, the Civil War... We're the most warlike nation in history."

Frank shrugged. "At least since the Romans, maybe more than them. We're a violent civilization, I guess."

"Yes, and those ISNA bastards are finding out the hard way that we're not the soft people their leaders told them we were. But I've seen enough blood to last a lifetime."

"It's the end of the world as we know it," Frank said, nodding. "The Dying Time isn't even over yet and here we are looking to fight not just invaders but other Americans, too."

"All of which is why I don't think reminders like these bullet holes help anyone. I'll see if we have people available to patch these up."

Frank used his crutch to tap the stump where Peter had cut off one foot with an axe to prove a point. "Still itches all the time," he said with a wry grin. "There's one reminder we can't patch up. Anyway, I got word from Ethan, down in the bunker. He says we got radio confirmations from the Confed allies about tonight's meeting. They'll be here in time for the video chat with Taggart. I swear, video conferencing seems like some kind of magic, now."

"It might as well be magic. Once the stuff that still works breaks down, we'll be truly back where we started. The guns will last longer but they'll stop working too. Eventually. It'll be flintlocks and swords again, or maybe longbows and swords, by the time I hit great-grandmother status. How's Taggart doing out there in New Jersey?"

Frank shrugged and sat with a groan of effort on a log that had been set out in front of Cassy's house—the Clan's HQ, as well—to serve as a bench. "He's a colonel now, with the size of his force. Maybe even higher since Ethan last got an update. A few thousand soldiers, mostly ex-military from the Gulf War, the rest guerrillas he's training up from the slaves he's been freeing all over upstate New Jersey."

"Good. The Invader cantonment in New York City will hopefully get real hungry, real soon, without their slaves to farm all that land they stole." She glanced at Frank and saw he was shivering. "I'll let you get back to trying to keep warm, Frank. If you see Michael before I do, tell him to make sure our guards are doubled today. We want a show of force for our visitors. Thanks for the update."

Frank nodded, and then Cassy left to go check up on the work detail at the east pond harvesting cattails. These were long past edible now, but still made great insulating filler for the quilts some in the Clan had begun making. They made good trade goods for more gasifiers from the Falconry, or Lebanon as they used to call that tiny Pennsylvania town. Other survivor groups congregated in the trading center there and it was getting easier for everyone to find what they needed, if they came with suitable goods to trade in return. International trade and high finance had degenerated these days into bartering blankets for generators... Cassy shook her head and walked on.

* * *

Jaz put the last of their remaining supplies back into the covered wagon and shivered. Zipping up the blue quilted jacket she wore over her customary hoodie, she walked to the other side of the wagon where Choony was going through his "packing checklist." It was a morning routine he had developed the very first morning on this horse-drawn journey. He was methodical, no doubt about it. They were well along now, heading steadily south, but she missed the Clan, her family now as she reckoned it. Their mission was more important than her homesickness, she had to remind herself.

Restive now, she decided to prod her companion. "Choon, do we gotta do that checklist thingie, like, every single day? We need to get moving. That one farm we passed on our first day out said it was only like, a few miles ahead now. Why didn't we just keep going?"

Choony looked up, his bright, almond-shaped eyes lighting up when he saw her. They always seemed to do that and she loved seeing it. He replied, "We can't afford to have things bounce away if we have to ride for our lives again. Unless you feel like giving stuff away for free to the next batch of bandits or cannibals that chase us. I'm sure they'd be very grateful." His smile gave away his fake-stern tone of voice.

Jaz grinned at him. Such a cute idiot sometimes. "Yeah, yeah. They'd probably make me their queen and cook you for dinner."

Choony chuckled softly.

"Well," Jaz continued. "I still want to get going. Maybe we can trade some stuff in that enclave, if they're still alive when we get there this time. Too late for the last one."

"No, they couldn't drive away the bandits—but that's

why we have to make sure everything is secure before we move on. It would go faster if you helped…" He raised one eyebrow, a challenge.

"You lie! You'd double-check my double-checks," Jaz said, laughing. "Net zero time saved and lots of time wasted. I'd rather stand here and complain, because I know how much faster you go when I entertain you."

Choony mock-growled at her good-naturedly, then went through the rest of his checklist. She taunted and cajoled him the entire time but it didn't really take long, maybe five minutes. They both knew there wouldn't be much chance to joke around once the wagon got moving for the day. When traveling, you kept your eyes and ears open if you wanted to live, and these days you weren't looking out for state troopers with speeding ticket quotas to meet.

Soon enough they scrambled aboard and the wagon got rolling, Jaz and Choony swaying back and forth on the wooden bench seat. Jaz sat on the right, keeping her rifle next to her, eyes scanning restlessly out to the horizon and back seeking movement or other signs of the living. Lots of people still survived outside the cities, not all of them friendly; other travelers they had encountered told some pretty harrowing tales about what the cities were like now for the few who still lived there.

As the wagon rolled on, the horses' hooves clopping softly in the dirt like a metronome, Jaz let her mind wander back to Clanholme. It truly was her home now, she had decided, a new experience for this former Philly street dweller. The last time she had been at Clanholme, she had shared a lunch with Cassy, the Clan leader, in the HQ, and they had talked. Mostly it had been relaxed give-and-take about business—but before they had finished eating, they had planned the rough outline of this trip all over creation to find other survivor groups willing to join the new

Confederation. She remembered some of their small talk, too. Eventually, they had gotten down to personal matters.

Poor Cassy had her leg in a brace, one of several mementos from a recent battle that finally slaughtered a small army of foreign invaders who had tried to make their home in Confed territory. The Clan and their allies had driven the unwanted settlers out. As they retreated, the 'vaders had burned Adamstown to the ground and killed most of the townspeople. The Confederation got its revenge, but it was not done without some losses. And for Cassy, not without a leg brace and a healing scar on her cheek from a bullet graze. The new scar was not by itself; Cassy's scarred face had become a symbol of Clan toughness, an association that Cassy did nothing to discourage among Clanholme's enemies and allies.

Jaz wondered now whether the graze had healed up yet. She totally hoped so—Cassy had been so nice to her while they talked. Whatever bad blood remained from when Jaz had first met Cassy (and robbed her) was gone, finally. They had even talked about Choony...

"Don't wait too long to decide if you want him," Cassy had said, "or I might make my own move." Which was totally hilarious because Choony was Jaz's age, or maybe twenty-four, and Cassy was totally middle aged, or whatever. At least thirty-five. That made Cassy one of the older people to have survived so far, which made her simply old as far as twenty-year-old Jaz was concerned.

Jaz glanced at Choony for a moment and he caught it, smiled, and nodded to her. She nodded back as a return smile reached her lips, and went back to scanning the horizon for threats. She really didn't need to look at him, though, because she had memorized every line and angle of his face by now. For a second-generation Korean immigrant with more education than experience, and a pacifist

Buddhist on top of that, he had a surprising appeal. But his personality and what was inside made him shine. She had never met anyone like him, not in the tough Philly streets.

But she couldn't help wishing she knew where she wanted to take her friendship with Choony, the hardworking Buddhist pacifist chemical scientist and part-time combat medic, wagoner, ostler and animal-loving veterinarian. She wondered if he ever suffered an identity crisis and made an involuntary little choking sound holding down a laugh. Choony looked over, a question on his face, so she grinned, said "Never mind," and went back to scanning the landscape. Damn. She really needed a distraction.

* * *

Ethan sat in his squeaky chair facing the small computer desk, deep in the Clan's underground bunker. It wasn't really a bunker in the way his own had been, back in Chesterbrook before the 'vaders found his property, but it was better than most he had seen. It also held the Clan's communications center, and had been EMP-shielded, so the electronic and binary gear all still worked. Cassy had put the bunker in before the EMPs, when Clanholme was simply her second home, a place where she made a hobby of learning the arts of prepper readiness and permaculture gardening. Now it was home to the Clan, with over a hundred people, and had absorbed the now-vacant lands around it. The bunker wasn't very well lit but it had sturdy walls and was fairly deep underground, so it felt like a nice, cozy cave to him. Safe. No one felt safe aboveground nowadays. Ever.

Ethan adjusted his green *Ready Player One* vintage gaming tee shirt—one of his prized possessions—and decided it was time to establish his data connections through HAMnet and see what was going on out in the Big Wide

World. Usually he heard nothing, or very little, but every once in a while he'd connect with some distant group of survivors. It was nice to know there were still people out there, nice people who didn't want to eat him or kill him for his stuff. Well, probably not—they were far enough away that it was never an option, so he got along famously with them. They weren't often on at the same times he was, but they had agreed to each be online at a specific time once weekly so that they could trade news if there was any.

Ethan turned on his HAM radio and launched his HAMnet apps. At first, there was no connection and he felt a moment of panic, but then his signal strength spiked to normal, and the hourglass appeared. He waited for a few seconds while his chat app loaded and popped up on-screen. Later, he'd get on the HAM radio itself to talk with whatever HAMheads still lived, but he wasn't thinking of them just yet. He ran through his VPN net, masking his trail as best he could, then showed up in the chatroom that someone had left up since right after the EMPs hit. It was probably some prepper type, maybe sitting alone in a cabin in West Virginia with some creative way of getting online, and hosting the chats as his way of staying social. In these chats he did away with Dark Ryder and posed as "E-Clan1," just another survivor from just another enclave.

E-Clan1 >> *Anyone on? Still alive?*

He sat and waited as the minutes ticked by, wishing this chat setup had an alert when people logged in. On the bright side, when you logged in you saw whatever had been written in the last ten minutes. After that, it erased itself. At eight minutes in, he got a reply and then another—

MooseLand >> *Hi 2 u both, Alaska inna hizzouse!*

E-Clan1 >> *lol good 2 c u both. We're hanging on here in PA. How's FL and AK?*

MooseLand >> *Still holding on. Winter made it easy for us to hold off our Chinese and Korean friends. Spring is coming, but the other round of EMPs evened up our odds a bit.*

SgtFlaughter >> *We got our commie bastards on the run. Normalized relations my ass, half a million Cubans and Russians still alive, holed up in Orlando. Not for long tho.*

MooseLand >> *Ha! Go get im FL. Soon I hope. Then u can turn to Georgia and the rest of the Gulf Coast yah?*

SgtFlaughter >> *That's the plan. Kill these guyz then go north*

MooseLand >> *Wish we were doing as good as u all. We got them stopped at the Calif Oregon passes, and the Cascades, but they still got south AK, western WA, and like half of OR. Got some bases in E. WA too, and Anchorage is theirs. We get a survivor once in a while wander out of there, talking crazy. But I believe it. Slave labor, people eating their kids or parents, vaders working the rest 2 death. Just bad. Go go, Free Alaska!*

E-Clan1 >> *Rock on Free Alaska! U can do it! We're OK 4 now here. Good news coming from NY, guess the vaders there r hemmed up in NYC. Freedom fightrs makn a New America starting in NJ, and they* *say they r coming into west PA soon. Can't wait.*

SgtFlaughter >> *Hope they hurry eclan, u got spring coming 2. We heard of this Empire out of Ft Wayne, u no about them?*

E-Clan1 >> *Yah, they r comin this way in spring. We will hold them off long as we can. Sucks they r Americans tho.*

MooseLand >> *No they r not! Americans fight vaders not us. We r hoping 2 get help from Colorado, there's Army there!*

E-Clan1 >> *He isn't going 2 help u much, he is working with Empire guyz*

SgtFlaughter >> *No way*

E-Clan1 >> *Way. its legit. Some of his troops scouting we talked 2 them, they told us.*

SgtFlaughter >> *Damn. We need 2 b careful then. CO dudes r fighting vaders in TX but not r problem 4 awhile. We got bigger probs here tho.*

E-Clan1 >> *Like wat?*

SgtFlaughter >> *Too many chefs, not enuf cooks. Evry group wants 2 b the leader here. Hope we hold it 2gether after the big push*

E-Clan1 >> *Wish I could help u both...*

He felt a twinge of guilt for lying about how he knew the Empire and the Mountain were pals, but they didn't need to know that. They spent the next ten minutes talking about the old America, the one with stores that sold pie, and the last movies they had seen. It got kind of sappy and way too nostalgic. Ethan finally logged off feeling a bit depressed. The Northwest was on the ropes and Florida was probably worse-off than "SgtFlaughter" had let on. Getting the Russians and Cubans out of Florida was great, but if the survivors fell to fighting each other, it could be years before they stopped looking like a tropical Somalia, bloody warlords and all. Damn.

Ethan turned to his other computer and loaded up a game. Killing zombies would take his mind off America's troubles. For a while anyway. Maybe.

* * *

From her makeshift podium—really just a laptop stand—Cassy glanced out through her window and cursed the early nights of winter. It was black outside, which matched her mood. The cheery living room was well-lit by LED bulbs running off her solar array, or rather the deep-cycle batteries that stored the solar power. Some irrational part of her wanted to smash those lightbulbs to dust. She took a deep breath and calmed herself, then focused on keeping a relaxed, friendly expression on her face for the benefit of her guests, the Clan Council.

Technically the Council had some authority, but everyone knew Cassy's final word was law. Her valley, her rules. In this day and age, you had a leader with claws or you died, and Cassy had claws. But the Council were her friends, her family—she'd never step on their opinions unless absolutely necessary, and despite the confidence she showed everyone, all day every day, she was all too aware that she sometimes made mistakes. *Had* made mistakes that got good people killed. But life went on, she was the leader, and the pipe dream of Frank stepping up as Clan leader had faded long ago. This was just her lot in life, for however long she lived. She was a far cry from the trusting, mid-thirties marketing executive she had been on the day the EMPs hit. Another lifetime, another life...

"Alright, I call the meeting to order," Cassy said. "Let the minutes show that Frank, our manager, is here. Joe Ellings is here for the White Stag survivors and is our agriculture foreman. Grandma Mandy is here, as usual—thanks for coming, Mom—and will be our devil's advocate since Choony will be gone with Jaz for quite a while yet. Ethan, our intel and communications guy is here. Nice shirt, by the way." She smiled as Ethan preened a bit in his geeky tee-shirt. "Michael, our security director. And me. I'm glad you're all here. And we bid welcome to our Confederation allies."

Cassy looked around the room and saw the envoys from their Confederation allies taking note of who was who in the Clan. She gave them about five seconds to sort it, then continued. "I'd like to personally thank our guests for coming here. Liz Town is here, as is Brickerville, Lititz, and Ephrata, each representing the survivor groups under their care. Lebanon couldn't make it, unfortunately, due to distance and weather."

Cassy noted that the Liz Town envoy wasn't the usual man, but another man she hadn't met before. By custom they called the envoys by their town name, and Frank was the Clan's rep, but she'd liked the old Liz Town rep.

Ephrata stood then, which was unexpected. All eyes turned to him as he said, "I'd like to thank the Clan for inviting us. It's important that we all have unfettered access to this Colonel Taggart and his New America, and I am happy that the Clan has recognized this need."

As he sat back down, Cassy kept her relaxed, friendly expression in place, but only through iron will. She was about to reply when Frank spoke, though he didn't stand. By agreement, due to his missing foot, he stayed seated during any meetings. "Thank you, Ephrata. Although I figure it's our relationship, and it's certainly our equipment that makes it possible, the Clan has never hoarded resources we didn't need for ourselves. Colonel Taggart has made it clear he will deal with the Confederation only through Cassy here—he doesn't want to widen the risk to his own operations, but we are happy to share. The way I see it, keeping this leaky boat afloat is more important than old-world-style politics, don't you think? We're in it to win it, for *all* of us."

Cassy noted that Ephrata and the other envoys nodded when Frank spoke up. He had neatly reminded everyone that this was the Clan's resource, Clan equipment, Clan everything—but that the Clan wasn't going to try to play power politics with its allies, nor should they play politics back. Times were different, Cassy mused. Open discussion would be a losing game in pre-EMP politics, but everyone who still played those games was now dead or dying. When people were alive on a razor's edge, you said what you meant, and said it clearly, or you didn't survive. Some day that would change, but not today. In the meantime, she was grateful for Frank's diplomatic, unifying ways.

Cassy coughed once, then said, "We are here, as you know, for a teleconference with Colonel Taggart, who's busy operating a guerrilla army of current and former military people at the core, plus thousands of liberated civilians like ourselves being trained up as they go. Upstate New Jersey had been blocked off by the Korean and ISNA invaders, and two million slaves from New York City were clearing it for spring planting. Now the slaves are being freed and the invaders are on the run."

Lititz stood, waited a second, then said, "I was under the impression that he was in New York City, yes?"

"The 'vaders in New York City had Taggart hemmed up, but he escaped when he figured out how they were staying one step ahead of him. He used their spies against them, and got himself and his ex-military people out of the city into New Jersey. He has reclaimed a lot of territory since then and has been liberating civilians whenever he can, or avenging their murders when he wasn't fast enough."

Lititz nodded. "Yes, but what has this to do with the Confederation, and what's he going to do with all that territory? How do we know he isn't just another General Houle in sheep's clothing?" The envoy sat down again.

Cassy frowned, but recovered quickly. Lititz didn't know Taggart like Ethan did, and she trusted Ethan's judgment. She had to. "Our hope and dream is that this Taggart is founding a New America. We all know General Houle at the Mountain in Colorado is claiming to be El Jeffe and wants to be Caesar, but he's clearly a bastard and unfit. Taggart is playing a balancing act, trying not to earn traitor status with the Mountain but not obeying their orders, either. He says when he sees a legal Constitutional government again, he'll submit to its authority. In the meantime, anything we can do to help him, we must do. All agreed?"

Raised hands from the envoys and from Frank showed unanimous agreement, or at least compliance. But that was the slow ball, the easy home run. If only all the issues were so easily resolved.

From the back of the room, Ethan said, "It's up and almost time. They'll join us any moment."

Cassy nodded, and watched as Ethan brought a tiny laptop and a sleek-looking device up front. On the coffee table he placed the device, a projector, and connected it to the laptop; it then projected an image of the living room onto the wall behind her. She turned the podium around, not liking the fact that the envoys were behind her now where she couldn't read their expressions, and waited.

Two minutes later, the image flickered and was replaced by a shot of two men in Army field uniforms. One was a burly, light-complexion black man with the unmistakable aura of authority—Michael had the same aura when dealing with his Marines or the other Clan warriors. Slightly behind him was a younger white man with no facial hair and somewhat Irish-mutt features. Neither had facial hair.

The man in front said, "Greetings, is this thing on?" When Cassy gave a thumbs-up, he continued, "I am Major General Taggart, commander of the Army of the United States, Reformed." He looked directly at the camera and said, "Please introduce your team."

Cassy said, "I am Cassandra Shores, but everyone calls me Cassy. I am the Clan Leader, and nominal representative of the Confederation, an alliance of survivor enclaves in Pennsylvania working together to maintain our independence from all enemies, foreign and domestic." She then introduced the other envoys, but didn't introduce her council members except for Frank, whom she listed as the Clan's representative while she stood for the Confederation. On screen, in the background, the younger soldier took notes as she spoke.

Then Taggart nodded, and said, "Behind me is Sergeant Major Eagan, who will be my day-to-day liaison with your Confederation and with the Clan directly. Thank you all for coming, and allowing me to speak with you today."

On the projection, Cassy saw that the envoys behind her were nodding in approval. Good, another bar cleared, and Taggart was showing himself not to be the egomaniac some had feared. "Thank you for your time, General Taggart, and congratulations on your latest field promotion. From what we've heard, it was well earned."

"It is what it is, Cassy. The more I liberate, the more I command, and we have to have a rank structure. Sometimes it's just easier to ask for forgiveness than permission, and the Mountain isn't here—that's what your man calls them, right? The Mountain?"

Cassy replied, "Yes, sir. We understand the delicate situation you have there, and will do what we can not to complicate your life in that regard—but we won't bow down to this General Houle, sir. He isn't here, and he didn't help us or anyone but himself, to go by our limited intel."

On screen, Cassy saw that Taggart made no expression, but his sidekick Eagan had to turn away to hide a grin. That was good to know. Cassy immediately felt a sort of kindred spirit in the young man, and if this Taggart officer relied heavily on Eagan then it spoke volumes about the kind of leader Taggart was. What kind of person he was, really.

Taggart nodded, and his eyes smiled for a second but the rest of his face was solidly neutral, unreadable. "I understand your feelings in the matter. I can't say that I blame you, but one way or another the Mountain is a reality we will all have to deal with. Although there is some question about the chain of command and the legitimacy of his claim to be the Commander-in-Chief, it doesn't change the fact that General Houle outranks me. I walk a fine line, and until certain issues are decided, I prefer not to kick the hornet's nest."

Out of the corner of her eye, Cassy saw Michael stand. She glanced over and saw him standing ramrod straight, feet together, hands at his sides, the way the Marines did when Michael gave them orders.

"Sir," Michael said loudly enough to carry across the room, "Major Michael K. Bates, USMC Retired, Force Recon. I am the Clan's military C.O."

All eyes turned to him as he spoke, but he paid no heed. Cassy's eyes went wide—she had never known his rank and had only guessed at his Force Recon status. Even Frank looked surprised, and they had known each other for a few years before the EMPs.

Michael continued, "Sir, from one grunt to another, what is the status of the New United States Reformed? We've heard rumors that you've established a civilian chain of command in parallel to your military command. Is that true? It's a question with deep implications, considering the claims of General Houle, sir."

Taggart's huge face, projected onto the wall, grew a big sloppy grin. "Hooah, Marine."

"Oohrah, General," Michael snapped back, but he too now wore a grin. Michael's whole body language relaxed, though he kept his 'position of attention,' as he called it.

"I'm glad you asked that, Major. In point of fact, I am not forming a New United States. I have, however, been elected President of the existing United States by the citizens within my operational area. It's a formality, really—I run this show here simply because no one else can—but it gives my people hope that America is going to rise from the ashes, and we haven't lost everything. This complicates my relationship with the Mountain, however, and I haven't reported this election to them. Not until I decide how I will proceed regarding General Houle's claims."

He paused and glanced off-screen, away from the Sergeant-Major, and murmured "later" to whoever it was. Turning back to the camera, he continued, "We have functioning governmental bodies in place now, though they're crude. We've taken in a lot of refugees and have no way to feed too many more. Those who can't work in the fields or carry a weapon are being turned away, which I deeply regret, but soon we'll have to turn away the able-bodied as well. I doubt I'll be a well-loved president in the future history books. In any case, it is only a title of convenience. It maintains a link with the civilians yearning, as the statue said, to be free."

Michael nodded, listening carefully as Taggart spoke, and then replied, "Is the General aware of the Clan's method of agriculture? This intensive 'permaculture' has the potential to produce on par with, or out-produce, the best commercial farmlands. It requires more people labor, but without tractors and the ability to ship in tons of fertilizer, it may be the only way agriculture can resume in the post-EMP operations environment, and I've seen the proof of concept right here, sir. Cassy can tell you about it if you like."

Michael then sat, and Cassy looked to Taggart. When he said nothing, she raised an eyebrow and pursed her lips. Damned if she was going to be the first to talk—if Taggart wasn't on board with what Michael had said, she didn't want to put him on the spot, nor did she want to suffer a hit in front of the envoys if he wasn't interested in the idea.

Then Taggart, who had been looking away, returned his gaze to the screen. "Actually, that's an excellent question. Yes, I am aware of the Clan's farming method, although I don't know any details. Eagan just told me your man said it's sustainable and productive even without fertilizer, which commercial agriculture never has been, not even when the tractors and long-distance transports were working. Is that accurate, Cassy?"

Cassy nodded slowly. "Yes, in essence. But it requires knowledge. You can't just plow a field and put down seed the way your farmers have always done it. Just doesn't work that way, General, but you can expect some resistance from your farmers. It's a big change."

Taggart nodded, his projected image filling the wall. "I've been advised of that. In fact, one of my rescued civilians is a permaculture enthusiast. He's only read a lot of books on the topic, never in practice—he lived in an apartment before the war and dreamed of a homestead like yours. I have a plan in mind, however. Cassy, I'd like to name you my Interim Secretary of Agriculture. You'd need to work closely with my guy, who will be your deputy and number two man for permaculture. We need to get up to speed quickly, because spring is coming."

Cassy stared at the laptop, jaw agape. She blinked hard twice and snapped her jaw shut. "I'm honored, sir..."

"I sense a 'but' coming, Cassy," Taggart replied.

"I have a Clan to lead, and I'm kept pretty busy trying to teach people from the Confederation's enclaves so they can get started in the spring. I want to help—"

Taggart interrupted her with one hand held up toward the screen. "I won't try to tell you what to do, but if America is going to rise again—the America we want—then we're all going to have to start worrying about more than our own small corners of the world. Why don't you train people from each of your enclaves at the same time you instruct the Deputy Secretary of Agriculture? Turn it into an accelerated course, help everyone get the basics down pat so we can at least begin without delaying your own Confederation."

On the screen, Cassy saw the Brickerville envoy stand up behind her. "Sir, and Cassy, if I may offer a suggestion? Why don't we each send a person to Clanholme to study under Cassy directly? Perhaps a couple hours per day of instruction would suffice to get us up to speed for spring planting. They can carry the knowledge back and spread it on from there."

Cassy felt all eyes on her, both those behind her and on the video conference, and her cheeks flushed, her jaw gritting. How could she do everything needed? She was only one person, dammit, and the Clan was her first responsibility. And how could she teach them what they needed to know in time? No one could miss her frustration so she spoke her thoughts aloud to the screen. "They'd have to dig swales and berms to retain water, and catchment ponds, using nothing but A-frame levels to keep the swales on contour. It takes practice and hard work, not classwork. There's no way I could see the land everyone will have to dig on—it'd take months we don't have to go to each location to evaluate local conditions. I don't see how I can make it work from here."

Frank's deep voice rose behind her. "Cassy, this is a chance to save thousands. Maybe millions, someday. A chance to redefine how we all do agriculture. Imagine the future generations who will live better and healthier lives because of what you can teach us? If you need more time... Well, you can delegate your Clan responsibilities to me. This is more important."

His words hung in the air between them. Frank was offering publicly to step up to handle much of the Clan leader's responsibilities. She had been trying to get him to do that for as long as she had known him, through ups and downs, crisis and peacetime, hunger and plenty. He had always refused, on grounds that it was her farm and she was a better leader in his estimation. Now, when she didn't want to do something that would put *more* responsibilities on her shoulders, for *more* people... Now he steps up?

She realized her shoulders had hunched up and she had made her hands into fists, and took a deep breath to calm down. Part of her still wanted to leap across the living room and choke the crap out of him. Not only would this add to her burden, but she didn't want to be the agriculture secretary, or whatever. All she had ever wanted was just to raise her family on a nice, quiet homestead, healthier and more self-sufficiently.

To get that for her family after the EMPs hit, she'd had to

get that for the Clan as well. There were all of fourteen people in the beginning. Now the Clan had nearly two hundred people, only half of whom were survivors of the Clan's enslavement under Peter; the rest were newer. And then the alliance. And when that became the Confederation, many hundreds more, even if they were far away and had their own local leaders. She was still ultimately responsible for them.

Cassy let out a long breath between clenched teeth, then finally spoke. All eyes were on her. "General... Mr. President... I accept, and deeply appreciate your confidence, but I have certain firm requests."

"By all means, if it's possible, I'll meet your requests." Taggart smiled, but it was tight-lipped. His eyes looked kind, however. Maybe he felt the burden of responsibility as much as she did. That was a novel thought. But she realized it was probable he did understand.

Cassy looked at Taggart intently for a moment, and for the first time, she saw how bedraggled he looked. Exhausted, with a faint hint of gray starting in his close-cropped hair. Yes, the man knew precisely how she felt about this. She let out a sigh.

"Very well. Firstly, I'll need our training to begin after evening chow—anytime after seventeen hundred hours will do."

"Our chow is a bit later. Will eighteen-hundred hours be okay?"

Cassy nodded. "Yes. Secondly, I'll need you to provide the manpower for the Deputy Secretary to put the things I'll teach him into action quickly. As you say, spring is coming on fast. Preparation takes a lot of digging, in the beginning—and then cutting starts from the food-producing trees. You'll need to make a survey of the fruit and nut trees in your area right away, find out what grows well locally and find new starts if the invaders destroyed existing orchards. That can be done while your man is in training and then passing the training on to others. And then there's the design work, which depends on the local terrain."

Cassy went on with her list. Gather all the shovels and picks they can find. Seeds. Hay. The list was endless, and Eagan nodded dutifully as he wrote it all down.

When she ran out of steam, Taggart said, "Very well, Cassy. Your second, here, can consult on any problems. Is there anything else you need in order to make all this happen?"

Cassy felt her stomach flip. She had saved the best for last. Her marketing training before the war had taught her to get the easy yesses in the beginning, then ask for the hard things. And here she went. "Lastly, I request that you send two companies of troops to us. One under my direct command, or rather Michael's, and one to divide among the other enclaves. The more our people work with yours, the easier an eventual integration will be. We can cross-train between your troops and ours, and we will all be stronger for it."

Taggart didn't bat an eyelash. For a long moment, he stared silently at the camera. Just when Cassy thought he was going to balk, he nodded once, a curt motion. "You will provide for their ammunition, food, and other necessary gear, of course?"

Cassy felt a flood of relief wash over her. *Two companies* of troops, already armed and experienced fighters even if they weren't his ex-military people. She felt the odds of surviving this spring rising even as she nodded back. Her mind was already elsewhere tallying odds and considering deployments. She knew General Houle was sending a battalion through her territory in dribs and drabs gathering them to the north and supposedly awaiting Taggart's arrival with a second battalion. Now she felt confident they could be repelled if needed, at least until Houle sent his own vanguard at them from the Mountain. They'd be able to give the Empire a fight they had never expected when their troops showed up, she thought with satisfaction.

But the general had asked her a question. "Yes sir, I think we can make this work. It has been an honor to meet and get such a positive measure of your plans. I thank you for giving us so much time." She turned to the envoys. "Do any of you have questions at this point?"

The envoy from Liz Town raised his hand. "I do." Cassy nodded. "I'm Liz Town, General Taggart. What I want to know is, what do we call you? General, or Mr. President, or what?"

Taggart broke into an obviously spontaneous laugh. "When you feed me a line like that, all I can say is"—he gave a Groucho Marx eyebrow waggle—"call me whatever you like, just don't call me late for chow."

The room erupted in laughter, and Eagan could be seen on the screen, grinning behind the general. On that cheerful note, Ethan cut the connection and the meeting disbanded. Cider and a meal awaited everyone in the kitchen, the work of Grandma Mandy, Cassy's daughter Brianna, and Brianna's younger friend Kaitlyn. The envoys were chattering and getting to know each other as they followed little Kaitlyn into the kitchen to pick up their trays.

- 2 -

0700 HOURS - ZERO DAY +188

SMOKE STILL ROSE from the corpse of Cincinnati as Samuel Pease looked at it from the passenger seat of an ancient Jeep. The damn thing still ran despite the EMPs and was as old as his parents. The thought of his parents sent a shiver down his spin, and a wave of sorrow and regret tinged with anger.

He had made it to their house all right, after the EMPs, but not soon enough. When he arrived with his accidental companions, Mike and Brett, the place had been ransacked and his parents were dead—stabbed to death in the old yellow kitchen over whatever scraps of food had remained. In that whole neighborhood of Chesterbrook, what little hadn't been burnt down had been ravaged.

Samuel persuaded his companions to head with him back home to Decatur, right outside Fort Wayne. Over five hundred miles in under a month, on foot. Somewhere in Ohio outside Lima, he and Brett had decided that pansy-ass Mike was the weakest link, and they had killed him. Spent two days smoking the meat they had carved off Mike while they ate his heart and liver, and promised each other they'd never speak of that horrible time again.

In the driver's seat, Brett drummed his fingers on the steering wheel. "You thinking about the Hell Run again, boss? Or your parents?"

"Both. How'd you know?" Samuel asked. "And I told you, it's Captain now, not boss."

"Sure, Captain. Can this sergeant speak freely, Sam?" Brett grinned sardonically, still drumming his fingers.

"Sure." Samuel clenched his jaw and resisted the urge to just kill Brett. The man had never looked afraid of Samuel, and that was a pisser. After everything they had been through together over five-hundred miles of raping, looting, and killing, the asshole ought to have a bit more respect for Sam Pease, because dammit, Samuel Pease was a stone-cold monster. Everyone knew that, except this piece of shit. "What's on that tiny little brain of yours? You're boring me."

Brett ignored the jibe. "Why the hell we here again? Seems like a lose-lose game to me. We're in the goddamn Midwest Republic, feared by everyone for five-hundred miles in every direction, but Carlos—"

"First Citizen Carlos, if you know what's good for you."

"Fine, First Citizen Carlos, he's sucking up to those assholes in Colorado. Why? Dude's a thousand miles away, and the only army he's got here is that pissant battalion he's got moving east. We could mop them up, but instead Carlos kissed their asses and here we are, getting ready to run some bullshit joint training exercise with their last company-sized unit. Why we gotta go through Cincinnati? Place is a morgue, and what's left are scary mo-fos."

"Think about it, numbnuts. Out there in the wild, we were scary-ass monsters, right? Didn't want to kill all those people but you do what you gotta do to survive. And you might as well enjoy yourself when there's something you have to do, and we sure did. Going to Hell anyway, I figured. But we never took what we didn't need, and we only played with our food—never bothered people when we didn't have to. Right?"

"Yeah, so? We're swell people, stand up guys, me and you. We only killed the people we had to rob, and I figured we were doing them a favor. Better quick by us than slow by starving. So what if we had a little fun with a few of them? They were dying anyway. And we always did it quick, when we killed them. None of that bullshit torture some other guys like so they can hear 'em yell."

Samuel said, "Yeah. Well, now we're in the Army of the Republic, and we don't have to do that shit anymore at all, unless there's some enclave that doesn't figure they need to vote 'yes' on joining the Republic. When's the last time we had to just straight murder anyone?"

Brett frowned as he thought back. "Maybe two weeks. And another two before that."

"Yeah. And in the month since we got back to my hometown, we've risen in the ranks. Played it square, got promoted. They even kept us together, me and my right-hand man. So I figure, this is just the Major giving us a little R-and-R. We slip down into Cincin, show these visiting Army fucks what we're about. They report back to NORAD what a bunch of crazy maddog killers we all are, and they decide maybe they don't want to mess with the Republic. Maybe it's best if they just let us follow orders and leave us alone the rest of the time."

"Shit, Sam. Why didn't you say that before? So there's a reason to mess with those freaky-ass losers in Cincin. Well, if there's a reason, we might as well enjoy it, right? If you're right, then the more we enjoy ourselves down there, the more we'll impress those Army shits."

"Yeah, that's about right. Although," Samuel said with a

big happy grin, "I didn't exactly ask for clarification on that little detail. They might say no, after all."

"Better to ask for forgiveness," Brett said, nodding. "Alright, I see our Army friends. Three hundred yards at one o'clock and about to meet their nightmares."

Samuel squinted to see so far away, but Brett was right. Three platoons in Army field uniforms marching toward him, three abreast. "Cool. Brett, jump out and spread the word to our guys what the plan is. You think those screwballs in Cincin are crazy, wait till the Army sees what we got up our sleeves. Hate to do it, but they'll leave us alone once they report back the crazy shit we're about to pull."

Brett hopped out and walked back toward the company of troops behind the jeep, all swagger and whistling happily. The guy was dumb, Samuel knew, but he was loyal, and down to do whatever. What more could you ask for in a friend?

He didn't tell Brett that he hated the idea of working with those Army assholes, or that he had complained loudly about having to do it. Something about these guys, coming here from so far away, just didn't sit right. They were up to something, or scouting them so the general-in-the-mountain could eat Samuel's beloved Republic later. His C.O. had told him to follow orders or walk, and Samuel had no intention of walking away from his cushy post in the Republic's army. But he'd damn sure follow those orders in a way that served the Republic best, even if his commanders were too stupid to realize these Army shits were basically spies. He'd do his best to make every one of them vomit by the time this day was done. And if one or two happened to disappear in some dark Cincinnati alley, well, that could hardly be traced back to Samuel.

And if it did, he'd just blame Brett. The guy was a monster and an idiot anyway, and deserved it. What Brett did with that one girl in Ohio... Whatever happened to him would only be Karma. Even if he was Samuel's friend.

* * *

Nestor strode through the farmhouse like an avenging angel, destroying everything of value, personal or practical. The old man downstairs, now bound to a chair, deserved it. He had tracked the cannibals here, but they were gone when Nestor arrived. He and his *Night Ghosts* guerrillas—the invaders' name for his band—were always a step behind, always just missing the murdering scum. Today, though, there were horse droppings still steaming in the barn here. The old man knew them, helped them, and they were so close now that Nestor could almost smell them. But they weren't here, another miss, and that old man knew where they had gone. He was damn well going to tell.

Downstairs, Nestor could hear the old man shouting that he didn't know who they were. The people Nestor was tracking had just come in, forced him to feed them, taken what they wanted, and "skedaddled." After he finished going room by room upstairs, Nestor headed downstairs. He walked by the bound-up old man, ignoring the shiner growing over the man's left eye, and went to the door into the garage.

As Nestor's hand went to the door handle, the old man grew suddenly frantic, thrashing feebly against his bonds. "Don't go in there!" he cried out. "You get out of my house! I didn't do nothing!"

Nestor drew his pistol and motioned to one of his fighters; he came over and on the count of three, kicked the garage door open and stepped out of the way, while Nestor rushed inside with weapon ready and turned to the left. The fighter followed him in and turned to the right. No movement, no threats inside. They both looked around the garage...

Nestor's eyes fell upon a picnic table in the center of the garage, and he froze. A chill shot up his spine as he realized what he was looking at. The table was covered in blood and gore, bits of flesh... and teeth. Wicked knives and a sickle lay bloody on the table, giving the scene an unearthly, terrifying aspect. "Something out of a damn horror movie..." muttered the fighter next to him. Then Nestor heard his fighter vomit.

Nestor grabbed his stricken fighter by the shoulder and half-dragged him back into the house, away from that terrible scene, and closed the door behind him as far as it would go after being kicked in. It blocked the view, at least. Had the person butchered there been alive when the cutting began? Nestor felt his stomach churn as he visualized the cannibals pulling their victim's teeth out one by one while he was still alive and screaming for mercy. Nestor's stomach flip-flopped.

All eyes turned to Nestor, but he only stared at the old man, jaw clenched, free hand in a fist at his side. He felt his cheeks flush, and his throat was dry. The old man stared back, eyes wide with fear rather than anger now.

Nestor didn't take his eyes off the old man as he said, "Go get Ratbone."

A woman near the door said, pausing, "Are... you sure, boss?"

Nestor merely nodded, and the woman darted out the door. Nestor said, "Old man, tell me where they are."

"Who?" the man cried out, voice cracking.

"You know who. Tell me and we'll go easier on you."

The old man's eyes teared up, and one strolled down his cheek. "If I tell you anything, you'll kill me anyway... Please, I just—"

"Silence!" Nestor roared, taking a step toward the

prisoner. He stopped himself, looked down at the ground and clenched his jaw as he opened and closed his fists. "I don't think you understand, mister. Once you tell us where they are, then you get to die. Quickly and painlessly. Until then?" He shrugged. "How long this will go on is entirely up to you."

The door opened and a man walked in. He was short and wiry-thin. He wore wire-rimmed glasses and a wool trench coat over a dress shirt. A nerdy bow tie, pressed jeans, and red suspenders completed his lack of style. He looked anything but dangerous, but Nestor knew better. Looks are deceiving.

"Ratbone. Find out where his guests went. We'll wait outside. Do what you must, but don't let him die until he tells you. Only then, kill him quick and make it painless. Understand?"

Ratbone's eyes narrowed and he licked his lips, nostrils flaring. "Oh yes, boss. Oh, I do understand." He looked at the old man and smiled, but it was far from friendly. "Cannibal scum."

The old man began to scream. "No! You can't leave me in here with him!"

Ratbone pulled a leather tube off his back and unrolled it on the kitchen counter. A dozen metal instruments gleamed. "I'll get what you need, boss. Go wait outside. You shouldn't be here for this." He hummed softly to himself as he laid various instruments out on the counter.

Nestor nodded, watching the little man prepare for his evil work, then shook himself free of the fascination and he and the other fighters walked outside, closing the door behind them. They withdrew about a hundred yards—far enough, he hoped, to not hear what was coming. The idea of getting information this way went against everything he had believed in before the EMPs. Now, however, there weren't police to wear a prisoner down over days and days to get more reliable information, and in that delay more people would probably be murdered. No, he had decided that the goal outweighed the means, and he'd just have to live with the guilt—because he'd protect some other innocent family through his willingness to carry that awful burden. And it would be a burden for the rest of his life, however long that would be, he knew.

He could have just released the Other, the evil no-Nestor who rode around in his mind all day trying to get loose. That one might enjoy doing what Ratbone did, but he would be just as likely to kill the guy outright. What did the Other care about information? Nestor couldn't trust the Other with even the simplest of tasks. Besides, Nestor mused, bringing out the Other would just sidestep guilt that would still be his to bear, and that wasn't right. If he was going to sentence a man to die this way, using the Other couldn't buy freedom from guilt.

Forty-five minutes later, smoke began to wisp from the broken front window, and Nestor half-stood. Had something gone wrong in the house? But no, Ratbone walked calmly out the front door, his leather roll of tools slung across his back.

As he walked up, Nestor saw that Ratbone's pupils were dilated, cheeks flushed, and his breath was husky. His hands, held in front of him, fidgeted and shook slightly. Nestor decided that when this was all over, Ratbone would receive the Other's special treatment. But not now... not yet. For now, the deviant was useful in a war that had turned Nestor into everything he would have hated back in the good old days, before he knew about the Other. These were not the good old days. For now, Nestor would be who his Clanholme friends, the people who had given him redemption, needed him to be. He would willingly bear the guilt later.

Ratbone broke into his thoughts. "Boss, I got what you

asked for."

"Go ahead." Nester said.

"It seems there's four of them. They're the old man's two sons, a daughter, and a son-in-law. They have a cabin about ten miles from here where the old man thought they'd be hiding. Got compass directions and everything."

"Good," Nestor replied, nodding. He forced himself to smile, then said, "You've done well, Ratbone. Remind me to give you a raise when money works again."

"Will do, boss," Ratbone replied, and bounced on the balls of his feet with a wide grin. "I did my best, I know we're on a deadline."

Nestor slapped the other man's shoulder. "I know you did. I can count on you for the hard things, Ratbone, and I appreciate that." Then he turned to his two dozen fighters and shouted, "Mount up! We got some hunting to do!"

As the men and women of the Night Ghosts whooped and hollered, swinging up into their horses' saddles, Nestor wiped his hand on his jacket, as if his hand were soiled just from touching the Ratbone's shoulder. Or maybe it was to wipe away the old man's blood, which was surely on his own hands as much as Ratbone's.

Climbing onto his horse, Nestor swung around to the northwest, and kicked his heels into the horse's flanks, spurring his mount away from the grisly scene. Behind him, the old man's home became engulfed in flames, but it couldn't ever burn away his guilt.

* * *

Cassy stood before her Council and the assembled Confed envoys, looking at a map tacked to the wall behind her. With a laser pointer, she went through the accumulated changes they knew about in enemy dispositions. She pointed out areas where raiders were active, places where survivors might be at risk, and all the usual SitRep information she had on hand. She'd be glad when the envoys went home—they had been at Clanholme for three days now and she wanted nothing more than to wave goodbye in the morning so Clanholme life could get back to normal.

"...and as you can see, the cannibal activity has been within this twenty-mile area, covering much of the western Confederation. We've had cannibals before and we will have them again, I'm sure, but both our scouts and the Night Ghosts are chasing them hard."

Brickerville's envoy said, "I got twenty bucks says the Night Ghosts beat you to 'em," and there were a few chuckles at the good-natured ribbing.

"You're on," Cassy said, grinning. "Next up, regarding the joint op on the invader encampment west of the Falconry —"

The door opened with a bang, propelled by heavy winds outside, and all heads turned as one of her guards stepped inside with a woman Cassy had never seen before. The guard looked confused and embarrassed, but didn't act like this was a dangerous threat, which was good... Cassy banged her fist on the podium. "What is the meaning of this?"

The woman wore a woolen cowl over a sharp-looking black knee-length coat, and when she pulled the cowl off, it revealed she was in her early forties. That was unusual by itself since not many that age had survived unless they had been blessed with fantastic luck. This woman had clearly once been a classic beauty but a large scar, still healing, went from the center of her forehead at the hairline to just under her left ear, narrowly missing her eye. She stood tall, erect, proud.

As she pulled off her gloves, she reached into her inside jacket pocket, causing the guard to tense, ready to rush the woman, but she only pulled out an envelope with a bright red wax seal on the flap. "I'm aware that Confed envoys don't use names. Therefore, if it pleases you, my name is Liz Town," she told the assembled group.

There was a murmur. Then the Liz Town envoy—a man who had been there for the past several days—stood and glowered at the newcomer. "What do you mean by that? I am Liz Town. Explain yourself." His jaw clenched tightly, and he held his hands in fists at his sides.

The woman said, "Sorry, but you *were* Liz Town. Things have changed in the last couple of days. In the interests of time and accuracy, our leadership sent me to relieve you. And Carl? Pamela said to tell you, 'thank you for your service,' and said you'd know what that meant."

Cassy saw the original envoy's face turn white. What in the hell was going on in Liz Town?

The woman walked up to Cassy and presented the wax-sealed envelope. Cassy broke the seal and unfolded it—the envelope doubled as the letter itself, in the pre-industrial style. She read it carefully, brief though it was, and grew increasingly confused. It was in the Liz Town leader's usual handwriting and it had the right seal, but to remove a standing envoy? That made no sense. The letter said only that the current envoy was relieved of all duties and directed him to return to Liz Town as quickly as possible to report directly to his "band leader." Liz Town was organized into bands, she knew, much like clans within a tribe. The letter named the bearer as the new Liz Town envoy, effective immediately.

Cassy looked at the newcomer, and paused. What could be done? Nothing. Not the Confederation's responsibility. To challenge it would alienate Liz Town, and that was not an option. "Welcome to Clanholme, Liz Town. Please, be seated." Cassy turned to the old envoy, and pursed one side of her mouth as she shrugged. "I'm sorry—Carl, was it?—but the directions from your leader are clear. Please feel free to stay the night before heading back to Liz Town, though. I'm happy to share a meal with you."

In these dark new days, that was tantamount to calling him a friend, and she hoped it would take some of the sting out of his demotion. It was all she could offer.

He nodded, and gave her a wan smile. "Thank you, Cassy. Your hospitality is much appreciated. I would be delighted to take you up on your offer and, if you find yourself in Liz Town someday, I hope you will impose on me during your stay. You would honor me if you did."

As he walked out of the meeting, the new envoy walked across the room to her predecessor's seat, chin up, and sat. "So, where were we?"

Cassy said, "You couldn't wait to do this until after this meeting? I mean no offense, but it was rather disruptive."

The woman shrugged, and raised her eyebrow. "I'm sorry, but my orders were specific. I didn't wish to disrupt your Confed meeting, but when given a clear, direct order, what is one to do?"

"Obey, of course," Cassy replied. She let out a long breath and then said, "Very well. As I was saying, we will soon raid an invader encampment west of Falconry. They've been hampering trade with the Empire but since Falconry has proclaimed themselves a neutral free-trade zone—to all of our benefits—it's their negative impact on Liz Town's traders that makes Confed action necessary. The enemy is estimated to number only about fifty. The Clan is allocating eighteen people to this. Taj Mahal will send three. Ephrata, thirty. Brickerville, twenty. Lititz, twenty-five. Lebanon, forty. And Liz Town, thirty. That gives us—"

"Pardon me," said Liz Town, raising her hand.

Cassy replied, "Go ahead. Here, we stand to speak,

except for Clanholme—he is an amputee so he stays seated, of necessity."

The woman nodded, stood, and said, "Liz Town offers its deepest regrets, but due to recent developments we will be unable to allocate any people to this mission. We have the utmost respect for the Confederation and acknowledge our duties within it. We ask that you please accept our apologies at face value; they are sincere."

Cassy gripped the edges of the podium, knuckles turning white, but her face remained expressionless. "The Confederation acknowledges Liz Town's respect for their duties to the Confed. Why, may I ask, is Liz Town unable to perform that duty and dedicate fighters for this operation, which we will fight specifically to help Liz Town itself?"

For the first time, Liz Town didn't have her chin in the air; she looked down at her feet and said, "I wasn't told why, only that our fighters were needed closer to home right now. I was told to say that Liz Town will send more than its share of fighters for future missions, but that for the time being we will be unable to participate in Confed missions. That will last 'until further notice,' "

"And you have no idea why?" Cassy asked. Something was going on, that much was clear, but apparently they weren't talking. What could make Liz Town, the most militaristic member of the Confederation, shirk duty on a mission aimed at helping them? Cassy was certain that the envoy knew more than she was telling them.

"No ma'am, I have no reasons to give you. Only what I was instructed to say." Liz Town shifted uneasily in her seat and looked at her shoes as she spoke, unable to meet Cassy's gaze.

Cassy guessed the new envoy was not easy with her stonewalling, but the Confed had no choice but to accept it. She banged on the podium. "Very well. In light of Liz Town's inability to contribute to this mission, I must ask the other envoys a question. Do any among you wish to decline to participate, now that the numbers have changed?"

Only Lebanon's hand stayed down. Everyone else was backing away, and Cassy struggled against an urge to walk up and spit in Liz Town's face. It probably wasn't her fault. None of this crap made sense, and now the whole mission was a wash—the invaders would stay, unopposed and impeding trade to Falconry—trade that the rest of the Confederation needed. Maybe she could find an alternative way to drive them away, but she had no idea where to start looking for it. Maybe Michael could help.

She let out a long, ragged breath. "Very well. Given this new information, the mission in question is scrubbed. I'm sure no one is happy about it. And on that note, this meeting is adjourned. I'll see you all in a bit over some of our famous hard apple cider."

Cassy rapped the podium to make it official. And curse Liz Town for backing out now, rather than earlier. Now the whole Confed knew something was up with the Confed's strongest west-border member. Liz Town damn well better figure out what they were doing before spring or it would stand alone against the Empire. She shuddered to think of what that could mean for the rest of them.

Damn if she didn't need a good, stiff drink right now. She followed the others out to where they were serving the cider.

- 3 -

0700 HOURS - ZERO DAY +190

CONTACT WITH THE latest survivor group yesterday morning had gone really well, and Choony had been thrilled to get Strasburg's agreement to send a rep to Clanholme. Since then, he and Jaz had scouted another enclave and now prepared to wander into the outskirts of Intercourse, Pennsylvania.

Every new meeting with unknown survivors was stressful because one never knew how the residents would react to newcomers. Choony kept it in mind that meeting strangers—especially strangers with a survival stake in protecting their holding—always carried the risk of a fight.

Choony, like Jaz, was a bit distracted of late. Not by the risk of new encounters—he did try to keep his mind on the mission at such times—but because part of him still mulled over his feelings about Jaz. They'd been growing closer for a while now, having been solidly in the "friends" category from the start. Choony decided early on that he wouldn't push her. As a street kid of striking beauty, she had been through enough to make it hard to trust others. With her rough history, she didn't need her best friend to start hitting on her.

So, as much as he wanted to be with her as more than just a friend, things were as they were, not how he'd like them to be. If it grew into something more, it would do so on her timeline, not his. He was resolved on that.

Immersed in these thoughts, he finished packing their gear into the covered wagon and then gently shook Jaz awake. "Hey there, lazybones. Time to go meet the natives." As she sat up and yawned, he handed her a cup of nettle tea. It was a somewhat bitter brew but healthful and good for warming up fast, first thing on a cold morning.

Jaz smiled at him sleepily, took the cup and sipped slowly as she came awake, her blanket draped about her shoulders. Soon her tea was finished and she rose to stretch, then turned. "What's for breakfast?" She grinned at him.

It was a rhetorical question, of course. "Oatmeal and eggs," he replied out of habit. Shifting his tone to sound like a snooty pre-EMP waiter, he added, "With hot muffins and butter, madam."

Jaz giggled at his very phony British accent and smoothed an imaginary tablecloth, looking up at him with eyebrows arched expectantly like an impatient and over-privileged socialite. He did a poor job of hiding his urge to laugh and handed Jaz her metal camping cups and a spoon. She ate it all quickly and, glancing sidelong at Choony, straightened her back and dabbed daintily at her lips with an imaginary napkin because snooty restaurants required it, don't you know. When all was done, she cleaned her cups with sandy dirt and a trickle of water, gathered and packed away her gear. "Ready when you are, Sir Choony."

Climbing onto the wagon, the two then slowly made their way down the wooded hill toward the nearest cluster of smoke plumes on the outskirts of Intercourse, a small town with a name comedians had loved, back in the day. It took only twenty minutes or so to get within easy weapons range of the survivors, always a point of peak danger. It would only take a single nervous finger on a trigger to ruin his day. Choony grew tense, looking for signs of aggression. Next to him, Jaz's left leg bounced and her hands gripped her rifle tightly enough to whiten her knuckles.

It was show time, folks...

Choony saw that the residents had somehow pulled a bunch of big-rigs into place to block off several suburban blocks. Two stacked cars at one end made a gate; the cars had been rolled aside to allow entry and exit to the community. As they approached, four men emerged, weapons at the ready but not directly aimed at Choony and Jaz. Choony nudged his companion. "That's a good sign."

Jaz nodded but didn't say anything, as she kept her focus on the four men, and two more men prone on the roof of the largest trailer blocking the main entryway. The four on foot approached slowly, obviously sizing up the newcomers as they came.

When they got within about fifty feet, they stopped and one called out, "Stop your wagon, please."

Choony drew the wagon to a halt. Then two of the men continued forward, while one flanked left and the other flanked right, forming a strong defensive position. Choony simply waited. If they were going to kill him, they'd do it soon, but so far his instincts said they didn't intend to kill him and Jaz, not yet anyway. When the two approaching survivors got within conversation distance, Choony said calmly, "Well met, survivors. We come in peace, as envoys."

"Please drop your weapon, miss," one of the men replied.

Jaz slowly set the rifle down on the wooden runner in front of her, normally a foot rest. "You got it, mister," she said, and smiled. "We're not here to make trouble."

The man who had done the talking replied, "So what are you here for? We got no food to trade or to spare. I think you had best find another town to trade in, if that's your aim."

Choony nodded. "Of course. No one has enough food these days, and we're not here to beg or to offer trade for yours. We have enough to last until we get home and no more, but it's enough. Pretty boring fare, but sufficient." Best not to give them the false impression the wagon was loaded with fresh food and hard-to-find trade goods, or anything else of much value. "We're here to make contact with your community leaders, nothing more."

"Oh yeah? What do you want to talk about? I already said we don't have anything worth trading right now."

Choony put his hands up before him, palms together, and bowed slightly. It was a formal gesture that transformed him suddenly into an unthreatening Asian shopkeeper. Jaz, watching, blinked every time she saw him do this magic. Rising from his bow, Choony continued, "If it pleases you, we are from the Clan, north of you, and represent an alliance of independent survivor groups, and we're traveling out here to make contact with whoever we find still alive and surviving on their own. Not all your neighbors are hungry for your bones. We had our share of raiding cannibals before, but we and our allies chased them out and now any still living stay away." Choony hoped that the implied strength through numbers came through loud and clear.

In the Before times, such a statement might have caused shock or consternation, but in this dark new era assurances about rejecting cannibalism had become almost a standard greeting between strangers. The man nodded and seemed to relax a little, standing a bit easier, shoulders lowering. Choony could feel some of the tension falling away.

"Very well," the speaker said and turned to the man to his right—the one to Choony's side—saying, "Go let the boss know we got two people visiting from another group. They want to talk to him." The other man nodded and jogged away, and then there was nothing to do but wait.

Something about these people troubled Choony, but he couldn't put his finger on it. He put it down to nerves but also knew it was best to listen to instincts, and he kept alert while trying to look relaxed.

Shortly, the messenger jogged back out of the compound and stopped by the speaker. They spoke quietly for a moment. Then the speaker turned to Choony. "The boss will meet with you—he's interested in news from other places in the region, as you can imagine. Hope you're entertaining. We all want news. I'll take your rifle, but you can have it back when you leave. Kosher?"

Choony nodded, and Jaz picked up her rifle to hand to the man butt-first. They then followed their escort toward the wall of trucks and on inside. Choony looked around with a practiced eye. Experience had taught him what to look for in a survivor enclave. Signs of starvation, people missing limbs, groups with more guns than needed to defend themselves. Stacks of salvaged household goods that could have been found abandoned, but might also have been stripped during warlord-type raids.

This enclave had everything he'd expect in a peaceful enclave except piles of salvage. Possibly they kept it elsewhere, out of sight and protected, but still it felt odd. Salvage at abandoned farms meant life, for most survivor groups. The Clan had been no exception. Well, it all looked more or less as he would expect from a stable group. He'd simply keep his eyes open.

They reached an open area near the gate, where the group drew to a halt. "The wagon stays here," the speaker said, "but it'll be safe. Our guards will watch your stuff. Follow me, please."

Choony said, "My friend here will stay with the wagon, then. I mean no offense, but we don't know you yet and the little we brought with us means survival. I hope that will be okay."

The guard pursed his lips. "Sorry, but we don't know you, either. The boss said both or none. It's up to you, though. We can walk you both out, or we can walk you both to the boss."

Choony felt a certain tension in the air. Probably he and Jaz would be killed if they declined now, just on the off chance they were raider spies scoping out the defenses. Regardless, his mission was to make contact, so he made a snap decision. "I totally understand. We really do want to meet your leader, that's our mission. We would be delighted for you to lead both of us to your boss. Please do keep our wagon safe."

Jaz, nodding, added, "Trust has to start somewhere. Your house, your rules."

The escort led them one more block in and one to the right, to what seemed the center of the walled-off section of town. Along the way they noticed piles of something or other, covered by tarps and cardboard. Those must be their stockpiles, Choony decided, and felt much better.

They came to a large, ornate home with too many dead plants. Even the evergreen tree in the front yard looked brown and dying. Water must be an issue for these people, despite a stream that lay half a mile north of town. Maybe that kind of infrastructure would be something worth trading. He filed it away in his mind for possible future use. First things first.

One of their escorts knocked, and a deep voice from within called out, "Enter." The guard opened the door and led the way in while the other guard brought up the rear and closed the door behind them.

Inside, the house was warm from a fire crackling in the fireplace, and well lit by several storm lamps. It had once been the living room but now was dominated by a large L-shaped desk with filing cabinets to one side. Behind the desk sat a man who had obviously once been obese. He wasn't now, but his skin hung from him like melting rubber. It did not look healthy. The EMPs had led to everyone losing weight, of course.

The man rose behind the desk to his full height, just shy of six foot, and ran his left hand through thinning brown hair. He leaned across the desk and extended his right hand. "I'm Bradley, the Boss of Intercourse. That's my temporary title until I find something better. And that shouldn't be too difficult." He smiled and Choony relaxed a little.

Choony took the offered hand and then Jaz, smiling politely, shook his hand as well. "I'm Choony and this is Jaz. We're envoys from the Clan, up to the north a bit, and we speak for the greater Confederation our local groups have put together. They sent us to reach out and make contact with other survivor groups. Thank you for taking time to see us, boss."

"Have a seat then, guests from the Clan. We've heard of the Clan, and of this Confederation too, from traveling merchants. We used to have items to trade, but now we're set until spring planting and only that. Nothing's left we can trade."

Choony nodded, thinking. It was certainly possible they had heard of the Clan, which had become something of a local legend, after all. But the Confederation? Only the story of traveling merchants could explain that, so maybe he was being honest. Falconry merchants were roaming far from home now, after all, and the new Confederation would be just the sort of news to open doors.

"I hope you traded well," Choony said with a friendly smile, trying to be disarming. It was a type of dishonesty, he had reasoned early in this trip, but it was for an honorable cause. Still, he wasn't very good at it. Maybe he should turn it over to Jaz now.

"Bunch of horses and loads of hay, in exchange for some extra firearms we weren't using and had little ammo for. Guy said they had more ammo than guns back home, so it seemed fair. Come spring, those horses will serve us well plowing some fields or something. I leave that to my farming gurus."

"Makes sense," Choony commented, but Bradley spoke before he could continue.

"What doesn't make sense is why you're out here with two people and one gun. Doesn't add up. Care to elaborate?" He still smiled, but Choony noted that his eyes had narrowed just a fraction of an inch. He was wary, just as Choony himself was. It was a reasonable question.

"At least that question has an easy answer," Choony chuckled. "I'm a devout Buddhist, and will not participate in violence. I have no need of a weapon, since I will not use one."

"You want me to believe you've survived this long without ever getting violent with someone? I've met religious folks before, and most of 'em give up those fancy ideals as soon as their precious comfort gets threatened."

"Perhaps. But I have been lucky. I was accepted into the Clan during its earliest days, and have made myself useful in other ways since then."

"So this woman is your bodyguard, then?" Bradley asked, raising one eyebrow.

"I'm not ashamed to have a woman protect me, if that's what you mean. She's brave and capable, and she fights if people shoot at us, though that hasn't happened on this trip. More importantly, she's an envoy as well as me. Sometimes people would rather talk to me, others to her. So we both go, and it works out however it works out."

Jaz, sitting in the chair beside Choony, said, "I know you're thinking he's, like, a coward or something, but nothing could be less true. He's one of the bravest people I know."

Jaz glanced at Choony, and saw him give a faint smile and nod, so she continued, "Yeah, he won't lift a finger to do anything violent, but I've seen him run across an open field toward attackers, under gunfire, to retrieve a wounded Clanner, or to bring more ammo to a Clanner pinned down in a foxhole. He's also a capable medic."

As she spoke, Choony shifted in his seat awkwardly. He wasn't the kind of guy who liked to hear his own horn tooted, but it was important this leader knew Choony was no coward. "He speaks his mind regardless of the danger, but always manages to do so in a way that inspires people so they rethink. I've never seen him make anyone angry even when he totally disputes what they said. He's a member of the Clan's leadership council for a reason, and the Clan doesn't tolerate cowards."

Bradley, both eyebrows now raised, cocked his head at her, smiled good-humoredly and leaned back in his chair. He looked at Jaz for another long moment, and then turned to Choony and chewed on his lip. Finally he sat upright again and smiled. "Choony, I'm going to take her at her word. She's very convincing." He shifted his gaze briefly to nod an appreciation to Jaz, then returned to Choony. "I wouldn't offend the Clan by insulting a member of their Council. They surely see a good reason to keep you around. Now that I have Clan people in my office, I figure the rumors about both the Clan and the bigger alliance forming must be true, and that we have you all to thank for making our northern and western outposts a lot safer."

Choony's ears perked at that. Outposts? That implied a better level of organization than he'd have imagined from what he had seen here in town. And that made them a greater potential threat—or a greater ally. "I'm glad we could help our neighbors, even indirectly. The alliance you heard of is real. It was the Clan's leader who forged the idea into a reality. She is a remarkable woman and I'd love to introduce her to you personally someday."

Jaz nodded her agreement. "The things Cassy's led the Clan to do, the problems she's overcome, the enemies she's driven away or killed—including invader troops. I suppose she is, I mean, she's a mother bear about the Clan, with emphasis on the bear."

Bradley chuckled at the image and Jaz paused, waiting for a comment, but he waved her to go on.

"The thing is, she has a knack for finding ways to solve any problem we've come across so far, and our allies each owe the Clan their own lives one way or another because of her leadership." She paused to openly examine Bradley and added, "She acts kind of like you do, actually. I mean, when we're not under attack, she doesn't shout or bully people or act like she thinks she's special. She's always friendly and open to reasonable ideas, which is the feeling I get from you. No offense."

Bradley laughed and replied, "How could I take offense at flattery like that?" Holding his smile, he added, "Why do I feel like this is a sales pitch? A good one, because I actually believe you from the rumors I've heard, and you, Miss Jaz, are completely charming. But it still feels like a sales pitch." Then he turned back to Choony. "What does the Clan want anyway with little old Intercourse, Pennsylvania?"

Choony smiled, and gave Bradley a slight bow. "You are observant. That's a good quality in any leader. First and foremost, the Clan seeks peace between herself and her neighbors. Peace requires understanding. Other than a couple raiders and cannibal groups, most of the people we've met are happy to come to an understanding with the Clan and our allies in this regard."

"Oh, so you've met a lot? Other than the people in your Confederation, I mean."

"Some, yes. Most are simply doing what they must to survive. They're reinventing some of the old, lost crafts, and work hard to leave their kids in a less threatening world. They're just people. The survivors we've found who don't raid others have proven themselves to be courageous, able to adapt quickly, and sensible. It's been encouraging. That's why I volunteered for this travel. There is strength in numbers and we want our Confederation to thrive."

"Plus, I really like to meet new people," Jaz added, smiling winsomely at Bradley.

Bradley said, "Given the Clan's good reputation, and its resistance to the would-be conquerors of America, I suspect we can easily come to a peace agreement with you. Assuming, of course, that the Clan will honor our two-mile-radius boundary. That's our land, and we'll protect it, of course. Please don't misunderstand me—that's not a threat. It's what we claim as ours, just as the Clan claims its territory and wouldn't tolerate strangers settling next door without their approval. Or I assume they wouldn't, since no one thinks them fools."

Choony smiled. "Of course. The Clan is no fool, and we do just as you say. We've actually invited some refugee groups to settle on nearby abandoned farms, if they seem honorable. Every group we've added has made our security more solid. From my map, I believe we'd be willing to honor your two-mile territorial border. The Clan isn't looking to expand its territory, only its alliances and peace agreements. The Confederation has grown because mutual trade and support are vital to survival in our region. That's probably true in every region these days."

Bradley leaned further back, placing his hands behind his head and crossing his leg casually. "Very well, then. Let's talk about the nitty-gritty."

Choony smiled politely, but masked the giddiness he felt. A major enclave with its own outposts, and every sign that they might be a fine addition to the Confederation. This would secure the Clan's southeastern border, if an accord could be reached. He leaned forward and prepared for the real negotiations to begin. This part wasn't his strongest suit, but with Jaz at hand he never had to worry about slipping up. She knew people better than anybody.

* * *

Ethan burst out of the HQ—Cassy's house—and bolted for the outdoor kitchen. It was lunch time, and Cassy would be there shortly if she wasn't already. She wasn't in the kitchen or the chow line, so he entered the giant Army-surplus pavilion tent that served as a chow hall, and spotted Cassy as she sat down next to Frank. Michael's wife, Tiffany, was also there. He crossed the distance in half a dozen paces, and plopped down on the picnic table bench next to Cassy.

Cassy took one look at Ethan and grinned. "You look excited about something. What have you come to tell me, oh great Elfen Paladin Warrior?"

"It's Elven Shadow-Knight," he grinned back, "and it's hard to play online games without any online to speak of, but the great Shadow-Knight shall never–*never!* I say–be forgotten." He declared that last in a booming, speech-making voice, and got a chuckle from those at the table. "But yes, despite your teasing, I have great news," Ethan added in a staccato blast of words.

When Cassy raised an eyebrow, he continued, "I just got news from Florida by way of one of my HAMhead friends.

Care to guess?"

"They solved the problem with their lack of pythons in every bathtub?"

"Funny, ha ha. No, but almost as good. Last night the survivor group alliance in Florida, which had Orlando's invasion zone bottled up, launched a massive counter-assault on the city. The fighting went on all night, but a couple hours ago the last of the 'vader defensive lines cracked, and Americans are surging through the city, mopping up the Russian and Cuban forces in detail."

Frank slammed his fist on the table. "Yesss!" he hissed, and cocked his head. "I assume 'in detail' means something specific?"

Ethan replied, "Yeah, basically it means 'one piece at a time.' They're going from building to building now, slaughtering 'vaders wherever they find them. By tomorrow morning there won't be a Russian or Cuban foreign fighter left alive in Orlando, or anywhere else in Florida."

Cassy clapped Ethan on the shoulder. "That's fantastic news! It doesn't help with our ISNA-Korean problem, but it could mean a strong American core to occupy the invaders from Louisiana to Virginia—and that can only help us in the long run."

Tiffany smiled, but her tone was somber. "Well, let's pray to the Flying Spaghetti Monster, or Thor, or the god of your choice, that Florida keeps their act together and they don't fall apart from politics, now that the immediate threat is gone."

Ethan's grin faded. "Damn, Tif. You're such a TPKer."

The others stared blankly at him. Oh for crying out loud. Of course they wouldn't know even that simple gaming term... "Total Party Killer, Tiffany. A buzzkill. It's when the Game Master—"

"I get the idea, Ethan," Tiffany said, laughing. "You and

your games. If you weren't such a great fighter, too, I wouldn't know what to make of you."

Frank added, "Thanks for sharing the great news, man. It makes lunch taste so much better."

Tiffany nodded enthusiastically, then took a bite of her bacon, lettuce, and tomato sandwich, closing her eyes to savor the flavor. "Mmmm...." escaped her lips as she chewed.

Actually, after a winter of Constant Stew and bread, a B.L.T. sounded amazing to everyone... The next batch of cold-frame produce must have been harvested! It'd be a couple weeks before there was more, but the scouting teams were gathering up more fast-food trays as quickly as they found them because they made perfect cold frames.

Ethan, always ready for good food, looked around and blurted, "If you'll pardon me, I'm going to celebrate America's latest win by getting my own sammich! I'll be right back." His stomach growled loudly just as he got up, to the good-natured laughter of the others.

* * *

Cassy sat outside later, in the last full rays of sunlight for the day. It had been warmer than usual, a sure sign that spring would soon be on them.

Spring, with days full of sowing seeds in the raised beds of the Jungle, which Cassy had designed to become the farm's intensive gardening section and the Clan had taken as proof of Cassy's genius despite her protests that she had learned it from books.

Other teams would keep busy throwing out seed bombs that would sow dandelions and other opportunistic "weeds" that would soon restore the soil for thousands of acres all around Clanholme itself. Weeds were merely early succession plants, as she had taught her Clan classes, and would give way soon enough to other more human-useful plants as the soil improved from the barren, starved dirt it had become under modern farming practices.

Meanwhile, dandelions themselves were delicious as fresh produce, and the other seeds in their weed bombs started plants with either food value or medicinal uses, or might germinate into flowers to draw pollinating bees into the self-sustaining ecosystem... and spring was when the new, half-random plant groupings took form.

Also a result of such projects, spring was almost as busy as autumn. This current brief window of relative warmth in the sunlight would be one of the last she could enjoy at leisure until after the autumn harvests were in. She had no trouble lazing back to enjoy it.

Her little handheld radio crackled, and she brought her mind back to focus on Ethan's voice. "Charlie One, this is Charlie Two," Ethan announced. "We have five riders inbound from the south—Lititz just alerted us. They'll be here in about twenty mikes, coming up via Newport Road. They say they're envoys sent by Choony, but no additional information."

Cassy's heart leapt with joy at hearing that Choony still lived. She figured he would, or she wouldn't have sent him on his mission with Jaz, but confirmation was a glad and welcome bit of news. "Received. Get a squad to meet them outside the southern Food Forest zone, disarm them or turn them away. We're eager to talk but not if they're walking around as armed strangers."

Ethan acknowledged and the radio went dead. Cassy wasn't sure which one she wanted to deal with more, the last full rays of sunshine or new envoys to meet and greet. Probably the sunshine, but too bad. Duty called. She let out a long breath, then got up from her lawn chair and hurried inside to spruce up.

Half an hour later, Cassy watched from the guard tower with borrowed binoculars, waiting for something to happen. Then she saw people emerging from the Food Forest south of her house—her ten guards, five on each side of five new people. The newcomers walked in a row pushing mountain bikes. She handed the binoculars back to the tower guard with a nod and climbed back down the rope ladder to await their arrival.

Michael joined her as she waited. Ethan had of course alerted the head of security about the intrusion. Her military C.O. was armed only with his pistol, however, and Cassy was grateful that he thought better of bringing his usual rifle. Greeting guests was often tense work, and leaders carrying rifles didn't shout trust or confidence.

Cassy muttered, "Thanks for joining me."

"Of course. Any idea who they are?"

"No. Lititz radioed ahead to say these guys were coming, but all they said was that Choony and Jaz had sent them. But they have mountain bikes, like those raiders from Hershey, so we need to be on our toes."

"I just hope they're of more use than yesterday's," Michael replied. "Those people were nice, and very happy to join under Lititz's banner, but I couldn't see they'd be of much use."

Cassy nodded slowly. He was right. They needed someone strong farther south in order to expand the Confederation's borders in that direction, but so far Choony's contacts had been with isolated, sometimes hurting homesteads. Not that they weren't welcome, of course, but they weren't terribly useful. "They sent five people, though," she said thoughtfully. "That's a hopeful sign, if they had that many to spare."

Cassy and Michael stood in silence until the three columns approached, and then she strode forward to greet them, Michael right behind her. When she got close enough, she stopped and waited for them to come the last few feet. Let them send out their leader, rather than trying to guess.

The second man in line set down his bicycle and walked up to Cassy directly. He extended his hand. It was hard and calloused, like her own. "You must be Cassy, leader of the Clan and the Confederation, am I right?"

Cassy shook his hand and smiled. "I am, thank you. And you are?"

"I'm Thomas, but I guess by your custom my name's Intercourse. Your envoy, Jaz, told me to say that."

Cassy choked back laughter. Of course Jaz would do that. What a wonderful name... "Hello then, Thomas. She's right, and we'll call you by your home enclave name from now on, at least when you represent your group. An interesting name," she added, grinning. "I bet you've heard every possible joke already so I'll refrain. Won't you and your companions please come have some water or cider, and we have some leftovers from lunch if you're hungry."

Intercourse smiled back. "We'd love something to drink to wash the road dust away, but we brought our own provisions. Thank you for the offer."

Cassy nodded, approving. It was another good sign. These days you could tell much about a person by whether they accepted an offer of food or not. The greedy and the needy accepted; the polite and self-sufficient did not. "Very well, friend. Why don't you and I retire to my house, and our Clanners will take care of your people while we talk." She turned to Michael and said, "Can you have someone send us some water, cider, and a bottle of wine? We may ask you or Frank to join us in a bit."

Then she led Intercourse into her home. Closing the door behind her, she said, "Please feel free to take a seat on the couch." She sat in the reclining chair, facing the couch. "So,

Intercourse. Where is that place? I haven't heard of it. I spent most of my life in Philly and Chesterbrook, before the EMPs."

"It was a small town about eight or ten miles east of Lancaster. Religious people settled it before that word took on new meanings, and named it for the sociable, cohesive nature they hoped for in their new community. Now it's an even smaller town."

Cassy raised an eyebrow. East of Lancaster... "Oh, so you know the people at White Stag Farms?" She said it casually, but it was anything but casual. White Stag people had fled their farms after the invaders sprayed it with their deadly brown-haze defoliant, and had conquered her people for a time. Now their leader, Peter, was long dead and missed by no one.

"Yes ma'am. They're just east of us, maybe two miles. I knew them before the EMPs, and they were pretty good people. Tight-knit, though. Now that area's dead and empty. We don't know where they went, or if they all just died when the enemy sprayed their farm. I've kinda wondered about what happened to them."

That was the right answer. Cassy smiled at Intercourse. "Yes, a few of them eventually joined the Clan but the rest died, I'm sorry to say. So tell me, how did your people meet my envoys?"

Michael entered with a cloth grocery sack containing water bottles, a sealed-top pitcher of fresh-drawn apple cider, and a bottle of some white wine or other. He handed Intercourse a water bottle, then set about pouring cups of cider. "Don't mind me," he said. "Happy to play the role of server today." He nodded to Intercourse and added, "My people are busy getting to know your people. They seem to be hitting it off."

Intercourse nodded to Michael and then continued to

Cassy, "Your envoys, Choony and Jaz, came to us. Walked right up to our walls all calm and casual, unafraid. They didn't even look nervous. That's rare. It got our Boss's attention, and out of curiosity he had us let them in. The Boss and they talked for a good hour at least. Choony gave assurances that your alliance would respect our two-mile border. He said you're open to trade and so we thought, isn't that great, because so are we. So as of right now, we have agreed with your diplomats to a peace treaty, and we want to open trade as soon as possible."

Cassy nodded, her eyes sparkling. "We'll abide by the agreement they made, pending verification from them of course. What sort of things do you have to trade?"

"I'm afraid that we currently have more things we need than things to offer, ma'am, but the Boss had an idea to balance the books out, so to speak."

Cassy pursed her lips. Damn. Maybe freeloaders after all, despite what their manners would indicate. "We don't trade for free, of course. As you probably know from experience, handing out supplies is a sucker's bet. Everyone is barely getting by, so trade right now is more about swapping things you have for the things they have. Yes?"

Intercourse smiled at Cassy, seemingly oblivious to the unfavorable implications and blind to the expression on her face. "Of course. How else could subsistence communities do it? What we need isn't food. That, we have enough of. What we need are odds and ends. Junk siding, pipes, duct tape—miscellaneous stuff you can use to make things, repair things, keep old technology working, even make into art or jerry-rig into useful stuff right on the spot. It's crap you might have tons of, just lying around or piled up under tarps. Most of that stuff in Intercourse was looted by other towns before we got ourselves organized a couple months ago. Some of it got sprayed or stolen by the invading troops, too.

We're rebuilding now and we need that stuff."

Cassy sipped her water, then accepted a cup of cider from Michael with an appreciative glance. "So what does Intercourse have to offer in return? It doesn't sound like you have much."

Intercourse shrugged. "Only a few things. A warehouse full of tarps of various sizes, perfect for building cover, for patching roofs, collecting or holding off rainwater, frost-protecting crops, collecting stocks of next year's seeds, catching nut and fruit tree windfalls, whatever. We lucked onto a fully-stocked Army Surplus Store with bins full of all sorts of this and that. We're happy to trade any of it at good value for us both. And lastly, we have something we know you want because Choony and Jaz told us all about it."

"What might that be?" Cassy asked as she peered at her surprising guest over the rim of her cup.

"We offer you an alliance. A strong, well-organized southern neighbor that has survived these hungry times, outlasted the threats all around us, and is fully equipped. Between our compound in Intercourse and our outlying bases, we have about three hundred able-bodied adults under arms, mostly with civilian weapons but also with a few of the invaders' AK rifles, or however you call those. We noticed we were getting fewer and fewer raiders from the north and west, and now we know why. It's because you all got organized and cleaned house. Just like we did to your south. So let's be allies."

"And that makes you want an alliance? Could you explain further? It seems as if you've got a good handle on your territory, and we have ours locked down pretty tightly as well. I'd expect you to be *less* likely to need an alliance, not more. Just a thought." Really, she wanted to gauge his response to her skepticism.

"The Boss figures that makes us all kindred spirits. Plus,

he was impressed by your envoy's pacifist ways. You still took him in even though he won't fight, and you just don't see much of that these days, especially not for someone who looks like one of the invaders. And on top of that, the invaders are still out there somewhere, plotting and getting ready to pounce. A stronger alliance means safety in numbers. And one more thing..."

Cassy nodded, but kept her face expressionless. She'd recognized Choony's "safety in numbers" phrase, of course, but that actually strengthened their believability. Whatever the envoy said next would be their true motivation, she decided, based on her pre-EMP marketing expertise. Maybe it would be reasonable, maybe not, but in any case it would speak volumes about what kind of people they were. "Go ahead, please. Speak freely."

"As your diplomats have no doubt discovered, there are small homesteads and farms scattered throughout our corner of Pennsylvania and many are still occupied. Choony explained that when you add smaller groups to your Confederation, you place them under the wing of the nearest, strongest group of survivors. For our region, that's us. We would ask that survivor groups in our neck of the woods be put under our, what do you call it, sphere of influence? By going through us, we improve communications, speed up reaction times and make our region more tight-knit."

That wasn't bad, Cassy mused, nodding thoughtfully. That was her exact reasoning for the way the Clan assigned small holdings to bigger nearby partners in the Confederation for protection, trade, and diplomacy. She could live with that. Of course it also meant they were trading their strength for free holdings in their area, negotiated by Clan envoys rather than spending their own manpower on it. "I think that, pending our agents' report when they return, your proposal sounds reasonable enough.

We'd also want to send one of our military leaders to your enclave to take a look at your defenses and supplies. You can say no to that, but I think it would greatly help in building trust from our people to yours, and it would let us know in more detail what we can do to help improve your defenses. We have some top-notch military talent among us. Marine Corps officers, for example. Michael, today's so-called server, is a former Marine Corps Major and the Clan's military C.O. His people are well qualified to actually help you with field-tested advice. And maybe we can pick up some ideas from how you do things as well. We're all in this boat together; might as well act like it."

"Well then," Intercourse said as he raised his glass in a toast, "I think we can come to an arrangement. I'd like to celebrate this moment by sharing one of my granola bars with you, if you'll join me?"

Cassy smiled, and nodded. That offer, too, spoke volumes about what kind of people these were. They would share food with their friends, and that helped greatly to put her mind at ease. Jaz and Choony really outdid themselves, bringing in this new ally. "Of course, that's generous of you. But only if you'll join us for evening chow." She smiled, visualizing the looks on their faces when they got served B.L.T. sandwiches and fresh cider.

- 4 -

2230 HOURS - ZERO DAY +190

CARL REINED IN his horse as he approached the Liz Town southern gate. It was still damn cold outside but the snow had mostly melted earlier in the day, the first warm day in quite a while. Now everything was starting to freeze, turning everything icy, and the deposed Liz Town envoy was glad he made it back home in one run instead of having to camp outside. To either side of the Liz Town gate, shipping containers were stacked two-high, filled with rubble, and the interior facing had tons of rubble piled up against it; the rest of the walls were made of rubble, but they were slowly reinforcing it with more shipping containers just like at the gates.

He needed sleep, a bath, and food, and in the morning he would need to talk to Pamela. She obviously knew something about why he had been relieved as the Liz Town envoy to Clanholme, judging from her cryptic message she had sent via his replacement. It was cruel irony that even here and now at the end of the world, his damn ex-wife was still around to make his life miserable. And so far, still trying to "win him back." She should have gotten the hint when the woman Carl had left her for died of dysentery early on. Carl hadn't truly left Pamela for another woman a year ago—he had just left. The other woman was a symptom, not the cause, but Pamela didn't seem to understand that.

Carl shouted up to the gatekeepers, "Carl Woburn, Citizen of the Timber Wolf Band, requesting access. I come home with open hands."

One of the guards shouted down at him, "Liz Town welcomes her wayward Wolf-brother. Why are your open hands empty?"

Carl replied, "Because Liz Town and my Band fill me with all I need."

Having exchanged the passphrases correctly, Carl heard the flurry of noises from the horses on the other side, harnessed through a pulley to a big-rig truck, which now slid aside to grant him access. He made two clicks with his tongue and nudged his horse forward, and rode into Liz Town; the creak of the gate being closed again echoed behind him.

Before him stretched the Clear Zone, a 100-yard expanse where everything had been torn down to build the town walls, both exterior and the smaller walls that divided the town up into Band Territories. Only the remaining roads were public access, as they wound through all the territories. Timber Wolf turf was on the west side of town, and thus often faced the brunt of raids from Hershey and elsewhere, a fact of which his Band was mighty proud.

Carl wound his way through Diamondback Band turf and on through the narrow gateway into Timber Wolf territory. His home was one room in a very nice house that he shared with other moderately high-ranking Band members. He was high enough that he didn't have to share a room, an uncommon privilege. Once inside the house, he gathered an MRE, two gallon-jugs of water, and the washbasin, and went to his room. First he ate and drank his fill, then used the remaining water for a cold "bath." Fresh clothes on, dirty clothes in the trash bag for laundering later, and then just before midnight he collapsed onto his bed in total exhaustion…

…and sat bolt upright, whipping out his pistol from under the bed. But his pistol flew from his hands and landed across the room, and Carl sat in the dark, his mind befuddled by sleep, dumbly trying to figure out what the hell was going on. A soft female voice in the darkness said, "Welcome home, Carl."

He rubbed the sleep from his eyes. It was pitch black. He snarled, "Pamela? What the hell time is it?"

"Time for you to get your reflexes back. If I had wanted to kill you, I might have actually succeeded tonight." Pamela sparked her lighter and the small flame was blinding. She lit the storm lantern on his night stand and turned it down low so there was just enough light to see by. "And we need to talk. I told you to come see me when you got back, or did you not get the message?"

Carl replied, "I did get it. But I needed sleep and food before I came to find you."

"No time, sweetie. We may be divorced but I still care about you. I wouldn't want to see something awful happen to you."

That got Carl's attention and cleared his mind. She wasn't here to cajole him but to warn him. "I appreciate that. Okay, what was so important that you had to break into my room in the middle of the night?"

"I know you. First thing in the morning you'd head to the Wolf Den to complain to our Alpha about being replaced as the Confed envoy. It's important for your business interests. But you have been away long enough to miss an important development."

Carl swung his feet off the bed onto the floor and rested his elbows on his knees. "I'm all ears."

In the dim light, he saw Pamela purse her lips, faintly shaking her head. "Our Alpha Wolf doesn't know it, but he's about to be deposed as both Band leader and Speaker of Liz Town. Diamondback's leader will replace him. Much of our Band and three others have decided that we need a change—a new Speaker and a new direction—if we're to save ourselves from what's coming."

Carl froze. The hair on the back of his neck stood up, and he felt goosebumps along his arms. What the hell was she saying? It made no sense. Things were going well and the other Bands were happy with the Timber Wolf leadership over Liz Town. Or so he had thought. A growing fear lurched in his stomach. "Pamela, I'm not awake enough for riddles. What's coming, and why are you telling me?"

"The Midwest Republic is coming, Carl, and they're too powerful to stop. They'll burn down anyone in their way, including Cassy and her Clan. It's time to survive, Carl. There are enough of us who see the reality of the situation and if that means a new Speaker, so be it." Pamela paused but Carl just stared at her. She placed her hand on top of his. "Carl, I want you on my side. You need to know that our people are watching you. If you go to our Band leader, they'll know, and your life will be in danger. So please, stay in your room until I call for you. I couldn't bear to lose you a second time."

Carl's mind spun, but it was stuck in neutral. The engine revved but his mind went nowhere while Pamela's words replayed themselves in his mind. Pamela, his ex-wife, his most loyal pack-sister... and she was a traitor. There was no way around it. She was too deeply involved to walk away. He knew she'd only feel guilty later about her treason, and her conspirators would certainly kill him to protect the cabal she had gotten herself involved in. It might put her at risk, too, and they may be divorced but... wait... this meeting was a test as much as an attempt to rescue him. She had put him on the spot just by warning him.

But then the thought struck him that if the cabal held the majority view, they would already have struck. They stayed in the shadows because they weren't yet coming from a position of strength. If he could just warn the Alpha... But to do that, first he'd have to pass Pamela's test. Okay, do one step at a time.

Carl smiled at Pamela now taking both of her hands into his own. "You know I still care deeply for you, right? Maybe I fell out of love with you just before the invasion, but that doesn't mean I stopped caring. Thank you for warning me. I've... I have concerns about the Empire as well. I've shouted to any who would listen that we need stronger defenses, more people, more guns, if we're going to stop the Empire. And the Alpha hasn't listened, not to me and not to anyone else. I can't say what will happen between you and me, but who can tell the future?" He cocked his head and added, "But at least we do know what's likely to come at us when it warms up, and it needs to be handled the best way for Liz Town. I'd rather be an ally with them than conquered."

Carl paused a moment, then continued, "I have one question. If I do this—if I step out of the way and let this happen—will my people and my business be taken care of? I'm responsible for them, and though some won't understand why I did it, they'll still be alive to figure out it was for the best."

Pamela's grin grew wide, and when she spoke her voice seemed to soar with joy. "Of course. Those who steer us in the right direction will be rewarded, both by the new Speaker and by the Empire. They've made us specific offers and assurances, and you stand to make a great many profitable barters under our new arrangements. Liz Town will be made the next Falconry, and we can dominate east-west trade the way they do now. You're in line to take a piece of that. Oh, Carl, you've got to join me! It'd crush me to lose you."

Carl nodded as though giving serious thought to her words. Then he said, "So, it was you who had me replaced as envoy to the Confederation. To get me here, to warn me."

Pamela squeezed his hand. "Of course. The woman we sent as your replacement is one of our people, too. She's gathering intel there before separating Liz Town from our Clan entanglements. The more we help the Republic, the better off we'll be when it's over. It's inevitable. The Midwest Republic will win—they hold all the high cards. But we have a choice about whether we survive and thrive or die."

What a stupid thing to say. No one ever got to choose whether they lived or died. Just ask Adamstown. They opened their gates to the invaders and cooperated with them, only to be lined up outside and slaughtered while their town burned.

Sometimes it simply comes down to fight... or die. Sure, the Confederation took revenge for Adamstown, slaughtering the invaders who did it down to the last man as far as anyone could tell. But Adamstown was still a smoking graveyard. And now some in Liz Town were trying to go the same route. He had long ago decided that appeasing evil never spares you from that evil—only hard, bloody resistance has a chance. Of course, first he had to live long enough to warn the Speaker.

"Sounds brilliant. I was so angry when you had me replaced, but when she gave me our code for meeting, I knew there had to be more to the story." He gave her his most sincere smile.

Pamela smiled back, and Carl knew he had her. She had been his wife for years and he knew her well. He continued, "I know logic when I see it, and what you have going here... It can ensure our survival as a town. I'd been racking my brain for so long about how we could begin to beat something as big as the Empire, this Midwest Republic. I don't like what you're doing, but you're right. It might be the only way we all get to live long enough to find out what the future holds for me and you. For all of us here in Liz Town."

Carl stretched his arms out and they embraced in a hug, which he held for a long minute with his chin resting on her shoulder. He counted backwards from *ten... nine...* and thought about how much he'd like to plunge a knife in this traitor's back right now. This sort of disgusting character defect was the reason he had left her in the first place, after he figured out what a self-serving, conniving bitch she really was... *two... one...*

Carl separated himself from her, then put his hands on her shoulders and looked her in the eyes. "Thank you, Pamela, for seeing a way out where I did not. What do you need me to do?"

"Just stay in your room or at chow until I call for you, sweetie. I'm so happy to have you with me on this! I'll let you know when you have a part to play in this. You'll see me again in a few days."

Carl smiled at her, nodding, but hell no—she wouldn't be seeing him again until it was time to hang her and the rest of her traitors off the north gate walls as a warning to the Empire. Thinking about that day, it got easier to make his smile believable.

* * *

0545 HOURS - ZERO DAY +193

Cassy peered through her binoculars from the crest of the hill, surveying the skirmish going on some eighty yards away, below. A dozen scrawny, bedraggled men with hunting rifles were either lying prone in the dirt or hiding behind bushes and rocks, firing into Taj Mahal, the enclave of third-generation Indians she had settled near Clanholme and helped get on their feet. "Glad we got word of these guys from your scouts, Michael. Taj Mahal will be hard-pressed to repel them on their own without bad losses."

Michael grunted. She heard him telling the other Clan troops, including his Marines, to move up to the crest, and assigning targets already visible. "On my count, fire at will," he said.

When he hit three, a deafening barrage of gunfire erupted to both sides of her, then the staccato *bang, bang* of continued firing. Down below, she saw most of the raiders fall, go limp, or roll around screaming. Their cries were cut short as her fighters continued firing, and ten seconds later it was all over. Cassy turned to look at Michael. "Well done. It's amazing what crossfire from elevation can do when they don't know you're there."

Michael nodded somberly. "It's a crippling force amplifier, for sure." He then ordered the troops to descend, spread out with weapons ready in case any raiders survived to return fire. None did.

As Cassy followed down to the secured battlefield, she saw the Taj Mahal people coming out from behind cover. Their leader, Barry, spotted her and walked toward her, and they met in the middle.

"Cassy, thank goodness you made it on time," Barry said, grinning.

Cassy shook his hand eagerly. "I'm glad we made it, too. A scout happened to see them on the move, and we were out to ambush them. I guess we did, in a way."

Barry looked around the field as both his and Cassy's people double-checked the bodies to make sure they were dead, and they divvied up whatever supplies were gathered without any direction from their leaders—there was a deal, after all, and half of all battle loot was owed to Cassy. She didn't ask for more just because she had been the one to decide the battle. He said, "These are Hershey raiders, if I had to guess. Weird they wound up here."

Cassy frowned. "What the heck are Hershey's people doing so far south? Usually Liz Town gets them before they can bother the rest of the Confederation."

Michael approached as she said it, and shook his head. "Ethan talked to them this morning, so we know they're alive, but they either didn't see these guys or didn't tell us about them. I expect to see more of these types of underfed raiders in the future."

Cassy mulled that over. In his terse, not always direct style, Michael was saying that Liz Town wasn't being effective, that he expected them to let slip more bands of hungry raiders. That bothered her because today's raid, combined with the scene at the last Confed meeting, didn't bode well. "I'm sure they just slipped by, Michael," Cassy said, mostly for Barry's benefit.

Turning to Barry she said, "Alright, the loot's divvied up. I'll let you get back to your people, they'll want to celebrate I'm sure. You need anything, friend?"

Barry smiled, but shook his head. "A working microwave? Short of that, we have what we need. Our earthworks for spring planting are coming along great, so we're nearly set for spring planting. We found tons of clover seed nearby, which we'll use for ground cover everywhere we don't plant something else."

"Alright, Barry, that's great news. Radio Ethan if you need anything, okay?"

They shook hands and Barry left back to his own people. Cassy turned to Michael. "Let Ethan know about this when we get back. Something isn't right. Between this and the sudden replacement Liz Town envoy, I wonder what the hell those people are up to. Something feels very wrong about this."

"Whatever it is," Michael replied, "I'm telling our Confed allies to double up on their scout patrols."

Cassy nodded but didn't reply. What was there to say? If Liz Town was sloughing their duties, everyone else would have to pull more weight to keep everyone safe. If that continued into spring, it would mean fewer people working the farms. Bad all around.

* * *

Captain Samuel Pease, Midwest Republic Army, sat near a fire with his sidekick, Brett, and warmed his hands. His breakfast tray sat in the dirt beside him. As always, he was still hungry after eating everything they gave him. There was never enough, dammit. The last time he had been full was after raiding Cincinnati with those troops from the general-in-the-mountain. Both the soldiers he and Brett had killed on the sly had MREs, which of course he didn't turn in for Division of Spoils. That was more of a guideline than a rule, if they didn't know you had loot or where you got it...

Brett's annoying voice interrupted Samuel's thoughts. "When are we going on another joint-training mission? It was loads of fun, but I haven't been full since then." He tossed his tray into the dirt again.

It was for the Indentured to pick up after soldiers, one of the great perks of service. Samuel nudged his tray with the toe of his boot. "You remember those soldiers' faces when they saw what we did? That one family had to die, of course, and when you gotta do something—"

"—you might as well enjoy it!" they said in unison.

Brett said, "Yeah, Sam. It's on my highlights reel, the

whole thing. Those tough-boy Army guys have been hiding up in their mountain base this whole time. I bet they never saw anything like *that* before, Cap'n. You figure that's why we got assigned to this unit?"

"Naw. The major told me we did a great job, so I doubt it."

"What'd the major tell you?" Brett asked, eyes bright with anticipation of a good laugh.

"He said damn near everyone in that Army unit we cross-trained with filed a complaint about us and almost all of us who went on that mission. I guess we weren't the only ones to have a good old time down there in burning Cincinnati. He said they 'got a much better understanding now of the Republic's operational tactics and capabilities,' which I figure means they all went home to puke and cry to momma."

Brett laughed, happy the story ended with a punchline. "So then why did we get reassigned here? I didn't think we were going to be doing much more expanding to the east anymore."

Samuel nodded. "I thought so, too. I figured they had enough of invading others for more land, but I guess once you have a taste for conquest, only more of it will do."

Brett grew quiet and stared into the fire a moment, then said, "I have mixed feelings about that. On the one hand, it means we get to have more fun and games, which I more or less thought we were done with. On the other hand, I don't figure it's necessary. We got enough land and then some. It's like those people we met during our travels... We never took what we didn't need, right? We were friendly and all unless we had to take something."

"Yeah, I know what you mean," Samuel said. "I have mixed feelings, too. But then again, orders are orders, and that makes it necessary. Assuming we get such orders again."

"Damn, Sam. We're bound to get orders like that. Have you seen who all makes up your new command? Half of them are scouts, for crying out loud. The only reason for scouts on a border unit sure isn't for defense. And more units are trickling in since we got here. I think we'll be on our bikes real soon, chewing up miles and making all those little towns Republic."

Samuel nodded. Brett was probably right, and they'd soon invade the free lands to the east. The Republic mostly used bikes instead of horses because horses were scarce, and because bikes were faster after about the first three days. They didn't need supplies, whereas horses ran out of saddle-feed in a couple days and had to graze. It was a good thing bikes were better, Samuel mused, because most of the Republic's horses were now being used to pull railway cars or wagons. Any operational orders would put a high priority on railway stations, to resupply their forces.

Samuel said, "Yeah. With all these scouts, we're probably going to go invite more survivors to vote on joining us."

Brett frowned. "Don't make sense. We got all the land we need. But like you said, the higher-ups probably got a taste for conquest now. And not all of those survivor towns out there are going to vote the smart way. We'll have to put on our game faces again, because you know how the Republic 'requisitions' all the supplies of those who don't join, like a tax. They're better off joining and only paying half of what they got, but a lot of those idiots got it in their head they can do as they like. Life isn't like that."

Samuel shrugged. "There's always someone bigger, badder, and more organized telling folks what to do." He laughed. "I think they call it government."

"Sam, I hope you're wrong. We got what we need. I don't much like putting on our game faces just because. We only took what we needed when it was just you and me. I miss those days."

"Me too, Brett. Me too. But we take care of us first, right? We may be hungry, but we sure aren't starving like most of those folks out there." Samuel used his thumb to motion east, beyond the Republic's control. "Of course, that's because the Republic kills off what we can't support. If we can't take it, we burn it."

"It's a shame," Brett replied, staring into the fire.

It was indeed a shame. But Samuel was no fool. When you gotta do something, you might as well have fun doing it.

- 5 -

0345 HOURS - ZERO DAY +194

CARL STRETCHED HIS back after crouching by his third-floor bedroom window for the last hour, peering out to look for movement, any sign of watchers. He'd spotted one earlier, after chow, posted hiding across the street from the front door, but he was fairly sure there were no spies in back of the house, where his bedroom window faced. He picked up his rappelling rope and at one end tied a Tumble Hitch knot around one of his bed's steel legs. Grabbing the correct length, the side that would hold, he climbed out the third-story window and slid feet-first down, using his booted feet to control the descent. Once on the patio at the bottom, he stashed the rope's trailing ends out of sight as best he could among the standing evergreen trees that lined the patio.

Then he bolted toward the back fence line, jumped up, hooked his elbow over the top edge, and rolled over the top, landing on his feet in the pitch-black alley behind the house. There, from one of the derelict trash cans that lined the alleyway—no one had ever bothered to take them in after the EMPs—he pulled out a black jacket and a shemaugh that he kept hidden there. In moments he was suitably clad in mostly black, and the shemaugh would partially obscure his face without being obvious that was what he was doing. He jogged to the end of the alley, then slowed to a brisk walk, slow enough to seem casual but fast enough that he hoped anyone looking would assume he had somewhere to be.

He spared a moment to be thankful that the Speaker of Liz Town was a Timber Wolf Band member—had he lived in another band's territory it would have been nearly impossible to get to his house without being seen and challenged. As it was he walked down the street, heading three blocks north to the right cross street. Halfway there, he heard a scuff of shoes behind him, but he managed to avoid looking, or skipping a step. His pulse picked up; someone was behind him and at this time of night it was probably no coincidence. At the next alley, with only a block to go, he took his time turning right, and off the street. After three paces, he spun on his heels and drew his knife, a simple five-inch fixed blade with a Tanto point, ideal for punching through the thick jackets and layers that everyone wore this time of year, but far less useful for slashing attacks. Still, slashing wasn't ideal anyway when everyone was padded for winter weather.

He waited, heart pounding, trying desperately to breath quietly despite his body's adrenalized need for air... Several seconds later, a man came around the corner at a half-run, clearly trying to catch up to him, and Carl thrust his knife straight forward. Between his thrust, the heavy tip of his knife, and the man's momentum, the knife slid through the other man's ribs almost effortlessly, sinking up to the hilt. Whoever this man was, he stared at Carl with eyes open wide with shock and surprise, then slowly fell to the side, his weight tearing the knife blade free. He was dead by the time he hit the ground, landing on his back.

"Amateur," Carl muttered.

He threw the knife over the fence into the overgrown shrubs of the abandoned house there and stuffed the corpse into a dumpster, being careful not to get blood on himself. There wasn't a lot of blood. That done, Carl put his hands in his pockets and casually strode out of the alley and continued on his way toward the Alpha's house.

Of course, there would be people watching there, too. Even if Pamela's cabal wasn't watching, every Band of any size would have the building under observation, noting who came and went and how long they stayed. Knowledge was power. He patted his jacket and felt his other knife resting comfortably within its sheath, but hoped not to have to use it. He'd have to find a way to get inside unobserved.

Fortunately, Carl knew this layout like the back of his hand. A narrow path, supposedly an alley but too narrow for two people to pass side by side, ran behind the Alpha's house. It was completely overgrown—had been for years—but before the EMPs it had been tunneled out by neighborhood kids as a play fort. He zipped his jacket and tucked his shemaugh in like a scarf so it wouldn't catch on anything, and pushed aside a bush. As expected, there was a tunnel, easily large enough for a kid but cramped for a man Carl's size. It was his only real hope of reaching the Alpha unobserved, though, so he took a breath and crawled in. In the time since the EMPs, a few ambitious branches had grown into the chopped-out tunnel, but with some effort and his knife he removed them. That took longer than it should have, but Tanto-tipped knives sucked at that sort of work.

Twenty minutes later he was at the brush that hid an opening into the tunnel, adjacent to the Alpha's fence. A jump and a tumble later, he found himself inside the Alpha's backyard and bolted for the rear of the house. He knew there was a cast iron downspout from the roof there, and he shimmied up it to the balcony, flipped over the railing, and peered into the blacked-out room of his leader, the Alpha of the Timber Wolf Band, Speaker of Liz Town. Inside, nothing moved. He pulled an old credit card and had quickly opened the double French doors, slid inside, and closed the doors after him. Then he froze, and simply stood listening to the noises of the night. Nothing sounded out of the ordinary; he had made it undetected. Now for the easy part...

Carl crept to the four-poster bed in the center of the room, against one wall, and drew aside the sheer curtain. He whispered, "Hey boss, got a minute?"

The Alpha sat bolt upright and as he did so he withdrew his hand from under his pillow, a revolver in hand, but Carl half-expected that. No one slept deeply these days. Carl, being fully alert, disarmed his Alpha with a quick maneuver that used both his hands and left him holding the gun. "Whoa, not here to hurt you, boss."

The Alpha said, groggily, "What the hell? Who? What?"

Carl grinned in the darkness. "Take a minute. It's Carl, and we're in your bedroom."

"Goddammit, Carl. You scared me half to death. What time is it?"

"It's four thirty a.m. We gotta talk."

"So make an appointment—"

"No, it can't wait. No one can know I came to you with this."

The Alpha rubbed his eyes and glanced around in the room's dim light before turning his gaze again to Carl. "You'd better have a good explanation."

Carl nodded. There was a reason Carl wasn't the Alpha and his friend was, and that reason was aggression, drive, ambition. Things Carl didn't pride himself on and didn't want. But the Alpha also prized his integrity, and that was something Carl did respect. "I do, trust me."

"Well? Out with it." The Alpha stood from his bed and

put on his robe, then walked to the desk in his room. From it, he pulled out a bottle of Wild Turkey bourbon. "Want a snort?"

"Sure," Carl replied, and took the offered glass with a nod of thanks. "Right to the point, then." He paused to take a sip of bourbon, and sighed, "Ahhh..."

"This isn't a slumber party, Carl. I sure hope you do actually get right to the point."

"You know there's people here who feel we shouldn't stand against the Empire."

"I know that, but those people aren't in charge. I'm the Speaker, Carl, not them. Don't worry about it."

"One of them *is* in charge. Can I worry now?"

"What, the SecDef? He's my brother-in-law, and loyal to a fault. Our troops are solidly behind me."

"Not the SecDef, not that I know of anyway. But your SecState is one of them. She—"

"Pamela? Your ex wife? Don't be foolish, Carl. She's been loyal and one of our core people since the very beginning."

"She's loyal when it suits her purposes. It doesn't suit her anymore. You don't know her like I—"

"She's loyal!" he said, raising his voice, but then took a deep breath and turned to listen toward the door. When no noise of rushing guards came, he continued in a quieter voice, "She's always been loyal. She's your ex, so you hate her and see the worst, but—"

"That's not it, dammit! She *came to me*, to try to recruit me. There's a conspiracy and it goes up high. She said you'd be out of office pretty damn soon, and then she and the cabal are going to buckle to the Empire. Says it's the only way we all get to live, because she's convinced we can't hold off the Empire."

"Bullshit. They can be beaten, and have been already. Springfield stopped them cold in Illinois, and God only knows how many thousands of Chippewas are in northern Michigan, but it was enough to stomp the Republic's troops into the bloody dirt. Chicago Militia's, too. Tell me again why I should believe this story, Carl. Are you sure you aren't letting your emotions get in the way? Or are you just jealous of Pamela's position?"

Carl clenched his jaw. This was not going as planned. "I'm not jealous, dammit. Pamela's a damned traitor. She called me home from Clanholme and replaced me with one of her own plotters."

"Pamela told me you'd been acting funny lately. It's why she had you relieved from your envoy duties. She thought the pressure was getting to you, and I think I think I see it too."

Carl's jaw dropped and he stared at the Alpha wide-eyed. "Sir, you can't mean that. I'm here trying to warn you, risking my own life to do so, and—"

"And now you think people want to kill you?" the Alpha said. "Enough of this nonsense. Carl, I know you. I believe that *you* believe the things you're saying, but I need you to return to your quarters and stay there until I summon you. I have to decide what to do with you. Maybe time away from the stress of your duties will help."

"But sir, if I—"

"I said that's enough," the Alpha snapped, his hand up as if to say halt. Then he sighed and lowered his voice. "Carl, I'm going to put you under house arrest, and you are relieved of all your duties for now. Go home, get some sleep, read a book."

"But Pamela—"

The Alpha's face turned bright red. "This is a damn order, not a suggestion. Now get the hell out of my room."

The Alpha stared at Carl, eyes unwavering as he met Carl's gaze. After a few moments, Carl looked away and let out a long, deep breath. "Yes, sir. I hear and I obey."

Neither said another word as Carl left the way he had come in. If he said another word he'd probably end up getting an escort home, and that would be the death of them both shortly afterward, in all likelihood. Carl shimmied down the cast iron pipe and quickly vanished the way he'd come.

But in the tunnel, instead of turning right to go home, he turned left. The tunnel let out amidst rubble from a burnt-out section of town, and from there Carl began to run. He had a safehouse set up out here in the supposed barrens, stocked well enough to keep him going for months. It would give him time to decide what to do next, and who could be trusted. Among his large business enterprises he had several rough, shady people who took care of his "odd jobs." He'd have to figure out how to contact one of them and get updates on what was going down in Liz Town. He suspected it would happen sooner rather than later, whatever Pamela had in mind, once she realized he was gone. The Alpha would probably call Pamela in to tell her all about the nighttime visit. Carl had to be well hidden before morning.

* * *

Nestor walked around the inferno that was once a cabin. They'd found it without much problem, and one of his people had doused the building's perimeter with gasoline from two jerry cans on the back of the very dead 4x4 SUV parked outside. The building had gone up almost immediately, and he and his people only had to shoot one person attempting to escape from a window in the loft. Everyone else inside, the fire claimed. Now the blaze was beginning to lessen, since the building had collapsed in on itself.

Nestor turned to two of his people, and pointed at the barn. "Go clear it, make sure no one is hiding in there. Find anything of value and let me know. Then we'll burn it down too."

As they ran off, Nestor opened the SUV and rummaged through it, checking every space in the slowly dawning morning light. Not much of value, of course. He didn't expect to find anything, but it passed the time and it had to be checked anyway.

The cabin had probably held a lot of useful items, but a siege would have taken forever and rushing the house would have been an unnecessary risk. Why take the chance of losing a fighter to gunfire when they could end it safely with one match?

As his people scoured the area, checking every shed or outbuilding, and any place that looked like a possible stash spot, the two he'd sent to the barn returned. One held a small metal box, like a money lockbox. "Found this buried in the hay, boss. The hay is too fresh to be from before the lights went out, so they put it there since then."

Nestor examined the box; it was a simple thing, rectangular and not too tall. A round-key lock set flush with the box surface secured it. "Good work. It might be important. Maybe medicines, or who knows what. Find a way to pry this damn thing open," he said, and handed the box back.

Ten minutes later they returned, but they looked tense, even spooked, and their eyes darted everywhere, searching. "It's open. You aren't going to like it." One handed the box to Nestor.

He set the bent, twisted box on the SUV's hood and flipped open the lid. Inside was a huge pill bottle stuffed with tiny pink pills. The label read, "Oxycodone 10mg tablets."

There was also a map with bold, red writing on it. A glance told him it had pinpointed the settlements in the area, rough population, how well supplied they were, and also pointed out important features throughout this little pocket of Pennsylvania.

Four large gold coins lay inside the box, each weighing about an ounce, with the rough image of some dude he'd never seen. It certainly wasn't U.S.-minted coinage. It looked homemade. The faint inscription read, "MWR - A New Dawn."

Most tantalizing of all, he found a note handwritten on printer paper. It consisted of text in three neat columns, the writing small and precise, with alternating numbers and letters. Some sort of a code, maybe. "What the heck. Any of you seen anything like this before?"

Nestor showed it to his people one at a time, but none admitted to knowing what it was. "We'll have to make a trip to Clanholme," he announced. "They have a guy there who might be able to make sense of this. What do you make of the rest of this stuff?"

There was a long moment of silence before Ratbone hesitantly suggested, "Maybe the MWR is the Empire. You know, the Midwest Republic. I think that's what they're calling themselves."

Nestor nodded, staring at the map. "I think you're right. And this map, all of this is stuff the Empire would want to know ahead of time. Spies, d'you think?"

"Damn, boss," Ratbone muttered, sounding shocked. "These candyballs were working for the Empire?"

Nestor grit his teeth. If he could burn those assholes alive again, he would. "Even cannibals have a price. Especially cannibals, in fact. That's probably enough gold coin to set them up nicely in the Empire. And the pills, those were the bribe for here and now. Well, take them. That stuff makes good barter, you know. We'll take the note and the map to Clanholme. Cassy will want to know that the Empire is hiring traitors. You can bet your sweet knives that these guys aren't the only people the Empire bought, Ratbone." Nestor handed the box to one of his fighters. "Pack it all up.

Get all the hay we can carry and then torch the barn. Let's get the hell out of here, this place feels like it has evil oozing from every crack."

Nestor resaddled his horse and gave it the last of the hay in his saddlebags. They'd soon be full again, to the horse's probable delight. At least this simple creature would be happy with today's results—Nestor sure wasn't. The Empire was coming, no matter what platitudes and promises they'd given to Cassy. Spring would bring more blood. It never seemed to end, the blood he had to spill. Even now at the end of the world as they knew it, the killing was the one thing that hadn't changed. The Other loved it, but Nestor only hoped he could stay strong through the times that lay ahead.

* * *

Ethan heard the bunker door open and hastily threw on a pair of sweatpants and an old tee-shirt. With a quick kiss to Amber, he left the bunks area, closing the curtain behind him. Seconds later, Cassy emerged from the tunnel to the surface. "Evening, Cassy," he said with a smile. "Your timing is terrible as always."

Cassy gave him a smile and said, "Har dee har har. You and Amber will just have to wait. We just had a visit from one of Nestor's Night Ghosts, and got something for you."

That got his attention. Nestor was technically part of the Clan, but the reality was that he and his band of Adamstown survivors were their own guerrilla operation, running around like nomads, taking the fight to the enemy. Very exciting stories to tell the kids, when he visited, but not great for one's longevity. "I hope it's a pony. Or an MMO server."

"Ponies won't fit down here in your Cave of Justice, and we don't have the power to run a server farm. Sorry, not this time. He did send some intel, though. He just got done tracking down that band of cannibals we've been hearing about, so there's that."

Ethan frowned. "A pony would have been nice. But those people have been a thorn in our sides for over a month. I assume they won't be eating anymore Long Pig."

"Nope, the messenger said the Night Ghosts burned the house down with them in it. Bad way to go. They say they got some intel for us, too. It seems the cannibals had a lockbox with a bigass bottle of narcotics inside, half of which he sent to us. The box also had a map of the area covered in the sorts of notes an army would need to know in an invasion. And four hefty gold coins, freshly minted, with what they think is a picture of the Empire's leader on them." Cassy handed him two of the coins. "They sent us half, of course."

Ethan felt the cool, heavy coins in his hand and examined them. They felt soft, like only fairly pure gold can. The edges were smooth, not ridged against paring away a little at a time like American money had been since the days of gold and silver coins. On one side the coins had an inscription with the Empire's acronym and motto—A New Dawn—with crude crossed rifles as decoration. On the other, he saw the profile image of a man's face. The Emperor, or whatever they called their leader, no doubt. Their founder, or whoever was taking credit for it.

"Cassy, these are newly made coins. I imagine they used a rubber mold to create a casting, then pour molten gold into it. Slow, laborious. I used to make coins like that out of Zinc for my Saturday roleplaying game sessions. I used 'em for Bennies for the best pen-and-paper game in the universe, Savage Wo—"

Cassy abruptly cut him off. "Save your pretend-war stories, Ethan. But they sent something else I figure you'll love." She pulled an envelope from her back pocket and handed it to Ethan.

He opened the envelope and pulled out a single sheet of printer paper, which had three columns of neat, small writing. It was a series of letters and numbers. "Some sort of code?"

Cassy nodded. "Think you can crack it?"

"I can try."

"Good, I'd like to know what they're up to, and whether the cannibals killed an Empire spy to get this stuff or, as Nestor thinks, they were collaborators selling out to the Empire. Hopefully this can give us some answers."

Ethan looked up from the note, locking eyes with Cassy. That would not be good. "You mean the Empire is infiltrating Confed territory with spies? I figured they would try, but to see evidence of it... how many more spies are there?"

"We knew the Empire was coming though, right? Spring will be on us soon, and then the fighting starts. Not just enclaves against the Empire but everywhere. We're back to campaign seasons, like in medieval times. People who only want to peaceably farm always suffer the worst in times like that."

"Like all the times, ever, before the industrial revolution," Ethan agreed. "Whatever this code says, I doubt it'll be something we can use to our advantage. The Empire isn't sending vital military secrets to Confed renegade cannibals, and even if they ate an Empire spy to get this stuff it's not going to be their plan of attack. But it could still be useful, so I'll get right on it. I have no idea if I can crack it, but I have software that gives us at least a shot in hell. Maybe two."

"Alright. Do your best. This is classified, by the way. I don't want everyone knowing about this–it'll spook people. And we definitely don't want our Empire envoys to know."

Ethan took a deep breath and let it out slowly. He felt the muscles in his neck tense. "Great. Now we're keeping secrets from the people for their own good. Sounds familiar."

Cassy's eyebrows furrowed, her lips tight. "Don't give me that. Until this is decoded we don't know if they simply ate a spy or they're collaborators, and wild speculation is the only result of telling people half a story. Figure out what this says and I'll let you tell everyone yourself if that's what you want. But make no mistake, Ethan, we're in a war now. The side that wins will be the side that wants it more, and I won't have you spooking our Clanners based on some half-assed theory. Or having it leak back to the Empire."

Ethan looked away, and nodded. It didn't sit well with him, good little anarchist that he was, but she had a point. He'd go along, for now at least. "Alright. Let's get the whole story if we can, then, but we have to at least put our scouts on high alert. And by the way, there's news out of Florida."

Cassy's expression softened. "Really? That's fantastic." She caught Ethan's frown. "Not fantastic? What's going on in Gatorland?"

"Right after taking Orlando, two factions got to squabbling over loot. Who got how much food, that sort of thing. It spread from there when other factions didn't want to be left out. Why let those two decide, right? The whole thing has been falling apart. The Russians and Cubans may be dead and gone, but they found new enemies. Each other."

"Crap. It's like former Yugoslavia. If they don't get that under control, it'll be years of low-intensity bloodshed that will take a century to get over, even after someone wins. With personal feuds left between families forever." Cassy let out another sigh. It was her most annoying habit.

Ethan said, "Also, I reached out to Liz Town by radio. It's not promising... They have it manned of course, but when we asked to talk to the envoy, we were told she's unavailable. They didn't even pretend to go find her and ask—he just replied and said she's not available to talk to us. He offered to take a message. I said we'd like to talk to her about all the raiders filtering through their turf into the rest of the Confed, and asked whether we can help with anything. Still no response."

Cassy looked up at the ceiling for a moment, then back to Ethan. "So, Empire spies, Americans fighting Americans, and now Liz Town dropping the ball and stonewalling us. Probably turned their coats. The day just keeps getting better and better." She let out yet another sigh. "I'm going to go hit the sack."

"Okay, I'll get started on that message but no guarantees that I'll be able to decode it."

"Thanks, Ethan," Cassy said. "And hey, don't you forget to sleep either, mister." She headed back toward the tunnel to her house and disappeared.

Ethan, now alone in the bunker's living area, held the sheet of paper and the two gold coins. That note must be important, despite what he'd told Cassy. It wouldn't be encrypted otherwise. Hopefully they weren't using a cipher based on using identical source books for coding and decoding, because those are tough and he'd probably never get it decoded—the local book copy would have burned down along with the cannibals' house. Probably not, though, or they'd have left the book in the strongbox. Tomorrow, he would begin transcribing it onto his computer to begin running code crackers on it. For tonight, he had other things to do.

Ethan set the paper on his computer desk and then headed toward the bedroom, stripping off his shirt as he went. It was late and he was tired, but Amber didn't stay with him overnight as often as he'd like, so he was damn sure going to make the most of that time with her.

- 6 -

0900 HOURS - ZERO DAY +195

LEANING AGAINST A tree for support, Joe Ellings used his foot to flip over one of the corpses. The guy's neck was half gone where someone got a damn fine shot in. Around him, the bodies of half a dozen other scrawny-looking city boys lay, twisted up where they fell. "I reckon these raiders ain't gonna bother us no more," he said and the other Clan fighters with him cheered in agreement. "Like shooting fish in a damn barrel, I tell you what."

One of his fighters, off to his left, shouted, "Heya Joe, you gotta take a look at this one. He's got a map and some sort of weird writing. Like a note."

Joe sauntered over and bent down to take a look. Sure as rain, the guy had him some papers. There was a map and a sheet of white printer paper, all right. He picked up the map and, heedless of the blood on it, opened it halfway. Pencil-writing all over the map showed the location of Confed towns and had a number next to them, which he figured was their populations. Other markings showed freshwater ponds and streams. Still others had a bunch of little red X-marks.

From over his shoulder, one of his fighters—a woman,

but he never did hold that against no one—said, "Joe, one of those X-marks... Isn't that here in this copse of trees?"

Well, he didn't know what a copse was, but figured it to be a small clump of trees because that's where they all were. "Yeah, maybe so. Looks like it. Take this and see if you can't sniff it out, whatever them marks are. Got a hunch we need to get these to Michael, fast."

She took the map and wandered off, staring at it, and Joe turned to scrounging whatever he could off the corpses. The growing pile of gear so far had seven hunting rifles—two were only bolt action—and three pistols. Also a few backpacks, couple of rucksacks, and some wool blankets. Those would all be useful to someone back home.

Funny, this was the third bunch of raiders he heard of in the past few days. Them folks in Liz Town sure weren't doing what they ought to, letting all these teams slip past them like greased pigs.

A woman shouted, and Joe's head whipped around 'til he spotted her. It was the woman with the map and she must've dug something up. He walked over to check on it, and saw a 55-gallon drum buried at the base of a tree. "Well, I'll be damned. What do you reckon that is? Open it up, girl!"

The woman undid the tension clasp at the barrel's lip then lifted the blue plastic lid off, revealing the contents, and she let out a low whistle.

Joe moved to get a better look, and he too let out a whistle. Inside there were half a dozen of them AK-47-type rifles, probably two dozen loaded magazines, and the rest of the space was crammed damn near full with boxes of ammo. "Bless us, if these raider folks had done found this stash before we got here, we might be the ones with them pennies on our eyes," Joe said, then chuckled. "Ain't no luck like good luck, y'all. Get them rifles up, we're taking 'em back home with us. Grab them blankets and backpacks, too, and any other gear we can scrounge up. Waste not, want not, my daddy always said."

Wasn't that just a kick in the pants! Another half hour, them boys would have found that stash and used 'em on good ol' Joe and his boys. His *people*, he corrected himself—the ladies sure did their part with the fighting and whatnot, so they deserved credit where it was due. Question was, who put them AKs there, and what did it mean?

Ten minutes later, Joe and his band were mounted up and riding hard for Clanholme. It wasn't too long before they reined up at the stables atop the hill south of the Complex—the walled circle of them sandbag houses Cassy was so fond of—and handing off their mounts to the people there on stable duty. He told a couple of his fighters to go turn in their loot, but he grabbed up the map and the funny-looking note himself and headed downhill. He had to talk to Michael. He couldn't find him, though, so set about taking care of his gear.

A short while later, Michael found him cleaning his weapon. Michael said, "Hey, Joe. I heard you got rid of another band of raiders. Good work, friend. They said you were looking for me?"

Joe nodded, and glanced around to make sure no one was nearby listening. Then he set down his rifle and pulled out the map and note, handing them to Michael. "Yessir. We found these here papers on their bodies. One is a map and seems to rightly show us our neighbors, places to get them some water, and so on. The other one I can't make no sense out of. Just gibberish but I thought maybe you might figure out what it means."

Michael examined the map and then the paper, and frowned. "You're right, that map is full of useful intel. And that paper seems to be some sort of cipher. That means code."

"I know what cipher means," Joe said, a bit irritated by the comment but Michael ignored him.

"Maybe Ethan will be able to crack it. I'll give it to Cassy to decide. Thanks, Joe."

"We also dug up a mess of them AK rifles and a boatload of bullets, from one o' them Xs on that there map."

"Really? Hm... looks like the Empire may be supplying the local bandits in exchange for military intel for a possible spring invasion." Michael paused, lost in thought for a moment, then continued, "Come find me later, okay? I have a mission in mind. But this is need-to-know, so let's keep this between us. We'll talk later."

Michael left Joe alone with his thoughts. It was a peculiar mix of pride and fear, knowing that he had done well and would be tagged for a secret mission with Michael. That boy was all about secret missions, and if Joe was good enough to come along, well, that spoke right highly about him, didn't it? But then again, them Empire folks was prowlin' around outside like wolves, and they'd need to get dealt with sooner or later. The rest of the Clan would have to be told. But maybe not just yet.

Oh, to hell with it. Let Michael do the comtemplatin'. Joe felt his stomach growl like a bear, and went to dig up some chow.

* * *

Taggart walked the long row of troops and examined them casually as he went, Eagan at his side taking notes. He wouldn't call most of them real soldiers, but they were what he had and were sufficient enough.

As they walked, Eagan said, "You're really sending them an entire battalion, sir?"

Taggart didn't take his eyes off the troops and kept

walking as he replied, “That’s affirmative. They’re not at full TO&E, of course. Thirty per platoon, two per company, three companies. They’re short at every level. Two hundred combatants is only half of the minimum battalion size, really, but no one’s at full strength so it’ll have to do. Those people are expecting to see action this spring.”

“And all those truck-bed wagons, and all those supplies…”

“Yes, Eagan, I know. We need all of them. But what good will it do us to defeat the invasion forces here, only to get mopped up later by this Empire they told us about? General Houle’s lapdogs, no less. If we can help nip that in the bud with a surprise battalion of reinforcements, we’ll just have to make do.”

“Understood, sir. But why send them with more supplies than they need for the trip? Surely we need them more than this Clan, or Confederation, or whatever.”

“They’re not for the Clan. They’re to sustain our forces while they’re deployed. You think the Confederation could easily support so many extra mouths? I don’t believe they can. They’re a bunch of farmers sustaining themselves.” Taggart paused to chew out a “soldier” who hadn’t remembered to put his canteens on his combat webbing. Then he added, “We fought a revolution partly because a king was making farmers feed his troops, remember?”

Eagan, still playing devil’s advocate, replied, “What if they don’t want to come back? This Clanholme sounds like a paradise compared to our ops area. Sir, I really have to tell you that I feel this is a bad idea. We need these troops and supplies, and if you send them anyway, we’ll need them back when it’s over out there.”

Taggart frowned. Eagan had turned into a damn fine NCO, his right-hand man in most every regard, and his outspoken—some would say insubordinate—nature was something Taggart valued, but Eagan sometimes didn't see the Big Picture. "I understand your concerns, Eagan, but this is happening. We're sending them. If they don't come back, then they'll have to face some penalties someday when all of this is behind us, but we still have enough to continue our program here. We made sure of that. We're sending troops where America most needs 'em. So get with that program and just make it happen."

They reached the end of the inspection line, and Taggart said, "Alright, let them fall out. They'll move out toward their new objective in sixty mikes."

Eagan stepped away to bark out orders, leaving Taggart with his thoughts. He hoped Eagan was wrong about needing these troops locally, but the die was cast. It wouldn't do anyone any good to win the battle with Ree but lose the war against the Empire and Houle for America's future.

* * *

1330 HOURS - ZERO DAY +195

Joe Ellings sat cross-legged far to one side of the Complex, near the western tool shed and water pond, a tarp stretched out before him assembling "seed bombs," as Cassy called them, for the spring plantings. Tap out a small circle of clay. Add a fat pinch of compost and a small pinch of mixed seeds to the center, then wrap it all up in the clay. It wasn't hard work, but it was boring. Later, the Clan would scatter these things all willy-nilly around the outskirts of Clanholme, and the spring rains would open 'em up so the seeds could sprout. Not all the plants would make it, but nature would sort out the best ones for the soil conditions in any particular place.

He had made about fifty of the things so far, and

reckoned to have about that many more to go before his knees gave out and he'd have to take a spell to stretch and walk around. Getting older wasn't no piece of cake, that was surely true.

A shadow fell across the tarp and he looked back to see Michael coming up behind him from the ponds with an armful of them cattails. For some reason, the Clan's quilts stuffed with the fluffy bits of cattails traded really good. People liked 'em. Heck, might be time to trade for one himself and find out what the ruckus was all about. Michael reached him, set his load down, and popped a squat.

Joe said, "Howdy, Michael. Time for that talk y'all wanted to have with me?"

Michael grunted, and picked up some clay. "Yes, I've done some thinking."

Joe patted another clay ball smooth. "Well, what's got you all riled up? You wouldn't want to jaw out here away from the others, less it was for something important."

Michael set his freshly made ball aside and began another. "You're a straight shooter, so that's how I'll tell it to you. You know those Empire envoys that Cassy told us to leave alone? Well, they're putting their nose into things they have no good reason to know. The sorts of things that make them more spies than envoys. If their bosses are prepping to invade us, we can't risk them finding out we know about it. I've already told your team not to talk about it, and especially not to the envoys."

Joe shrugged. "Well, them envoys been askin' me and everyone else about how we run our guards, our scouts, all of that. They say it's so's they can take what's good back home with them so they can fix what's broke with their own ways of doing. But I can't figure it that way. I think they're spying, too. Glad to know I'm not the only one who thinks it."

"Nope, you aren't. My Marines feel the same way. They

need to go or go down before they learn too much. They already know about the cars and the gasifiers."

Joe looked over at Michael, and locked eyes with him. "Lord knows that's a risk. But Cassy says we need to treat them like guests, and just put away the dirty dishes so's they don't see 'em, if you catch my meaning."

"Cassy's looking at it as the Clan leader. She has to consider politics. I have to look at it from the security director's point of view."

Joe paused. He had a sneaking feeling he knew where this was headed, and he didn't like it one bit. "So what are you saying, Michael? Out with it. I ain't got all day for you to find your point."

Michael smiled for a moment, then looked deadly serious, eyes locked with Joe's. "My duty to the Clan is to kill them before they can report back. They might leave any time now and bring our secrets with them. I'm of the opinion that my general duty to protect the Clan—a duty Cassy gave me to fulfill as I see fit—outweighs my obligation to obey her situational command about leaving these envoys alone. The situation just changed. You follow me so far?"

"Yessir, I reckon I do. You figure you got a higher duty that outweighs the other thing. Seems simple enough, however you dress it up. And you may be right. That don't answer what all this has to do with me, though. Pardon me for sayin' so but killing them who done nothin' to me ain't really my style."

Michael shrugged. "No need to apologize, you're being honest. And you're right, I do have a higher duty to keep all of us alive and free. And you are correct that your duties and mine aren't the same. However, and I say this with respect, you *do* have a duty to follow my orders, inasmuch as you're a guardsman. So I'll ask you this once and then leave it be. If I order you to assist me with this, will you obey? I won't ask you to make the kill, Joe. That's a burden I'll carry so no one else has to. But I could use your help setting it up. If you can't do this as a volunteer, but you will obey an order, I'm happy to make it an honest-to-god order."

Joe frowned, and Michael continued, "Just think about that map you found, and what might happen to the Clan if they bring back everything else they learned at chow or just walking around with their eyes open. Can I count on you with this mission? It goes without saying that this is Top Secret. No one can know about this, and we don't need to talk about it after it's done. But I need to know if you're in."

Joe stared at the lump of clay in his hands. What was the right choice? It was hard to ken which way was right. Was it murder if they weren't shootin' at him first? No, the Empire and the Confederation would be scrapping with each other soon enough, he figured. War was war, and that's all there was to it. But what about Cassy's orders to let them Empire folks be? She wanted them left alone, so long as they weren't doing nothing bad. But then an idea struck him like a bolt of lightning. Those folks *were doing something bad.* They were sneaking around being spies. Maybe Cassy didn't know. Maybe killing those folks would be what she'd want, if she had proof. There wasn't any proof, of course, but Michael was right. Any fool could see what they were up to. That being the case, then he ought to follow Michael's orders...

"Alright, Michael. You're right about them. They need to be dealt with. So, y'all give me the order, and I'll do my part. I figure sometimes you got to break an order to get behind the spirit of the order. What do you want me to do?"

Michael smiled, and put his hand on Joe's shoulder, a friendly gesture. "I need you to convince them to follow you out to the copse of trees, you know the one—where you killed that one White Stag slaver during Peter's days in charge. You get them out there, and my Marines and I will handle what needs handling. Those trees thrive on blood, and we'll do the watering. Get them out there after evening chow tonight. I'll be ready."

Joe nodded. "You can count on me."

Michael rose and walked off, and Joe was left with his seeds and his own dark thoughts. It would be chow time soon, and it'd be best he sat with the envoys, the better to get their trust up. If he could get 'em curious, they wouldn't be joining the Clan for morning chow.

* * *

Ethan scraped his tray as best he could into the bucket, from which scraps would usually be fed to the pigs, but this time of year it would go into the compost piles instead. Then he dumped the tray into the first 55-gallon drum, set over a low fire. Thank goodness he didn't have kitchen duty this month—those poor saps had to scrub the dishes off in the hot barrel, then dump them into the soapy second barrel, rescrub them, and dump them into the freshwater third barrel, before stacking them. Then they'd do it all over again in the morning. Ha. Better them than him.

From there he made his way down into the bunker. After chow, he usually spent a couple hours both on HAMnet and on the HAM radio to talk to whoever happened to be on. It was also when he'd receive routine orders and info from the 20s, that secretive group that he once thought were freedom fighters but had since realized they almost certainly worked directly for General Houle. Self-proclaimed Commander-in-Chief of the USA "for the duration of the crisis," hidden deep inside a mountain fortress in Colorado and seizing power. Houle was a bastard, for sure.

When he had used Ethan to hack systems to launch an EMP counter-strike over the U.S. to level the playing field against the invaders, eliminating the advantage they got from having the only planes in the sky, the only tanks in the field, Ethan had *also* unwittingly launched EMPs over almost every corner of the globe. He had used Ethan to plunge the world into darkness, sentencing billions to starvation and death. Together they had ended the world to save the U.S., and he'd never forgive that bastard for it. Or stop having nightmares.

But the Mountain knew where Clanholme was, so he had to walk a fine line with them, at least appearing to obey orders. Look like a good trooper. He had already caught them testing him once.

Reaching the bunker, he glanced at his U.S. wall map full of pushpins and flags, and made a mental note to update it tomorrow. He had a few new bits of intel to add to it. Then he booted his laptop. After loading his virtual machine, an operating system within a system, and connecting to a chain of VPNs that were still up and running for the moment, he connected to the internet at large. These days it was much smaller than it had been...

As expected, within moments several musical dings announced messages and emails. The first was from Taggart, via the backdoor they had arranged by going through some old, poorly-secured satellites. He was sending troops! That was fantastic and he'd have to let Cassy know during the morning meeting. It was a journey of 150 miles, roughly, and would take four or five days on foot. One person could conceivably make the journey in three days, but larger formations took longer, had to worry about setting up defenses before encamping for the night, deal with sprained ankles, and a million other things that would slow them down.

Then his HAM crackled—it was his buddy in Florida, who had nothing good to report. His faction had a hold of southwest Orlando and had taken over two smaller groups that joined them rather than fight them, but they were losing some ground elsewhere to aggressive neighbors. The whole situation reminded him very much of post-Yugoslavia Bosnia. Hopefully it wouldn't drag on for years, but the world moved slower now that the cars and planes were lawn ornaments and metal parts.

Then an encrypted message came through from Watcher One. Whoever it was, they had started out pretending to be just another survivor, but it had since come to light that he was Ethan's handler for the 20s. Or rather, *Dark Ryder*'s handler, that being Ethan's hacker name. Ethan loaded the message file into a sandbox, a virtual environment that would contain any virus or malware that hitched a ride on the message. He loaded up Cipher P1776 and decrypted the file. It turned out to be only a text file, however, so all the precautions had been unnecessary. Oh well, better safe than sorry. He opened the file.

To: Dark Ryder
From: Watcher One
February 16
Priority: Beta

Dark Ryder:

Be advised there is a new paramilitary group active within your operations area. Intel suggests they are called *Night Ghosts*. Approx. 35 combatants, horse mobile, armed with AK-47s and misc civilian weapons. They are functioning as a guerrilla force, but have recently begun to target other small survivor groups as well as invader forces.

```
This unit has the capacity to become a destabilizing force in your region. Therefore, several UAVs have been allocated for the purpose of eliminating this force. To be effective, however, the target must first be located.

You are tasked with using available resources to locate the Night Ghosts forces, and you will then relay coordinates through me for the UAVs to engage target.

Although this has been allocated a priority of Beta (high, non-essential), please consider this to be an urgent mission. The Night Ghosts must be stopped before they eliminate additional survivor elements.

END
```

Ethan scratched his head. So they had found out about Nestor and his Night Ghosts, but didn't know they were operating with Clan approval. They either didn't know the "survivor elements" the Night Ghosts destroyed were traitors for the Empire, or they did know.

The latter option was more likely and it sent a chill down his spine. If the 20s knew, then the General knew, and that would be confirmation that the Empire was working for General Houle. But if they didn't know those victims were working for the Empire, then that would disprove his theory that they were working together, the Empire and the Mountain.

Did the 20s know about the spies the Empire planted, or did they not? It was maddening not to have the answer to that critical question.

Either way, there was no way he could obey this order.

He'd have to make it look like he was, and the Mountain had satellites over his area. That meant wasting manpower on sending scouts out on wild goose chases. Dammit.

Then an idea struck him. What if he gave them the coordinates of a survivor group that was working for the Empire? Finding one of those might be hard, but maybe not impossible. And if the UAVs took out that group, then he'd know the Mountain wasn't aware they were Empire assets. It wouldn't rule out Mountain-Empire collaboration, but it would at least keep the question open. On the other hand, if they didn't take out the target, then they *did* know the target was an Empire asset. It would change the whole game.

So the Clan's scouts had to find some survivors who were working for the Empire, and Ethan knew just the person to get that job done. Nestor himself, with his Night Ghosts, were in the best position to find the right target for this. He'd only have to convince Nestor not to just kill them...

Ethan took out a piece of paper and a pen, and began to write a letter to Nestor. He'd have to figure out how to get it to him, but that was a problem for tomorrow.

* * *

It was still plenty warm when Joe got his chow. Biscuits and gravy, which suited him just fine. He skipped the apple cider. Enough was enough. It would have been mighty fine if Cassy had thought to make some other drinks, too, when she set up the farm. Next year would be great, though. His mouth watered to think of all the berries and fruits on the farm that would be harvested next year. Until then... water and cider. He never got tired of water, at least.

Looking around, Joe spotted the Empire envoys, Oscar and Jason, sitting at one "table," a rock a little away from everyone else. Looked like they weren't much welcome among the Clanners.

He put on a smile and walked over. “Howdy. Y’all mind if I sit with you?”

Oscar looked up at Joe and nodded. “Certainly. We’re always happy to enjoy a meal with someone from the Clan. It’s why we’re here, after all.”

“Y’all are here to eat our food with us?” Joe smiled, putting his best good ol’ boy spin on it.

Oscar laughed and said, “No, of course not. We brought our own food, but the Clan’s hospitality over the past month has been most welcome. I am told that biscuits and gravy is a rare treat right now, and so far it’s been mostly stew.”

“Yeah,” Joe replied, “stew is the best way to get all them nutrients out of it, you know.”

Oscar nodded somberly. “We eat too much of it back home, too. So how are you this fine day?”

Joe looked over both shoulders and when he saw no Clanners were around, he leaned forward, hunching over his chow like he was eating. Instead of shoveling grub into his mouth, he said, “Y’all know I’m not originally Clan, right?”

“Yes. You were part of the White Stag people, weren’t you?”

Joe took a small bite and ate it quickly. Then he said, “True. Survival, you know? But don’t be fooled. The Clan has big plans, bigger’n what they tell me or you about, but it’s a small place. Thin walls. A fellow hears things.”

Oscar shrugged. “We’ve been here a month, and haven’t heard anything about that.” He put his elbows on the rock and fiddled with his food. Joe saw him surreptitiously glance around, then they locked eyes. “I wouldn’t want you to betray a confidence,” Oscar said. “The Midwest Republic isn’t here to spy.”

“Of course not. But I reckon y’all wouldn’t turn down news that might help decide how close an ally y’all want to be. Am I wrong about that?”

Oscar stared at Joe for a long moment, but then seemed to come to a decision. He shook his head. "No, you aren't wrong. Anything you care to share that might help our superiors make informed decisions is welcome, of course."

Joe picked up a piece of bread and, elbows on the rock, held the bit of biscuit near his mouth as though eating. He smiled. "Of course. Well, seems the Clan got themselves a secret stash. They found rocket launchers, buried in that there PVC piping. Big ol' stash of ammo. And radios, working ones. The kind y'all hook up to cars, and the ones folks carry in satchels, got them a couple miles in range to transmit. I hear folks tell they got encryption. Ain't nobody can bust through that, not without big computers or what have you. Got it all stashed away from pryin' eyes."

Joe then went quiet and focused on his food. He took his time eating and felt like a cat playing with its prey. Let them make the next move, he figured, while he enjoyed them biscuits.

Finally, the other one, Jason, said, "That's mighty interesting, Joe. Why would you tell me this? I'm not sure I understand your motivation. Is this a warning or a carrot for alliance?"

Joe glanced up, then looked back at his wooden trencher. "I told y'all, I joined the Clan out of survival. But they killed my friends, and I ain't got no loyalty to that. I want out, but I got nowhere to go. If I tell you where the Clan done hid this gear, y'all gotta promise me you'll take me with you back to the Republic and set me up. I ain't afraid of hard work, and I can work good. I just need me a grubstake to get set up, and a way out of here."

Jason stared at him, then said, "That's it? Nothing else? That seems like a small thing to ask for such big news."

Joe shrugged. "I don't want these here Clanners to get bushwhacked, but I ain't exactly puttin' my neck out for 'em either. A way out, a way to start over—that's all I want. Every time I look at these folks, all I can see is my friends' faces when they done got strung up, after the Clan tore free again."

"I see. That's an interesting proposition. I'm not saying we will or won't take you with us, Joe, but if you could tell us whereabouts you think this supposed cache is, and we confirm it, then when we leave, I'll take you with us. If—and only if—the cache turns out to be the real deal."

Joe nodded. "Fair 'nuff. Tonight, after chow, there ain't no one out there. Y'all head north 'bout a mile as the crow flies, there's a big ol' bundle of trees growing. It's like a little forest, old and dense, but it ain't that big. It's near the trail outta here, and it's the only one, so I reckon you can't miss it. The stuff is all dug up, and they covered 'em with tarps. Easy as pie to find. Take a gander, then take me with you."

Oscar leaned close to Jason and whispered in his ear for a moment, and then Jason nodded. He looked at Joe and said, "We hear you aren't exactly on the inner circle. You're on the Council so you can keep the other White Stag survivors in line, but otherwise they don't much lean on you for anything important. You're the outsider, even after saving their skins. How's that ring?"

"It rings true," Joe said with one small nod, and looked at his plate. "They don't trust ol' Joe Ellings, so I can't hardly trust them."

Oscar smiled. "Joe, if what you say is true, Jason and I will bring you with us. We'll set you up somewhere nice. And we'll set up people under you—you'll never be the outsider again. You'll be in charge, where you belong. A man who sees opportunities shouldn't be squandered like this."

Joe nodded, and put a sad expression on his face. "Yessir. I feel the same. I don't like turning on these here folks, they spared us White Stag that joined 'em, but I reckon this is a small thing. You treat me better'n what they done,

I'll prove my worth to y'all."

Oscar said, "That's good to know. I'll tell you what... Why don't you lead us there? I'd feel a lot safer wandering around Clan territory if we were accompanied by a council member."

"I'm not sure I could get away without being noticed," Joe said, "but y'all can find it easy."

Jason shook his head but wore a polite smile on his face. "No. If you want to earn your place, be at the north food forest at nine o'clock."

Joe nodded, and his thoughts ran amok, wondering if he was doing the right thing. Michael had seemed so certain, though, and the man knew things Joe didn't. Well, the thing was done. No use fretting about it now. He'd show up and lead them to the copse of trees, and the chips would fall where they wanted to.

- 7 -

2100 HOURS - ZERO DAY +195

JOE ARRIVED AT the northern food forest, and it took only a couple minutes to find the envoys, Oscar and Jason, both armed with hunting rifles. They must have had those stashed. It didn't matter, though. They shook hands, said greetings, and headed north.

Joe led them on a cautious path that kept the faint track just barely in view. Soon, the tiny forest could be seen in the distance. Joe nudged the envoy and pointed. They didn't speak, however. They just kept walking. Soon, the copse grew larger, and they were almost there.

Oscar whispered, "Joe, keep close when we go in. If anyone's there, it's better if they see you—I don't want anyone inside to shoot us."

Joe nodded. He felt a chill down his spine. There were Marines in those woods, but he reckoned they wouldn't shoot him. They were good enough to tell the difference. He hoped they were. "Let's go."

They walked in the deepening gloom of the woods. The thing was only about five acres, total, but it was fairly old, a mature forest. Lots of underbrush to get through, but the

Clan had hacked a number of decent trails throughout the place. Joe led them along one such path. Almost halfway through the woods, Joe saw ahead a number of mounds with tarps staked out over them.

"There they are," he said. "Rockets and radios. I reckon you'll want to lay eyes on 'em."

Jason nodded and turned to his assistant. "Pull back that tarp there," he said, pointing to the nearest pile. The group moved closer, and Oscar approached the covered mound. He bent over, took a hold of the tarp, and yanked.

In the next moment, a crossbow bolt pierced the man's back, where his neck joined the rest of his spine. The tip protruded from the front of his neck. He gasped, a bubbling, wet sound.

At the same time, there was a sudden flurry of movement all around them. In the gloom, Joe had a hard time seeing what was going on. It was as though parts of the forest just came alive and attacked Oscar. His cries were quickly silenced. Jason turned to flee, but ran right into one of the living, moving pieces of forest. He stopped abruptly, a surprised look on his face, and looked down toward his belly. Something glinted there briefly, and he toppled over, moaning. Then there was silence.

A second later, the living pieces of forest called out, "Clear," one after the other.

Then one approached Joe and, though he knew it was foolish, he felt a primordial fear racing through him. His mind told him these were just Marines in ghillie suits, but the ancient, lizard part of his brain saw monsters.

The monster pulled its hood back, revealing Michael's face. Joe felt a tingling in his fingers as the adrenaline subsided. "Joe, you've done well."

Michael patted Joe on the arm.

Joe nodded. "We had to get her done," he said, wiping

the sweat from the back of his neck. He glanced at the tarp, now pulled back on one corner. Beneath it was only a pile of leaves and branches, of course. "They were spies, like you said."

Michael grimaced, lips tight. "Of course they were. But no more." He turned to one of the other monsters and said, "Sturm! You go ransack their gear. Any intel, anything unusual, you bring it to me, okay? Go now."

"Aye, aye, sir." She let her ghillie suit slide off of her, stepped out of it, and headed south at a jog.

Joe watched her leave, and stared after her for a moment. "Michael, y'all have ice for blood. You scare me. I'm glad you're on our side."

Michael didn't smile. He only nodded and said, "Training. We fall back on our training."

Joe looked at Michael and said, "Still glad we're in this together, Michael. If you don't mind, I need a drink. I'll see you later."

Michael nodded, patted him on the shoulder again, and then turned away, ordering the remaining Marines to break out their shovels.

Joe turned and trudged back to Clanholme, thinking about that sweet, hard apple cider every step of the way.

* * *

In the morning, Cassy fumbled her way through the chow line with the rest of the Clan, eyes still puffy. She prayed today was a coffee day—the Clan had only a little, and it wouldn't last forever, so it was rationed. She looked down the line and saw the rocket stove on which the half-dozen percolators were set. The stove wasn't lit. She let out a sigh, disappointed, and forced herself to smile when it was her turn to receive breakfast. More constant stew, but with a side of fresh-baked bread. At least they had bread. And it tasted way better than the pre-sliced loaves from before the invasion.

She looked around, scanning the room for a seat, and noticed that the Empire's spies—the "envoys" they'd sent—weren't there. For the first time in the month they'd been here, they weren't sitting to the side by themselves. She looked around and saw they weren't at any other table, either. She felt a bit of worry worm its way into her mind.

No envoys, but she did see Michael and Sturm at one table, half-done with their meal. She wandered over, nodding and waving as people greeted her when she went by, and then sat next to Sturm, opposite Michael.

"Good morning, Marines. How's it going?"

Sturm shrugged, and wore a smile. "It goes very well."

Michael shot Sturm a glare. That was odd... He turned to Cassy. "Good morning. Going well, except for the damn stew. After biscuits and gravy, it's hard to go back to slop."

Cassy laughed. How true that was. "Yeah. I hear that. Say, Michael, where's our guests?" Of course Michael would know. It was his business to know. His job.

He shrugged. "Not here."

Cassy frowned. That didn't answer her question. "Are you saying you don't know where they are?" The idea was worrisome.

"No, I didn't say that. They left Clanholme last night." Michael took another bite of his stew and frowned, but ate it just the same.

Cassy's eyebrows knitted. "Michael, you're playing word games. You know where they are, and they left Clanholme. They said nothing about leaving. Did they find out something they shouldn't have? Should I be worried?"

Sturm gave Cassy a half-smile and said, "I wouldn't worry."

Michael again shot a glare at Sturm. Then he said to her, "Why don't you go get me another cup of apple juice, Sturm."

"Aye, aye, sir." Sturm got up and left.

Cassy was used to the weird way Marines gave each other orders, or even just talked to one another, so she wasn't surprised that Sturm hadn't even paused at the tone in Michael's voice. It was normal, to her. Cassy watched her leave, then looked at Michael.

"You're our head of security. I know you would never lie about official business, but stop playing word games. Tell it true—where are the envoys and why did they leave?"

Michael let out a long breath. He set his spoon down and gave Cassy his full attention. "It is this Marine's duty to inform the Clan leader that he and three other Marines left Oscar and Jason in shallow graves deep inside the north copse of woods. They left because I instigated a lie that lured them to the copse, specifically so that I could kill them."

Then he picked up his spoon and began eating his stew again, as though he hadn't just told her he'd disobeyed her direct order to leave them alone.

She said, "So you follow my order to tell me the truth, but disobey my direct order to leave them alone? Do you know what you've done?" She felt her face flush, and felt suddenly hot.

Michael sighed. "That's correct. They've been here a month. They have surely found out more than we'd have liked. Cassy, we *are going to war*, whether we want to or not. Whether we try to appease their spies or not. That being the case, it's my job to protect the Clan, not to obey you. I did what I felt was required to do my job, and I'd do it again. You want to exile me, go ahead. I'll leave with a clear conscience. Maybe you should just let me do my fucking job and back the hell up."

Cassy's jaw dropped. Michael had never, ever spoken to

her like that before. She felt her hands clench into fists, but stopped. She counted to three, taking deep breaths and looking at her bowl as she did so. Finally, she felt her pulse slow a bit. This was not the time to make rash statements.

"Michael, I give you orders, and you follow them because that's the chain of command, not because I'm somehow more important than anyone else. You feel you have a higher duty to protect the Clan than to follow that chain. Is that right?"

Michael nodded, staring into her eyes unflinchingly.

"What's done is done. But Michael... If this bites us in the ass, the Clan will hold you personally responsible for the consequences of your actions. Unless and until that happens, I am going to simply trust your judgment. You have counterintelligence training, and I don't."

Michael nodded again.

"Okay. Time to move on. But one more thing... This Clan will never survive with too many chiefs. Next time, I want to know ahead of time, before you want to break the chain of command and risk war with a foreign power all by yourself."

Michael was silent for several long seconds. At last, he said quietly, "Very well. Next time, I'll talk to you before I go kill our enemies."

Cassy nodded. "Good enough. Done is done. You going to eat that last slice of bread?"

Michael's lips turned up at the corners. "I sure am," he replied as Sturm returned with two cups of juice. "But I'll split it with you."

Cassy reached across and accepted the half-slice he offered to her. But she couldn't get past the nagging worry of what would happen when the Empire's official envoys didn't check in with their masters, but that was a problem for the future. And Michael was right—leaving them alive wouldn't have changed the outcome. She just had wanted as much time as possible in between now and the start of the war.

- 8 -

0900 HOURS - ZERO DAY +198

CASSY WATCHED AS Thomas, the Intercourse envoy, left her "HQ" and closed the door. Michael, sitting on the couch, grunted.

"What's on your mind, Michael?" Cassy sat back down in her recliner and let the footrest up, leaning back.

"I have concerns," he said. "Some things aren't adding up."

Cassy nodded. Of course, she had her own concerns. "For one, they're pretty damn eager to join our Confederation. Most people need a bit of convincing, but not Intercourse."

"There's that, certainly. But I've got the report back from one of my men who went to Intercourse to evaluate their defenses and see where we could offer advice to shore them up. Now I think we should give them bad advice. Make them vulnerable if we can, not secure."

"And why do you say that?"

"They've got no salvage. Name one established survivor group that has no piles of useful things they've scraped together. Everything from old window frames to tarps to scrap iron. And then there's their rifles. My guy says fully half of their rifles are the same model, firing the same round. It's remotely possible they found a gun store that specialized, but I don't buy it."

"That bit about the salvage," Cassy said, "sounds like they just appeared there. And why had we not encountered their people before? At least, we should have run across their scouts before now. It's not like we don't patrol to our south."

Michael nodded. "And the report I received says that their defenses seem recent. There's gashes in the muddy ground still from where they moved big rigs into place to wall off part of the town. It implies their defenses were set up only recently."

Cassy frowned. It sounded worse and worse. "So, they may have only recently appeared, only recently built those defenses, they're well organized, and their weapons aren't random enough. They were supplied with those weapons. And who has enough horses to move so many semitrucks around? I would have thought they'd have eaten most of their horses over this past winter. And finally, we never encountered them before now."

Michael said, "So we're thinking similar thoughts. I'll make sure we keep an eye on that Thomas guy while he's here. If we catch him snooping, I'll take him to the Smoke Shack."

"Only if it's necessary, Michael. Understand? Check with me first this time—but if it's needed, we'll do that."

Cassy shuddered—thinking of that dreaded place always had that effect on her. She swore she could feel the blood and pain that place had soaked up. If there were ghosts around, that's where they'd be.

* * *

Jaz sat next to Choony on the wagon, the repetitive thump of the wheels over ripples in the Newport Road asphalt feeling hypnotic. Rifle in her right hand, she swept her gaze back and forth ahead of them and to either side, looking for movement. Every so often she would stare at some distant point for three seconds, the better to catch movement in the foreground. So far, nothing moved out there.

Choony had the reins loose on his lap and was looking at their map. "Kinzers should be just ahead, so keep your eyes open," he said. "After that, a bridge over some stream or other, and onward to Gap. That's where the real danger will be—it's a large enough town to have hungry survivors, maybe."

Jaz grunted in acknowledgement. The warning wasn't necessary, but not unwelcome. It was good to know what lay ahead, but she assumed all survivor groups were murderous cannibals until they showed otherwise. Someday, she figured, she and Choony would get ambushed and become someone's dinner. Until then, she'd just do her best to keep them both alive.

The wagon slowly approached Kinzers. A large building on the left looked like a school. Then she saw a single plume of gray smoke rising from further east, past the school. Jaz said, "I think people are alive in there. Look."

Choony turned his head, then picked up the reins and drew the wagon to a halt. "I suppose we should say hello, then. Yeah?"

"That's what we're here for," Jaz replied. She checked the safety and small magazine of her rifle. "All set."

Choony turned the wagon eastward, skirting the south end of the school. A large sign came into view proclaiming it a high school, but it had no obvious signs of inhabitants. Once beyond the school, they saw the "town" was really not much more than a few scattered businesses. They turned left again, trying to find the source of the smoke, and passed a huge grain mill, which Choony noted on the map. Then, on the right, they saw a cluster of buildings that looked like some sort of medieval manor. A winery, perhaps, or some weirdly-placed mansion. And directly ahead of them lay the source of the smoke plume—another school. The sign said it was an intermediate school. It was far too large for just the few pre-EMP locals who had lived nearby.

Jaz said, "It must have served practically the whole county. Look at those wide open fields around the school. And across the road is nothing but farmland. I wonder if it was sprayed with that brown haze the 'vaders used when their airplanes worked."

Choony pulled the wagon into the parking lot of the school, which ran parallel to the road, came to a stop, and waited. Jaz could see that the plume of smoke came from inside one large segment of the school, the roof of which had a large hole cut into it. She imagined it was the communal living area. After sitting still for some five minutes, Jaz was about to suggest they wander inside but then she saw movement. Four people came out of the school armed with rifles, which they aimed at the wagon while they approached; they had a clear shot at Jaz, but with the way the wagon was parked they had no shot at Choony. Jaz aimed her rifle back, focusing on the person in front. Hopefully he was the team leader...

At about twenty yards away, they halted and three of them kneeled, keeping weapons aimed at Jaz and the wagon. The man still standing—the one at whom Jaz had her own rifle aimed—shouted, "Who are you and what do you want? You are trespassing on Outpost Alpha territory."

Jaz didn't know what the hell Outpost Alpha was, but shouted back, "We come in peace. We're here to make contact with other survivor groups—"

The man interrupted, "Where you from?"

"Up north. We're from Clanholme, and—"

One of the kneeling men shouted, "It's them!" and opened fire, his first bullet tearing a chunk out of the wooden pole next to her head that held the wagon's canvas cover.

Jaz's return shot struck their leader in the face and he flopped over backwards, even as Jaz felt the surge of the horses straining against their harness. The wagon quickly began to roll. The three men kneeling fired one more time, but missed her, and she fired two rounds in quick succession, causing her attackers to slide face-first into the dirt as they went prone. The wagon suddenly veered right, and Jaz glanced ahead. Choony had taken the wagon around the corner of the school, between it and the winery or mansion they'd passed, and in seconds they were out of sight from the shooters. The wagon never slowed.

Jaz felt the wagon veer south again and onto the road. Ahead lay the bridge. She stood in the seat and turned around to look behind the wagon, and saw five people on horses far behind them, but catching up quickly. "They're coming, Choony," she said and swung her rifle up to rest on the wagon cover's supporting crossbeam. They fired at the wagon intermittently, but never came close. She fired, but also missed. At this range, with the wagon at full speed, their pursuers would be almost right on top of them before she could be sure of hitting them, so she sat back down. No use getting tossed from the wagon on a bump. She figured fifteen seconds would be enough time for them to get close enough to hit, and began the mental count. It also helped steady her nerves. Fifteen... Fourteen...

The wagon reached the bridge and as the wheels crossed over, the whole wagon jerked wildly. She realized she would have been thrown, had she still been standing, but lost her count. Where was she? Screw it. Ten... Nine...

As the wagon half-bounced off the bridge and back onto level road, Jaz saw half a dozen people ahead, kneeling, rifles aimed at them. They couldn't possibly miss...

Bang, bang came the rapid sounds of six rifles firing. And then the wagon was roaring past them. To her amazement, they all missed. She was still trying to get a good grip on her own rifle after being bounced around so much when, ahead, more people. At least four more. Frantically she scrambled to get her rifle to her shoulder, but once she did she saw that they held their own rifles up in the air. Behind her, more shooting, but these people would be in the line of fire of their own people... Jaz was a bit confused from so much adrenaline coursing through her, but then she felt Choony grab her rifle barrel and push it down, spoiling whatever shot she had.

Jaz's head whipped around to glare at Choony, but he only smiled. She took a deep breath... and then the sound of voices penetrated her adrenaline fog. "... all right, people? Whoa!"

Choony brought the wagon to a halt. "Thank you for chasing them off," he said to the men.

Looking at them, Jaz's spinning mind finally caught up—these men weren't shooting at her, but at the people chasing her.

The man in front said, "You're lucky we've been watching those people, keeping them on their side of the river. We don't need the Empire snooping around on our side."

Jaz blurted, "The Empire? Those guys?"

He nodded. "That's right, miss. Our scouts had everything between here and Intercourse as being vacant, and then one day those people showed up. We sent a guy disguised as a trader. Turns out they were claiming they'd always been there, which we know is bullshit."

Choony said, "Interesting. And the people chasing us,

they were from Intercourse?"

"Yeah. They got three or four outposts like that one. They said they'd always been there, yet they didn't have a thing to trade, not even for food. No scrap, nothing. Tell me one group of people still alive who don't have stuff they've gathered, and who don't need more food? I figure them to be spies, and a beachhead."

Choony turned to Jaz and said, "I wonder why they didn't just kill us when we were in Intercourse. It makes no sense."

Jaz had a sudden thought, and a shivering chill ran down her spine. "What if… Maybe they didn't kill us then because they didn't have orders to, yet, but now they do?"

Choony's jaw dropped. "That would mean…"

"Radios," Jaz finished for him. "The Empire has at least a few radios. We've lost an advantage."

The speaker in front of them said, "Well, you're welcome to join us back in town, folks. The Gap welcomes any enemy of those bastards."

Jaz nodded slowly, mind still reeling. "The Clan would love to talk to your leaders."

* * *

Frank greeted the incoming patrol as they rode into Clanholme. It wasn't easy on him, hobbling around on his crutch.

"Welcome home," Frank said with a smile as Michael reined up near him.

Michael dismounted and shook Frank's hand. "Thanks. We found them right where the scout said they'd be. Twenty people from the Empire, judging by the coins we found on them. Same gold coins Nestor sent us a few days ago."

"Twenty? And you attacked them with only ten people? Ballsy."

Michael grinned and winked. "That's ten Marines, buddy. It's amazing what you can do with a well-timed surprise attack. It's a great force multiplier. We got one injured, but I think it's a flesh wound. Anyway, the Night Ghosts showed up while we were searching the bodies. Nestor said he's run into a couple bands of Empire scouts recently, too, and figured there were even more that he missed."

"That's bad news—them being Empire scouts, I mean—and you should let Cassy know about them and what Nestor told you, right away."

Michael raised one eyebrow at him. "Chain of command, buddy. You go tell her, and then tell Ethan, so he can let our allies know. It's all part of the job you volunteered to help out with."

Frank was stunned for a moment, but then felt his cheeks flush red. Michael was right, of course. "Okay, I'll tell them both. This is going to take some getting used to. I'm used to actually being able to pull my weight—you know, go on raids and all. And now..."

Michael shook his head, and Frank felt the weight of his disapproval. "And now you've got to start thinking like a leader again, because when Cassy's busy doing her agriculture thing, you *are* the leader again. It's who we need you to be. Got it?"

Frank nodded, and looked away. "Yeah."

"Good," Michael said. "Anyway, I'm off. Need to water and brush down the horses. And Frank? Come see me later if you need to get some shit off your chest, okay? We've been friends since long before all of this, and I'm here if you need me."

Frank nodded. "I may take you up on that." He turned and headed toward the HQ, feeling a little embarrassed that he had let his physical handicap become a mental one, and that just wasn't like him. He may be missing a foot, but his mind was intact. It was time to quit whining about things he couldn't change and make the best of it. By the time he got to the HQ, he was done feeling sorry for himself. Now that the Empire was bribing all the locals and it was becoming more difficult to know who to trust anymore, he knew it was even more vital that he listened to Michael's advice. Now, more than ever, he knew he had to be a real leader.

- 9 -

0900 HOURS - ZERO DAY +201

CARL SAT LEANING against one wall in his decrepit safehouse, deep in the unclaimed sectors of Elizabethtown outside the Liz Town walls. Although he had some storm lanterns, he didn't use them. Light would only draw attention from the starving Bums—those who hadn't managed to join a Band before Liz Town got its act together —and the occasional band of raiders.

He was enjoying a cold breakfast of canned raviolis, which he split with one of his contacts, Sunshine. She had turned twenty-one after the EMPs hit. She was a ratty-looking thing, dirty and scrawny, but even through the grime he could tell she had once been beautiful, and still would be if given a bath, and some clothes that weren't torn, dirty, and four sizes too big. Before the war, she would definitely have been his "type"—a bit tomboyish, high cheekbones, almost almond-shaped crystal blue eyes, and a strong but not manly jaw that curved gracefully down to a sort of pointed, elfin chin.

That didn't matter now. More importantly for Carl's purposes, she was cunning and smart. He had snuck food to her for months now when he was in town, along with a revolver, and she helped him get things in the wild that he couldn't find in walled-up Liz Town. She also provided news, and was part of a gang of ten or so other Bums, all of whom worked for Carl from time to time, like in setting up this safehouse (though Carl had stashed the food under the floorboards). She swore up and down they had never resorted to cannibalism, and he chose to believe her because it was expedient to do so.

"Thanks for the grub, dude," Sunshine said with her usual gap-toothed smile. Starvation often caused teeth to fall out, and she had lost two. The rest were still neat, perfect, white.

Carl smiled back at the waif. "No worries, girl. You know I got your back, whenever I can. Thanks for having mine."

"Pshaw. Of course I got your back. My crew and I wouldn't have made it this long without your help, probably. Want some Ecstasy? I got a few bars."

That meant batches of three Ecstasy pills. Despite the misconception before the EMPs, "X" didn't necessarily make one want to hump trees or whatever, but did give the most intense euphoria. Carl didn't want his mind clouded for the next twelve hours, though. "No thanks. Not in the mood." That was the easiest way to say no without pissing people off, or risking them thinking he was being judgmental.

"One of these days I'm going to get you to smash."

Surprised, Carl grinned with sudden embarrassment. She had been trying to get him in bed for months, and he always said no. He didn't like the idea that it could be taking advantage of her—she'd do anything to eat, after all. "Maybe, but not today, beautiful. You and I both need a bath before that could happen."

Sunshine laughed, then caught herself. "You and I both know I'm the one who needs the bath. I can't wait for spring, when the daytime will heat up enough for me to scrub down in the streams. Then you'll be all smitten, and I won't have to ask. You'll take me like a pirate and plunder some booty."

"Ha! That's hilarious. Arrr... Then maybe you'll stop trying to shiver me timber."

Sunshine gave an uncharacteristic giggle, probably her kid coming out, the one everyone without dead eyes still had inside somewhere. He grinned back.

The two talked cheerfully for a while about normal things like finding food, whether rats were edible, and how best to hide from cannibals. Carl was glad for the company because the worst part of hiding out in a safehouse was the boredom. There was quite literally nothing to do. He'd almost have slept with Sunshine just to relieve the monotony, but he suspected she was crushing on him, and he didn't want to give her mixed messages. That wouldn't be right.

Then, mid-sentence, Sunshine froze. Carl had a moment of confusion, then he too froze, listening and looking around. He didn't see anything... He whispered, "What?"

Sunshine held up her hand for silence. A moment later, Carl heard a faint noise outside, like boots on gravel. Sunshine drew her revolver, the one Carl had given her a while back.

Carl drew his 1911 pistol, a heavy .45-caliber handgun. He preferred a slightly smaller round such as a .40-caliber, but ammunition was easier to scrounge for the 1911. He rose to his feet, slow and silent, then went back to listening. The odds were good that it was just one of the many feral dogs that roamed the streets, but maybe not.

Carl took two light steps to a window. It had been spray-painted black on the inside, but he had put a few small pieces of tape on each window. When lifted, it allowed him to look out without being too obvious. Pulse racing, he lifted one piece of tape and put his eye to the window. Nothing.

He moved to the next window and did the same. He saw a blur of movement outside but it went immediately out of view. Then through the window, he heard faint footsteps outside. Definitely a person, though he hadn't seen them long enough to get anything about him or her.

Carl waved at Sunshine to get her attention, then raised both eyebrows and pointed at her. Was it one of hers? But she shook her head, then went to a different window and lifted a flap of tape. Carl did the same. He didn't see anyone outside, but dammit, he had heard at least one. Where were they?

Sunshine crept across the room to the area just in front of the fireplace, avoiding one particularly creaky floorboard, and moved the small rug there. Carl saw the outline of a trap door there, though he would probably have missed it if he didn't know it was there. She swung the trapdoor open on its well-oiled hinges, and stuck her head through. She looked all around before she came back up, then left the door open and got to her feet.

She whispered, "I see eight legs out there. Four people, eight if they're amputees."

Carl gave her a half-smile. Sunshine always had that sass, that attitude, and it was one of the things he loved about her. Her personality was the reason he thought of her as a friend almost as much as an asset. "No one should know we're here," he whispered back. "Maybe just scroungers, but that's a pretty big coincidence. How can we get out of here?"

"Either hide in the crawl space under the house, or out that window," she replied, pointing at the south-facing ones. "There were two on the north side, and two on the west side, so we can bolt out the window and to the left. There are some bushes for cover, but not much until we got across the street. Then only abandoned houses, so we could maybe ditch there or find another place to hide."

"Opening the window will make noise. Maybe under the house is the better bet," Carl whispered. "C'mon, let's go. You first."

"Always the gentleman," Sunshine said with a smile, and slid quietly through the hole into the crawlspace beneath.

He heard a crash from the other end of the house, someone kicking in the door. Time was up. He dropped through the hole and closed the trapdoor. He pulled a string attached to the rug, which moved it back over the trap door—even as well hidden as it was, the carpet would help.

Below, he and Sunshine kept pistols drawn and aimed toward the trapdoor. Either they'd find it or they wouldn't, had seen it close or hadn't, but now he was trapped. There was nowhere to run. For long minutes that felt like hours, his heartbeat drumming in his ears, Carl and Sunshine waited. They heard the clomping noise of booted feet going back and forth above them on the hardwood floor. Crashes and the sounds of shattering glass made it clear that the people above were searching carefully, and not being careful about what they broke.

Sunshine tapped Carl's shoulder then pointed to his left. He looked in that direction and, through the fine mesh wire of the air intake opening, a pair of booted feet. He glanced behind him and saw another—they had posted two at opposite corners of the house, able to see if anyone ran out. Never mind the noise the window would have made, if they had tried to flee they would have been seen. Hiding had been the right decision.

The two inside spent some fifteen minutes both searching and looting the place. Thankfully, most of his food was down here, but of course now Sunshine knew where it was hidden. Anything up top would no doubt be taken by their visitors.

A voice above his head shouted, “Clear.” Another at the other end of the house shouted the same thing back. Footsteps as they met in the middle of the house. “How the hell did he get out?”

“I don’t know. A window, maybe. A hidden exit.”

“Well, we aren’t getting paid without at least his corpse, man.”

“There’s a lot of crap here that’s worth something. We can get paid that way.”

“We’re supposed to burn the house down after we catch him.”

“Did we catch him? Don’t think so. Maybe he’ll come back. We can set up a stakeout and then if he comes back, we catch him inside. If we burn it down now, he sure won’t come back, and then what? No body, no payday.”

“Fine. Grab that box of food, I’ll get this one with the other crap, and then we can get the hell out of here.”

Once he heard them leave, he and Sunshine peered through the screened ventilation holes. He didn’t relax until all four had gone, headed north somewhere. Then he let out a long breath, releasing tension. “That was close,” he said.

“Sounds like you made some new friends,” Sunshine replied, eyebrows furrowed. “Where will you go?”

Carl paused to think, but there wasn’t really anywhere he could go. Liz Town was too dangerous, and now his bug-out house in the “wildlands,” the parts of Elizabethtown that weren’t walled off, had been compromised. How the hell they knew about his safehouse, he couldn’t say. “No idea. I have the food in this crawlspace, the clothes on my back, and my gun. I’ll have to get it out of here and to a new vacant house, somewhere no one knows about. Or leave and try to get somewhere else.”

Sunshine said, “I’ll tell you what. Give me a quarter of your food and I’ll help you carry all this out to another place

I know. It's two blocks away, and I'm the only one I know of who ever goes into it. It should be safe, so long as you stay inside and away from the windows."

"You'd do that for me?"

"I'd do that for food. Don't flatter yourself, you aren't that cute."

"You know I am," he said with a grin.

"Maybe. Probably. But I'm hungry. Let's get the hell out of here." Sunshine grabbed a box of canned raviolis and set it up through the trapdoor, then went to get another. Within fifteen minutes they had it all stashed out of sight across the street, so they could move it more easily at their leisure.

* * *

Samuel rode at the front of the troop column, winding along the road. A squad rode ahead to scout the way, so he could relax a little and enjoy the scenery.

At least until Brett interrupted his reverie. "So, Cap, how long before we get to where we're going?"

"Slept through my briefing, did you?" Samuel replied, and shot Brett a disgusted look.

Brett shrugged. "If you weren't so boring I wouldn't have to."

"We should make Canton, Ohio by tonight. They're a recent Republic addition, after seeing what happened to that graveyard we just passed, Wooster."

The road hit an incline, and the conversation stopped long enough to crest the hill. Then Brett said, "Wooster was stupid to vote no. So after Canton, we'll be in Pennsylvania, right?"

Samuel let gravity do the work, the bike accelerating without pedaling. "Yup. From there we'll spend half our nights outside, and the other half with friendlies. It'll take us about a week to get where we're going. The towns will resupply us."

"Since when do we have friendlies in Pennsylvania?" Brett took his hands off the handlebars and coasted, arms outstretched.

"Knock that off. You eat pavement out here, I'll leave your ass. Anyway, the Republic sent some settler groups to claim vacant homesteads along the way. They'll farm in the spring so we have supply lines into the west and south Pennsylvania. Right now they're acting as independents, and I heard one got set up to join the Confederation we'll be fighting. So we're going there to cause havoc in the meantime."

"Pretending to be bandits—that'll be fun."

"Well, orders are orders," Samuel said. "And when you gotta do something..."

Brett grinned. "...You might as well have fun with it! I can't wait. We haven't seen any real action since Cincinnati."

"Oh, believe me, we're going to have a *ton of fun*. Our orders are to scorch the earth on anyone who won't join the Republic, and we got a hundred people on bikes to make that happen."

Brett was quiet for a moment, and Samuel figured he was relishing the thought. Then Brett said, "Sam, we're going to be like modern-day Vikings, with the roads as our rivers. I almost wish we had swords so we could do it up close and personal. I like to watch the stupid looks on their faces when they get a blade shoved through 'em."

"Yeah, that's great, but these days the peasants have guns. You don't bring a sword to a gunfight."

Brett nodded, the wind flipping his hair around wildly as they pedaled onward. "A guy can dream, Sam. A guy can dream."

Several hours later they saw the unwalled town of

Canton ahead of them, and Brett let out a whoop. Samuel felt pretty happy about it, too—getting off these damn bikes was the best part of his day. A member of one of the scout teams was riding back toward the main column, and Samuel slowed to a halt to pull up next to him.

He said, "Captain, all is well. They're expecting us, and will have supplies and houses ready for us. I get the feeling they want us out of town just as soon as possible."

"I'm sure they do. They only voted to join the glorious Midwest Republic because of what happened to their neighbor, and because they were next in line. I call it a motivational tactic."

"What, burning down their neighbors?" Brett said, smirking.

"More or less," Samuel replied. "Okay, let's move out. Brett, get them moving." To the scout, he said, "Let them know we're coming. And I'll expect some entertainment from the locals, or a bunch of rowdy, armed bandits are going to be awfully hard to control. Think you can remember that?"

The scout nodded, saluted, and rode toward town, and Brett went down the line getting the column straightened out. He liked to enter a town looking as impressive as possible.

Two minutes later, the column began to move again, Samuel at the head. He rode in and headed toward the "town square," an open area in the center of the still-inhabited portion of Canton. Several buildings had been cleared out, turned to rubble for the beginnings of a town wall that was still far from complete. The vacant space left behind had been converted to a market and storage area. It also provided a central area to park their bikes.

While Brett got busy assigning the night's guard posts, Samuel met the Canton leader, a middle-aged man whose name he forgot as soon as it was mentioned. Why bother with it? The unit would be gone in the morning. "You have the supplies we require?"

The town's leader said, "Yes, sir. All your supplies are over there." He pointed to a pile of canned and dried goods and some gear. "You realize this means some of us will go hungry before spring, don't you?"

Samuel put on an expression of pained sympathy, put his hand on the man's shoulder, and said, "I do, and for that I apologize. I follow orders just as you must. I hope that when we come back through here next year, we will have a lot of gear and supplies we can give you to make up for the terrible inconvenience. Thank you for putting us up for the night—our mission is important, and you're a key part of making it possible. The Republic thanks you."

The other man looked away, and only nodded.

Samuel walked away and found Brett organizing bicycle storage. He was lining them up neatly, making it easy to guard them overnight.

Brett saw Samuel and said, "Nice of them to give up their stuff for us. Did you give him the 'Republic thanks you' speech or the 'we all have duties in this world' speech?"

"The Republic one. Of course he probably didn't give two shits about the Republic's thanks, not when his people might go hungry before some crops come up."

"Do you care?" Brett smirked.

"Not really, just so long as we get to eat."

Brett shrugged. He probably didn't care much either. "Hey boss, do you think they got some chicks here? To the conqueror go the spoils, if you know what I mean."

Samuel paused, then said, "Come to think of it, they were supposed to entertain us. You should go let their leader know how much we'd *appreciate* some companionship tonight. Give him the 'we all have duties' speech. And let our troops know that rank has its privileges—I'm not getting stuck with some fugly chick. I think I'm in the mood for a blonde or maybe a redhead."

* * *

Nestor turned once to see the friendly folks of Manheim waving goodbye. He and his guerrillas were welcome there, so long as they didn't overstay their welcome and put undue burden on the town, a Confederation member. To them, he was protector, not parasite. It felt good.

Riding beside him, Ratbone said, "You sure it's good to run around outside Hershey?"

Nestor nodded. "Yes, I'm sure. Liz Town has let too many hungry bands of refugees through into Confed territory and they're not all kosher, so we have a target-rich environment there."

"Too true. I figure we'll probably run across some when we get up around I-76, really. Are we going to camp out in those State Game Lands again?"

"Yeah," Nestor replied. "It's about the halfway point, so a good place to set up for a while. Fresh water, too."

They rode on for another couple of hours before approaching the Interstate. As always, Nestor sent four riders ahead to scout both sides of the roadway, and the rest of his unit didn't cross until the scouts gave the signal. This time, crossing the freeway was uneventful. Then they rode on for another half-mile before turning east toward the forest, which was once a wildlife refuge.

After a couple scouts rode out again to make sure the area was clear, all of Nestor's thirty-four guerrillas rode in and, from long practice, went about setting up camp with hardly a word spoken. Not until it was set up, tarp lean-tos in place, kitchen established, and patrols set did any of them relax. Then it was time to cook up some chow, meager though it would be. A couple hours after nightfall, Nestor lay under his tarp lean-to, wrapped in his wool blanket, and drifted to sleep.

He bolted upright as echoes of gunfire bounced around the forest. Sweet, sweet music! The opening score, and now it was showtime. *The Other* grabbed his rifle and sprinted toward the source of that deadly, beautiful music. Free at last! That putz who rode around in his mind with him must have been sleeping, and it was about damn time. His other actors rose up from their shelters as he ran past them, and they'd be along shortly.

Ahead, he saw two of his own actors crouched behind a fallen tree, shooting into the dark. No problem. The extras gave away their positions by their muzzle flashes. The Other sprinted toward a spot to their right, and circled around. Four men lay prone, firing back. Oh sweet fate. Distracted, they hadn't seen the Other.

He crept to the nearest and plunged his knife into the back of the man's neck. He went limp instantly without so much as a cry. Sonofabitch, the bastard had screwed up his lines. He was supposed to deliver a believable scream of pain and terror. The script in the Other's mind said so. Best to try again, then.

The Other slid his knife into its sheath and crept forward, but as he approached the second man, the bastard looked up in time to see him coming. No knifey-knife this time. The Other pulled the trigger, his rifle kicked, and the man's chest spouted a pulsing geyser of beautiful blood. Such perfect special effects! And this guy delivered his lines flawlessly before exiting stage left.

The two remaining men turned at the noise and looked to their partner, then with wide eyes they boggled at the Other. The Other grinned and snap-fired two rounds, striking both men. Two more rounds finished them off, and that was the end of the marvelous scene.

His people began to rise from their prone positions, but then one pointed past him into the dark forest beyond. The Other spun, and saw a dozen more charging through the dense underbrush toward him. Rifle empty, he dropped it and drew his knife. Then beyond the fast-approaching line of people he saw one man slightly farther back, shouting. That would be the so-called leader of this little improv troupe... stupid word, "leader." They never led—behinders is what they were. Meant they're liars, but they still played in the symphony.

The Other bolted behind a tree but didn't slow down. He came out the other side and made a sharp left turn off his right foot, went between two rather startled-looking actors, and in four steps and one giant leap he crashed into their leader. The two tumbled to the ground, and the Other cackled with glee. He came up to one knee before the other man could sit up. He rushed his target as he struggled to his hands and knees and jumped, landing on the man's back, forcing him face-first into the dirt.

The Other grabbed a clump of the man's hair and then slid the blade of his knife across the man's forehead. Lifting with his whole body, the Other pulled the man's scalp clean off his head, leaving his bloody skull exposed. And oh, the sweet, beautiful lines that man delivered!

The Other turned to look at the man's companions, half a dozen facing him and the other half holding off the Other's men as best they could. Now outnumbered greatly, however, they fell one by one. The Other grinned, put the scalp on top of his head like a toupee, and shouted, "And... Action!" before bursting into a full run at the six facing him. Blood oozed down the Other's face as he ran and in only a few steps he crashed into the closest man. The other five turned to run, but went straight into the Night Ghosts' hail of fire; they dropped to the ground like bloody marionettes.

The Other slid his knife into the man's belly, and they screamed together, one in pain and fear, the other with savage, mocking joy.

Nestor rose out of a fog, fighting his way into consciousness. He opened his eyes and saw everything in red for a moment, until like a camera lens clicking, the red slid away. He looked down, confused, and saw that he straddled a dead stranger. His knife was in the man, but there were half a dozen other knife wounds as well. "What the..."

You're welcome. Another fine play we put on, pansy-ass.

"Shut up," Nestor said from between clenched teeth.

A voice next to him, Ratbone's, said, "Pretty sure he isn't talking anymore, boss."

"What happened," Nestor growled, still groggy and trying to make sense of what his eyes and ears were telling him.

"Looks like your little brain-hitchhiker came out to play. Good thing, too, because you were the fastest one of all of us to get out there to back up our guards. They were about to get overrun."

Nestor became aware of something wet and warm on his head, but when he reached up he felt only hair. "I'm wounded," he said, but it was more a question than a statement.

I gave you a pretty hat. Say thank-you...

Nestor felt something shift on his head, and frantically rubbed his hands over his head to get it off, whatever it was—and the scalp he unknowingly wore fell off his head, landing hair-down on the face of the dead man beneath him. Nestor scrambled back, off the body and away from that horrible wet, hairy thing. "Oh, goddammit," came out in a whiny shout. In his mind, the Other sent him waves of laughter.

Good thing you were asleep or your buddies would all be dead now, you chickenshit.

Nestor shut his eyes and shoved the Other back down where he belonged once combat ended. Ratbone had watched Nestor go through this sort of cycle before, right after a fight, and kept quiet until Nestor opened his eyes again.

Then Ratbone stepped up to Nestor and held his hand out to help him up. “That Other guy is one nasty sonofabitch, sir.”

Nestor nodded, and grabbed Ratbone’s hand, struggling to his feet. “Yeah. Creepy. But useful sometimes.”

“We’d have lost quite a few people without him here, tonight. Come on, let’s get that crap off you. I got some shampoo in my bag and the creek’s right over there.”

“Hey boss,” shouted another man, who was rummaging through all the dead men’s pockets. “Look here, more of those gold coins. Think they knew we were here?”

Nestor said, “No, I think they just stumbled over us on their way into Confed territory. This Empire is really starting to piss me off.”

They’re great actors, though. Better than you, jerkoff, the Other whispered in his mind.

Nestor ignored him, and followed Ratbone back toward camp, wanting nothing more than some shampoo and a pan of heated creek water.

- 10 -

1000 HOURS - ZERO DAY +202

AS THEIR WAGON rolled on, Jaz sat quietly beside Choony. They had been growing closer, the sort of close that had been in his dreams for quite a while. Yet lately, quiet was all there was between them. It was all very confusing, but he suspected there was something that had made her feel too vulnerable. She was from the streets and stunningly beautiful, and she had some invisible scars. Some walls. That was understandable.

He sat quietly next to her without pushing. As always, he would let her take the time she needed, the path she wanted. If she felt about him the way he now realized he felt about her, she'd come around. Or she wouldn't. Whether she did or didn't, he could do nothing about it, and worrying about it would only upset his inner harmony while accomplishing nothing. Or so he told himself—the truth was, he was finding that letting go was a lot harder than it was for most things in life. One's desires were what made a thing painful or not, stressful or not—not the thing itself. Yet still, he hung on.

He spent a lot of time meditating, these last couple days.

"Penny for your thoughts," Jaz said, startling him. She

hadn't spoken all morning, until then.

Choony wouldn't lie, not to her and not to anyone. Lying put bad karma into the universe, and brought bad results and inner turmoil. The truth would stand on its own. "I was thinking of us, what we are, and what your silence means. I'm supposed to let such thoughts go, but that's sometimes easier to say than to do."

Jaz smiled at him, and he wished he could tell what she was feeling. Sometimes he doubted even she fully knew what she felt, as she didn't seem to be very in tune with her feelings.

"I thought so," Jaz said. "Half of me hoped so. It's kind of confusing, and I don't really know how to explain it, but I'm really sorry for being all quiet-like lately. I've just been thinking too, trying to figure things out."

Far in the distance, Choony saw the hill that marked home—Clanholme was on the far side. They'd be home in less than an hour, at least briefly. Their mission wasn't done, but they had urgent news for Cassy.

Choony nodded to Jaz. "Self-reflection is important. Sometimes what we think we want isn't what we need, isn't even what we truly want, but it can be hard to realize that." He tried not to care whether that was it or not, but somehow couldn't. Buddha would be disappointed.

Jaz grinned, the first real smile in a while now. "Fishing for compliments? Fine, I'll bite." Then her expression grew somber. "I do want you, Choony. That's totally not what's going on. I just, like, worry?"

"Is that a question or a statement?" Choony asked, and turned to face her, showing that she had his full attention. The horses would be fine trudging north on their own for a minute.

Jaz looked down at her hands, which held her rifle across her lap. "Both, I guess. 'Worry' isn't the right word. I just never felt so open and easy to hurt. Not with anyone before. I worry that I got too attached to you. Sometimes it's better when you don't feel anything, then you can do what needs doing and nothing can hurt your actual deep-down heart."

"So, you're afraid that I'm going to hurt you? I can't promise that I won't, but I can promise that I'd never do anything intentionally that would hurt you. I hope you know that."

Jaz nodded slowly, still looking down at her hands and fidgeting. "I never worry about that anymore. You keep it real, one-hundred percent. The problem..." she said, and her voice trailed off.

Choony felt a turmoil unlike any since junior high and his first solid crush. "You sound confused. You worry I'll hurt you and that you let yourself get too vulnerable, but you never worry I'll hurt you. There must be more going on, then."

Jaz looked away for a moment, but said nothing.

Choony continued, "You can tell me. Or is it that you worry I care more than you do, that I'll cling to you?"

He braced himself for her answer, whatever she said, and reminded himself that it wouldn't actually kill him if she said yes, he was clingy. It would only feel like it.

Her spontaneous laugh, high-pitched and beautiful, surprised him. She looked at him and said, "No, that's not even possible. Listen, we came close to dying when that Intercourse outpost tried to ambush us."

"True, but neither of us died."

"The entire time, all I could think about was whether, if they killed you, I might be happier if I died with you."

Choony opened his mouth to speak, but Jaz continued unabated. "What we're doing out here is dangerous, Choony. Like, probably-going-to-kill-us dangerous."

"I know."

"One or both of us will die out here in the wilds, sooner or later, and I'm okay with that. I need to be okay with that because what we're doing is so damn important. Save the world kind of important, maybe. But..."

"...but if we're too close, you're afraid of getting hurt, should I die, or of hurting me by getting killed?"

Jaz nodded, and closed her eyes tightly for a moment. Opening them, she looked at him and he saw they were red and bleary. "I can't do this job right if I'm more worried about you than the mission, Choony. I know I'm tough, I've been through more things than I'll ever talk about, but it's tough-like-diamonds—nothing can scratch me, but hit me hard enough or in the wrong place and I'll shatter."

Choony fought a flash of anger, then went stone-cold as he fought for control of his emotions. Finally he calmed himself. He couldn't blame her for her feelings, they were what they were. "I'd like to suggest that if we know we're going to get killed at some point, it's better to die with love than fear. Isn't it better to have our shining moment together first, even if it's brief? As long as we're going to die anyway, I'd like to die happy and... And in love," he added, and felt his throat tighten.

He hadn't said that to her before because he didn't want to pressure her. He didn't want her to say it back just because it was the thing to say at the moment. But if she was going to wall herself off, she deserved to know how he felt, first, and what she would be giving up and what she would cost him, too.

Jaz let out a muffled cry and turned away from him. He put his hand on her knee, and she didn't move it away. He only wanted to comfort her, but had no idea what to say to make it better.

"I know. I feel it, Choony. I just... I need time to figure things out for myself. I feel like everything is louder than everything else. Do you know what I mean?"

"I do."

"Good, then you understand why I just need some time."

Choony nodded his understanding, though she couldn't see him. He decided to let her be for a while, and he took his hand off her knee. He tried to be calm, but it was hard. "Of course, Jaz."

After that, they rode on in silence as they approached Clanholme. In a way, he felt a sense of dread at the thought of arriving. Surely people would shout and cheer, smile, clap him on the back. There would be joy, and he'd have to smile a smile he couldn't feel right now. It wouldn't be right to take their happiness because of his own stupid turmoil. Ha. Maybe he should worry about his harmony rather than his *other* desires. Desire was the source of all pain and conflict in the world, after all. He knew that.

The wagon wound around the base of the hill, and the guard tower slowly shifted into view. He and Jaz would have to deal with heartfelt reunions with true friends. They'd have to tell Cassy about the Empire's fake survivor group at Intercourse, and their real new allies at the Gap. And worst, he'd have to tell Cassy that the Empire had some radios—and one was at Intercourse.

He took a deep breath as a crowd began to gather around the guard tower. Reunion time. Show time. Shutting his eyes a moment, he tried to access that inner acceptance but, as Jaz put it, everything felt so *loud*...

* * *

Carl huddled inside the otherwise vacant house two blocks from his compromised safehouse, in the wildlands of Elizabethtown. The sun had gone down a couple hours earlier and, as the temperature plummeted, he shivered and wished he had a blanket. Those bastards sent to kill him had taken his, along with some of his food and his lantern.

He knew he couldn't stay there forever. He would run out of food, or get eaten, or Pamela's hired goons would find him. He worried about the Alpha, leader of his band, the Timber Wolves and Speaker of Liz Town. Was he deposed yet by Pamela's cabal of co-conspirators? She'd tried to recruit Carl, and of course he'd thrown his life away by trying to warn the Alpha, that fool. Why had he been so stupid as to think the Alpha would listen to him? Just because they were friends?

His thoughts were interrupted by three knocks at the back door, Sunshine's idea to let him know it was she who was coming in, not Pam's goons. He welcomed the break from his pity party.

When Sunshine came in, she was carrying a thick comforter and a decent-looking wool blanket. Maybe one he had given her group back when he was still welcome in Liz Town.

Sunshine smiled at him and said, "Honey, I'm home."

"Ha. Okay, dear. Dinner's in the oven and the kids are asleep already. How was work?"

"Funny. Ha ha. I brought you blankets. Care to break them in?" she said, wiggling her eyebrows at him.

Carl feigned indignation as he replied, "You, missy, are a tease. Holding out blankets and then not giving it up."

She handed him the comforter and wrapped the wool blanket around her shoulders. It was gray, and Carl suspected that was its actual color rather than just being filthy and faded. "I never tease," she said with a smirk, then sat down leaning against a wall.

Carl did likewise, sitting next to her. "Thanks. I was freezing."

"Yeah, I figured. We had a couple extras from the blankets you gave us last month. It's the least I could do for all you did to help us."

"Oh, the very least, I agree," he said with a pursed-lipped smile.

Sunshine bumped his knee with hers. "Got news for ya. You probably won't like it, but it could be good for you."

"They're turning the power back on tomorrow? What's not to like about that?"

"I wish. No, I'm sorry to be the one to tell you, but the Timber Wolves' Alpha got himself killed."

Carl froze. That was news, and not the good kind. "I tried to warn him, dammit."

Sunshine put her hand on his arm and squeezed lightly. "I know. You did what you could. But what's done is done, and maybe now whoever's chasing you will stop."

"Doubtful."

"With the Alpha dead and a new Speaker election coming up, they might be too busy to care, and of course now you can't stop them from killing him. Not your concern anymore."

"How did they kill him?" It was a morbid question, but he felt like he owed it to his friend to know that. To know what failure had cost the Alpha.

"Rumor has it you killed him. Snuck into his room early this morning, tied him up, beat on him a little bit, then slit his throat and ran away."

Carl's hands turned into fists. From between clenched teeth, he said, "My knife. They found my knife, right?"

Sunshine nodded.

Dammit! He'd left that already-bloody knife in the bushes, but they'd found it. He'd hoped to pick it up later—the Tanto-tipped knife with which he had killed one of his watchers was among his favorites.

Carl said, "Do my packmates believe the rumor?" It was an important question, as the answer could well determine how long he lived and would definitely determine what options he now faced.

"No, most Timber Wolves are saying it was a Diamondback assassin. Diamondback is considered the frontrunners for a new Speaker, so they had the most to gain. But the other Bands believe it. They didn't know you."

Carl frowned. At least his packmates didn't believe this nonsense. He'd have to make his next moves carefully, but at least other Bands weren't likely to pursue him. They wouldn't much care about who killed another Band's leader, other than that it meant an election they could hope to win, whatever the odds.

His jaw set like iron, Carl said, "So I have friends in the Timber Wolves still. With Pamela off my tail, or at least distracted by the election preparations, I have a chance to contact some of them. Maybe I couldn't save my friend, but I can try to get revenge for his murder. And for betraying me."

"I can help you sneak in. We wildlanders know some secret ways."

Carl nodded, wheels turning in his mind. "Good. If it's the last thing I do, I want to bring that bitch Pamela down."

Sunshine leaned her head against his shoulder and let out a deep breath. "If you must, then I'll help you. I owe you my life. Besides, maybe if I help you survive, you'll let me get you drunk enough to smash."

Carl chuckled at that. Would it really be so bad if she was crushing on him? But it wasn't something he wanted to deal with or even think about right now. Besides, it wouldn't be fair to her if he got her hopes up and then went and got himself killed. But maybe after this was all over... A man could do worse than stick with someone he really liked and knew he could trust with his life...

* * *

0900 HOURS - ZERO DAY +203

Cassy walked toward her house and felt a strange mix of happiness and dread. She'd missed Jaz and Choony's return because she was still dealing with the damn conflict between Lebanon and the Falconry, but she had met up with the two travelers later in the day. Their news was mixed—the survivors at Intercourse were Empire spies, basically, which she had suspected but now had proof of. It was alarming that they had radios, and Ethan had sent riders out to all the Confed allies with new frequencies and spoken code words for sensitive matters. Michael said keeping up some chatter on the old radio band would help them mislead the enemy when the time came. That made sense but it wasn't enough to turn the news good.

On the other hand, Jaz and Choony were alive, and that was fantastic news. They'd squeaked through another close one, it seemed. Cassy had chatted with Choony for a long time, catching up and just getting reacquainted. It was nice having him to bounce ideas and internal conflicts off of. He always seemed to lead her to her own right answers just by asking questions, never lecturing unless she needed a lecture, and he seemed to always know when to lead and when to lecture.

Just as importantly, the new large settlement at the Gap was a priceless find. If they became allies or joined the Confed, which Jaz thought was likely, they would help secure the southern flank, something the Clan especially wanted to see. They covered a bridge, a natural choke point, and they were mostly self-sufficient. They also had helped Choony and Jaz escape the Intercourse ambush purely on principle, which spoke well of them.

As Cassy approached the door to her house, she put those thoughts aside and braced herself for the storm she was about to face. Lebanon and the Falconry were still at each other's throats about Lebanon taxing traders leaving Falconry territory, and both sides had sent envoys to Clanholme to plead their case. Cassy was pleased that they turned to Clanholme to arbitrate the matter, but irritated at the time it had taken, and would still take. It also made the Clan responsible for the outcome. She'd have to tread lightly.

Opening the door, she stepped inside and smiled at the man and woman seated in her living room, who sat on opposite sides of the room. Cassy could feel the tension between them. "Good morning to you both," she said cheerily.

The man from Lebanon, with characteristic charm and tact, said, "Let's not blow smoke up each other's asses, okay? I wish to go home, and to do that we need to resolve this. Lebanon thanks you for mediating this simple matter, and if you can just tell Falconry the facts of the matter, I can get out of here."

The Falconry woman smirked. "Yes, Cassy," she said, pointedly using the Clan leader's familiar name, "I think two days is long enough as well. You have so much more important matters to attend, I'm sure, so once you explain to Lebanon that they can't go around taxing allies of the Confederation for passing through, we'll both be out of your hair. Sorry for the ridiculous circumstances of my visit."

Cassy let out a sharp breath. These two were night and day, and both frustrating in their own ways. She stepped up to her podium and then said, "Thank you both for your patience. This is an important issue for all of us and I've had to think long and hard about a resolution since hearing both of your arguments yesterday."

Lebanon, irritation in his voice, said, "Fantastic. Like Falconry said, let's get this over with."

"That's not what I said," snarled Falconry.

Cassy raised her hands, palms toward the two guests appeasingly. "Please, I do have a verdict. One which is fair. It has taken a while because this sets a precedent, and I have to be sure that we sail forward in the best direction."

Cassy paused and waited, until both representatives nodded in acknowledgement. Then she said, "Lebanon. You feel you have the right to a fee for passage from non-Confederation traders moving through your territory, is that right?"

When he nodded, Cassy continued, "Falconry. You feel that as our secret ally you should enjoy the same protections as Confederation members, and you feel that your wagons moving west and northeast don't travel through Lebanon's territory. Correct?"

"More or less, yes. They can't claim everything. We have claims, too."

Cassy nodded, and put on her most sympathetic, wistful smile. "It is the Confederation's decision that Falconry controls all land within one mile of their survivor enclave. Lebanon may not collect passage fees from wagons within this zone. Additionally, it can't collect from caravans headed west along the edge of the forest—they're headed toward Liz Town, a Confederation member. Fees on those wagons affect prices Liz Town has to pay."

The Lebanon rep frowned, while his counterpart smiled with tightly-pressed lips, a smug expression.

Cassy continued, "However. The Confederation claims all other territory within our borders, outside of Falconry's one-mile radius. These territories belong to the closest major Confederation member. Falconry, Lebanon controls the Confed territory outside your one mile. They may collect fees as they wish, so long as those fees are reasonable and necessary. They do, after all, patrol all that territory to make it safer for your traders and they keep the roads clear. Unless those wagons are heading west along the forest between itself and Liz Town, Lebanon may apply reasonable fees for passage. This is the Confederation's decision." She slapped the podium, which made a sharp bang. "That is all."

The man from Lebanon shook Cassy's hand and left, all smiles, but the Falconry woman stayed behind. After Lebanon was gone, she turned to Cassy and narrowed her eyes. "You've made a mistake, Cassy. One you'll likely regret."

Cassy looked up at the ceiling and let out a slow, frustrated breath. "Listen, I don't like them charging you, or any trader. We *need* trade to grow and recover. But if I arbitrate against Lebanon, what if they pulled out of the Confederation? Would your people be safer without them standing strong to your north, defending you from the hordes? No."

"We stood against those raiders and refugees before the Confederation, and we could do it again. We—"

Cassy interrupted, "And they'd be free not just to collect fees from you, but to seize your goods. They're a lot bigger than you, and closer than the rest of the Confed members. We couldn't protect you from *them*."

Falconry was quiet, and stared at Cassy with one eyebrow raised. The look on her face did not inspire Cassy's hope that she would go along easily with this decision. Cassy continued, "Look, I gave you territory. Now we have a border and you're safe within that border. And I gave you an exemption for your westbound traders, even if they aren't ending their journey at Liz Town."

"Because it benefitted the Confederation to do so. Please don't spit on me and tell me it's raining."

Cassy nodded. The envoy had a point, after all. "Fine. Then the truth is that I gave you all that I could, because we're allies and because the Clan has special trade arrangements with Falconry. And because it was the right thing to do. But I can't do more for you. Lebanon is in the Confed and ultimately, the Confed needs to take care of its own before it takes care of outsiders. That's the reality we live in, and you know it."

Falconry's nostrils flared and her cheeks flushed. "We have a trade arrangement that's more important to you than us, Cassy. You really need to think about what you're doing. The Falconry will remember this, if you let this decision stand."

"Sorry. Whatever the consequences, my hands are tied. I can't afford to lose Lebanon. Now, if you wanted to join the Confederation then things would be dif—"

Falconry interrupted, snapping, "Shove that! You've shown whose friendship you value more. Cassy, I'm shocked and disappointed. I think you can forget about getting first dibs on our gasifiers, or anything else. From here out, the Falconry will do just like you said—we'll look after our own before we look out for you outsiders."

Cassy could only nod. It wasn't unexpected, but still sucked. "I understand. Just don't cut off your nose to spite your face—we're still the biggest, closest markets you have, and we still welcome your trading wagons. And you still get the benefit of being pretty safe now, surrounded by strong Confed groups to shield you from the hungry world out there."

She held open the door, and Falconry left, taking great strides toward the horse stables. No doubt she was leaving immediately. Damn Lebanon and their fees. They should be looting enemies, not friends, and they'd just made Cassy's life a lot more difficult.

If Choony were still in Clanholme, he'd have something to say about this that would put things into proper perspective. She thought of him and smiled, almost hearing his voice in her head saying, "Do you really need Lebanon?" knowing the answer was yes, and then he'd smile all Buddha-like at her until she had some personal epiphany.

But Choony wasn't in Clanholme anymore, having left earlier that morning after delivering the unwelcome news of spies or maybe shock troops posing as residents, and she would have to find her own epiphany. Damn Lebanon again...

* * *

1800 HOURS - ZERO DAY +205

Nestor and his fellow "traders" sat across from the town's leader, Bradley, the "Boss of Intercourse," in the man's office. They'd gotten along famously, despite his crazy mind-companion's continual warnings. That didn't mean he ignored the warnings, but so far, they seemed like circumstantial evidence at best. There weren't a lot of children among them... The Dying Times weren't easy on kids and the elderly, so that wasn't definitive. They didn't have stockpiles of salvage... They had at least a plausible explanation for that, and had told him they traded it for food in autumn of last year.

Still, he kept his eyes and ears open, and felt a lot better knowing his five best fighters were right outside the house chitchatting with Bradley's two guards.

"So," Bradley said, his loose, flabby neck jiggling as he spoke, "I can't believe I'm really hosting some of the famous Night Ghosts. We've even heard of you down here, from traders and refugees. They talk about the bloody path you cut right through the heart of those invaders around some town called Brickville."

"Brickerville," Nestor corrected. He smiled wanly. "It was

a rough time but we did what we had to, just like everyone else. Thank you for offering to trade a few supplies with me and my little crew. I'm glad I thought to bring those gold coins from the Empire."

Bradley's left eye twitched once, but a big grin spread across his face. "Well, I figure we'll be trading with them and your Confederation soon enough."

Nestor shrugged, and kept his face neutral, eyes locked onto Bradley's. "Not my Confederation. I'm friendly with them, but not friends." No point giving away intel if he didn't have to...

"So for the gold coins, we owe you enough cans to feed your band. We'd be happy to deliver them, if you'd like." Bradley now wore an easygoing smile.

He lies. Let's kill him.

Nestor ignored the voice of the Other bouncing through his mind. "Oh, no thanks. It's kind of you, but when my guys and I leave we can just take it with us. The rest of them can wait. We do have some food, after all."

Bradley gave no sign of disappointment, only nodded. "As you wish. I'm glad you're staying, though. I have my lunch coming, and it'll be great having someone from out there in the wilds to talk to while I eat. We don't get a lot of visitors."

Before the EMPs, eating in front of guests without offering them any would have been the height of rudeness, but the EMPs changed everything. Nestor's stomach growled at the thought of hot food. "My stomach seems to agree. But yes, we spend most of our time north of here, or did before."

"So what brings you down here, then?"

"We're trying to move around a lot, meet everyone in the region who isn't with the Empire or the 'vaders. You'll have to tell me where you found all these trucks... Pretty clever, walling off part of the town like that. Other places I've been to have used rubble for that, but the trucks are quicker and faster, I bet."

There was a knock at the door. "Enter," Bradley said loudly, and the front door swung open. A man and a woman entered, each with a tray carrying a bowl of soup and a small pile of honest-to-goodness broccoli.

Nestor's eyes went wide. "Broccoli? How on Earth did you get that?"

"Been frozen all winter. We found them in the freezer of a collapsed restaurant. They seemed fresh enough when we opened one, so we've been enjoying them as special rewards and treats."

"Awesome. I can't wait to eat something green that isn't rotten. But just for the record, I didn't ask for food," Nestor chuckled.

"Duly noted," Bradley replied, his voice full of mock severity. He looked at the man carrying a tray and tipped his head toward Nestor. The man nodded and carefully set his tray down before the Night Ghost leader, then stepped back. The woman set hers in front of Bradley, who then dismissed them. The two servers stepped to the side and stood with their backs to a wall to wait for their leader and their guest to eat.

Don't eat it, dumbass. The Other's irritating voice bounced through Nestor's mind again.

Nestor ignored the voice. This was broccoli, after all. He picked up a steaming-hot piece and raised it to his nose to smell the goodness. "I haven't seen broccoli in forever," he said, smiling.

Bradley leaned back in his chair and put his hands behind his head, intertwining his fingers. "Yeah, it was really quite a score. I'll be sad when it's gone, which will be rather too soon. But spring is coming, and then we'll plant."

The Other's voice rang through Nestor's mind. *He isn't*

eating his. Why wouldn't he devour freaking broccoli, *man? Why aren't his fields plowed if he's planting in the spring?*

Nestor paused. That was a good point. Still smiling, he set his broccoli down on the tray before him. Bradley's eyes narrowed. It was just for a moment, but Nestor was sure he'd seen it. "What all are you planting in the spring? Maybe the Clan can offer some seeds to cover your bases."

Bradley's smile faded a bit. "I'm not sure. I have people who take care of that. I don't really care as long as it gets planted."

"How many seeds do you have? Is it enough?"

Bradley lowered his arms, setting his elbows on the desk in front of him. "I'm told we have enough, yeah. They chose me as their leader, not their farmer. I delegate to people who manage the parts I don't know enough about."

Nestor pushed the tray away a little and scooted his chair back a few inches, enough to allow him to rest his own elbows on the desk comfortably—and still give him room to jump up if necessary. Damn the Other for putting doubts into his head. That broccoli had looked so delicious. "That makes sense. I delegate too," he said, thinking back to the old man in the farmhouse, and what he'd had Ratbone do. Still, a leader who didn't know details about his food supply was a crappy leader—unless he was just keeping his stockpile a secret from outsiders, which was possible. "While I appreciate the offer, I can't eat your food. You know how the new rules work, I'm sure. I don't want to owe anything to anyone."

Bradley pursed his lips and raised one eyebrow, but it wasn't exactly a hostile expression. He rested his hands in his lap. "Now, I offered you food. It'd be rude for me to eat before my guests. Not everything has changed since the war came."

Nestor shrugged. "Sorry. Where I come from, we don't

take food we don't need and haven't earned or traded fair for. So—"

Bradley interrupted, "Just consider it a bonus. Those coins are actually worth a lot. You bargained badly, friend. But a deal is a deal so don't go asking for more. Still, I can throw in a bowl of soup. I'd hate for it to go to waste." He leaned forward again, resting his elbows on his knees.

Nestor slowly sat upright, taking his elbows off the desk, and his eyes narrowed at Bradley. "No thank you. Like you said, a deal is a deal, and this meal wasn't part of the deal. Do me a favor, please, and take your hands out from under the desk."

"Oh come now, I thought we were past all that. A nice, trusting—"

There was a loud bang and the sound of splintering wood. Nestor's head whipped around and he saw his companions swarm into the room, weapons out and aimed at Bradley and his two companions. Nestor also saw that one of the servers had a knife in his hand. "Knife," he said simply.

Two of his people disarmed the man, then shoved both servers to the floor. Then they slit both their throats. One of Nestor's people aimed a pistol at Bradley. "Get up."

Nestor calmly said, "What's going on?"

Ratbone, wiping the blood from his knife on the pants of a dead server, said, "They kept insisting that we eat their damn soup..."

Bradley shouted, "You come in here, refuse my generosity, kill my people. We're going to kill every last one of you little vermin. We're going to—"

The man with a gun pointed at Bradley shouted, "Stand up or die."

Bradley stood, and in his hand was a pistol. Nestor noted that his hand shook a little. Good, the asshole was scared. He should be.

Nestor said, "Ratbone, it's time for Plan B. What a shame."

Ratbone bolted outside and raised what looked like another pistol. Pulling the trigger, there was a burst of light and smoke that streaked upward, and then the area outside took on a red glow.

Bradley turned pale. "A flare gun? What—"

Nestor couldn't hear the rest of what his "host" said over the deafening roar of several explosions, which added their own hellish light to the scene outside the window. Then the sound of weapons being fired, and screaming voices far away.

Nestor grinned. "You should have gone with rubble, Bradley. Dynamite is everywhere these days, and it just tears right through cargo trailers. You know, like your walls. Right now my people are swarming through the wreckage of your gates and walls."

Sweat beaded on Bradley's forehead and his knees almost gave out, he shook so bad. "You can't... I have an envoy at Clanholme, for chrissake! We're trying to be *allies,* damn you. The Confederation will hunt you down for this!"

Nestor coughed, then recovered. "Ha. You don't know much, do you? I'm not part of the Confederation. Anyway, like that old movie said, I think they'll just chew me out. I've been chewed out before." He turned to the man who had Bradley covered with his pistol and winked.

Bang. Bang.

Bradley toppled with a look of shock and rage etched on his face, then hit the floor and didn't move.

Nestor said, "Coward never did use his gun. Alright, let's go join the fun out there, guys. Say hello to my little friend..."

About damn time. Now it's my turn. Then the Other laughed out loud and pointed at the shattered door. "What are you bitches waiting for? It's showtime."

- 11 -

0800 HOURS - ZERO DAY +215

CASSY FOUND FRANK as he directed a crew expanding the Complex, adding more insulative, bullet-resistant earthbag domes and walls to the network of interconnected, walled small dwellings. Even when done, the Complex would only be large enough to hold half the Clan—another walled complex of small earthbag houses would eventually have to be built somewhere nearby before next winter.

She waited until he finished talking to his crew before intruding. “Hi, Frank. Got a minute?”

He smiled and nodded. “Sure do. What’s up?”

“We’ve got ten cars and a dozen old crop dusters, but only six gasifiers for the cars, and only half of the planes have been refitted or were already airworthy when we found them. Six more gasifiers are under construction or refit, though.”

He raised an eyebrow. “Okay. What’s the question, exactly?”

“I need to know what our timeline is for getting the planes refitted, for one. Second, when can the rest of the cars be fitted for wood fuel?”

“Dean says he’ll have the other half of the planes done by

spring. As for the gasifiers, he's on standby."

Cassy frowned. "Damn. I know we aren't getting half the parts we used to from Falconry, since they took away our preferential treatment. But we need those cars up and running. They'll have the armor, the turrets, the guns... but we have no way to drive them until the gasifiers are working."

Frank let out a deep breath. "Look, Cassy, I know how important it is. But you know what Dean is like. I can't tell him anything. He says he can't make them until we have the copper tubing, the drums for burning, all that. He can't make them without parts, you know."

Cassy looked down and clenched her jaw. Looking back up to Frank, she said, "Have we searched any of these abandoned farmhouses near us? Some of them have to have copper pipes for plumbing, and I know damn well there has to be fifty-five gallon drums at some of them."

"Probably. We could strip them."

Cassy nodded. "Okay, we had better get started. Send out scouts to find what we need. Get Dean to make a list. If you don't keep your foot up his ass, he won't get them done."

He chuckled. "How will I get around if I leave that one up his ass?"

Cassy laughed. Then, with a thoughtful look, she said, "Let's find out if Dean has enough helpers, too. If he doesn't, we had better get him a crew to put this stuff together."

"It's going to be hard to spare the scouts and a set of workers for that right now," Frank said. "You know Ethan has them running wild goose chases up north to look like we're looking for the Night Ghosts."

Frank was right. They were short scouts due to the decoy they had set up in the north while Nestor was busy wreaking havoc on the Empire's fake settlements to the south. It was working out well since The Gap had just joined the

Confederation, giving them a strong southern neighbor. Traders were even starting to make occasional runs that way since Fake Intercourse was out of the way.

"Take half the people Ethan sent out and put them on this, okay?" Cassy said. "It's way more important than playing mind games with the 20s. Pipes, drums, fittings, and anything else Dean says he needs. Get him to make that list. And find out if he'll need more helpers to get it done."

"You got it."

Cassy nodded, and the two went their separate ways. Frank was obviously irritated by the task, and she knew he'd run into some resistance at the change in people's tasks, but she couldn't help that. She really wished she could take people off the construction project, too, but that was critically important. Everything seemed critical, and there were never enough people or supplies to get everything done. But if she had more people, then she'd need to do more... A cycle of failure. She pursed her lips, frustrated. She'd just have to find a way to make do with what they had, as always.

She had an hour or so to kill before her next video conference with Taggart's people on her duties as his so-called Secretary of Agriculture. Maybe she should go talk to Grandma Mandy about the problem of allocating people for all the tasks that had to get done. Grandma Mandy was a bit of a whiz when it came to organizing things. Yes. She had time...

But no, Cassy didn't have patience to listen to her mom's lectures about religion right now. Grandma Mandy meant well, and she was the nicest person ever put on this Earth. She taught the kids during whatever little schooling time people could spare for their kids, and led the team babysitting the littlest ones. But Mandy's religious faith was absolute. Normally that was kind of a good thing, a steadying thing, and she didn't mean to cram her religion down people's throats, but to Cassy that often felt like the result of a conversation with her.

Instead, Cassy found herself heading to the outdoor kitchen, but when she got there, she found the cleanup had already finished. She let out a long sigh. But then she saw a little girl sitting on her heels in the corner, between the rocket stove oven and the big drum where food scraps were kept, to be dumped later into the compost piles. It was Amber's seven-year-old daughter Kaitlyn, peering intently at something on the dirt floor.

Cassy liked the little kids. They were used to her appearance and never seemed to even notice the scars on her face, unlike adults. Cassy was still a good-looking woman, but her scars were noticeable—mementos mainly of her battle with their former conqueror, Peter, and his psychotic rapist sidekick Jim, plus a few smaller scars from various other battles.

She sat down on a bench nearby, and Kaitlyn looked up at her and smiled. "Cassy, is your leg still bad?"

Cassy couldn't help but smile back at that innocent, sweet girl. Well, not innocent—no one was sheltered the way they had been before the war—but hopeful and bright. It lifted Cassy's spirits just to see this child. She said, "Oh, my leg is fine, honey. What are you looking at?"

Kaitlyn scooted to the side with a funny little duck-walk, not rising from her crouched position, to let Cassy see better. The girl had been looking at a swarm of ants battling a beetle. Both sides were oblivious of the huge watchers above them.

Kaitlyn said, "It's like the goons fighting the Confederation. See, the ants are like all of us. And the beetle is so big, but it can't fight so many little biting things. It's going to lose, and then they'll drag it into their hole somewhere and eat it. Gobble it up and feed their little ant kids."

It was unsettling to realize that this little girl framed her child's play in terms of a war that hadn't really even started yet. It was an outlet for fear, Cassy supposed. All the kids probably did it, just as a way to cope with their fear of an unknown future. She imagined them playing "Empire and Clanners," and no doubt the Clan always won their version of Cops and Robbers.

Cassy said, "How do you think they can get something so big down their tiny little ant hole?"

Kaitlyn shrugged and immediately replied, "Oh, they'll cut it up into little pieces and drop them down the hole and then all the little ant kids will be happy the beetle attacked them, and they'll have lots to eat, and their moms will make armor from all the little shell pieces."

The thought of these little ants having enough to eat seemed to fill her with joy. Cassy was happy too, but for another reason—if the ants were beginning to emerge again, it meant spring was right around the corner. Time for planting and celebrating warm weather and swimming in the ponds. A time of life returning.

But for Clanholme, it was also a time of danger. The Empire would come with spring, and who knew what the invaders planned? Spring could bring the invaders back, too. She wished she could take some joy without worry like little Kaitlyn, but Cassy knew better than to think that was in her cards.

* * *

Just after morning chores and lunch, Ethan returned to the bunker and noticed a message waiting for him via the popup chat box that Watcher One, his handler from the 20s, would sometimes use to contact him directly. He had located the bit of malware that allowed it, way back on his own farm, before the Clan and the invaders and all of this had even happened. He had left it in place, but had put it into a "virtual machine" as a type of "sandbox" so those on the other end couldn't hack him—they'd only see the pristine fake system he had set up for them. He huffed in frustration and opened the chat box. As expected, it was from Watcher One.

> ***Watcher1*** >> *Hi, need status on Night Ghosts location. Update?*

Ethan frowned. He had been avoiding this particular issue, sending scouts riding north to Nestor's old location since the Ghosts were now running around to the south. It was a dangerous game because the Mountain had at least a dozen UAVs armed with missiles, which could be as easily used on the Clan as on the Night Ghosts, and the 20s knew where Clanholme was.

> ***Dark Ryder*** >> *I have scouts going out into his last known op area performing grid searches. I have a file of the grid coordinates, patterns, and progression. Shall I send that to you via HAMnet?*

> ***Watcher1*** >> *Negative. He isn't north of your position. Subject relocated to the south. Didn't you know that?*

This was a loaded question. If his 20s handler somehow knew that Ethan did know about Nestor's migration, he'd be caught in a lie and proven untrustworthy. But Watcher1 didn't seem to have spies in Clanholme... Best bet? Feign ignorance.

> ***Dark Ryder*** >> *We had heard a rumor but have*

not received confirmation from down there. Attention focused on area we last had confirmation of Night Ghost operations.

Watcher1 >> *Check HAMnet, collect incoming file. I'll stand by and wait.*

Ethan grimaced. Beyond being a pain in the butt, he really didn't want to see whatever they were sending. He had no choice, though, and ignorance in this case wasn't bliss. He connected to HAMnet and a zip file began to download. Once it was done, he opened it inside another protective "sandbox" so that if it carried viruses or malware, they wouldn't infect his system. Unzipping the file, he found a folder containing dozens of image files.

As he opened them in order, a chain of events became clear—Nestor and his Night Ghosts had gone to a settlement, sent some people inside, then blown the settlement walls and swarmed inside. They killed every man, woman, and child. Or, it looked like they were children judging by their size compared to the others.

At least he assumed it was Nestor, or else Watcher One wouldn't have sent the images. So the Night Ghosts had sacked a settlement. That was new, they had never done that before...

Ethan also noticed that the images were from a satellite. A chill ran down his spine as he had a sudden realization—if the 20s didn't know where Nestor was, that meant they'd had satellites covering the settlement already when Nestor attacked, rather than having tracked him there. It stood to reason that they had birds covering other major viable survivor enclaves, not just over Clanholme. Thank goodness he had been sending out actual scouts like clockwork to "look for the Night Ghosts."

His chat box dinged with an incoming message, and Ethan switched screens.

> ***Watcher1*** >> *That was done by Night Ghosts. By luck, we found and tracked from your last confirmed area of operation. Unless they're Clan, then they have to be Night Ghosts. The only known motive for this mass killing is looting. Last images show Night Ghosts looting the settlement and the bodies.*

Ethan opened the last couple of images and saw definite looting. Both were moderately zoomed in, so many details were clear. The first showed a guy kicking in a door, his muzzle flash caught on camera as he shot up whoever had been inside. A woman pulling boots off a body. Two men pulling a tarp off a pile of salvage, revealing wooden crates. The second showed the raiders moving out of the settlement in a column, heavily laden with loot. Ethan flipped back to the chat box. He paused before replying because he was about to risk antagonizing Watcher One, but the answer would tell him a lot that he didn't know right now.

> ***Dark Ryder*** >> *The UAV strike would have been timely just then, since their coordinates were known.*

> ***Watcher1*** >> *The images have a delay, only retrieved once or twice daily, and then take time to review. By then, they were out of bird's searchable grid area. They're sacking survivor groups now, not just lone homesteads. Need to deal with this before invader OpFor returns to your region.*

> ***Dark Ryder*** >> *Affirmative. We will shift search grid south. This must be stopped.*

> ***Watcher1*** >> *Agreed. Why have you not found them yet? It seems like a large group of people would be easy to find in such a small region. Perhaps motivation is the issue. We can arrange additional motivation if you think it would help.*

Ethan froze. That was definitely a threat. Maybe it was time to double down on his efforts to backtrace Watcher One. Long ago, Ethan had pinged him as being in Virginia somewhere, but since then he had appeared to be coming from all over the world. Those first few pings, though—the ones from Virginia—were probably from before Watcher One had time to better scramble his location. Ethan felt almost sure of it. Not that it helped him right now, but someday he'd want to get this monkey off his back...

> ***Dark Ryder*** >> *As you said, he relocated from our search area. We will transition grid pattern search to the south.*

Watcher One then logged out from the chat. Ethan spat curses at his monitor, wishing he could reach through the damn thing and strangle whoever was on the other end. It took him ten minutes of pacing and a cup of coffee before his pulse was down to normal and he didn't feel like destroying his own stuff in a fit of rage.

As he calmed down, however, a new thought struck him. Maybe Nestor had gone rogue. Maybe there was another explanation. But the part about killing children, that was too much. Nestor had been kind of creepy when he was at Clanholme, actually. And the way he had taken to the nomad life of a guerrilla, rather than settling into Clanholme when he had been offered a spot, it all just raised more doubts about the man as far as Ethan was concerned.

Very well. If Nestor really was sacking settlements now, he truly did need to be stopped. Ethan loaded an overhead map of the sacked town's region and began drawing out the grid for the pattern search, highlighting a few of the most probable areas. Time to find the man.

* * *

General Ree enjoyed the fresh afternoon air blowing past him as he motored south from his fortress in the City, heading toward the bridges into New Jersey. There weren't any other running vehicles and the roads had been cleared. His driver couldn't go too fast due to occasional road hazards, but if his driver went too slowly he risked surprise raids from bike-mobile guerrillas who could swarm out of nowhere by the dozens. Guerrillas began seizing all the bikes they could about a month ago, and Ree had cursed himself for not thinking of that himself. Still, he now had four cars running and if an ambush came, he could speed away to safety.

These journeys to visit his People's Worker Army were dangerous but necessary. He had to keep his officers motivated, some through fear and others through flattery. Also, his American workers were kept in fear through occasional glimpses of their own Great Leader, Ree—all had heard of his occasional slaughter of P.W.A. units that were unruly or in danger of being taken by that traitor, Taggart. Ree learned long ago that fear for one's life was a wonderful way to motivate most workers, especially these lazy Americans.

As they drove through the quiet city, Ree thought about the people who had lived there. Once there had been nearly eight million in the city, but now it was hard to even visualize so many. It was nearly a third of his beloved country's population, all crammed onto this tiny island. At most only three million remained, the rest having been enslaved in New Jersey, killed, or been eaten by their fellow Americans—his analysts said Americans were devouring twenty-five-thousand of their own people daily now!

But that number was a little high. His nemesis Taggart had several times seized the tunnels and bridges that allowed access to the city, and Ree's scouts estimated that Taggart had gained upwards of ten thousand new refugees on each occasion. Forty thousand or so was small compared to the millions who remained, or even compared to Ree's slaves and former-slave guerrillas in New Jersey, but even assuming half wandered away to live or die on their own, Taggart had still gained a corps-sized unit from his raids. The only blessing was that those few people didn't come at the expense of the People's Worker Army.

The tunnel entry came into view. It was named after an old American president who had, according to his schooling, crushed the hopes and dreams of half the nation and began the process of destroying the states' freedoms, centralizing power and shoveling money into the hands of his capitalist-pig cronies. Ree hadn't bothered to rename the tunnel—he enjoyed the irony of using the tunnel named after a warmongering American president to contain and control Americans, just as the tunnel's namesake had done one-hundred-fifty years or so before. Ree considered himself a connoisseur of irony.

His heart rose now in anticipation. A minute later, leading to the tunnel entrance, his favorite creation came into view—a quarter mile of road where every street light had skeletal human remains hung and bound to the pole with barbed wire.

These were the bodies of the worst of the worst, those who embodied everything that was wrong with America and made it weak, degenerate, and corrupt. Bankers, Wall Street master traders, and of course actors and musicians and other willing tools of Wall Street oppression. So much wealth, invested not on making the nation great but squandered on making yet more money for those who had no need of more. So much talent, wasted with sloth and drugs and sex, and held up by a feeble-minded public as examples they should strive to emulate.

Ree once had those people in his prison camp, trying to re-educate them and tear away their blinders to see the truth, but almost all of them had resisted mightily. After Taggart had fought his way free of New York City, those prisoners had begun whispering about revolt, about hope Taggart would rescue them, about revenge. Ha! Revenge for what? He had tried to help them, but they were not grateful. That's when he quit wasting time and resources on those people and just had them strung up. Their message had once been greed and violence and degeneracy, but now their message was "Keep Out." They were more useful dead than alive, in that way.

Early on, Ree had hoped that, once their misguided idols were dead, his Americans would see clearly again and understand the great mission for them that Korea and others had offered when they attacked their country, but those hopes had been dashed.

Americans deserved no mercy, as far as Ree was concerned. Only those who would bend to the will of the People, through harmony with the intellect of the Great Leader, could be redeemed. Only those who would bear the yoke he placed on them would survive. The rest would be burnt like chaff after harvest time, or like those dead capitalists and entertainers he drove past now. Men like Taggart and those who followed him were just the last, dying gasp of Capitalism. They fought for corporate masters who were long dead or in hiding, just as America had always been hiding from the truth. The Worker, who held the true power, insisted on kneeling to the bankers and the singers. Bah.

The drive through the tunnel to what remained of his upstate New Jersey holdings was uneventful, and his driver was too scared to engage in small talk, afraid of Ree and of guerrillas, so Ree spent that time bored with his own thoughts.

Finally he saw his compound ahead, the massive complex built in less than two months, around which he had expanded his holdings. It had let him gain the land he needed for his Worker Army. Not a fortress really, it was nonetheless well protected from ground attacks, but its main purpose was storage and processing. All the food he would grow would come through that building before being transported to wherever Ree wanted it. Much would go to his stronghold in New York City and more would go to feeding the Worker Army, but the rest would be used for the good of all the people, by bribing their neighbors to submit to Ree's rule. For food they would join him peacefully, and then Ree would burn away their chaff just as he had with the rest of his American subjects so far.

They entered the complex and parked, then his driver opened his door for him and he climbed out of the car. It was a great car, but soon the fuel would spoil and it wouldn't work anymore. At least, for now, it worked great for quickly shuttling him back and forth.

Ree strode to the briefing room as his driver sprinted ahead of him to alert people Ree was coming, although the whole base probably knew before he ever got out of the car. His personal guards trailed behind him.

Entering the room, he saw Pak Kim, the Major in charge of clearing out land for spring farming. Most of the base's command staff must've been present, judging by the crowd gathering, even some of the ISNA leaders. They were mostly lieutenants and a couple of captains.

As Ree entered, the room stood to attention and Major Kim saluted. Ree returned the salute and walked to the podium while the others sat down. “Major, update me on the guerrillas. How fares the people’s war against the criminal Taggart and his capitalist servants?”

Kim stood again and said, “Leader, we are pleased to report that we have rescued half of our People’s Worker Army.”

“This helps us how?”

“By reinforcing the valuable areas and putting token strength in the useless areas, and diverting the Worker Army from those areas, we have saddled Taggart with unproductive land that he has to guard, without allowing him many additional recruits.”

Ree smiled. “Congratulations, Major. So we now have half the land we did, and twice the men per kilometer?”

Kim’s eyes went wide for a second but then he recovered. With a strong, steady voice he said, “Yes, my leader. We are well prepared for spring. Some of the People will starve before first harvests, but it is unavoidable.”

“I’m sure they are happy to spend themselves in the great cause of the People’s liberation.” Ree’s face was carefully expressionless. He prided himself on showing only what he wanted others to see.

Kim paused. He was probably trying to decide how Ree felt about that. Finally, Kim said, “Yes. It is a worthy sacrifice. Giving one’s self up for the good of the people is noble.”

Ree fumed inside. The major had really just tried to tell him Americans understood the need to sacrifice all for the People. That wasn’t at all like the Americans Ree knew. “Major, thank you. However, I believe there is a flaw in your logic.”

Kim withered under Ree's stare. After a short pause, he replied, "Of course, my leader. I bend my will and my thoughts in harmony with your own. I would be honored to learn of my mistake, so that I can correct it."

Ree favored him with a smile. At least the major could grovel properly. Ree counted to three in his mind and then said, "When the American workers get hungry, they will not welcome the chance to spend themselves for the greater good. No, they will organize and rebel. A few here, a few there. Nothing we can't handle. But it will divert our strength from the war with the American criminal Taggart. Nothing can be allowed to harm our great war against the capitalists."

Kim nodded automatically, and bowed. "Yes, my leader. We will spread the workers out and try to find more supplies for them, to last until early harvests."

Ree put on an expression of displeasure. Kim couldn't meet his gaze, and Ree resisted the urge to smile at the idiot's discomfort. "No, Major Kim. That will only require more of our troops to watch them, and there is no more food, no more supplies. We must make do, or do without."

Kim bowed again. "What is my leader's will?"

Ree grimaced. Kim's incompetence was stunning. Unfortunately, he was popular with his troops and probably the best administrator and organizer Ree had ever commanded. Kim was necessary. So instead of just shooting him, Ree put on the face of the patient father explaining to a wayward child.

"Major, we can't keep the Americans in the rear to starve, and we can't spread them out to starve. Nor can we spare the fighters to guard the useless. The only solution is simple. You must mercifully exterminate the workers we can't feed. Half of them, you said?"

Kim said, "We have a million and a half workers. Nearly half are unsupportable."

Ree smiled at him. “I commend you on your knowledge of our supply situation. It is why I value you as I do. Very well. Take four-hundred-thousand of the Worker Army and exterminate them. Don’t use bullets—we can’t afford to spare so many for this.”

Kim didn’t reply for a moment, and Ree could see from the faraway look in his eyes that he was thinking of solutions. Then Kim looked up and smiled. “Yes, we can do this. We can put them into railway cars, telling them they are being relocated. They will go quietly. Once in the cars we can use our defoliant spray to quietly and quickly end them. It will be terribly painful to sacrifice so many workers, but such is the price of victory for the People, my leader.”

Ree was surprised, though of course it didn’t show on his face. He hadn’t thought of that. “You see? With some thought, you have brought your will in line with your leader’s. I commend you in front of all these officers. We have many canisters, enough to balance our numbers. Please begin immediately.”

Kim bowed and Ree saw he had a faint smile of pride. It was a weakness, but a useful one.

Ree turned his attention to the others present and said, “Thank you for your attendance, everyone. Kim, see me to my quarters so we can discuss some other issues. Everyone else is dismissed.”

The major escorted Ree to his quarters and the ensuing conversation was friendly and light. Inside, however, General Ree seethed at the need to kill so many otherwise valuable workers. Once his plan to deal with Taggart was finished, he’d oversee the collection of new workers from among New York City’s survivors, so it wasn’t a total loss, but it was damn inconvenient and his goals for spring planting would have to be revised. Oh well—such was the burden of leadership.

- 12 -

0800 HOURS - ZERO DAY +216

CAPTAIN SAMUEL PEASE stared at the written orders with a wide grin on his face. Finally, he was going to war! Okay, not real war, but the kind of guerrilla war the Midwest Republic so excelled at. Samuel had an itch to scratch, having not had the chance to enjoy some ultra-violence in quite a while. Hell, Brett seemed about ready to kill a few of their own troops just for something more to do than endless pedaling across empty miles of nothing.

Brett tapped his foot nearby. “Dammit, Sam. What’s it say?”

“Captain Pease, please. There’s people around.”

Brett laughed aloud. “Fuck them, *Captain*. So? What does it say?”

Samuel let out a long breath. Brett was an irritating shit sometimes, like an angry Chihuahua bouncing and barking at the end of its leash. But when chips were down, he grew into a Rottweiler. “I’m getting to it, give me a damn minute.”

He had already read the orders, but for another thirty seconds—as long as he thought he could push it—he stared at the page pretending to read it.

"Sam, I'm gonna shove those orders up your ass if you don't tell me what they say!"

"That would make it hard for you to read them, wouldn't it?"

"Fuck you, asshole. You know I can't read much. Rub it in, you gotta sleep sometime."

Samuel grinned and looked up. "Oh fine, I'll tell you. They're taking off our leashes. We get to pedal our asses into this 'Confederation' and start tearing into those assholes. It looks like me and my ancillaries get to have a lot of fun, coming really soon to a Confederation near you."

"Abso-muthafukkin-lutely," Brett said, louder than he should have, and slammed a fist into his palm. "So... what the hell is the Confederation?"

"I see you slept through briefings again. You are a lazy piece of crap, Brett."

Brett only grinned. Of course he had slept through briefings. They were boring to Samuel, too, and everyone was always exhausted while on the march. Or bike. Or whatever.

Samuel said, "Fine. You remember hearing about the Clan, right? They killed our diplomats, so now it's time for Plan B? Well, the Clan made some allies with their neighbors, got together and made a Confederation. The briefing said it was Elizabethtown, Lebanon, Cornwall, Lititz, Manheim, Ephrata, and the Clan itself. They're close to some dink-shit village called Penryn."

Brett's grin faded a bit. "I mean, we'll still have a great old time, but that sounds like we'll do some real fighting. That's not as much fun."

Samuel nodded. "Yeah, but we're not trying to conquer all that, we're just raising hell and having our kind of fun. Creating chaos and confusion in the operational area, as the bosses say, and messing with their trade and supply lines. Then our real army comes in. We mess 'em up, the army cleans 'em up. Works every time."

"Maybe they got some bitches in them places, too."

"Probably," Samuel said with a leering grin. He waggled his eyebrows and said, "I bet you one gold Rep I can get my first bitch to scream louder than yours. And she'll *like* it."

Brett punched Samuel in the shoulder. "Aww, look at you, all brave and shit. You're going to lose that bet. Yours is only gonna scream with pain, but mine's gonna be all like, 'oh daddy, you're the greatest and your junk is huge.' "

Samuel laughed hard, then, and gasping for air he said, "You are *such* a dreamer. I bet she does shout that out, but only because you're going to bribe her with food. Bitches will say or do anything for food."

Brett smirked. "You didn't make that part of the rules, so yeah. Shoot, I'm so hungry I'd blow a donkey for a quesadilla."

Samuel let out a loud sigh. "Man. Why do you always bring up Mexican food? I'd kill your mother for the Dinner Special platter from *Los Amigos*, a great little joint around the corner from my mom's house."

Then Samuel grew quiet, frowning. Damn. Now he was thinking of his mom, and how pissed and hurt he felt when he finally got to her house after hundreds of miles on foot, only to find the neighborhood burnt down and his mom's blood and intestines decorating her kitchen. She was the best damn woman in the entire frikkin' world, and none of those other bitches he had met came close to the angel his mom was.

Brett put his hand on Samuel's shoulder. "Sorry man. Reminded yourself of your mom, huh? I know you'd rather have her back than even some homemade Mexican buffet. But at least she went quick, and didn't have to live through all this crap we gotta deal with."

Samuel nodded. Brett was right, and anyway there was

nothing to do about it now. "Yeah, thanks, man. You're a great friend. But hey," he said, brightening, "at least we have a job to do now, and you know what they say about doing what you have to do."

Brett said, "Yeah. 'You might as well enjoy it.' Might as well take the good with the bad. When do we move out?"

"First thing in the morning. By noon, we'll be in the Confederation and no more goddamn leash holding us back. Once our army comes in and takes over, we got a channel to all that food we heard about in New Jersey, not to mention flanking those invader assholes up in northern Pennsylvania. But you know what? I think all this raiding is gonna be like therapy."

Brett nodded and gave him a wan smile. "Totally. Cathartic, even. You and me, kicking ass and taking names."

"Stop pretending you know what 'cathartic' means, you ignorant fuck."

"Whatever. I got one gold Rep that says I get the first Clan kill between us."

"You're on," Samuel said glumly. "Maybe winning one of your Reps will make me feel better."

"Dream on, Sam. You never get the first kill. I wonder what I'll spend your money on..."

* * *

Nestor held the bandana over his mouth and nose to shield himself from the acrid smoke of burning wires, insulation, and a million toxic irritants. The four houses on the homestead cast red and yellow light onto everything, overpowering the overcast day's sunlight. This was the third Empire settlement in as many days, and he had destroyed them all to the last person. On this third one, he hadn't even had to let the Other take over to get it done. It was becoming routine.

Thinking of the Other brought him back to thoughts of his daughter, his little pumpkin. She had been the only light in his life after his wife died in an accident. He still believed that one was an accident, that the Other hadn't taken over and killed the love of his life. But as for his daughter... he could no longer deny it. They had been right to put him in the asylum, after what he had done to her. Nestor shuddered and felt a wash of nausea crash over him as flashes of the dream he'd had came back to him.

The terrible nightmare he had once thought of as nothing more than his mind torturing him in his sleep, piecing together things he had heard on the news or from the police as they investigated. Details he had learned about the terrible, gruesome way in which some monster had killed his little pumpkin. But now he knew better. Now he knew that the nightmare was a memory. The Other had come and destroyed what was left of Nestor's world after his wife died, and the Other was him.

When he had first made that connection and realized what had actually happened, he vomited and then sobbed for two days, neither eating nor drinking, not even sleeping. He tortured himself and considered eating the barrel of his gun. His people, his *Night Ghosts*, had left him in peace, knowing something was wrong.

The houses burning around him cast a light that reminded him of the hue that washed over everything he saw when the Other was at the helm. Reminded him of his daughter.

But just like at the end of his two days of soul-destroying misery, the thought no longer brought him to the edge of suicide. Now it enraged him. *It hadn't been him.* Not Nestor, but the Other who had killed his daughter (and maybe his wife). His family might be gone, but the Confederation was full of other families, other daughters and fathers. They needed protection now, in this new world, and the Other could do a lot to bring them that protection.

Nestor hadn't killed his daughter, but he now lived to make sure no other Little Pumpkins got killed. The Other had destroyed his world, and now he used the Other to help him protect good people by unleashing it to destroy the bad ones.

The Other couldn't be redeemed but maybe Nestor himself could be, now that he could control the Other. He silently vowed to dedicate himself to that.

Briefly, he thought about the implications of not needing the Other for this one. It meant Nestor was becoming used to all of this, perhaps. Or maybe all the killing and violence was destroying who he was, burning him out from the inside. Certainly he felt very different than he had when he first emerged from the insane asylum, long after the invader war had begun, being chased by a dozen people bent on revenge for killings he had no recollection of.

Even if he was becoming numb or burnt out, Nestor was indifferent now. He didn't really care whether he lived or died, so how was it relevant? He had nothing to live for anyway other than the vague wish to redeem himself, so he was fine with the idea of dying in this terrible war. At least he would be dying for something worthwhile and his struggle with the Other would end.

Nestor turned to face his troops as they mustered just outside the cluster of buildings, carrying loot as they returned from searching for survivors to kill. He had surrounded the place with his new people while his original core of thirty or so conducted the attack itself, and the new people had earned another couple of kills when residents had tried to flee.

It was nice having so many people. He saw his original Night Ghosts, or what was left of them, but also saw dozens and dozens of new faces. Other survivors of the Empire's attacks, just as the originals were survivors of the 'vaders sacking Adamstown. From his original thirty guerrillas, he now had nearly one hundred. They were men and women who had lost everything they had built up since the EMPs, people who hated the 'vaders and the Empire for killing their friends, their families. They wanted payback, and Nestor could help them get it—his reputation had spread wide, and people were flocking to his war banner. The Night Ghosts had become a force to be reckoned with.

This attack was finished, but ten miles east his scouts had found another homestead occupied that had been empty a week before. Their story had been the same as this farm's, according to the scout, and showed the same signs. They weren't just people settling down, they were Empire plants and spies. And by day's end, they'd be dead like the twenty-person force who had claimed to live here. The Empire was stepping up its infiltration and Nestor was determined to stop them wherever he and his Ghosts could.

* * *

Ethan opened the file and found more day-old satellite pictures with file names like "Night Ghosts attack 1A" or "Night Ghosts burning 2C." Taken together and in order, they painted a clear picture—Nestor was killing homesteads and then burning them down, looting food.

The very first satellite images of such an attack from before today's batch of photos had turned out to be Empire spies, according to Cassy, so that was a good kill, but now it seemed that Nestor had gotten a taste for how easy it was to take out unprepared little settlements. He had gone bandit. His forces had also grown much bigger since the first one, at least tripling in size from what Ethan could see. Maybe more.

Now, with at least ninety or so bandits, he was becoming a significant player in the area.

Ethan put his elbows on his desk and his face into his hands, and struggled with himself. Nestor had seemed nice enough, but how well did anyone really know him? He had gone missing after a battle shortly after coming to the Clan, and had gone guerrilla, taking to it like a duck to water. He had once saved two Clan children, but that didn't really mean anything. And with the heavy pressure the 20s were putting on Ethan... They weren't going to let it go.

Yeah—he was risking the Clan's safety by protecting Nestor. Hell, his *duty to the Clan* said he now ought to give Nestor up, right? After all, he was sacking homesteads and even a settlement. He had gone rogue. The Confed would have to deal with him sooner or later. Maybe giving Nestor's position away would kill two birds with one stone—prove his loyalty to the 20s, at least as far as they were concerned, and get rid of a growing bandit threat.

Ethan let out a long, slow breath of resignation. Fine. He had to do what he had to do. Ethan loaded the chat box and typed out the coordinates for the golf course just north of poor, dead Lancaster. He had overheard Cassy telling Michael that's where the Night Ghosts were encamped. They'd be gone by the time the 20s could bring UAVs or satellites to bear, but it was a start point, and would buy him time with the 20s.

Briefly, he thought of bringing all this to Cassy's attention. Normally he would, but with the evidence against Nestor piling up and with the 20s now making threats if he didn't get results, he couldn't afford to wait for Cassy's "let's make sure" attitude. Plus he'd have to explain about the 20s threat, and there was a risk she'd misinterpret that to mean Ethan was playing double agent. He was, but not the way she might think—his loyalty was to the Clan.

Sorry, Nestor. He'd crossed a line, and Ethan had the Clan to worry about. The new standard was to care for your own first, outsiders second, and Nestor had become the outsider.

- 13 -

0815 HOURS - ZERO DAY +224

THE SOUND OF an engine carried far with no background hum of civilization to mask it. Cassy caught it right away, although it took a moment for her brain to click on just what that noise was. She grabbed a dozen Clanners and they headed toward the gravel drive at the northeast end of the property. Everyone carried weapons at all times nowadays, so there was no scramble for guns. When she got to the gravel drive, she saw a familiar burly F-series pickup coming up the driveway and spewing smoke and pulling a trailer.

Two mounted Clan guards rode ahead and two behind the truck, which rolled to a stop about ten feet from Cassy. A short, wiry black man climbed out of the driver's seat, and a burly, rough-looking white man with a shotgun climbed out of the passenger side and then set his shotgun on the seat before closing the door.

Cassy grinned. "If it isn't Terry and Lump, traders extraordinaire. To what do we owe the pleasure?" It had been Terry, the Falconry wandering trader, who first introduced Cassy to the idea of using a gasifier to run a vehicle.

Terry grinned back. "Cassy, leader of the Clan and what's left of civilization! How have you been?"

"Pretty good, lately. Can I offer you some breakfast? We may have some left over."

Terry smirked. "Thank you for the offer, but I have my own," he replied. It was a standard sort of exchange when greeting people, both the offer and the refusal. "I also have some news for you, and thought I'd pass it on while I was in the area. And maybe get some trading done, of course."

Cassy nodded. "Certainly. Can you have Lump open up the wagon? My people will be coming through any minute, I'm sure, once news of a visitor spreads."

Terry looked at Lump and then jerked his head toward the wagon. Turning back to Cassy he said, "So have you heard the news up around Liz Town?"

Cassy frowned. "We haven't been in contact recently, so no. Their envoy left a couple of days ago on some urgent business or other. What's going on?"

"Seems like quite a few of the homesteads west of Liz Town have been attacked. Everyone dead, but the buildings left intact. Rumor has it Liz Town isn't patrolling out that way anymore and has pulled their people back to just their own holdings."

Cassy huffed through her nose in frustration. "Damn. What about Renfar? They're under Liz Town's watch. Are they being supported? Those Renaissance Faire grounds are cool and all, and a natural choke point on the road, but they don't have many defenses other than their own armed people."

"Nope. Renfar has had to fight off a couple of small raids, the first in two months. Liz Town isn't stopping them in the north and west before they head south and east, so it's getting pretty wild out there. But they're building a log wall around the core grounds and the winery, so it isn't as open as it used to be."

"Thank goodness. They're nice enough people. Any idea why Liz Town isn't patrolling? None of us can afford that, you know."

"Tell me about it," Terry said shaking his head. "At least Lebanon has stepped up their west patrols, so Falconry hasn't had to deal with all those bandits. My leaders may not be happy you mostly sided with Lebanon during that trade dispute, but I'm sure glad. It gave the Lebs good motivation to keep patrolling, keep protecting us even if it isn't intentional."

Cassy frowned again. "Yeah... Leaders and their people sometimes have different concerns. I try not to let that be the case here, but it happens. I'm glad you guys are safe, though. We do like Falconry, you know. Good people."

Terry nodded. "Yep, glad you feel that way too. I was lucky to fall in with them early on. I'll pass that remark on to the Head Falconer, Delorse."

Cassy replied, "Be sure to give Delorse my best wishes. I may have had my hands tied, but I respect her as a leader." An impish grin spread on Cassy's face, "And tell her she's always welcome to join the Confederation."

Terry laughed, and put his hand on her shoulder. "I'll let you tell her that. Anyway, that's all I got on my end. What have you heard?"

Cassy began sharing what rumors she had—sharing news was one of the best things about these old-style wandering merchants, tinkers, and traveling salesmen, because they spread news between settlements. She was especially sure to note, very casually, that Manheim really needed nuts and bolts for some current project. If Terry could supply them, he'd make a fortune on the trade value. Telling him was a nice reward for coming by basically just to share the news and let them browse his wagon—and maybe Manheim would get the bolts it needed.

* * *

Ethan grabbed a bowl and a plate of food before the lunch bell—really a blast from the guard tower's air siren—and headed toward the HQ to go back down to the bunker below. He was busy compiling numbers and troop movements, deciding what to tell his 20s handler Watcher One, and updating his maps. He didn't have time to sit through the usual lunch rush, and as a member of the Clan's council, rank had its privileges.

"Hey, Ethan," he heard from behind him. Michael's voice.

Ethan turned and nodded. "I'd shake your hand, but my hands are full."

"How will you get a bowl of soup down the ladder?" Michael asked, smirking.

Damn. Ethan hadn't thought that far ahead. He was a little scatterbrained from number crunching. "Good point. Maybe Cassy has a thermos in her house."

"Probably. But I need to talk a minute, Ethan. Can we grab a seat?"

Ethan walked over to the split-log bench outside Cassy's house and set his food down, then sat. "What's up?"

"Just needed to share some intel with you, Cassy's orders. A trader came through this morning with news."

"I heard," Ethan replied. "It's always news when someone visits."

Michael frowned. "It seems that Liz Town pulled in all their patrols. They aren't patrolling to their west and now only guard their own actual territory. Meanwhile, lots of homesteads are getting raided, killing the people but not burning down the buildings. I suspect Empire infiltrators."

Ethan furrowed his brow. "Damn, that's awful. Has anyone sent out scouts to find them and wipe them out?"

Michael nodded. "Yes, there's several bands of scouts now, mostly from Lebanon. But rumor has it there's a bunch of bike tracks, and Lebanon thinks they're raiders from the Empire, like I do. I think they're softening us up for the big offensive. These Empire raiders are fast and mobile, hitting hard and fading away. Bikes would explain that."

"What are we doing about them? The Clan, I mean."

"Before we do anything, Cassy wants you to radio Liz Town. They're not attending Confed meetings, not patrolling for raiders. Find out what the hell is going on with those people."

Ethan grimaced. "I can't just radio them ask what the hell they're doing. Bad diplomacy. We need to send an envoy."

Michael shook his head. "No. We will send one, but Cassy was specific. Establish comms with Liz Town and get a SitRep first."

Ethan let out a long breath. "Fine, I'll do it."

Michael got up and left, and Ethan decided to finish his meal up there instead of in the bunker, mostly to give himself time to think on how he would approach the problem.

* * *

Choony and Jaz sat on the well-worn wagon bench as they rode away from Clanholme once again. Their last week out on the road had netted some new homesteads, which Cassy had put under both Clanholme and the Gap's oversight and protection. It had been productive, but the discovery of several burnt-out homesteads littered with corpses had been depressing, and sobering. It meant bandits were active in the area, and if they were on horses there was no way the wagon could outrun them. Because of that, they had been staying close enough to Clanholme or the Gap to make a break for it if they must. At least give them a chance at surviving. Choony had also rigged up a quick-release on the wagon itself. If needed, they could try to climb up to the horses and release the wagon. Maybe. If they didn't fall, if they didn't drop the quick-release, if the horses didn't freak out and overturn the whole enchilada. If, if, if...

The loud boom of Jaz firing her rifle made Choony practically jump up, startling him out of his thoughts. "Status," he quickly blurted.

Jaz laughed, and the sound to him was like the music of a crystal-clear waterfall in some faraway tropical paradise. "Stop the wagon," she said. "I bagged us a bunny. Fresh meat tonight!"

Choony was careful not to frown. He didn't like killing anything, much less when they still had a fresh load of supplies, but Jaz greatly preferred fresh meat to the dried vegetables and pemmican, which was a mix of dried-out meat that had then been crushed almost to a powder, mixed with rendered fat with spices like a touch of dried chiles or black pepper for character—it kept nearly forever. It didn't need refrigeration and had been the world's original energy bar, especially when mixed with ground nuts and dried bits of fruit like theirs were.

"Well, it's no use arguing with you about it," he said. "But I won't let the rabbit go to waste, either. Stew or roasted?" Her answer would determine how early they stopped for the night, stew taking quite a bit longer.

"If I never eat more stew, it'll be too soon. Definitely roasted. Maybe we can use a couple of our potatoes for a hash."

Since they'd been on the road, Jaz and he both had learned to cook much better over a small fire and had definitely gotten more creative. You had to when your supplies only included a cast iron frying pan and a cast iron

Dutch oven for cooking.

"Very well," Choony said.

The wagon rolled to a stop and Jaz walked out to get the rabbit. She spent a few minutes skinning and gutting it—the nearly freezing temperature would keep it fresh until they stopped to cook it. She used dirt to clean the bunny gore off her hands, then wiped her hands on her pants.

Jaz climbed back onto the wagon, and a moment later Choony flicked the reins to get the wagon moving again. "So where do you want to head this time?" he asked.

"We should totally head south. Like, skip the Gap entirely. I want to see if there's anyone alive in the Georgetown area. If not, we can head north again, go through the Gap before checking out that area between Highway 30 and Highway 322. What do you think?"

"I think that takes us about two miles farther from the Gap than I want to get. What's got you so fearless today?"

Jaz smirked. "Not fearless. Just, I know you won't let anything happen to me. You'll totally jump in front of a bullet, and then I can run away."

Of course she'd never do that, Choony knew. Jaz joked about it precisely because she'd never do it, he had realized early on. It was one of the many things he loved about her. That thought startled him. He had already decided he was in love with Jaz, but every time the thought crossed his mind it still was jolting.

"One-Hundred Percent, as the kids used to say," Choony said. "I'm a 'Gee' like that."

Jaz giggled for a second before catching herself. "You're, like, the farthest thing from it. It's what I like about you, *yo*." She added that last 'yo' with emphasis, making fun of him even more.

It occurred to Choony that Jaz had opened up over the last week, and was again her flirtatious, cheerful-but-warped self. But there was something different, too, something new about the way she played word games with him, teased him, played pranks on him. A new confidence, an added measure of trust. And he loved every second of it.

The next few miles were filled with the most pleasant thoughts, and his heart raced. He only hoped she didn't notice the flush he felt in his cheeks.

* * *

Taggart looked down at his map, where little colored wooden blocks showed the locations of his units as well as known enemy positions. Two civilians he had rescued during a major raid two days earlier had told him about a tremendous troop movement scheduled to get underway today or tomorrow. A large part of Ree's forces were apparently clustered now, up in the rough terrain northeast of Ridgefield, New Jersey. They could go around Taggart or fight snipers and raids all along their lines for most of their journey. They were going to march into New York City. Taggart figured they would head east to Norwood near the mighty Hudson River before heading south, to avoid Taggart's territory.

Betting on this, Taggart had stationed thousands of his fighters in a wide arc of intermittent, heavily-wooded areas. Closter Nature Center. Alpine Park—complete with a wooden and stone fortress at the Scouts camp nearby. Rockleigh. The dense woods all over within a half mile of Norwood. There were more, but those held his largest units for this operation. He had many fallback positions south of those—Ree's troops would either push through a strong defense-in-depth or turn back and face continual assaults and raids.

Either way, the trap would close around the invaders when they reached Broadway and Piermont Road, where dense woods surrounded a cluster of suburbs close to the Hudson River. Units north would move laterally to encircle the invaders from the rear, and then positions before and along the invader line would surge forward. If the battle went well, they'd press the assault. If the invaders maintained unit cohesion and assaulted together in one direction—the worst case scenario—his units would melt away and rally at fallback points, where the invaders would have to rally and assault again.

Ree's troops would have to maintain a high-intensity assault with good unit cohesion to stand a chance, but they'd become more exhausted with each position they had to assault. And Taggart's troops would simply melt away each time, replaced by fresh troops as needed. It was the advantage of the native homeland defender.

That was the plan, anyway. If Ree stupidly tried to cross the reservoir east at Old Hook instead of at Broadway to the north, then Ree would be slaughtered with nowhere to retreat. Taggart was certain that Ree was smarter than that. He had been an intelligent opponent so far.

One of their messengers ran up to Eagan to report. His messengers were drawn mostly from people they had just rescued, the same group that had told Taggart of this troop movement. Taggart didn't have weapons and gear for the additional thousand who had joined his forces, but he needed runners and lots of them, so he had told Eagan to assign them that duty.

Out of breath, the runner handed a slip of paper to Eagan. "The invaders been spotted moving down Broadway," he said between breaths.

Eagan looked at the paper and nodded. "Well done, private. Get some water and catch your breath, then stand by."

Eagan turned to Taggart and said, "General, rough

estimate is ten thousand troops under arms, and the forward elements are just now passing the trap entrance perimeter."

Taggart nodded. "Excellent. Stand by for more runners, and get ready to relay orders." Taggart had a system of paper slips for both reports and orders to unit commanders. The code they were using had been simple to explain, and simple to decode in the field, but if the invaders got hold of a slip they wouldn't be able to decode it right away. They wouldn't have the time and by the time they did, it would be outdated information.

Over the next ten minutes, more runners came in with reports. It turned out they were moving a huge supply of food and ammunition to Ree's position in the City—wagon after wagon loaded with goods. Too ripe a plum to pass up.

When Taggart estimated enough time had passed for the invaders to get into position, he issued his go orders to all five of his top field commanders for the operation. They'd relay to their subordinate unit commands, and so on down the line.

Taggart frowned, a bit worried. Without radios, big operations like this one were like Napoleonics but with automatic weapons and battle rifles. Heck, Napoleon's era had more advanced systems for relaying orders and information than what Taggart was using. They had used bugles and flags, mirror flashes from hilltop to hilltop, and shouts down the line. Even smoke signals sometimes. Taggart was reinventing the wheel, and trying to stay one step ahead of Ree's own reinventions, to boot. It was worrying—and very Napoleonic-era.

Taggart watched the swarm of runners take off in different directions with their slips of paper and anticipated the din of battle that would begin in ten minutes—but wasn't looking forward to the chaos of receiving intel and issuing orders, all while moving his cute little wooden blocks around on his map. He'd almost rather be in the thick of combat himself. Things got simple in combat.

He wished he had spent some time playing those miniature war games like that Clanner Ethan talked about playing on weekends over beer and barbeque, before the war. It might have come in handy now.

- 14 -

0445 HOURS - ZERO DAY +225

NESTOR CROUCHED IN the predawn darkness with five of his fighters. That left five on guard duty at their encampment —with one hundred fighters now, he kept ten on rotating two-hour night watch, and two of those patrolled farther out to ensure their perimeter was clear. It had been sheer dumb luck that his two roving scouts had found this campsite just before dusk the evening before.

The encampment was well hidden among tall bramble bushes—two pup tents on either side of a Dakota fire hole and four bicycles in the dirt on the other side of the fire hole. Two men and two women, no children, all armed with AR-style rifles. They had those big hiking-style backpacks, loaded with supplies, which sat adjacent to the tents. The rifles were in their tents with them. Nestor was positive these were yet another group of Empire scouts.

He had watched the encampment for the last half hour for any sentries or activity, but there had been none. The campers had trusted that their concealment would keep them safe. Nestor whispered to the woman beside him, "We'll approach from the fire hole side of the tents. They're sure to have weapons, so no screw ups. I don't want to lose anyone—we kill them, then search them for those damn gold coins the Empire uses."

Later, he would need to let Clanholme know about all these infiltrators. Fake settlements, fake homesteads, swarms of these two- and four-person scouting teams... Confed territory was swarming with Empire, and Nestor's Night Ghosts had spent days and days killing them. Yet there were still more, and he had no doubt that for every group he killed, two more were on the way. This was the prelude to war.

Well, if they wanted war, they'd get it...

Nestor's people got into place, he and four of them forming a semicircle facing the camp with their AK-47s at the ready. The fifth, Ratbone, moved with amazing silence to the tents' rear with a jerrycan of gasoline and methodically applied fuel to the back and top of each tent. Nestor could imagine the disturbingly gleeful smile Ratbone would have while doing it. The guy was definitely disturbed. A complete nutjob.

Ratbone used a simple lighter to ignite both tents. With a menacing *whoosh*, the backs of the tents ignited, the flames quickly spreading up onto the tops. It turned out the tents were canvas, so they didn't just go up in a fireball like Nestor had imagined, but that's why he and the other four were ready with their rifles...

From within the tents, a man screamed, "Fire!" A second later there were more shouts, and the noise of frantic people struggling out of their blankets and the entry flaps. The four presumed Empire scouts came tumbling out of the tents still shouting and sleep-confused. Two had brought their rifles, but they were looking only at the tents.

Before they had the chance to do anything, Nestor said, "Guns." He squeezed his trigger, firing one round that spread his target's brains over the now fully-engulfed tent.

Two more shots rang out from Nestor's fighters and the other armed scout, a woman, collapsed in a heap without uttering a word.

Confused, the last two scouts—a man and a woman—stared dumbly at their companions lying in the dirt. Behind them, Ratbone was moving their backpacks away from the inferno.

"Don't move," Nestor shouted, "you're surrounded. Put your hands in the air."

The woman raised her hands quickly. The man looked toward the voice and saw Nestor and his four fighters, then at his dead companions' hunting rifles in the dirt. A second later, his hands rose slowly into the air and he said, "Don't shoot. We surrender."

* * *

"Now then," Nestor said, "what unit are you with?" He paced back and forth behind the two surviving Empire scouts, who were on their knees. Their wrists and ankles were bound with rope, and they each had a shemaugh wrapped around their heads to blind them. Nestor had his revolver in hand and every so often he spun the cylinder to make a clicking noise.

The woman answered readily. "We're just refugees from out west," she said, and her voice cracked. She sounded about ready to cry.

The man nodded vigorously. "We lost most of our friends to the cannibals a month ago and we've been hiding out ever since." His voice was steady.

Nestor nodded to Ratbone, who stepped behind the man, pressed his shotgun barrel against the man's head. Nestor said, "Try this again. Mister, what unit are you with?"

The man tilted his head down, away from the steel barrel jammed against him, and turned his head toward the sound of Nestor's voice. "Please, man, we're just trying to survive the best we can. We haven't hurt anyone, I swear it."

There was a sudden deafening roar as the shotgun went off, the angle of Ratbone's barrel causing some of the gore to splatter onto the woman. The man's head was half gone, and he flopped forward into the dirt amidst a growing pool of red. The woman screamed, tried to rise to her feet to run despite being bound and blind.

Nestor gripped her roughly by the neck and shoved her back to her knees, then pressed his pistol against the back of her head. "You have one chance to live. This information is not vital to me, so I have no problem letting you join your friend. Let's try this one last time. Tell me what unit you're with, or die. You choose."

The woman's head and shoulders shook as she sobbed, and Nestor pushed his barrel against the back of her head even harder. "Crying won't save you. Talking might. Five. Four..."

The woman cried out, "Stop, I'll tell you!" She gasped for air for a moment, then grew still. Finally, she said, "Mister, we're just scouts for the Midwest Republic's Third Division, First Regiment. We mark up maps and bring it back to them, and they give us food. Supplies. We're not soldiers, we're just scouts."

"At last, she shows a will to live. How many divisions does the Empire—your Republic—have?"

"At least three that I've heard of. Different regiments are given territories to control and defend, but Third Division is the one that does all the fighting. They get the best gear, the best fighters, the most food. And rumor has it they're coming this way, though I don't know when."

"You've heard nothing? Tell it true."

"Just rumors. Everything from two weeks to three months. Who knows? Even the division commander won't know until they get the order to go, so it's all just gossip."

Nestor thought on that. It made sense. She was probably telling the truth, or most of it. He eyed the woman for a moment, then said, "Take off her blind and hold her down. Hold her tight."

His followers roughly removed the shemaugh and pinned her to the ground by her shoulders, wrists, knees and ankles. Nestor pulled out a large folding tactical knife and approached her.

Eyes wide in terror, she screamed, "You said you'd let me live!"

Nestor nodded, jaw clenched tightly. This would be unpleasant for him, but he dare not hand the job to the Other inside himself. "Oh, I'm going to let you live. But I can't have you infiltrating some survivor group, can I?" This next part would no doubt bother him for days to come, but he consoled himself with the fact that she would at least be alive...

With his fifth fighter pinning her head to the ground, he used his knife to carve into her forehead the word, "Spy."

Her screams of pain echoed across the landscape.

* * *

Midmorning, Cassy was in her HQ, hand-writing in the Clan's supply ledgers, when Ethan found her. It was good timing, as she'd have another training video conference with Taggart's people in an hour, around lunchtime. "Hey Ethan. What do you have for me?"

"I spoke with Liz Town. It's bad news. Adam, the Speaker of Liz Town, is dead."

Cassy froze and her jaw dropped. She stared at Ethan while her mind worked through what he'd just told her, pushing through the shock. Her forehead creased. "Dead?"

"That is what they said, yeah."

"Who's in charge over there now?"

"They have an Interim Speaker at the moment."

"So why the hell aren't they patrolling?"

"They said Liz Town isn't in a position to meet their Confed duties right now. They'll resume as soon as they can put together another election to confirm the new Speaker. I don't know for sure but I get the impression that they are having some kind of internal strife. Wouldn't be surprised if the Speaker was killed."

Cassy blinked three times rapidly. "They aren't pulling out of the Confederation, are they?"

"They said they'd resume their responsibilities, so I assume not."

"The timing could hardly be worse," Cassy said. "The Empire will roll right through them, and they're going to get caught with their pants down."

Ethan shrugged and held up his hands, helpless. "This will put even more pressure on Lebanon and Manheim—the front lines—if Liz Town falls. You'll need to let them and Lititz know what's up."

Cassy closed her eyes and took a deep breath. "How many cars do we have working, and how many are new and improved?"

"We now have twelve cars running on woodgas, and ten of them are rocking the '80s post-apocalyptic vibe."

Cassy nodded, but his cheerful slang didn't do much to raise her mood. "Keep them hidden from now on. Horse patrols only, until I say otherwise. There are too many Empire spies around these days and I want them to be a surprise when we mow them down with our pretend tanks."

Ethan left to go pass the word and would no doubt be back in his bunker in twenty minutes. The guy was practically a hermit, though everyone liked him when he was out and about. Her mind turned to their fleet of cars.

Ten "battlecars," each a two-person operation—one to drive the car or truck and one to man the weapons and swap out the nearly air-tight cylinders of wood clippings and toss wood into the rocket stove oven. It was the interchangeable canisters, extended fuel for the engine, that had been Dean Jepson's genius addition to the basic system they had first received from the Falconry traders. Those spare fuel canisters had changed everything—even made independent operation with extended ranges possible. And they didn't show from the outside, so even if people knew about the gasifiers they wouldn't suspect Dean's improvements.

The cars also had quarter-inch metal plates added over the doors and windows, and between the trunk and the hollowed-out rear seat area. These would stop most rounds short of a .50-caliber rifle, but they weighed a ton and took the range of the cars back down to only one hundred miles or so on the wood they could carry.

The last two vehicles were unarmored half-ton pickup trucks that carried loads of wood in the bed and pulled additional wood on special trailers, extending the battlecars' range to about five hundred miles before the fuel truck needed to restock. Brickerville was their main refueling station for that, since they had tons of wood already cut, cured and stacked for ready use. Clanholme had a couple full loads as a reserve, as well, though it still had to cure awhile.

Thoughts of Liz Town wouldn't leave her alone, though. She hoped she wouldn't end up using those battlecars against Liz Town, but if they fell to the Empire, she'd have to.

* * *

Carl walked between four other men, each armed with AR15s, the civilian version of the military's M16 rifle. They passed under the Liz Town wall into Kodiak Band territory via a narrow tunnel, which Sunshine's people had put in place. The entry from the wildlands outside the wall was hidden by a burnt-out car.

His guardians hadn't disarmed him, which was a good sign. Still, he didn't trust them, or anyone for that matter, so he kept alert for any sign of betrayal. When Sunshine had gleefully told him there was a Kodiak who had the support of Carl's own Timber Wolves band and their leader was maneuvering to become the next Speaker, he'd shared her joy. The Kodiak leader was a staunch supporter of the old Speaker and his policies about resisting the Empire, joining the Confederation, and more.

In a hushed voice, Carl said to one of his guards, "I thought you Kodiaks believed I killed the Speaker."

The man glanced at Carl. "Yeah, we did, but when your whole Band vouches for you, we gotta figure it was a setup. And that Diamondback asshole who set himself up as Speaker has argued before that we should join the Empire. Your ex, Pamela, is tied in with them. You do the math."

The man's clear logic and good sense left Carl feeling a bit brighter about his future. The rest of the short journey was made in silence. A few minutes later they arrived at a nondescript house with boards over all the windows. It looked abandoned. The guards led him around back, then up through the back door. If they were going to ambush him, the tunnel would have been the place to do it, Carl figured, so he was alert but not fearful.

Inside at the kitchen table sat two men and a woman. Carl recognized her. "Mary Ann, I thank you for your hospitality and protection." He bowed slightly, as was appropriate since she was leader of the entire Kodiak Band.

The woman grinned at him. "Carl Woburn, hero of the dark days. I've heard of you. Somehow I expected you to be a giant, muscled barbarian."

"I get that a lot. But I assure you, I'm at least fit for duty."

"I'm sure you are. You know why we agreed to meet you, of course."

"Yeah," Carl replied. "We both don't like this Diamondback plot, nor the Empire, and we want revenge for our true Speaker's murder."

Mary Ann nodded. "More or less. But more than that, too. You were instrumental in ending the neighborhood wars before Liz Town was established. You could have been the Speaker and you turned it down cold. You were one of Adam's most trusted advisors before your ex-wife whispered poison in his ears."

Carl shrugged uncomfortably and said, "That's all true, more or less. May I ask the point of bringing all that up?"

Mary Ann eyed him for several seconds, long enough for his feeling of awkwardness to intensify. Carl shifted his weight to his other foot. Finally she continued. "I want you with us, Carl. Openly. The future of Liz Town is at stake. Do we become Empire slaves, or stand as proud equals in the Confederation? Some of the Bands are strongly opposed to this new Diamondback usurper."

"What can I do? I'll do anything to help if I can, but I'm exiled and under a secret death sentence. Pamela has confidence that if they can put off the vote long enough, the Empire will arrive, the issue will be moot, and she'll be rewarded. That's all she's really about. She's made Diamondback their quisling and we'll all be stuck with that asshole at the top."

Mary Ann pursed her lips and her eyes narrowed. "Stop being defeatist. We four packs outside the Diamondbacks outnumber them, if we can just get our shit together. You've pulled that off before, during the neighborhood wars. The Empire's biggest supporter besides Diamondback right now is the Wolverine Band, and they're not married to the idea—they just want to be on the winning team. They know Pamela's pet candidate is an asshole and I doubt they want to be under him any more than we or your Wolves do."

Carl thought about that for a moment, then said, "If we can make it look like Diamondback is going to lose, their lukewarm supporters will flip sides like they did last time."

Mary Ann nodded, but her face twisted into a snarl as she spit on the floor. "Wolverines, forever going whichever way the wind tosses them. Bah."

Carl couldn't argue. No one much liked or trusted the Wolverine Band. "That leaves only the Pumas as a wildcard."

Mary Ann said, "They're not much of a wildcard. They've said that if we can put up a good candidate to oppose the Empire and Diamondbacks, and if we can get the Timber Wolves openly on our side, then they'll join us."

"So what should I be worried about?" Carl replied immediately. Nothing was that easy in this world, not anymore. And assurances of the "don't worry about it" type always pegged his suspicion meter.

She replied, "Diamondback and Wolverine will have heard of all this by now. Diamondback will already be gunning for me, maybe Wolverines too if they're more committed than I think they are. I want you to do for me what you did for your Alpha—keep me alive. We're pushing hard for a quick election, beating the Empire to the punch, but if they kill me first, it won't matter. There won't be time for anyone else to step up and win."

Carl studied Mary Ann for a moment. She didn't show any signs of fear, only a cold acceptance of reality. Acceptance and determination. "I assume you have a plan."

"Bright boy. I do indeed. I have this safehouse, as so many ranking Liz Towners do. Mine's been set up over time by the only half-dozen people I'd trust with my life, all of whom are here with us now. Stay here with me. If things go sideways, I believe you can get me out alive, and I know you have hideouts in the wildlands, contacts out there. People who can help you."

Carl closed his eyes for a moment, thinking, but the decision was really pretty easy. "Alright. If you oppose Diamondback and the Empire, then I will support you. My people will support you. But first we have to keep you alive, and I need to set up contingency plans. I'll need a Kodiak disguise and maybe a helper in case of a challenge."

Mary Ann nodded to one of her companions, who headed upstairs. She said, "Done. We'll replace those wildlander clothes with our boots and jacket, get you a brown hoodie, and the right rags. Bandanas make the man, you know. Wear them wrong, you'll give yourself away."

All the Bands wore black boots, black leather jackets slashed with different paint colors, and a bandana or two, usually around the neck and either wrist or ankle. How they were tied, where the knots were, even how they were folded or turned to the side, all those details were a secret handshake that mattered. With the right disguise, he could go anywhere in Kodiak territory unmolested and, with the hoodie, unrecognized.

It was a start, at least. Carl gritted his teeth. Finally, he had a glimmer of hope for some payback. He swore that by the time this was all over with, Pamela would die by his hand, preferably while begging. But everything in its time. First, he had to organize himself around this new plan. Damn, it felt good to have one again.

- 15 -

1800 HOURS - ZERO DAY +226

TAGGART SAT IN front of the tiny laptop monitor and waited for the connection. The process of finding VPNs, connecting, moving on, connecting elsewhere—masking the signal path took time. But when it finished, he was rewarded with a *ding* from the laptop and a video conference screen popped up. Cassy was on the other end, and she looked startled to see him.

"General," Cassy said, regaining her composure, "what a pleasure. I expected Eagan. How are you today?"

Taggart said, "Well enough. I'll turn you over to my Sergeant Major shortly, but first I wanted to share some news with you."

"By all means, General. Go ahead."

"Feel free to call me Taggart if that's easier."

"As you wish." Cassy's mouth turned into a faint smile at the corners.

"We just concluded our largest offensive to date. We lured and engaged a significant portion of the New Jersey invader forces near the Hudson River."

"You're still here for our regularly scheduled conference,

so I assume it went well?"

"Yes. We are still mopping up patches of resistance. Overall, though, we reduced their combat effectiveness to below the point of unit cohesion."

Cassy stared at the monitor, looking blank but expectant. Taggart suppressed a sigh. "In other words, we killed most of them and the rest scattered willy-nilly."

Cassy almost clapped. "That's great," she said. "Any idea what's next for New America?"

"Even though we just got a lot closer to having parity of force with the invaders, they still have plenty of troops left, so don't celebrate too much. Also, because we had them nearly enveloped, the lucky few survivors had to flee to the west and were unable to exfiltrate to safety."

"Does this affect us over here?"

"Maybe. Over the coming few days, you may see small units ranging from lone stragglers to ad-hoc platoons drifting through Confederation territory. You'll want to alert your people."

Cassy nodded. "Thanks for the warning. We will let them know. We're facing increasing pressure from the Empire here, by the way. That battalion you sent us could well be the difference out here, so thank you."

Taggart smiled at her and said, "I hope they do make a difference. It does me no good to battle myself to exhaustion out here defeating General Ree, only to get mopped up in detail by this Empire you face. General Houle and I are going to fight a proxy war through you and the Empire, it seems."

"It can't be helped," Cassy replied. "And we'd rather fight the Empire with your help than without."

"How are my boys and girls doing? You keeping them busy?" Taggart asked, holding back a yawn. He was certain the deep, dark circles under his eyes must have him looking like a meth addict right now.

"They're well. We set one company up here, the HQ company. The other two are split between Manheim and Lititz. They conduct their own scouting operations, but report to Michael Bates, our version of the Secretary of Defense. He tells me they're doing a great job."

Taggart nodded his approval. Cassy was smart enough to use his battalion before the big battle, and to spread them out. It was best not to have them all in one place, but close enough to rendezvous with each other if needed. "Alright, I'll turn you over to Eagan now for your permaculture thing. Thanks for your time."

Taggart climbed out of the chair and Eagan slid into it as he walked out, heading toward his War Room for a more local update.

The war room desk had new intelligence reports in a thin stack. Taggart rifled through the reports, skimming them. Eighty-five percent enemy fatalities, ten percent more wounded. Five percent had escaped to the west, unharmed. It was an unmitigated success by any definition, but the fighting had cost him ten percent casualties among his own troops. Most of those were wounded, rather than fatalities, but they wouldn't be combat-effective again for weeks, if ever. He'd need to make time to thank them personally.

He regretted their pain, their losses, but it was necessary He consoled himself with the knowledge that their sacrifices had not been in vain—Ree and his Islamist lapdogs were now greatly reduced, almost to the point of parity with Taggart's troop strength. Taggart's lip curled back as he considered the options opened up by his tremendous victory over Ree's forces. Not for the first time, he wished he could meet that man. Meet him, talk to get his measure, and then slit his damn throat personally.

* * *

1000 HOURS - ZERO DAY +230

Samuel sat on his bike maybe one hundred yards away from the carnage just ending, along with two of his troopers. Brett, of course, was enjoying himself over there with the rest of the troops and playing with the last survivors of the little fortified homestead. Not fortified enough, apparently. Soon, those survivors would be dead, too. Samuel himself stayed out of it, because he had noticed that the troops didn't play as hard when he was there. They mostly left it for him and Brett. Samuel wanted them all to get a chance for some real recreation because it bonded the unit together more tightly.

Samuel's other troops, those not playing around, were busy looting. When they were done, he'd mark the place on their map and take notes on what supplies he had to leave behind. Intel for his masters.

He overheard one of the two nearby troops complaining about not getting to join the fun, and laughed out loud. They turned to look at Samuel, and he said with a grin, "You got to have fun last time. Stop bitching. You know you all have to take turns. Just not your lucky day."

One nodded, but they stopped talking. Samuel turned back to the scene, and heard screaming. That'd be whoever was left getting toyed with, of course. A satisfying sound.

Then Samuel heard a faint whining noise, or rather, more like a buzzing sound. He looked around but saw nothing. He scanned the sky, but still nothing... Oh, wait. There it was—but what was it? Something flying. But then something glittering and metallic dropped from the dot in the sky. A second later, a small orange parachute opened up, slowing its descent.

Samuel tracked it until it landed, a mere couple hundred feet away. He turned to the two troops with him. "Well, don't just stand there. Go get it, and bring it here if it isn't a bomb."

The two exchanged looks and then pedaled toward the object, and Samuel resisted the urge to laugh. The looks on their faces when he'd said "bomb" were absolutely priceless. Shortly, the two came pedaling back, looking rather too excited. When they came within earshot, he gave them the thumb-up sign and shouted, "What the hell are you two morons smiling at?"

Pulling to a stop in front of him, they both began babbling at the same time. Irritated, Samuel held up his hands. "Shut the hell up. One at a time. You, go," he said, looking at the man on the right.

The other trooper looked disappointed, but the one on the right said, "Captain, I think that was a drone! It dropped a big metal cylinder—we can't even lift it. It had a cap and we unscrewed it, and guess what?"

"Idiot. What?"

"It had a couple M4 rifles and a boatload of ammo! Also, a sealed envelope." He pulled a simple white envelope out of his back pocket; it was pretty damn thick.

Samuel took the envelope and saw that on the front, his name was written. Or printed, rather. That was interesting. He opened it and took out the contents.

There were a half-dozen folded, thick-papered images that had been printed out. They showed a large group of people apparently attacking a homestead, the homestead burning, and finally, the group riding off on horses. It looked to be about a hundred people or so.

Next was a printed letter, addressed to him from some colonel, under the authority of General Houle, Commander-in-Chief of the United States. Whatever. Those Mountain boys were sure fond of fancy titles and patting themselves on the back... Samuel spit into the dirt next to him, then read the note.

"What's it say, Cap?" asked one of the men with him.

"Can I read it?"

"Maybe if you could read," Samuel said. "Hang on."

Samuel finished reading, then let out a low whistle. "Seems the Mountain Boys have a problem they want us to fix. Why the hell would they waste all that time and energy sending out a flippin' Predator to deliver mail? Or whatever it was. Must be an important mission, but it sounds stupid."

"Dammit, Cap. Just tell us, already!"

"Fine, fine. It's like talking to my kid nephew, jeeze. So, it seems there's this group called the Night Ghosts, and they're messing with our program, finding and killing way too many of the Empire forward bases. You know, the ones that look like normal settlers? Well, we have to go find 'em and kill 'em."

Samuel considered just ignoring the mission since it didn't come from his own chain of command, but hell—if the Mountain would send a damn drone to deliver a message, they might send one to deliver something else, like a missile, though he wondered why they didn't just hit these Night Ghosts with some missiles. Probably they were harder to replace than Samuel and his troops, the bastards. Then he remembered the op in Cincinnati—the Republic had bent over backwards to please General Houle. Samuel decided the Republic itself might string him up if he disobeyed. Every scenario for ignoring these orders was risky, and besides, Samuel never did shrink from a fight.

"Well," Samuel said, "it looks like they got about a hundred people on horses. We got a few more than that, on bikes. I never cared for even odds, so we'll have to rig an ambush."

Samuel stepped off his bike and opened his map, laying it on the ground. Based on the satellite images, he found where their raid had occurred. It was maybe ten miles away. The letter had said they were just loitering in the area. And then as he gazed at the map, an idea struck him. Not far from the enemy's suspected position lay a rail station. Those were a priority target for the Empire anyway, but maybe he could use it for more than just a mission objective. He'd have to lure them into a trap to improve his odds a bit, but that station could be just what he needed to accomplish that.

As Samuel studied the map and ran various plans through his mind, one struck him that made all the rest fall away. "My god," he muttered, "could it really be just that easy?"

The more he thought about the plan, the more he was convinced it would work. "Brett," he hollered, "get our people ready. I have a mission for you all."

"Good. About damn time. I'm bored already." Brett thumped Samuel on the shoulder. "What are we going to do?"

Samuel said, "It's insanely simple. That's how I know it'll work..."

* * *

0745 HOURS - ZERO DAY +231

Leaning against his saddle, which he'd removed and put on the ground, Nestor savored hot black coffee, a rare treat they'd looted from the last Empire homestead they'd found, along with enough supplies to support an entire company. Coincidentally, he had a company. It was a stroke of luck to be able to resupply in the field instead of having to go to Clanholme, which would have wasted a couple of days.

Then, in the distance, he saw two riders approaching fast, leaning far forward as their horses sprinted. His scouts returning. Nestor set his coffee down and climbed to his feet to await them. When they arrived, their horses were frothy and worn. Nestor ordered two of his people to take the horses for water. When they could, they walked the horses for a cool down, gave them a carrot or two to munch on as a treat, and brushed them. It was a way to say thanks—someone had told him it's important to keep a willing horse happy. Then he turned to his dismounted scouts.

"Report," he said simply.

"Nestor, there's a railway station a couple miles from here, under attack! The station flies the Clan's colors. About forty enemy, pinned down a hundred yards from the station. Twenty people in the station holding them off."

Nestor frowned as the man continued to lay out the situation and the terrain. It must be more Empire infiltrators. That railway station was important if the Clan had twenty people defending it. No one told him why they were important, but he was pretty sure it would be best not to let the Clan defenders lose the station.

Nestor shouted, his voice carrying far, "Listen up. We got a rail station under attack two miles out. Third Squad, ride like hell to the station and reinforce them. Ride like hell, but approach carefully and ambush the Empire bastards from behind if you can. Everyone else by platoons, flank the attackers east and west. They're on the north face of the station about a hundred yards out, backed by forest. Hit them from both sides, and don't let them get to those woods. First Squad, you're with me. Second, stay and guard the camp. Go, go, go!"

There was a flurry of activity as his people threw saddles on horses and grabbed weapons. They'd leave their gear behind, defended only by ten men and women, while the other ninety or so Night Ghosts showed the Empire how it felt to be on the defensive.

In two minutes the Night Ghosts were riding hell-bent for the station, the twin columns of Second and Third

Platoon stretched out before him. His own First Platoon's third squad was far out in front, aiming for the station itself. Nestor brought up the rear with his first squad. He liked to be in front, as the commander, but he often had to bring up the rear to make sure his units were deployed the way they should be.

Minutes later, he crested the low, rolling ridgeline and began the descent toward the station. Ten of his people were dismounting within the rail station's parking lot and rushed into the station itself. Then the rest of his forces reached the parking lot and dismounted. Half gathered at either end of the station and prepared to rush the enemy to the north. He'd have liked to just ride through them like the old movies, but with modern weapons, cavalry was mostly back to just being for transport. Like knights of old, they often dismounted before a battle began in earnest.

From his vantage, he saw his two units rush out, moving from cover to cover. With railway cars, sheds, and other debris, there was plenty of cover available. After exchanging low-intensity fire for a minute, the twenty or so enemies began to fall back toward the woods in an organized way, but every time they popped up, one or two fell to Night Ghost bullets. Then they broke and ran, and the Night Ghosts pursued. Nestor grinned—there was no way his people would let these bastards escape. They surged forward, whooping and yelling. The people in the rail station cheered.

Nestor turned to Ratbone, smiling, and opened his mouth to say something witty, when a huge volley of fire erupted from the tree line. Nestor's head whipped around, and his mind struggled to make sense of what he was seeing. It seemed like half his people fell with the first volley. The rest went prone or took cover and began to return fire at the unseen enemy in the tree line.

Then he heard intense firing break out in the station. He

frantically struggled with his binoculars, but got it zoomed in through the station's south-facing plate windows. His jaw dropped. The "Clan" defenders had opened fire on his squad inside. They fought back but the other side had surprise, and his people fell quickly. It was all just a trap.

Out in the field, despite being in cover, Nestor's remaining people were also dying. And with only ten people with him, there wasn't a damn thing Nestor could do about it. "Ratbone, get the squad ready. We've got to get back to camp, pack what we can take and burn the rest. They'll be coming for us."

Ratbone snarled. "We're just going to leave them down there to die? What the fuck!"

Nestor clenched his jaw and took a deep breath. He definitely understood Ratbone's feelings. "If you think you can save them with the ten of us, I'm game. If you want to save what can be saved to fight another day, I'm fine with that, too. What do you all want to do?" Nestor asked, looking around at his squad.

Slowly, first one and then another reined their horses toward the south and rode. Ratbone was the last of them to go, jaw clenched in rage. Nestor debated just riding into battle to die, but at last he decided he had a responsibility to those who could be saved. He, too, turned south and rode hard for camp.

Today was a very bad day, the worst in a long, long time.

* * *

General Ree wanted to throw things. He wanted to shoot the soldier in his makeshift office. But Ree never showed his emotions unless it was planned. To the soldier standing before him, he must seem preternaturally calm.

Ree said, "What were our casualty levels?"

"My leader, estimates are between seventy-five and ninety percent. Taggart took no prisoners, sir—those are fatalities. We have recovered between five and ten percent, and most of them had been wounded early in the battle while they were still able to retreat."

Ree nodded. "Very well, soldier. Leave the papers on my desk. You are dismissed."

The soldier left hastily. Thankfully it had been one of his own Korean troops to deliver the news of Taggart's ambush, rather than one of those disgusting, smelly Sandies. No unpleasant odor remained in the office to offend him.

So. Taggart had somehow caught wind of his troop movement and had managed to deploy in force, coordinating a complex battle plan with only runners to pass along orders. Americans had no style, but they were effective. Maybe because war was nothing but chaos, and the American military had always operated in such chaos every day. It was a miracle they functioned at all, but instead they could be surprisingly effective. Damn Americans. Plans were meaningless when one fought Americans, if they had a good leader.

Ree considered his options. Firstly, with almost a quarter of his troops either dead or injured, he no longer had an overwhelming advantage over Taggart. A smart commander, which Taggart certainly was, would shift to the offensive sometime soon. Ree snarled. He hated fighting defensively.

Maybe he didn't have to wait. He still held the advantage of numbers, though not decisively. But if he could strike fast, hard, and with a bit of surprise or just plain luck, he could defeat Taggart piece by piece, like dominos falling. Crush a portion of Taggart's forces, put him firmly back on the defensive. Maybe a drive toward Hackensack? He'd have to think on this. But there was no way he was going to let Taggart keep defining the operational tempo of this war. It was time to show Taggart that the tiger still has his claws.

Ree shouted for his aide, who came in and stood at attention. Ree said, "Get a SitRep from each of my division commanders, the latest reports. And tell them to stand by for orders. Tell them, 'the tiger prowls.' They'll know what it means.

When the aide saluted and left, Ree allowed himself to smile. The coded command meant taking off all their leashes, all the restrictions. It meant total war. Taggart would soon learn that winning that battle had been a terrible mistake for his people. It would cost him dearly.

- 16 -

1445 HOURS - ZERO DAY +242

CASSY SPOTTED ETHAN coming outside from her house HQ. The easiest tunnel to the bunker was hidden beneath her stairwell, so Ethan's emerging from the house when he hadn't been seen going in wasn't unusual. She waved at him, and Ethan headed toward her.

"What's up?" Cassy asked when he drew close.

Ethan craned his neck to look around. "I'm glad I got you alone. Got a minute?"

"Yeah. What can I help you with?"

"Well, I got in touch with Liz Town, finally. You'll never believe what's going on." Ethan's eyes narrowed, and at his sides, his hands closed into fists.

Cassy had a sinking feeling in her stomach. Ethan wasn't usually the angry type. He went with the flow on most things. "I would guess it's bad news?"

"More than bad. Liz Town's new leader is only temporary until they have an election, but he or she is—"

Cassy interrupted, "He or she? You don't even know which? Who is in charge over there, Ethan?"

Ethan looked away, unable to meet her gaze. "They

wouldn't tell me. They cited 'internal security reasons' for that. Can you believe it? But that's not what's important."

"That doesn't even sound like Liz Town."

Ethan ran his hand through his disheveled hair. "Cassy, I hate to say this but they're pulling out of the Confederation —"

"What? How could they do that?" Cassy said more loudly than she had intended. She lowered her voice and continued, "Don't they realize that without the Confederation, the Empire will chew them up and spit them out?"

Ethan shrugged. "You and I know that. They seem oblivious. But they haven't withdrawn officially and maybe not permanently. They said they're having internal problems. They can't deal with anything else right now, and their resources are stretched. I wouldn't be surprised if they're back to fighting block wars."

Cassy nodded. "If they had a coup, Liz Towners aren't the sort to sit back and let that happen."

"Maybe not. But the Empire is already here. Their terrorist infiltrators are all over the region, creating fear and chaos. You can bet the rest of the Empire show up soon."

"So you think the Empire may have had some influence on the new leader to back out?"

Ethan said, "I think it's plausible. Though at this point, we can only hope they have a vote soon, and that they elect someone else to be their Speaker. But they won't have the election until there's only two clear front-runners. Maybe not at all if the Interim Speaker is strong enough to just take over."

Cassy pursed her lips, shaking her head slightly. "Ethan, is there anything you can think of that we or the Confederation can do to help resolve the Liz Town situation?"

Ethan paused to think. "Well... I can't think of anything.

Maybe if we had a show of strength, like a victory over the Empire that we could spin into some huge moral victory. That might give a solid boost to the Liz Town loyalists and their candidate."

Cassy was silent for a long while. Finally, she said, "Call a meeting. I want envoys here from every group, no matter how small. Like a town hall meeting. We have to figure out what to do next."

* * *

1800 HOURS - ZERO DAY +244

As the sun lost its mid-day intensity, Frank sat outside the chow tent with his tray. The fresh air and warmer temperatures were a welcome relief from his day spent overseeing the Clan's preparations in the Jungle for planting.

Some of the beds were already planted, in fact. Many of the fields around Clanholme were being sown with thousands of the clay seed-bombs containing a wide variety of seeds, both for food plants and others—pollen producers, nitrogen fixers, biomass accumulators, the list went on. Many would have been considered weeds on a normal farm, but with Cassy's wild ideas on farming, they were just part of the ecosystem.

Her ideas had proven themselves so far—they got results. She got as much food per acre as the best pre-EMP commercial farms, although it took far more effort to harvest than did a thousand acres of one crop in neat rows. Well, even that wasn't true anymore—not since the EMPs had destroyed the infrastructure and most of the machines needed for mechanized harvesting became scrap metal.

The Winter Wheat and a couple of other spring crops were almost ready to harvest now, and then there would be so much good food he wouldn't know what to do with it all. That would be on top of the year-round salads they were getting from the cold frame beds. As farm manager, he'd have to figure out something. Cassy'd probably have some ideas.

They'd plant rice shortly, as well as Spring Wheat, though not in the same place the winter stuff was ripening. That would lead to plant disease, so it was important to alternate wheat and rice with other species of plants. But he was mostly looking forward to the fruit coming in—anything but apple cider! He never thought he'd be tired of cider, but months of drinking either that or water...

Frank's musing was interrupted when he heard a bit of a commotion over by the guard tower and hobbled over with his crutch to see what was going on. As he got closer, he saw two wounded riders being helped off their horses. They weren't Clanners, though. When he drew close, he saw their small face tattoos—a simple one-inch skull by their left eyes —and realized they were Night Ghosts.

"Get water, and fetch Sturm. You, get Michael here pronto," Frank said, his voice commanding. "Lay them down."

Once the two men were on the ground Frank began examining them. One had a bullet that had passed clean through his left arm, probably shattering the bone. Without hospitals, that one might require amputation. Frank thought of when his own foot was cut off and cringed.

The other had an entry wound on one side of his abdomen, but no exit wound. It might be a flesh wound, or it might be fatal. Sturm would be able to tell. At least he was conscious though, which was a good sign. "Relax, friends," Frank said, "help is on the way. You'll be fine, everything will be okay. What happened to you?"

The one with the wounded arm was pale and sweaty,

probably in shock. The other man answered, “We found a rail station getting attacked by Empire bandits and went to ambush the attackers. The whole thing was a setup, though. We were the ones who got ambushed. More than a hundred of them.”

Frank nodded. “Okay, son. You’re okay now, though. Did you see Nestor?”

The man closed his eyes. When he spoke, his voice was strong, though. “No, sir. I have no idea if he’s alive or dead.”

“Alright, son. You just relax. Help is on the way.” Frank stood, and saw Sturm running toward them with her emergency bag. Cassy was right behind her.

When Sturm drew close, he said, “Two gunshot wounds, one through the arm, the other abdominal with no exit wound.”

Sturm nodded and crouched down to attend the wounded, and Frank walked toward Cassy. When she came to a stop, he told her about the ambush, and that they didn’t know if Nestor was alive.

“Dammit,” she said. “This isn’t what we need right now. We need a strong victory to shore up Liz Town.”

Frank listened carefully while Cassy told him what was known about Liz Town’s situation, and Ethan’s idea. He nodded, but didn’t interrupt. When she finished, he said, “Yep, this is bad timing. Let’s not tell Liz Town.”

Cassy said, “Tell Michael to send out scouts, get the location from the wounded over there, and search for more survivors. And find out who led the ambush or where the ambushers are now. If they could take out the Ghosts, we need to deal with them. Last thing we need is that kind of force wandering around Confed territory.”

“You got it. I’ll tell Ethan to alert the other Confed members that there’s a company-sized unit raiding around here. The Gap is probably the closest, besides us, since the riders came in from the south."

"Good idea. We need to get scouts out like a swarm of bees, and put some units on standby. Let me know right away if we find any more Night Ghost survivors."

"Of course," Frank replied, then turned to go find Michael. There was much to do now, and it was all bad timing. Spring sowing was almost on them, and now this... Worst of all, the drain on time and resources would probably only get worse as the weather improved.

* * *

2145 HOURS - ZERO DAY +247

In the shell of a restaurant deep in Kodiak territory, Carl stood behind the impromptu stage where he'd be unobtrusive. He, three guards, and Mary Ann had left the safehouse with the Kodiak leader disguised as just another Kodiak. Two other teams had also left, all wearing the same clothes. After making sure they weren't followed, Carl's group had made their way to this meeting of the resistance, trying to drum up support for Mary Ann as the new Speaker of Liz Town and reinforcing her anti-Empire position.

The town hall-style meeting was a terrible risk for Mary Ann, Carl knew. Coming and going were the most dangerous, but even though the Interim Speaker probably wouldn't attack the meeting outright, that wouldn't prevent an assassin from slipping in. Carl kept alert, eyes roving the crowd and the doors for danger. The windows were blacked out, so at least a sniper wasn't likely while she was inside. Getting her back to the safehouse without being followed, or worse, attacked, would be the toughest problem.

The meeting went on for two hours, Mary Ann talking to the packed crowd and answering questions, not all of them easy ones. She handled it like a pro, though, and Carl felt confident she had won them over by the end. Almost all the people present vowed to recruit one other person for the cause of resistance, as well.

When everything wrapped up, Carl approached Mary Ann from behind and whispered, "Time to go. We should make a break while everyone is clearing out of here. It'll be harder to identify or follow you if we leave with everyone else."

Mary Ann didn't cringe when he said that. She only nodded and said, "Alright. Let's go, then."

As the crowd dispersed, Carl and the other three guards led her out the restaurant's front door with everyone else, forming a tight circle around her for protection. Once outside, Carl looked around for any threats. The area was dark and mostly uninhabited, but Kodiak Band had claimed it and walled it, so at least it was not in the wildlands outside the walls. Once free of the crowd, which was dispersing rapidly in all directions, they led her in the general direction of the safehouse, though not directly. He and the guards spread apart a bit, hoping to disguise that they were a group. Carl walked with Mary Ann, two other guards walked together twenty feet behind and to the left, and a fifth guard walked alone in a slightly different direction that would still keep him in eyesight most of the time.

Carl angled a bit to his left, heading toward the deep shadows of an alley. He couldn't see the alley from where he was, but he had seen it on the way to the meeting. The other guards would take a slightly different path and would be out of sight, but only briefly.

As they reached the derelict, debris-cluttered alley, Carl had the fleeting thought that Mary Ann was smart to go with him on this part of the journey. His life was now firmly intertwined with hers, and unless he wanted to live out in the wildlands as an exiled fugitive, he had to keep her alive, too. Her other guards were maybe less motivated, but he trusted her judgment when she had picked them. She knew her own people best.

Carl peered around the corner into the alleyway. Steam rose up from the old underground storm drain system, but nothing moved. After a few seconds, he stepped into the alley with Mary Ann and continued walking. They intertwined their arms and walked side by side, pretending to be just another amorous Kodiak couple. Carl kept the pace brisk enough to say, "hey, we're going somewhere specific," but slow enough that it didn't look like they were in a rush. Carl's training told him that was the best way to avoid being noticed—blend into the background, behave like everyone else, and you're practically invisible to anyone who wasn't looking right at you.

Before they reached the end of the alleyway, however, the situation changed. Two people stepped into the alley's exit, moving slowly. They seemed to be trying to look like two people chatting quietly with one another while on their way to somewhere. But their legs and arms were too stiff, their body language tense and ready for action. Carl turned his face toward Mary Ann as he glanced quickly toward the rear and saw two more people step into the alley behind them. This was obviously no coincidence.

Beside him, Mary Ann laughed out loud as though responding to something he had just said and took her arm out from his in order to punch him playfully on the shoulder. "Oh, you're no gentleman at all, are you," she said. She spoke in a normal tone of voice, sounding completely at ease, but in the silence of the night and in the alley's confines, her voice surely traveled to their soon-to-be attackers.

Carl grinned back and chuckled aloud. Mary Ann was obviously smart and cunning. By doing that, she had freed up his right arm without being obvious about it, and she hadn't missed a step as the other players showed up. She had played it perfectly.

When they got within a dozen feet of the first two, Carl heard the people behind them walking and guessed they were still about forty feet away. That gave him at most four seconds to deal with the first two before the second pair would be able to realize what was going on, react, and then be upon them—he'd have to do this fast. Strike first, strike hard.

In one motion, he drew his pistol and fired with his elbow at his side. The round struck the man on the right directly in his face, and he toppled backward. The second man's leg lashed out in a blur, striking Carl painfully at his wrist and sending his pistol flying. It nearly struck Mary Ann, then clattered to the ground.

Even as the pistol skittered across the pavement into the wall next to Mary Ann, Carl was already drawing his Tanto-pointed knife, thrusting it at his attacker, but he jumped back to the left and Carl's knife only brushed his leather jacket, ineffective. A knife appeared in the man's hand. He held it like an icepick, point down, and drew his arm up to attack.

Carl felt the thrill of victory rush through him—the other man was dead already, he just didn't know it. It was exactly the wrong grip, wrong attack. As his arm went up, Carl stepped toward him, thrusting his knife toward the attacker's chest.

The man's other arm swept across his body to block the blade, but it didn't. It only pushed the path of the blade from the left to the right. As Carl's blade punched through leather, skin, and bone with ease, he raised his other arm, blocking the man's clumsy downward stroke. Carl shoved the man backward, momentum then ripping the blade from his chest.

He hit the ground making a wheezing, bubbling noise. That was definitely a punctured lung—he'd be dead shortly.

Carl spun to face the other two and saw they had knives drawn as well, rushing toward him. Two on one with knives was a losing proposition, no matter how skilled you were, especially when they were ready for you and knew *you* had a knife, too. At least Mary Ann could get away, and her other guards couldn't be more than a few seconds away. Carl only had to delay these two motherfuckers for a moment.

The distance closed from twenty feet to six in only a moment—and Carl braced himself. He had already decided, right or wrong, that he was going to kill the one on the left, knowing the other would waste two precious seconds killing him. Then it would be only the last attacker and Mary Ann, with her having a great head start.

A deafening boom startled Carl, and one of the two—the one Carl figured would kill him—fell forward onto his face, skidding almost to Carl's feet.

Carl had no time to decipher what happened and swung his knife diagonally at the remaining one. He dodged to Carl's right, and the strike missed.

The man didn't stop turning, though, and finished spinning in a blur, his knife streaking toward Carl's face with a backhand strike.

Carl raised his right arm. It blocked the strike, but the other man's blade was no Tanto-point; the slightly curved blade cut through Carl's jacket like butter and bit deep into his upper arm.

Carl managed to keep his grip on his knife but felt immediate wetness in his jacket sleeve. It was a serious wound, he knew, but it didn't slow him down yet. Knife arm already up, Carl then thrust his knife point down and forward toward the other man's neck. His enemy's momentum from the last attack carried him forward, ruining his chance of defending himself, and Carl's knife sunk to its hilt into the man's back just below his neck.

The last foe groaned and fell forward slowly, toppling slowly at first like a tree. The fight was over, but there were sure to be more. He had to find Mary Ann and get her to safety.

Carl turned, ready to run after her, but saw her standing there, wide-eyed, holding the pistol he had dropped at the beginning of the fight.

"You should have run," he said. His voice was a deep growl from the adrenaline pumping through him and he felt like he couldn't catch his breath.

"Good for you I didn't," she smirked. "Let's get the hell out of here. Those shots will bring people."

Side by side, Mary Ann still holding the pistol, they ran from the alley, sprinting across the next street and up a block. They slid through one house's side gate into its backyard, then across the yard to the tall wooden fence. Neither of them slowed for it, leaping up and throwing an elbow over the top instead and using their momentum to carry their feet over the top before rolling off. They landed in a crouch on the other side.

Carl felt fire shoot through his arm, taking his breath away. The adrenaline was wearing off and he might go into shock soon if the wound was bad enough. There was no way to see it through his jacket, though, and no time yet to slow down. They kept running, though Carl quickly found himself a couple paces behind her. She didn't slow, however, so Carl put his chin down and redoubled his efforts. He didn't catch up, but at least he fell no further behind.

They crossed the yard and reached the house on the other side. Carl drew up short and kicked the back door open. It flew inward, one hinge flying away in a rain of wood splinters. He and Mary Ann stepped inside, and stopped.

Carl propped the door up as best he could and then tried to catch his breath.

"I guess I owe you a thanks," Carl said, panting. "Stay low."

Mary Ann leaned against the dead refrigerator, crouching enough to put her hands on her knees. Between whistling gasps, she said, "No problem... Guess we're even... badass."

Carl grinned. Mary Ann was turning out to be quite a remarkable person. He decided right then and there, she would make a fantastic Speaker for Liz Town. So far, she embodied everything Liz Town had stood for under his old Alpha. "...just glad you didn't miss that shot," he panted, "... woulda sucked for me..."

Carl counted his heartbeats. Forty beats later, his breathing had returned mostly to normal and his pulse was slowing noticeably. "We need to get out of here. Ideas?"

Mary Ann handed his pistol back to him and stood straight, stretching her back. "Well—"

The rear door, already halfway off its hinges, flew inward, narrowly missing Carl. A man wearing a leather jacket and Diamondback colors stepped through the doorway, gun drawn. He swung his pistol toward Mary Ann, to his left, ignoring Carl.

Carl leaped at him in a flying football tackle, but even as his feet left the ground, he knew he'd miss. He must have lost more blood than he thought, because suddenly his arms and legs felt heavy.

The other man stepped back, ruining his shot, as Carl landed on the kitchen floor and skidded into the lower cabinets. The other man growled and swung his pistol toward Carl.

Nothing he could do. Carl closed his eyes and waited for the bang. A half-second later he heard the resounding boom of a gun fired inside. It took another half-second to realize he didn't feel anything. Wasn't dead. He cracked one eye open. Standing at the front door was the lone guard, from whom they'd separated to avoid drawing attention as a group.

The guard grinned. "Lucky timing," he said. "Mary Ann, are you hurt?"

She shook her head. "No, but Carl got cut on the right arm."

More footsteps, but it was the other two guards. One said, "If we found you, they can too. Let's go."

Carl got to his feet. "I'm bleeding pretty bad. Must'a followed my blood trail."

Mary Ann nodded. "Take your jacket off. Do it now."

Carl shrugged out of the jacket and let it fall to the ground, and pulled his hoodie up over his head. He let it fall to the floor as well and looked at his arm. It was gashed to the bone and still bleeding heavily, but it wasn't an arterial cut. Take the good where you find it.

Mary Ann bent down, picked his hoodie off the floor, and pulled hard on one end of the hood's drawstring. It came out easily. She quickly looped the cord in half, slid the loose ends through the loop, and slid it up Carl's arm past the wound. When it got nearly up to his armpit, she pulled hard. The loop cinched down painfully, and after Carl's involuntary grunt he felt his arm begin to tingle immediately. No oxygen, but no bleeding out before someone could sew it up. *Take the good where you find it.*

Mary Ann tied the loose ends back around his arm, adding to the constriction and preventing it from coming loose. "No blood trail, now," she said, and used his hoodie to wipe as much blood off his arm as she could. It had taken less than a minute to apply the tourniquet. "Let's get out of here."

The group left together and headed toward the

safehouse, taking a circuitous route while checking for tails or rooftop watchers. They had to avoid leading anyone right to it. When they drew close, two guards broke off and slipped into shadows, waiting for followers cursed with a death wish.

Carl, Mary Ann, and the other lone guard got to their hideout safely. Once inside, she pulled a first aid kit and a sewing kit out of a kitchen drawer. "Sorry, no Lidocain. This is gonna hurt."

"Carl nodded. "Yeah, well, can't hurt worse than losing my arm."

"You wish," Mary Ann said.

Carl felt the cold air against his fresh, hot wound and let out another involuntary grunt. He sucked in a deep inhalation and held it. "Let's do this," he said, gritting his teeth.

"Alright, here goes," Mary Ann said as she sank the needle into his arm.

She was right. It hurt like hell.

- 17 -

0645 HOURS - ZERO DAY +249

CASSY SLID HER hand lightly over the rough surface of the biplane lower wing, feeling the hardened canvas with the tenderness of a lover. “Amazing. Two hundred years of technological advance, and this plane is back to being one of the most advanced machines in the world.”

Dean Jepson nodded and wiped his handkerchief over his sweaty face before stuffing it back into his pocket, sewn into the chest of his overalls. He spit, then grinned. “So glad you took a liking to her, Cassy. I call her Betsy.”

She didn’t care what it was named. “Fantastic, Dean. You did well getting her up and running.”

Dean was not a smiling man, far from it, but now his face lit in the biggest grin she had ever seen on him. “Ah, this old workhorse of a plane is the prettiest girl at the ball, I’d say.”

Cassy, Dean, and his wife may have once gone to court against one another before the EMPs, but they were all just Clanners together now. He was cranky and old, and the kids messed with him like they would any old codger sitting on a porch yelling at them to stay off his lawn, but she suspected he enjoyed that role. It was just the way he played with them, something he proved by working with Brianna and Kaitlyn when the two girls wanted to make "Medals of Generator" for Jaz and Choony.

"The only thing left is for y'all to figure out how to arm her and them other planes. We got ten, but the others are newfangled, and they ain't half so pretty. This one, though... She can fly almost as slow as a man might walk, and she can circle on a dime. She'll do better than all the rest when the fussin' and fightin' starts, you mark my words."

"And the fuel problem?" Cassy asked. "How are we handling that?"

"Ha. Missy, right now she runs on regular ol' gas, same as always. Them scouts got up cases of gas perserves, so she'll run right for another year if we're lucky. But by then we'll have more of them gas fryers, and I reckon I can rig her up to run on that stuff somehow."

Cassy stifled a chuckle at the way he said "preservers" and "gasifiers," but that didn't make him any less right, or less vital to the Clan.

So for now, the planes could run without major modifications. That was very good news, considering how scarce the high demand had made the small, efficient gasifiers that Dean built.

In fact, Dean's design was far better than the gasifiers out of Falconry or Brickerville, but Cassy reserved them for the Clan's battlecars. When there was a surplus, she'd think about trading them with more distant groups like Falconry and the Clan's client settlements like Taj Mahal.

She had set up the less efficient gasifiers that they had gotten by trade so far to generate power, turning the wind and solar power generators into backups. It had allowed the Clan to light most of the dwellings in the Complex, the HQ, and the Bunker—though the latter already had a generator that was now purely backup—and even the Clanholme water pumps. Now the reservoir at the top of the south hill could be filled without rain and without labor, saving hundreds of labor man-hours and giving the outdoor kitchen and the HQ running water at all times, and great pressure to boot.

Cassy nodded and said, "That's great, Dean. I'll let you get back to work. Tell your wife I said hello."

Dean grumbled, "You want to say hello to the missus, you tell her y'self. Bah. I don't know how you expect me to get work done if all y'all keep interrupting me anyway." He walked away, still muttering under his breath.

Cassy bit back a smile, shaking her head. There's the Dean I know, she thought as she left the hangar. Outside, Michael waited for her.

"How did it go?" he asked with a wry grin.

"Well, he smiled today."

"No kidding. But where are we with the planes?"

"All ten of the planes are running now, including the biplane, which he named Betsy," Cassy said with another drip of sarcasm at the end.

Michael chuckled a bit, shaking his head.

"Though, something interesting Dean had said to me just now—the biplane will fly almost as slow as a man walks, and will circle on a dime. I'm sure that's an exaggeration, but maybe we can use that to our advantage somehow."

Michael walked with her as she returned to their horses for the half-hour journey back to Clanholme. The planes were kept far enough away that only the scouts knew about them, even among the Clanners. Other than the Council, of course. They absolutely did not want word of the Clan's working airplanes to leak out to anyone outside.

"He's not exaggerating by much, actually," Michael said. "He might be absolutely right. His 'Betsy' might be our best plane. We studied different eras of warfare in the Corps. In World War One, they used biplanes by preference. They could stay in the air at surprisingly slow speeds and, with those two sets of wings, they generate enough lift to turn tightly for a long time before losing much altitude. That more than made up for their lack of speed."

The two Clanners mounted their horses and turned toward home. "If they are so great, why did we move to single-wing planes and jets?" Cassy asked, genuinely curious.

"Easy. Technology marches on. We got air-to-air missiles with ranges far beyond the pilot's vision, and radar to see the enemy very far out. With jets, speed is life. Biplanes just can't go that fast, and their quick maneuvering didn't mean as much when you could see by radar what was coming long before it got there, so we found designs that could go extremely fast."

Cassy nodded. "I see. We don't have air-to-air missiles and radar to worry about anymore, at least not outside the Mountain. If I'm getting this right, speed just means short attacks and long times between attacks now."

"That's the gist of it, yes. The biplane might outperform the others in every way that matters in this upcoming war. Not that the others won't do well—they're all crop dusters, after all. They were made for maneuverability."

"So we're reinventing air tactics from World War One and have to figure out how to arm these planes."

"Wait a minute." Michael paused in thought, then replied, "I think I have an idea. Earlier in the Great War they dropped bombs, but not like how you imagine them now. Their bombs were basically grenades that went off on impact, and the pilot or a passenger would literally throw them over the side to rain down on enemy positions. Sometimes they'd chuck a bomb right from the plane into a spotter tower and watch it go up in smoke as they flew away."

"Interesting," Cassy said.

"Yeah. We could rig up something with all that dynamite we got and maybe with shotgun shells—you know, like the boobytraps we have around Clanholme."

"I think the Brickerville people put something like that together to lob down from their drones during that fight against the invaders over at the quarry."

"Easy enough to set up. Impact drives a pin into the shell, which goes off and detonates the dynamite. We could attach fins to make them fall truer, as well."

"They won't be very accurate, but we just won't use them for precision stuff. Didn't the old warplanes have machine guns, too?"

Michael nodded. "Yes, but I have no idea how they got the bullets to go between the spinning propeller blades without just shooting off the propeller. Had to be a timing thing. I'll ask Ethan if he can find something about that, but I can't imagine there's much of the internet left."

Cassy frowned. That was a weird problem. Dean could probably figure out how they used to do that, but he was too busy on more important preparations and if she brought it up now, he'd grumble and mumble. Plane-mounted machine guns weren't the top priority, so she dismissed the idea. Maybe Ethan would find something. "At least we can put some semi-auto rifles up there with the pilots so they can shoot down at any easy targets."

Michael rubbed his jaw, thinking. "Yes, we should do that. Definitely. But I wonder if we could somehow strap weapons to the wings, too, far enough out so they don't spray the propeller, and then rig up a single trigger in the cabin. There would be no way to reload, but we could get one good strafing run per sortie. Better than nothing."

"Taggart's soldiers had a few belt-fed machine guns, right?" If they could be persuaded to give a few of those up, some of the planes might make multiple strafing runs...

"Yes," Michael said, "but they're more useful with those soldiers on the ground than stuck on an airplane we probably aren't going to use much after the first fight. We only get one shot at the surprise advantage. And besides, those are squad support weapons, not the big fifty-calibers. I think we should bring the planes out early in the war, not wait for a best moment, and then use them throughout the war, even after the surprise in the first fight."

Cassy shook her head. He had a point, but so did she. "No. If we use them too soon, they'll adjust their tactics to make our planes less effective and then, when the critical moment comes, our air force might not be able to get the job done. Or worse, the Empire might go find some old planes of their own. They have more resources than we do, for making war anyway. It's what they do."

"Very well," Michael said, shrugging. He clearly didn't agree, but he would follow her orders on this matter at least. Besides, they were both right. Cassy just had more strategic considerations to work with than Michael. It was the old "big picture" deal and that view was hers.

"So how are the Night Ghosts we found wandering around, and the two who found us?"

"A couple died. A dozen remain. There's two dozen unaccounted for, including Nestor. The enemy just vanished —they're on bikes, and they leave no trail or clue on pavement. They must be using the roadways to break up their trail. It's an excellent light cavalry strategy."

He almost sounded admiring.

"We have scouts out, like I asked?" She knew they did, but wanted to hear it from Michael.

"Of course. I have a dozen two-man teams from the Clan, Taj Mahal, and Taggart's troops. They're on horseback, they have most of our binoculars and maps, and they have strict orders to find Nestor or the raiders and then let us know."

"They know to go to an ally with a radio, if that's faster?"

Michael looked away, and his jaw clenched briefly before he said, "Of course, Cassy."

She heard irritation in his voice and knew she deserved it. Why did she feel like she had to manage everything herself? She had capable people whom she trusted. "Sorry, I know you know how to do your job. I guess I just like to hear our plans unfolding, sometimes."

"I give you reports," Michael commented, his voice deadpan.

She hadn't meant to insult him. "Sorry, Michael. I didn't mean to jostle your elbow. It's not you, it's me," she added, putting on a mock soap opera voice as she emphasized the last part.

He laughed at that, and the tension was broken. The rest of the trip had more pleasant conversation.

* * *

Choony stoked the small fire as they prepared to eat some more pemmican and dried fruit rings. They hadn't eaten much else since leaving Clanholme this time, but Choony had discovered that if he boiled a small amount of water and then mixed in chunks of pemmican, they'd dissolve into a meat-and-grease gruel. Adding some of their flour allowed him to fry it up almost like grits. Meat grits. Okay, not for gourmets, maybe, but at least you didn't have to chew it for hours.

Sitting on a rock next to the fire, Jaz munched her plain pemmican bar. "Just eat the damn stuff, Choon. You know it'll never be, like, *good*. It's still just meat and fat. Whether you eat it on a stick or in a bowl, it's still crap."

Choony glanced to the top of the hill, where they had stopped in the lee for lunch. It was rocky, which made it less comfortable but also easier to defend. "With the flour it's more like gravy."

"Crap gravy with an essence of orange, yum," Jaz said, rolling her eyes.

Choony set their cast iron skillet over the fire, resting on some rocks he had set up for the purpose. As his "gravy" heated, he looked down the hill and out over the little valley. "More like Dutch apple pie," he said, and got lost for a moment savoring the memory of that particular treat. Jaz looked wistful for a moment, too.

"Come autumn we'll have more apples than we know what to do with. And more hard apple cider," Jaz said, her voice rising at the end with excitement.

There was a glint down below, like metal or glass in the sunlight. "Did you see that?" Choony asked, straightening to a more alert posture.

Jaz dropped her pemmican for an answer and fell off the rock she had been sitting on, grabbing her rifle even as Choony sat taller. Crouched low now, she rested the rifle on her rock and peered through the scope. "Where was it," she asked quietly.

"From you, eleven o'clock."

Choony, realizing he had become a target sitting tall on his rock, squat-walked to another rock next to Jaz and opened the satchel she had dropped in the dirt next to her. Ten full magazines in this one, but they were the small five-round magazines that her semi-auto hunting rifle used, not the massive thirty-round magazines of the M4s and AKs. "Ready," he said. This had become routine, now, though he often wished a routine wasn't needed. See something, take cover, get ready to feed his warrior princess fresh magazines. Most of the time it turned out to be a broken bottle, or maybe an old license plate. Sometimes it was just a traveler. But once in a while, it was someone dangerous.

"Got it," she said. A moment later, she added, "Two men and one woman. Three AKs. Bikes in the dirt nearby. Backpacks on the bikes. They're eating. Looks like Empire."

Choony nodded. The bikes didn't mean they were Empire scouts or raiders, but it sure did raise the odds. The Empire raiders didn't have a standard armament, though—they used what they could, from AKs to M16s to bolt-action hunting rifles. He had seen one with a crossbow, even. Choony began smothering the fire with dirt—water would make too much steam and smoke. "Maybe they won't see us."

Jaz didn't take her eye from her scope. "That'd be awesome. I'm tired of getting shot at." Jaz froze, and remained silent. A second later, she fired her rifle.

"Shit shit shit. They saw us. One down, two coming." She fired again, but cursed.

"They saw you, you mean," replied Choony as he pulled out one of the small magazines, keeping it ready for a quick reload.

"Whatevs." *Bang. Bang. Bang.*

He handed her the magazine, and she had the expended one dropped and the new one inserted in less than two seconds. Down below, Choony heard the enemy keep up a steady rate of fire, but the ricochets were all over the place. "Good thing they have AKs," Choony said.

"At this range. Not so much good if they get closer." *Bang. Bang.*

Choony looked into the pouch to grab another magazine, but then Jaz let out a cry of pain. He looked up and saw her spin, landing face-first in the dirt. He felt his world shrink to a pinpoint and decided that if she died, he would go with her. But as soon as sound and time rushed back around him, he grabbed the rifle and brought the barrel over his own rock. He wasn't sure how critical Jaz's wound was but in order to save them both, he had to at least postpone their enemies' charge. He fired three rapid shots over their heads—it got them to crouch down, stopping their sudden rush which bought him little time to think of a plan. Then he heard Jaz cry out.

"Give me that shit," snarled Jaz as Choony reloaded. She had risen to her knees again, but had a growing red bloom over her left shoulder. His heart soared—she was alive.

He handed the rifle to her without a word and marveled at her toughness. Shoulder wounds weren't like in the movies, he knew. They could be some of the worst injuries with the longest recovery times, even if the victim didn't bleed out from a pierced major artery. They were dangerous. But Jaz seemed to have gotten lucky.

Jaz snatched the weapon and raised it to the rock one-handed, sighted in, and fired once. She grunted in pain and tears streamed down her face, but she didn't waver from her position. *Bang.* "We're gonna get overrun," she said matter-of-factly.

Choony reloaded for her after the fifth shot and handed the rifle back to her. That's when he noticed that the enemies' shots were now bouncing off the front of Jaz's rock instead of all over the place like earlier, and he realized they had gotten dangerously close. If Jaz tried to pop up to shoot, she might get one, but the other would mow her down.

Choony made a snap decision and it felt *right*. Things were as they were, and he would live or he'd die. He jumped to his feet, arms over his head, and screamed at the enemy. He saw they were a mere twenty yards away or so, now.

As their barrels whipped toward Choony, Jaz fired two shots and he saw one's head snap back as he toppled backward, but the other dove prone and Jaz's second shot missed. Had she not been injured, she might have got them both. She yelled, "Get the fuck down!"

Choony dropped down to sit on his heels again and

handed Jaz a fresh magazine. "If it's stupid and it works, it isn't stupid," he said. "That's what the Marines say."

"Yeah, yeah," Jaz replied, and fired again. "Just don't do that again. You may not be so lucky next time," she said as she reloaded, but Choony noticed it took her a heartbeat longer than before. Her injury was slowing her. Then she popped up and fired again, ducking as a round came back at her from the remaining raider. Her jaw was clenched tightly, and her hair was matted with dirt and sweat. But it was the sheen of moisture on her face and arms that alarmed him. She was beginning to look pale, colorless. That's when Choony realized she was going into shock, and there was nothing he could do about it right now.

Jaz reloaded again, bobbed her head three times as she stared at the ground, and then she bolted upright and snap-fired two shots. A cry from just downhill announced her victory. "Got you, fucker," she said.

And then she collapsed. Choony grabbed her as she fell and lowered her gently to the ground. He whipped his military field kit out of its belt pouch, took out the EMT scissors, shears, whatever those were called, and began to cut away Jaz's torn and bloody shirt. "Stay with me, Jaz," he said as his voice cracked.

Choony was definitely not centered.

* * *

General Ree sat in his tiny work center office, filling out paperwork. It was the bane of a combat general, but even as the world faded into a new Dark Age, he couldn't escape it. Without printers and scanners, it took even longer. For the thousandth time, he cursed the Americans for using EMPs on targets across the globe. The last gasps of a dying empire had plunged the world into darkness—including Ree himself.

Across the desk, in a simple swivel office chair, sat Major Pak Kim, who managed the day-to-day operations of the People's Worker Army. Some blind fools called them slaves, and maybe in some degenerate sense they were, but if so, it was for their own good.

"Big brother," Kim said, using the familiar-but-respectful honorific, "your forces in the City grow hungry. They aren't starving yet, but we need to get a lot of food to them and quickly. Your loyal troops have quelled some unrest already."

Ree could understand the feeling. Although his rank entitled him to food in plenty, he had cut his own rations in half. Every sandwich he ate could keep a member of the Worker Army alive for another day. He hadn't told anyone of his noble sacrifice, of course—the approval of his ancestors was reward enough—but eventually questions about his health began and he had to tell people.

He didn't mind the accolades he received for his selfless sacrifice, but worried that soldiers might follow his example. They had to stay strong to fight, to guide the Worker members, so Ree was thinking of issuing an order that all troops eat their full allotment.

"Of course. I appreciate your commitment to your duties," Ree said, putting his pencil down and folding his hands. "Let me ask you something. Should I commit another quarter of my forces to the journey to resupply New York? Let me hear your thoughts."

"No. I think another loss like that will be the end of us."

"What, then?" Ree asked. That hadn't been the answer he expected. The major was not the brightest man, outside of organization skills, but Ree would never overlook a good idea just because of the source.

"Sir, it seems to me that we are the trout swimming upstream in the Taedong River. We may make it to our destination, but we will struggle to do so and success is not guaranteed. Perhaps the General would consider an alternative."

"Perhaps. Share your thoughts, Kim. Let us see if your intellect is in harmony with that of the Great Leader."

Kim bowed, hands together. Then he leaned back in his chair and said, "Perhaps the General has been thinking of returning our entire army, and half of the People's Worker Army, to the safety of New York City. In this way, you may believe that we would all be safer from Taggart and allow him to starve without our supplies to steal to ease his burden."

Ree's eyes narrowed as he evaluated Kim. He looked relaxed, the perfect picture of calm. So then, he wasn't questioning Ree's plans. That was good for Kim's health. And the idea had some merit, though it created new questions in his mind. "I may have had that thought. If I had, little brother, how do you think I would plan to feed our army and our people?"

The corners of Kim's lips twitched upward for just an instant. He was no doubt pleased to believe that his thoughts were in line with what his leader had been thinking. "Sir, I know that it has occurred to you already that the Americans will eat one another, if they are hungry enough, and that it would be a simple matter to gather citizens of the City to feed the loyal Worker Army. Perhaps even presented in stew to make it easier on their consciences."

Ree nodded. That was indeed true. His workers wouldn't even need to know where the meat came from. They would guess, but they would also choose to believe Ree's official explanations. "And what of the vegetables and fruits? What of the nuts? How do you imagine I plan to bring those with us and then grow them in the City?"

Kim shifted in his seat, eager. Ree didn't show his displeasure, of course. But that lack of discipline was disgusting in an officer of the glorious Korean People's Army. Ree said, "Be calm, little brother. Tell me."

Kim nodded and said, "I know little compared to you, my leader. All I can think of is that we could easily bring all of our seeds and seedlings with us, and use Central Park as our new farmland. We could use rooftops and balconies, as well, because even without power, most of the City has plenty of water pressure. Most of the City gets its water from aquifers at higher elevation."

Ree favored him with a smile, and nodded. "You are not wrong, Kim. I have had such thoughts. I would of course need to rely on my favored administrator to organize such a massive migration."

Kim stood and bowed, holding the position until Ree waved his hand. Kim said, "I thank you. Such a compliment brings me honor in the eyes of my ancestors."

"Yes, yes," Ree replied. "You may leave me now. I need to return to considering how best to move so many people safely, if I do decide we should return."

Kim briefly bowed again and then headed toward the door. He grabbed the handle, but then turned around. "Sir... it occurs to me that we could bring all of our pigs, as well. They eat whatever is given to them, just like the People's Worker Army. I know you had the thought as well, but I would fail my duty to you if I didn't mention it."

Kim left, closing the door softly behind him and leaving Ree alone in the office. Ree leaned back in his chair and looked up at the foamboard ceiling. Could the answer really be so simple? Had stupid Major Pak Kim solved the dilemma Ree faced? The more he thought about it, the more the idea seemed like a solid solution to his problem.

Once safely back in New York, he could use up as many Americans as he needed to feed his workers. Pigs would provide meat, at least for some—such as for him and his officers—and could be carefully raised and bred for the future, as well. Central Park had plenty of open space, and even trees for lumber.

Ree thought of the many fruit and nut trees throughout his area. Branches could be cut and the ends kept alive in damp soil, in buckets, and he could plant those to create new food trees in the City. They could take the place of the useless ornamentals currently in the park.

Yes, this could work. Would Taggart dare attack Ree's entire force? He would need to use his entire army to do so and would probably lose such a battle. It would be all or nothing for Taggart, and he doubted his adversary would be so reckless.

Once in the City, Ree would be bottled up, but that was nothing. He'd have the island. Central Park. Fishing. It would be easy to raid across the river, putting that damned Taggart on the defensive for once. And with all the Worker Army gone, all the gear and equipment and seeds and food gone, Taggart would have to fend for himself instead of expanding at Ree's expense.

Another thought struck Ree. The Americans' delusional general, who thought himself their Commander-in-Chief, would have simple, direct access to Taggart once Ree's troops were no longer blocking them. Ree allowed himself to smile for a moment. "Taggart, you are the mouse. One shouldn't be friends with a cat, if one is the mouse..."

Ree pulled a map and a notepad from his desk drawer. Time to begin planning.

* * *

Taggart looked at the spreadsheet again, its rectangles on the laptop monitor silently taunting him. He would have liked to smash the damn thing, but of course he couldn't. Working computers couldn't be easily replaced, there being painfully few left.

"Eagan, no matter which way I go, no matter what plan I try, I can't see a way to feed everyone until harvest time. We have lots of land, but most of it was the stuff Ree hadn't cleared yet. We've captured lots of fortifications, all of those little mini-castles Ree built, but they were mostly already empty when we took them away from him."

Eagan nodded. "It's as though he has all his supplies gathered up somewhere in the middle of his territory. Our scouts haven't found it yet. Lately, we haven't sent scouts more than half a mile into the gook's territory without them going missing, presumed dead."

"Don't call him a gook, shitbird. When you belittle your enemy like that, you underestimate him. It's comforting, but we can't afford to fool ourselves that way. Leave self-comfort to the troops."

Eagan shrugged. "You got it, sir. But you know, he really hasn't done very well as a military leader. I'm not sure I could underestimate the man in that regard if I tried."

Taggart's eyes glittered with mirth. "Funny. And flattering, maybe. But I actually don't believe it. We've been lucky so far and a lot of things fallen our way. The NorKors wouldn't send an idiot for a theater as important as this one."

"Better to be lucky than good, they say."

"Yeah, until the luck runs out. Skill wins in the end, given enough time. Every time, Eagan."

"So don't give him time, sir. Let's flank him and get to where the good stuff is. He has seeds and livestock somewhere. A surprise raid deep into his territory, seize his goods, and then return to our own territory."

Taggart chuckled. "I see someone's been reading my railway condition reports and hypothetical operations notes."

Eagan smirked. "No, sir. I'd never read the stack of hand-written reports you keep in your locked drawer, the ones you never have me send out to Dark Ryder or the 20s."

Taggart let out a long breath, put his hands behind his head, and leaned back in his office chair. "That's not a bad idea you came up with," Taggart said, playing along with the game and pretending there weren't reports squirreled away in his drawer. "I suppose you think we should use the railways to move our entire force north of Ree and then push south, and hit him when he's travel-weary."

"That's my idea, yes sir, I thought about it all night," Eagan said with a poorly suppressed grin. "But seriously. If we could hit them hard enough by surprise, we could dislodge them, push them south out of midtown, and take over their operational area. It's got better land, more debris cleared, fields already plowed. It might not be farming Cassy's way, but if we took Ree's depots..."

"...we'd have enough food and seeds to see us through the year, and buy us time to show people how to put her radical ideas into practice."

"Yes, sir. It would be a shame, giving up all the earthworks we've done. Contouring, retainer ponds, all those things. But on the other hand, I don't think Ree would even recognize what the hell it was all for. He'd see it and laugh about how stupid we were, because as everyone knows, the best way to farm is to make everything flat and lined up in neat rows covering thousands of acres."

"You talk too much, Eagan. And I think all of that would look pretty familiar to the peasant farmers among his troops. But yeah, I think he'll just be pissed at how much work it'll take to undo what we did. He'll want quick-producing regular farms, not Cassy's thing."

"Yes, sir. I would love to be here when General Kimchi sees all this. He'll be super pissed."

Taggart leaned forward and rested his elbows on his knees. "We have to dislodge the enemy from his positions, first, so we can occupy his op area ourselves. And he's taking all the food he can carry for a reason."

"True. But your plan—the one that you didn't hide in your drawer—is a good one. A three-pronged attack that allows us to envelop a third to a half of his remaining forces and defeat that portion in detail, leaving us to face the rest of his forces at odds that favor us. Surprise is the key. It's also the biggest risk, because they've been spotting our scouts somehow. Why wouldn't they spot us and report to Ree? If that happens..."

"We'd have to send in the most experienced troops first to infiltrate and envelop. Then the less experienced troops can follow in part and smash into the pockets of enemy forces the more experienced troops created. We risk the core of our army at first, but if it all went sideways those are the same troops best able fight their way out, which our scout teams lacked the manpower to do. We wouldn't lose most of them, I think."

It would work. It had to work, because if they didn't try then Taggart would lose a significant portion of his forces to starvation and desertion before the end of summer, before the big harvests could begin. It was do-or-die for his half-civilian "army," but unfortunately Ree was in the same do-or-die situation. There was nothing easy about it, as Eagan knew perfectly well, but they really had no alternatives. Okay, failure not permitted.

Taggart nodded. "That's what my report would say, if I had written one."

The two men glanced simultaneously toward his desk drawer, then at each other, smiling.

- 18 -

0700 HOURS - ZERO DAY +250

SAMUEL LOOKED AT his raiders, sitting on their bikes lined up in three rows. Morning light filtered over the top of the hill but hid the rising sun. On the other side of that hill lay not just a clear view of the sun but a small settlement—close to Clanholme, capital of the enemy.

Brett nudged Samuel's arm with his elbow. "This ought to be a piece of cake, Captain," he said with a grin.

Samuel nodded. He had roughly one-hundred raiders, while the village had maybe forty people from what recon had revealed. Not all of the villagers were even armed. And Samuel would have the element of surprise. Best of all, the dipshits hadn't finished their wall, yet. The whole place was wide open.

"Only if we get in quickly. They have sentries, and they'll see us and raise the alarm. We have to get in there and buzz around like a swarm of bees before they can get their act together. Bust in doors, torch the buildings, the whole nine yards."

Brett lost his smile. He scratched his elbow as he said, "It sucks that some of their kids will get torched. I'd rather just shoot them, you know."

Samuel shrugged. What could he do about it? "I know what you mean, yeah. But we don't have time to screw around in there. It's gotta be a lightning raid. If you see any, kill them quick, but don't fuck this up. Go in, torch the place, kill everyone. Leave nothing but a memory that this place ever existed."

"I know, man. I know. We're too deep in Confed turf to screw around." Brett looked down at his handlebars, lips pursed.

Samuel understood Brett's feelings. He didn't like the idea of kids burning up either, but there was no way around it. Just as messed up, the strike-and-burn raid wouldn't leave any time to play with the pretty young ladies who were sure to be in there. Oh well, he'd had plenty of playtime at the last homestead they hit. Usually they left the buildings and supplies for the units who'd come after, and the settlers who'd come after that.

Samuel said, "Screw it. Might as well have some fun. I bet you half a coin that I can shoot more kids than you."

Brett grinned. "Fine, you're on. I get to spare some kids from burning, get some easy target practice, and take your money. Hells yeah."

Some of the lined-up troops, close enough to hear the conversation, chuckled at their exchange. Someone spoke up and said, "That half-coin's mine, sir!" and as news of the bet spread through the line, the words rose like a hushed chant, repeated over and over.

Samuel realized the troops were probably hating the idea of burning the buildings with children in them. What kind of monster enjoyed hurting kids? Samuel didn't, and even Brett hesitated unless they were pretty and almost adults. Every one of them knew shooting a kid was saving some little boy or girl from burning or starving. It was a way out from guilt.

Samuel let the chant go for a while, knowing they needed the release, before he raised his hand for silence and the voices trailed off to nothing. "Alright, you've all been briefed," he said when he had their full attention, "and you know what's expected. These guys are some of the Clan's best allies. On top of what we did to those people at the railway station, this blow will take the fight right out of the Confederation. It'll secure an alliance with Elizabethtown's survivors. And it'll clear the path for a direct strike against Clanholme when our army shows up. We can't afford to screw this up. Anyone who doesn't throw a torch, doesn't shoot their rifle, I will personally cut off your nuts and stuff them down your throat. Got it?"

"Yes, Captain," they said in unison.

Samuel smiled. This unit had become top-notch since this mission began. Tight-knit and a lot of combat experience. When they got back to the rear, they'd probably all get their own squads. It was a nice thought. "Well then. Ready arms, ready torches. Make sure you got your lighters handy. It's showtime. And—attack!"

Wordlessly, one hundred men and women pushed off and began pedaling up the hill. As they reached the crest, they pedaled even harder and, with gravity's help, they were soon going full speed. None made a sound, other than the faint clanging of gear bouncing around on mountain bikes.

Samuel himself reached the crest and stopped, three of his troops with him. Brett continued on, his right hand man making sure everyone did their part quickly and brutally. Samuel watched the cloud of bikes swarming toward the large homestead. Two-hundred yards. One-hundred-fifty yards.

He heard the crisp, clear sound of a rifle being fired, and cursed. Whoever shot early would be—

Wait. The puff of smoke came from one of the buildings'

upstairs windows. Then another and then a dozen. Samuel lifted his binoculars and scanned the scene. His troops dropped like flies, at least a dozen down. They began returning fire, but they were far from close enough to torch anything, yet.

He stopped, took a deep breath. At least two dozen people in various positions in the buildings, firing at his troops. They had cover and elevation. His people were on bikes and out in the open. Speed might have saved them, but they had slowed almost to a halt under the hail of gunfire, leaving them standing up and exposed.

Screw it. Best to lose a dozen fighters than a hundred. He whipped his air horn from his handlebar bag and blew three short, ear-piercing blasts, the signal for retreat. He waited two seconds, then did it again.

Through the binoculars he saw his people turn to run. More fell, shot in the back as they rode for their lives. And then they were beyond the one-hundred-meter mark, and fewer fell as the defenders' lack of real training showed—they weren't able to hit much at that range. He scanned the death ground between him and the village and counted about twenty people down. Not all were dead, but there was no way to go back for them. Sorry, people. He hoped Brett wasn't one of them.

* * *

Frank rode at a canter to keep his horse fresh for the actual battle charge. All around him, the hooves of one-hundred-twenty horses nearly deafened him. Every one of Taggart's soldiers who could hang on to a horse, and as many Clanners as could be spared. When the urgent radio call from Taj Mahal came in saying they were about to be attacked, Cassy hadn't wanted Frank to go. She had wanted to do this herself, but the Clan could lose him and the Confederation couldn't lose Cassy. He had put his foot down on that one.

He grinned at his choice of words, and glanced at his amputated foot, now a stump tucked into a special leather stirrup Dean had whipped up for him. That grumpy old man could make almost anything from scraps of nothing, just like Frank's best friend Jed had done before he got killed by 'vaders early on. Jed would have loved this Ride of the Valkyries. Then the notes of that old classic piece of music echoed through Frank's mind: Bum-dada-duuum-dum...

Ahead, possibly over the next rise, Frank heard the faint, random *tic-tic-tic* of distant gunfire. A chill ran up his spine as his heart pounded faster, eager for battle, eager to get payback on some Empire assholes. There would be no damn mercy given.

His horse galloped over the crest of the hill, and he saw below him several hundred yards away, the cluster buildings that made up Taj Mahal.

Frank saw what must be every able-bodied teenager and adult, up in the windows and on the roofs of the buildings facing east, pouring on heavy fire. They were shooting at dozens and dozens of people on mountain bikes, who were fleeing to the back side of a hill. From Frank's angle, he could see both the front and back of the hill, a side view, and saw a cluster of people there on the back side.

"Those must be their leaders," Frank shouted over the hoofbeats and wind, and he saw Michael turn his head where Frank was pointing.

Michael nodded, and turned his horse a bit east to make a beeline for the smaller group. "Follow me," yelled Michael, his gruff military-trained voice carrying over the din with ease, and the entire Clan wedge pivoted crazily.

Frank thought he could see one of the people on the hill's back side pointing toward him and his Clanners. A second later, both the cluster of retreating cyclists and the smaller group turned bikes southward, away from the oncoming cavalry, and pedaled furiously.

The Clan rescuers had already ridden hard for two miles, but at a pace that wouldn't wear out the horses. No doubt terrified, the enemy had all the adrenaline they needed to get moving, and quickly. They veered onto White Oak Road heading south, and Frank and his troops struggled to keep up. He only hoped the raiders would exhaust themselves before his horses did. A mile later, he and his cavalry had closed the distance quite a lot, now only a quarter mile behind, before Michael had insisted on slowing for the horses' sakes, saying that the horses would wear out the bike riders before they wore out, if they kept to the right speed.

So this was to be an endurance run, it seemed. Frank settled into his saddle and tried not to get too mesmerized by his horse's rhythmic gait.

* * *

Samuel felt his forehead grow damp despite the early morning chill, now that the sun was truly up. He glanced over his shoulder and saw that the horse mob behind him was trailing a little further back, now that he and his troops had hit a long, slight downhill stretch. He felt relief wash over him as Brett pulled up beside him, but knew he was far from done. His only real hope was to exhaust those horses in the chase, but had no idea whether bikes could wear out horses. He imagined they could—after all, that French bike race was, like, a thousand miles or something ridiculous—but some of his less fit troops were sure to fall out before that and would no doubt face a quick death at the hands of those Clan bastards.

A mile ahead lay Manheim, another Confed settlement.

Scouts had said they were well armed, but had only a few bikes of their own. They had plenty of horses, but scattered in stalls near the farming areas outside of town. Manheim had some weird system where a few people owned all the land and had sharecroppers under them. Their military was a militia system, with the officers being those landowners. The sharecroppers had to serve in the militia when called, if they wanted to eat. Feudal, really.

For a moment, Samuel thought of grabbing some horses from one of their farms, but decided against it. He didn't know exactly where they were, the horses chasing him would go much faster than he could off-road, and half his troops would probably shoot him themselves to get a horse. Screw it —he rode onward.

In the distance, he saw Manheim and was close enough to make out the individual buildings. The land leveled out and he began to slow a little, but as long as they didn't have to go uphill they should be fine.

Movement ahead. A jolt of alarm ran through him as he watched what appeared to be a dark, spreading mass emerge from the town—people, dozens and dozens, crawling out of their disgusting backwoods hole to get in his way. Samuel hissed at them through clenched teeth, and feverishly wished he could kill them all, beating them to death one by one.

There was no way his long, snaking column of bikes was going to get through that. He had hoped to punch through the deserted outer rim of the city, ditching the pursuing horses and losing only a few of his own people, but that option was gone. On his right lay a river, so he couldn't go that way, and to his left, he remembered, was a network of streams or rivers. If he went that way, he'd only be corralling himself and his people.

Just as he was about to give the order to charge, hoping some of his people might make it out alive, he spotted a bridge ahead on his right. A sign said "W. Henley Rd." Samuel grinned. That road led east to Old Line Road, and *that* road would take him to Elizabethtown. If they could get there, the burnt-out and abandoned northern half of the city would be the perfect place to lose his pursuers. Hell, the Confed troops might be unwilling to chase them into Liz Town's turf, and he knew the occupants weren't going to involve themselves. They were halfway to being Empire subjects, after all. He shouted, "Column right, at the bridge!"

The column slithered to the right, but had to slow almost to a halt in the rear. In a minute it turned from an orderly crossing to utter chaos as people struggled to get through, getting in each other's way and slowing the whole process. Samuel grit his teeth. Those were his troops... But to hell with it. At least they'd slow the chasers, and he and Brett were already across. He kept riding.

* * *

Frank saw the column turn and cursed—if they got across that bridge, this was going to be one long chase indeed. Michael must have had the same thought, because he shouted orders to spread out and move from a fast canter to a full gallop. Not a sprint, but still plenty fast.

Ahead, the bike column was getting itself twisted into knots at the bridge, and the swarm of Manheim soldiers—Cassy had stationed an entire company of Taggart's troops there—was rapidly closing on the column's other flank. Frank's heart surged with joy. They were going to slaughter these bastards, or at least a lot of them.

When Michael got within about eighty yards, he called for the unit to halt and dismounted. Frank stayed on his horse but pulled out his M4 from its leather saddle holster. As he called out to fire, the world erupted in noise and smoke as over one hundred men and women opened up on the cluster of raiders, who were bunched up at the bridge like ants swarming another insect. Manheim's troops did the same a few seconds later, and together they unleashed a full magazine. Frank fired small bursts until his magazine was empty. *Bap-bap. Bap-bap.*

Michael called for reloading, but there wasn't anything left to shoot at. When the smoke cleared, only a few enemies were moving at the bridge, and Manheim's troops advanced to finish them off. The bulk of the raiders were across and pedaling hard. Frank yelled, "Mount up! We got more of those assholes to catch. Get some!"

The troops cheered and mounted up. While the Manheim troops frantically cleared the clusterfuck of bikes and bodies, Frank and his unit snaked their way carefully through the carnage and across the bridge, avoiding the bikes still in their way. It was frustrating and damn slow, and every minute let the rest of the raiders get farther ahead. He did a quick tally and only counted some twenty bodies or so. Figure thirty dead, then, since he couldn't have seen them all —that left roughly fifty or sixty raiders still alive.

Frank waved to the Manheim troops as he went by and saw in the distance, behind them, little clusters of horse-mounted people riding toward him. The Manheimers were sending out what horses they had readily available, joining in the pursuit. Even better.

He and his cavalry kept up their steady pace, eating distance. After about a mile, the column of raiders turned right on what must be Old Line Road. If they stayed on that, it would take them through the deserted part of Liz Town, the so-called wildlands. He wasn't at all certain Liz Town would lift a finger to stop them, given the news he heard from Ethan in council meetings.

Michael, riding next to him, said, "If they hit Liz Town,

they'll scatter and we'll lose half of them."

"I know," was all Frank said in reply. It was true, of course, but spurring their horses to go faster would wear them out. They were closing the distance, but slowly. Still, Frank and his troops would be fresh when they finally caught up to the raiders while they would be exhausted. With the cavalry joining Frank from Manheim, he outnumbered the raiders roughly two-to-one. It would be a slaughter—if he could just catch them.

* * *

Samuel glanced again behind him, but the cavalry hadn't magically disappeared, and his own troops hadn't magically respawned. He still had maybe half his unit left, and they were tired. Hell, he was tired, and he was in better shape than most of them. They must be about ready to fall over. He turned to face ahead again and focused on pedaling. He worked toward getting into that Zen-like state where the rhythm of pedaling and the yellow lines on the road going by would act almost like a trance. "In the zone," Brett had called it. When he was in the zone, he felt like he could pedal damn near forever. He had gotten good at it riding all over the damn Midwest Republic, and the trip out here to this goddamn place.

Brett, panting, said, "How many... miles you figure...?"

Samuel didn't really know, but he could guesstimate. "Maybe two miles till Elizabeth." He didn't have the breath to say the whole damn name. When they went Republic, he was going to make them change it to something shorter.

Another mile went by, but then he saw the sprawl of Elizabethtown up ahead, smoke from dozens of small fires rising into the air on the south end of town, to the left, showing where most of the populated area was. A mile to go.

He glanced back again, but the horses were still there. Maybe even closer.

Abruptly the pedaling got easier, and he realized they had been on a slight incline for the last mile. Now they were heading downhill toward the streams that flowed through the town. Up ahead he saw a road sign: "PA-283 OVERPASS." Hot damn! His spirit soared, because on the other side of the bridge ahead was the abandoned part of Elizabethtown.

"Get ready," he shouted, and heard the call being repeated down the line of troops. "After the bridge, scatter northwest." The call was repeated once again.

He crossed the bridge going as fast as his tired legs would carry him with the slight help of gravity taking him downhill. As far ahead as he could see, the rubble wall of Liz Town lined the road. There were people on the wall, too, and more appeared even while he looked. They knew he was coming, somehow. He only hoped his intel was right, and they wouldn't open fire, but he wanted to get off that road and onto side streets going away from the wall as fast as possible.

He rode a few hundred feet more until he reached a promising-looking side street going north, away from the wall. This was it—time to fan out and whoever made it out alive could celebrate cheating death. He banked his bike, taking the turn as fast as he could. He almost hit the sidewalk curb on the other side of the street, but made the turn without crashing. He and the ten or so other lead bikes then headed north on Hickory Lane, according to the sign. Up ahead were dozens of cross streets, enough for everyone to fan out. It would make them hard to chase.

He also saw ahead that, along the power lines running on both sides of the street—or maybe they were phone lines?—were wooden pallets dangling from lengths of rope. That was odd, but he paid no mind; people did a lot of weird shit these days.

Sweet, sweet freedom was just ahead! All he had to do was get out of sight long enough to take cover in one of the many abandoned houses. Let the others keep running. They'd give the Clan riders someone to chase besides him and the few troops with him.

He heard what sounded like an elk call, which was weird —most of the ruins had enough people left that game either stayed away or got eaten. He shook his head to clear it. He didn't have time to screw around nature watching.

Abruptly, the pallets fell in unison. For a moment, everything seemed to shift into slow-motion. He saw the pallets falling. He saw something metallic glinting on them. And then, to his horror, he realized what the metal was—barbed wire had been strung across the road between pairs of pallets.

His view suddenly shifted from the road ahead and the falling pallets to the sky, and he became aware of a terrible yanking on his hoodie. His bike kept going. He heard it crash at the same time he landed on his back in the road. A sudden, sharp pain jabbed his neck, like a tiny stab wound and he realized with sudden clarity that he had landed on barbed wire, the same barbed wire that had snagged him off his bike.

All around him, he heard the crashing and cries of alarm from other riders also falling. He turned his head and saw a woman's front wheel impaled by the wire, momentum carrying the bike forward, and the wire was pulled up with it. It tangled into the axle and the bike jerked to a stop, but the rear rose up and flipped over the front wheel—she smashed face-first into the pavement.

Samuel struggled to his feet, but was knocked over by another man on a bike. The man crashed to the ground and managed somehow to skid ten more feet, getting caught up in multiple strands of wire as the road raspberried his exposed skin through torn leathers.

Struggling with the wire caught in his hoodie, Samuel got to his hands and knees but quickly gave up and, with desperate haste, simply pulled the hoodie off. He then crawled to the nearest downed bike, pulled the rifle from its handlebar holster and looked around.

The length of road was littered with his troops. A few people were wrapped in wire, struggling and crying out. Nearby, a man lay still in the road with a pool of blood spreading from his neck; barbed wire was wrapped completely around his throat. The sight made Samuel acutely aware of the hot, wet blood trickling down his own neck, and he shuddered.

Those fucking Liz Town traitors had turned on him. That was the only explanation. He felt his rage rise at the wall, visible in the distance back the way he had come from. When he got back to the Republic, goddammit, he was going make sure this entire fucking town burned...

A shot rang out to his left. His head snapped toward the sound, and he saw a ratty-looking man holding a pistol, leaning out of an abandoned house's window. He fired slowly and methodically at the nearest raiders, hitting every time. Fucker. Samuel snapped his rifle to his shoulder, planted his cheek on the stock, and scoped in on the man's heart. *Bang.* The asshole dropped without a sound, dead instantly, and lay half in and half out of the window.

Brett's voice behind him startled him. "Boss, we gotta get the fuck out of here."

"No shit," Samuel snapped. He saw that there were about ten men and women with him and Brett. Dozens littered the streets or scattered in other directions in small groups, abandoning their bikes. "Let's go," he told Brett, turning away from the window with its dead man, and headed toward another abandoned house. They could go through the yard, but first they had to get the hell off the street.

Horse hooves, lots of them. The noise reached his ears and he sped up his pace. Bullets bounced around all over the place, ricocheting, but didn't seem to be fired directly at him. That was common in battle. It didn't mean one of those wouldn't kill someone just the same, though. He heard hooves approach rapidly, and without looking back, Samuel and Brett dove over a low hedge. Samuel tucked himself into the hedgerow as best he could and held his breath—the hooves went by seconds later without slowing.

Brett whispered, "Damn, that was close."

"Let's get into that house." Samuel rose to a crouch on the balls of his feet, one hand holding his rifle and the other on the ground for balance. He counted to three and then Brett and he sprinted toward the side gate. Samuel didn't check to see if it was unlocked, and simply jumped up and rolled himself over the top. Brett landed nearly on top of him.

Samuel looked around and got his bearings. "Brett, the house on the other side—it faces an alley. Better to hide out there than here by the street."

"You think?" Brett bolted toward the back fence line with Samuel hot on his heels. They made it up and over, landing in a brown, winter-killed yard. The house looked empty, with a broken window. A door hung crazily on one hinge. Samuel said, "Looks good. Go!"

They crossed the backyard and dove into the house in moments. After a pause to let his eyes adjust, rifle at the ready, Samuel saw the house was indeed abandoned. It looked like it had been ransacked quite some time ago, and there was no sign of habitation since then. "Upstairs. Stay low, dammit. We can peer out the upper windows, but if anyone comes in we got a chance to get out before they know we're here."

As they went up the stairs slowly, rifles raised, Samuel wondered what would happen when he got back to the Republic. Would they give him more troops, or hang him? It could go either way. Keeping Brett alive had to be his priority right now, though, because if things went sideways when he got back to the Republic, he could always blame Brett. Sorry, buddy...

* * *

Frank watched the scene unfold from his saddle, but only took the occasional shot at an opportune target. The battle was a massacre, and the Empire raiders quickly went from disorganized unit to dead. People scattered in all directions, fleeing the carnage. Frank hurriedly coordinated with the soldiers to get a perimeter set up.

He looked at the barbed wire contraption—dozens of wires strung between pallets. They had been hung from a rope via loops of wire, the rope strung along the power lines by means of carabiners along their length. When the local wildlanders had somehow released the long ropes, the weight of the palettes made the whole thing—ropes, pallets, wires and all—come crashing down. It was crude but effective, and had allowed the winded cavalry to catch up, smashing into the raiders like a hammer.

He caught movement from the corner of his eye and looked. Two raiders were vaulting a back fence, and he saw them as they went up and over. "Soldier," he called, getting one's attention. "Take five men to that house," he said, pointing at the abandoned house he thought they had gone to. "At least two raiders just jumped that fence. Be careful."

The battle itself wound down to nothing. All that was left

was to put the wounded out of their misery and gather up all the weapons and ammo they could. It would be quite a score, Frank was certain.

Michael, on foot, came up beside Frank, panting. He had blood spatters all over his face, arms, and chest. "Add their guns to the supplies we confiscated. And with the supplies they stocked up in some of those abandoned farms, we'll be sitting pretty. The Empire won't have forward bases. Not bad."

Frank nodded. "It's a feather in our cap. And when you take a look behind us, look at the Liz Town wall. I saw dozens of people up there, watching. They didn't lift a finger to help."

"What about the trap? Pretty damn helpful."

"That wasn't Liz Town," Frank said, shaking his head. "That was the abandoned survivors out here in their 'wildlands,' not our supposed allies."

Michael shrugged. "Interesting. Let's be sure to parade past them on our way out, yeah? I think Cassy just got her show of strength she was looking for."

Frank glanced down at Michael. "Wow. Yeah, I think you're right. Let's be sure to salute them as we go by."

Frank saw the five troops he had sent after the two escapees. They approached, nodded to Michael—technically their military C.O. right now—and then to Frank. "Sir," one said, "there were two inside just like you said. They were upstairs. Two of us kept them pinned, while the others went around back and went after them inside. Short fight, two dead. We grabbed their weapons and left 'em there."

"Outstanding," Frank said. "Let's get all the loot up on the horses and get out of here."

Twenty minutes later, the enemy arsenal was packed up and the Confed wounded cared for. There had been a few losses, and a number of injuries, but for the most part it had been an Empire slaughter. They probably had fewer than twenty survivors, scattered in all directions. They weren't a military threat anymore.

At Frank's word, Michael commanded the column forward, and they kept the pace to a walk. The unit, stretched out like a snake now, slithered down the road toward the wall, and then along the length of that wall back toward the bridge. The wall was full of people who had watched the battle. Frank saw a knot of four or five people, standing tightly around another figure.

Frank figured that must be Liz Town's Interim Speaker. As he led the column past the man, Frank raised his rifle over his head in salute, and grinned. Then he pointedly turned to face the road again and continued on without looking back.

Just as he turned, though, he saw that figure punch the rubble and spin on his heels. Good, let that weaselly Empire-loving bastard fume. Everyone else in Liz Town saw it, too, and they seemed to have a different opinion, cheering down at the passing victors below.

Frank couldn't wait to tell Cassy about all of this.

- 19 -

1900 HOURS - ZERO DAY +250

CASSY SAT ON the recliner in her living room while Michael and Dean Jepson sat on the couch across from her. Outside, she heard the faint buzz of people coming and going with bandages, water, or other supplies to care for the wounded. Michael had just finished giving his report on the Battle of Liz Town. No doubt someday soon it would be called First Liz Town. It was a sobering thought.

Cassy said, "And you're sure the Interim Speaker was on the wall? They saw the battle?"

"Affirmative. I don't think it could have been anyone else. And he looked upset. I think it confirms your suspicions."

"That's bad news, but the good news is that the people themselves were cheering. There's still hope the whole town hasn't forgotten their own best interests, even if this dirtbag Speaker has."

Michael nodded. "No word on when they'll hold their election, but you know Liz Town. They're tight-lipped."

Cassy looked to Dean and was silent for a moment, considering the old man. He was rough-hewn oak, for sure. He could outpace a lot of the younger Clanners with his work, and his ideas were more valuable than most she heard. His curmudgeonly ways had grown on her, too—he was more entertaining than irritating now, a fact the kids had discovered long before the rest of the Clan adults did. They adored him and somehow he always had time for them.

"So, Dean. How are things going with the planes?"

Dean almost spat, but then apparently realized he was in someone's living room and reined himself in. He straightened himself, lifting his head, and answered, "If you can find some fool crazy enough to climb aboard, I got some new tricks for them to try out. But sure as hell, you ain't getting me up in one of them things. I call 'em death buckets."

Death buckets? Those words were surely his wife's and not his. Though it would make sense she wouldn't want him setting foot in one, and even if he wanted to, a good husband stood by his woman. After all, it didn't seem to change his enthusiasm about his work. As long as he got the job done it didn't matter to Cassy whether his wife had a few unfavorable words with him about his new project.

Cassy nodded. "Okay. What have you got?"

"Two things. First, I wired up some rifles under the wings. Now that we got all them AK rifles from the raiders, I'm gonna put those on instead of your pansy-ass M4s, all firin' at once. It'll work just like we talked. One good strafing run and they'll be on empty, but we got two on each side, so four AKs. It'll be a good run, they just need to make 'em count."

"That's great, Dean. I knew we could count on you." Cassy saw the older man seem to inflate with quiet pride, all while maintaining his dour expression. "How about the bombs?"

"Nothing doing. I can't figure out how to make the planes into bombers like in them old war videos with the doors underneath. They'll just have to drop 'em like we talked before. But," he said, with emphasis on the last word, "I did something the pilots might like. We didn't talk about this, but I didn't reckon you'd mind. I mounted two *more* of them AK rifles on the left wings on all the planes. They don't shoot straight, nope. Them things are pointed to shoot to the left. So while they're circling like vultures dropping bombs, they can shoot at the ground, too. I think the Army had a plane like that in Vietnam."

Michael broke in. "They did, but it was a chain gun basically. It relied on a huge volume of fire to suppress the enemy on the ground. I don't think it'll be as effective with AKs."

Dean sniffed. "Who asked you? What are you, seventeen?"

Michael smirked, but shut up. Cassy sighed. Thank goodness Michael humored the grumpy old man. Michael seemed to want nothing more than to keep such people safe. They were the ones who couldn't protect themselves without help. Maybe that was a Marine Corps trait, maybe a general military trait. Maybe it was just something found in any good man. Either way, Michael's affable good humor made her job easier.

Cassy said, "I still think it's genius. We'll give them a try in the first engagement and if they're effective, we'll keep them."

Dean grunted and calmed down.

"Thanks for the update, Dean. Is there anything else you'd like to add before we dismiss?"

"Yeah. The missus says you're doing this whole thing wrong, and you should have an 'action council,' on building more of them worm latrines."

The Clan's outhouses drained into small cement cisterns, buried and filled with earth worms and shredded paper, at least at the start. Then, liquids passed into channels lined first with filtering plants before the resulting clean water dumped out into the ponds, where more plants continued to filter as part of the detoxification process. The solids got eaten by the worms and turned into worm castings, an even better source of plant nutrients than most compost. When mixed with regular compost, the castings greatly improved plant growth and made the most efficient possible use of both castings and compost.

Installing the cisterns was difficult because they required the cement distributor boxes used by septic tanks—they were heavy and had to be transported by wagon from wherever they could be found. But keeping Dean's wife out of Cassy's hair without giving her something to do was even more difficult.

"Okay, Dean. Please let her know that I authorized her action council if she will lead it and find people willing to join in the effort. Improved efficiency is always good. Tell her we'll need about twice as many as we have now, and I thank her for thinking of a council to lead the effort. But it has to be volunteer hours—we can't afford to take anyone off the farming tasks, especially this time of year."

Dean smiled then, and Cassy got the impression he'd be glad to get her out of his own hair for a few hours here and there. "I always did tell the missus that you ain't as stupid as some folks say."

Some folks would be his wife, of course... Cassy grinned. "Thanks for that, Dean. I think."

She watched as Dean left, then turned to broach a more serious problem with Michael. "Do you think our victory on Liz Town's doorstep will make a difference?"

"With the Lizzies, it's hard to say. At the very least, it will motivate the loyalists. Nothing inspires bravery like success. Those people lining the wall were definitely glad to see us still living up to our promises. Of course, maybe they're just the local malcontents. We don't know enough about Liz Town politics to tell if the current leaders really have popular support."

Cassy nodded. "Ain't that the truth." She'd have to think of some way to get better inside intel. Maybe they still had supporters lurking in the main town. One more thing, always one more thing.

* * *

Ethan sat with his sketchbook open on his lap. He couldn't sketch worth a damn, but the pads were perfect for jotting down notes and writing out ideas to solidify them in his mind. Something about handwriting seemed to draw from a different part of the brain, and sometimes it helped for solving complex problems. Like the current one. How could he restore electronic communications with all the allies, securely and instantly? Secure email, especially, would be invaluable.

Amber sat in the other desk chair in a pair of his boxers and one of his tee shirts. That made it harder to concentrate, but he wasn't about to say anything that might make her go change. She had been watching him unconsciously rock back and forth in thought, knowing that she'd never completely fathom the way his strange hacker mind connected things up in new patterns. But perhaps it was fun to watch him doing it.

When he finally looked up at her, she said, "So you found a way to get hundreds of computers networked? Why not just use wifi?"

Ethan set his pencil down in the crease of his black faux-leather sketchbook. "Sort of. I think it'll work. You've heard of those simple computer boards the size of an Altoids tin? Raspberry Pi?"

"Yeah, they were in the news now and then, I remember."

"Well, we found a warehouse of something a lot like those. Each was sealed in mylar bags that acted almost like Faraday cages. Half of them still work, maybe more. Since I have computers that still work, down here, I could program the boards. The problem is telling them what to do. There's damn little internet left, and satellites are still up there working but you need the guts of a sat-phone to connect them to a computer. Not many of those left working since when in use they were wide open to the EMP."

"So, you have half of this, half of that. Can you just run ethernet cable? There's gotta be miles and miles of that stuff lying around."

"Probably, but the signal couldn't carry that far. They weren't designed for that. Those cables attract rodents, too, but I never knew why. I might try to connect to the fiber optic cables lying around everywhere, because they *were* designed for that, but I don't know how to make the link between those and the computer. It takes hardware we don't have."

"Nothing online?"

Ethan shook his head. "There's damn little 'online' left in the world. I haven't found anything trustworthy on it so far, but don't have endless hours to look, either. There's no big search engine working, you know. It's a matter of connect, look around. Connect, look around. It's internet, but it's not the Web."

Amber frowned. "I take it they aren't quite the same thing. Well, why not ask the Mountain? They think you're one of theirs, and they must have all sorts of useful knowledge stockpiled, just as part of their contingency planning."

Ethan started to shake his head, then stopped. Maybe

she was right. They did think he was one of theirs, and even if they had their doubts, the knowledge he looked for couldn't possibly harm them. He'd just have to come up with a plausible scenario to get them to take the time to search out what he was looking for and a good reason for them to give it to him. "Thanks. That's not a bad idea. I'll think about how to ask in a way that gets them to go look it up for me. If they have the knowledge stored somewhere, of course."

"Of course. Well, I need to go get dressed."

"Nooo!" Ethan cried out in mock horror. His cheeks reddened a little and he added, "I like looking at you dressed like that." By now, she was wearing a very large smile.

"Yeah, sorry," she said around the smile, "but I need to go help get all the kids tucked in and so forth. And I'm hungry again."

"I wonder why," Ethan said as he wiggled his eyebrows.

Amber laughed, then stood, her long legs uncoiling from where she had sat curled up on the chair. He watched her leave and wished they had more time together tonight. Maybe she'd sneak back later, if she could get away. Family obligations had to come first, of course, but that didn't make it less frustrating for him.

After she had dressed and left him with a kiss, he set down his sketchbook and opened up his laptop. He went through the motions, receiving information from the few places around the world where people could still connect to the internet. Then he went on the HAM radio and monitored for traffic, but nothing noteworthy came up.

He was about to call it quits for the night when his computer chirped with an incoming message alert. He set up the virtual machine, the sandbox, all the usual precautions, and then opened up the chat box. It was Watcher One, of course. The cursor blinked for a moment, and a message popped up. It consisted only of a string of numbers, which

Ethan realized were coordinates, a date, and a time. There was also a .txt file attached.

He opened the attachment and found a brief note. It said only, "Supply run heading to our friend back east. Will support important offensive. Provide escort through the region. Top Priority, Urgent."

The date was two days away. What the hell could be so important as to risk an overland journey to the east coast, all the way from Colorado? Ethan's curiosity was piqued. For whatever reason, he couldn't shake a nagging feeling of doubt. No one risked that kind of a journey unless it was vitally important. They had to know he wouldn't buy that story, but what was their game? Did they want to weaken Clanholme by sending people away just before the Empire mounted an attack? Or did they hope Clanholme would maybe lead them to Taggart's current location? That business of promising drones but instead setting up an invader ambush had led Taggart to stay as invisible to "the Mountain," as he called General Houle's Colorado HQ, as he could.

He'd have to tell Cassy about this and see if she or Michael had any ideas. And they'd need to arrange the escort to maintain credibility as allies of Gen. Houle. "Supplies, my ass," he muttered.

* * *

0900 HOURS - ZERO DAY +251

General Ree stood in the passenger side of the convertible "American muscle car," a vehicle festooned with high-quality art airbrushed lovingly onto the 1960s drop-top. His advisors had told him the art was "typical of vehicles for high-ranking members of America's Latino neighborhood mafias."

Apparently, in America every other block had its own mafia. Gang was a more accurate word for it. Now the car had a few bullet holes in it, mementoes of the battle with that Spyder gangster who had once been an ally of sorts. Ree smiled at the memory. Spyder had hated it when Ree talked to him as an officer to an enlisted man, so of course Ree had done that whenever possible. It had kept Spyder off balance.

As the car slowly crested the hill, Ree put away those memories to focus on the task at hand. He had gathered all of his troops and coordinated with those in the City, and they were about to launch a two-pronged assault on the traitor, Taggart. It would end his threat once and for all, and send him scurrying into the wilderness. Ree relished the thought of General Taggart once again being only a Captain. The man had no vision, no concept of how glorious the future would be under the Great Leader, with America's vanity, pride, and violence burned away. When Ree was done, America's old culture would be nothing but rotting bones, just like all those self-important celebrities hanging from poles outside the Lincoln Tunnel.

Ree looked down on the remnants of Hoboken, New Jersey. Like all cities, it was mostly vacant now. Clusters of houses with chimney smoke showed areas where survivors remained, though unlike most towns, Hoboken's survivors were split up in several different compounds. Intel said the compounds all operated under one leader, but independently for their day-to-day tasks.

What he didn't see was an open military presence. Taggart had turned this area into his headquarters after conquering it and the areas south of Hoboken, so Ree had expected to see thousands of troops in a cantonment. Ree raised his binoculars and examined the scene methodically, right to left, far to near. He could see open areas that had clearly been in use recently, but they were vacant now. Bits of paper blew across these open areas, swept along by a breeze coming from the river as the ground warmed up faster than the river waters.

Then Ree saw another large open area littered with pallets. They were in neat, orderly rows, mostly, but a few were tossed aside or smashed up. That area should be full of Taggart's troop supplies, but the pallets were eerily vacant.

In the driver's seat next to him, Major Kim said, "My general, what do you make of this?"

Ree grunted noncommittally. After a long pause, he let out a frustrated breath. "Somehow Taggart must have known we were coming. One doesn't clear out a base of this size in an hour—he had plenty of forewarning." Glancing over, he saw that Kim was recovering from an inadvertent flinch and was careful not to show his satisfaction.

Kim finally replied, "What if he didn't know, but relocated somewhere recently?"

Normally he'd play the master-and-servant game with Kim, but he lacked the energy. He felt like an old schooner that had the wind knocked out of its sails. He had neither wind nor current to guide him. Shaking off the discouragement, he answered Kim. "Either way, it's more important to find out where he went and what he's up to than to wonder why he left. Order Third Regiment to take Hoboken. Third has the best interrogators. Their mission is to find out all the intel we can regarding Taggart and where our old enemy went."

Ree felt a sudden chill of fear. He wasn't used to fear. Normally, he was the master of his world. Even when losing in battle, things proceeded in an orderly, nearly mathematically precise fashion, but this was an uncontrolled variable and he didn't have a solution for it. It was the unknown. The sheer oddity of it all—the strangeness—had Ree spooked and, to an extent he would never reveal to anyone, bewildered.

When uncertain, choose any direction and go. He had learned that as a teenager. Within a few hours, Ree had given orders to his regiments. Targets to take, towns to reconquer or burn, bridges to secure, everything important throughout the region. It had been his to begin with, until Taggart forced his units out, but now he had returned. It should have been a triumphant return, a parade across the corpses of his enemies, but instead Taggart was gone and Ree had no idea where. Yet the enemy undoubtedly knew where Ree was. It was a vulnerable position and the orders he had issued focused on reducing that vulnerability.

His officers finally gave the signal that it was safe for him to enter the town, and he told Kim to proceed. In the town's largest open area, long ago cleared of buildings, his troops had lined up the people still living in Hoboken. Those who didn't resist lined up in rough formation now, well guarded, while those who had resisted were lined up in a neat and orderly stack of corpses that needed no guards. The command elements of his units arrayed themselves in formation nearby, those not in the field to implement his orders.

The civilians, he noted as he drove slowly through the plaza, sullenly eyed the pile of corpses and the rows of officers. Let them eyeball their betters all they liked. These people needed to see the result of resistance. He otherwise ignored them.

Ree's car drifted to a stop facing his rows of officers, and he got out, climbed atop the car's hood, and with his hands behind his back, he let them see his gaze sweep over them all. Finally, he said in a loud voice that carried with the ease of a practiced battlefield commander, "Welcome back, gentlemen." He had no women higher officers—too much of a traditionalist for that.

He paused for the few Arab officers to receive the translation from their assistants, then continued. "The enemy has fled before us," he said, and had to pause as his commanders applauded. He never knew whether it was genuine applause or self-preservation, but it didn't matter. So long as everyone applauded, no one would know who was loyal and who wasn't. "They took as many supplies as they could and abandoned or burned the rest. They abandoned their civilians, as we knew they would."

One of his officers bowed low, and Ree waved his hand for the man to speak. He said, "My general, your victory is at hand. Our survey shows they left behind tons of vegetables, growing in makeshift greenhouses, or 'cold frames,' as the people call them. Shall we harvest these?"

"Of course," Ree replied. "Those glorious farmers who know about these cold frames should be consulted, so that we can expand that program."

Another officer, wearing the Korean emblem of an engineer, bowed and then said, "Sir, they've done extensive earthworks since we... left the area. We don't know what they're for, but—"

Ree cut him off with a raised hand, palm toward the officer. "Yes, I saw those. I don't know what they're for, but think about it. No one wastes effort these days, so you know it isn't for a park or a memorial. It must have something to do with food production. You only have to find out what. Question the liberated People's Worker Army for answers."

"And if they aren't eager to answer, or say they don't know?"

Ree forced himself to wear a smile as natural as the summer sun, but inside he wanted to smack the fool. "It was a huge project. Someone here knows what the ditches and mounts and patterns are for. If they don't want to answer, then... ask harder."

The officer bowed and said nothing further. Ree then looked up and down the line of officers and said, "They have used strange ways of farming, unlike what we've seen elsewhere. But we see it already raising food, unlike the more familiar farms, so I know that we will all have enough to eat, enough for our troops, and enough for your civilians. And when harvest time comes, I expect a bounty unlike anywhere else, because they wouldn't do all this for nothing. We will find out why, and copy it."

Ree paused, looking around the assembled men. Most of these officers would be given landholdings between Hoboken and New York City, while some would return with him to his base in the City. He'd presented land awards—hereditary awards—as a gift for a job well done. But the truth was that only those he trusted the most would come with him back to New York City, and whatever was learned about Taggart's nascent farms and their weird techniques would be implemented in open spaces throughout Manhattan island as well.

In reality, those who stayed in New Jersey were a buffer between Ree and his enemy, Taggart. Between them and the "gifts" his strange western ally would be sending soon, he was certain he could stabilize his situation. His island would be the start of a grand Korean empire in North America.

All he really had to do was institute feudalism under the guise of hereditary administrative leadership. Add the word "hereditary" and all of his officers were chomping at the bit to start their own little kingdoms—all for the good of the People, of course. Human nature, Ree mused, was very predictable. It was a useful trait.

* * *

"Dammit, Carl," Mary Ann said, "I can't believe our luck. Just when it looked like our supporters were wavering, a miracle on our doorstep. Have you been out since yesterday? Have you felt the energy out there? The silent majority, who want us to stand on our walls and piss on the Empire when they come—they're not so silent right now. You can practically hear the hum of a thousand whispered conversations right now."

Carl blinked at her probably unintentionally poetic wording. He shifted uncomfortably in the hard red plastic office chair in the safehouse living room. The dim light from the lanterns, necessary even in broad daylight due to the covered windows, seemed at odds with the excitement he felt. The Empire massacre might as well have been a gift wrapped in golden paper with a pretty red bow on top. Thank you, Clan. "I've been out there. I've felt it. And I've heard things. Like, Diamondback's allies are waffling on holding the election now, after promising it soon for weeks. That's bad news for the Interim Speaker, and very good news for you. We need to make sure everybody knows why, maybe have people insert it into all that whispering."

Mary Ann grinned as she stood from the couch. She paced in a circle around the coffee table, eyes on the floor, and held out one finger. "One, Diamondback can't say the Empire is unbeatable anymore, because we all just saw them get their asses handed to them." She held out another finger. "Two, the ones we questioned have all said the Empire got a bloody nose in Michigan outside Saginaw when they tussled with the Indians up there, and withdrew. Three," she said, with only her thumb and pinky left unextended, "Illinois is getting their act together, according to the prisoners we questioned, and they've stopped the Empire as well. It's the reason they're coming east, Carl—because they *can't* expand to the north or west. They *can* be beaten, and now all of Liz

Town knows it."

Carl sat patiently through Mary Ann's monologue, not wishing to interrupt her train of thought. He watched her as she sat down again. "You're right, of course. We don't need more whispering. We need to go rouse the rabble. Strike while the iron is hot, and get as many newly brave fighters on our side as we can. For once, I agree with you."

Mary Ann's eyes lit up as she watched him intently. "Yes! Do or die. It will be risky but worth it if we can get organized, then we can force that vote we've been delaying. We can elect a real Speaker and get our asses in gear preparing for the Empire."

"That would be you, of course," Carl said. He could barely contain his enthusiasm, but of course, those were precisely the times when it was smart to calm the hell down and think before acting. "You've got my loyalty, and the Timber Wolves back you as well. We need to get word to the leaders of the other Bands, the ones who aren't Diamondback supporters, and organize a sit-down."

Mary Ann leaned forward, sitting on the edge of her seat. "No. We need decisive action right now, not powwows. We strike while the warriors are ready. I'll go to them personally. I'll bring the message right to their doorsteps, where their fighters can hear every word. It'll be hard to play old-world politics with their warriors cheering for battle and an election to set them into action."

Carl's jaw tightened. He had been afraid of this. Typical Liz Town attitude... he had to rein her in if he could. "No way. The Interim Speaker and my ex-wife have already tried to kill you once, and damn near succeeded. How the hell can I keep you safe if—"

"That was in the middle of the night while we were scurrying around in the dark like scared mice. That's what happens when you play cloak-and-dagger against people who live and operate in the shadows. We need to stand in the spotlight and shout, not hide. Pamela and her puppet, Horace, won't dare attack me with thousands of Liz Town warriors clamoring for blood. It'd be civil war, Carl. She'd lose, and she knows it."

Mary Ann stood suddenly and made for the door. Carl half-fell out of his chair scrambling to intercept her. He slid in front of her just as she approached the front door. "Dammit, listen Mary Ann! Think about this, will you? Messages, we meet in safety and—"

Mary Ann reached both hands out, grabbing Carl by both shoulders, and cut him off again. "Carl, enough. It's done. I'm going. We can plan our moves as we go, but we need to act. Quickly, decisively, and *right now*. Now get out of my way." She tried to push him to the side.

Carl had a choice. Resist, and she'd do it anyway but without his advice and protection, or go with it and try to keep her safe. He let out a sharp, tense breath and let her move him to the side. "Maybe you're right," he said. He sure didn't feel that way, but Mary Ann was a good leader, maybe a great one, and she had great instincts. He had to allow that maybe she was right. Either way it was moot—she was doing this. "Okay, fine. I'm with you." Carl took a deep breath. He wanted his next statement to sound convincing. "Let's go whip up a storm and let Horace L. Wattleberger reap what Pamela sowed."

"There's the Carl Woburn I've heard so much about. Glad to meet you again," Mary Ann said, eyes crinkling at the edges with mirth. "Now, let's go start a riot!"

- 20 -

0545 HOURS - ZERO DAY +252

THE HOUSE ACROSS the street was virtually a mansion. The central portion was brick-built and looked ancient. To either side, angling outward toward the street like wings, newer additions had been added. They were more modern, yet still "classically inspired." The overall effect worked well, visually.

Before the house stretched a parking circle, paved with cobblestones with an opulent fountain in the center. Though the fountain no longer pumped water, it was still delightful, a beautiful masterwork of sculpture in granite, forming two swans facing away from one another. A couple acres of land surrounded the house, most of it in the rear, with garden plots, fruit and nut trees, horse stables... The entire property was surrounded by an ornate stone wall topped with a sturdy wrought iron fence, all of which was more for beauty and to tell onlookers "Keep Out" than for any real protective value. It predated any such need, after all.

"So this is where the Interim Speaker is staying?" asked the woman next to Carl, her voice low and raspy, almost like a whisper.

"It's where the Speaker must live, by our laws," Carl replied. "Sunshine, why did you agree to this? You and your people are outlawed—you could get killed."

"I wanted to see how the other half lived. You Liz Towners got it cushy," Sunshine said, trying to lighten the mood, then added, "If we die, it's still worth it for what my people might get out of this."

It made sense to Carl. He'd have made the same choices. "You realize if this goes sideways, no Band will claim knowledge of us. You'll be treated as an invader, and I'll be treated like a traitor." The thought almost made him shudder despite the warm layers he wore beneath his leather jacket.

"But the Timber Wolves will still help the rest of my small band. Food. Weapons. Allies. We'll be safer than the other groups in the wildlands, and safer from them, too. Besides, I can't let you go get yourself killed. Who can I mac on if you're dead?"

"Anyone but me?" Carl said.

"Don't even front. Someday I'm going to get you to smash."

"Maybe if we live through this, I'll surprise you," Carl said.

Sunshine smiled and pulled her long hair down over her left shoulder to hang over her breast, and fiddled with it nervously, wrapping a few strands around one finger and looking up at him through her lashes like a shy child. It was adorable, and awkward and, he allowed, tremendously appealing.

"Don't be a tease, Carl," she said, playing it off, but Carl had seen the moment of odd shyness.

Maybe she had been serious about it this whole time. He had never really been sure, but hadn't tried to find out, either. It felt wrong to try to hook up with a woman who might only be interested in hopes of getting food. So he had just given her what food he could, without strings.

Carl grinned through his own awkwardness. "Yeah right, you're the tease here, Sunshine. Anyway, we're about five minutes from showtime. You solid on the plan?"

Sunshine took a deep breath, but she didn't show any signs of being overly nervous. She had always been brave, every time he'd seen her. "Yeah," she said, "I got it. We're plausible deniability for the Kodiaks and your Band."

"More or less. And the rest of it?"

"We move out five minutes after shift change, kill anyone who resists, tie the rest up, and kidnap the Interim Speaker."

"Right," Carl said. "Then we force him to sign the election decree, authorizing a vote on a permanent Speaker within twenty-four hours so the vote happens now."

Five minutes later, ten men and women wearing Diamondback colors converged on the mini-mansion's front door and entered. A minute later, ten more left the building and departed in every direction, alone or in pairs, talking quietly. Carl practically stared at his mechanical watch as the seconds hand swept around the face. Each second took an eternity, and with each tick of the watch hand, Carl's tension level rose. Soon he was strung like a guitar, taut and practically vibrating with the urge to begin.

As the minutes hand ticked to twelve and the hours hand ticked to six, Carl's heart skipped a beat. It was mission time. He, Sunshine, and six of her wildlands group emerged from the dense shrubbery and headed toward the front of the house. He saw another, smaller group heading toward the right side of the house, and more drifting silently across the backyard. Yet another would hit the other end of the house, as well. The last group was in position, spread out, posted up at each of the house's four corners to kill anyone who escaped.

Without a word, one of Carl's group kicked the front

door by the knob, shattering the latch assembly and sending the door swinging inward. He stepped back as another of Sunshine's team bolted through the doorway. There was the boom of a shotgun, and Sunshine's man collapsed forward to the floor with a thud. Another boom, and a big chunk of wood was torn from the door frame.

Then from the right came the sound of two rifles fired and the tinkle of shattered glass. A scream inside, another thump, and Carl saw the shotgun slide across the floor in view of the doorway.

"Go, go!" Carl said, growling from between clenched teeth, and his team poured through the doorway, Carl entering next-to-last. He glanced to his right and saw that one could see straight down the length of the addition to the huge bay windows on the far side, where another team was coming in through shattered windows. It must have been one of them who killed the shotgun-wielding guard. He heard more gunfire from the rear of the house, and still more through the house's left wing although he couldn't see straight through it the way he could with the other wing.

And then, silence. All guards downstairs were dead or incapacitated. Now came the hard part—getting up the two arched stairwells in the foyer that led upstairs, where half the guards and the Interim Speaker would be readying themselves for the assault they knew had to come next. Carl and his people crouched behind cover as best they could, covering the upper landing from every angle—no one would pop out and surprise them without catching bullets first.

Though the target and his guards upstairs made no effort to come out—and why should they?—the upstairs doors that he could see were all open, making it difficult to head up without being fired upon by the people in those rooms, whichever rooms were actually occupied. Carl had no way to tell which ones were defended, or if they all were.

He had a little surprise ready for the Interim Speaker and his guards, though he'd give them the chance to surrender first. They wouldn't likely take it, but he had to try. "Surrender and I swear you won't be harmed," Carl called up the stairway.

There was silence for a moment, and then a man's voice called down, "I'm coming out. Y'all got the upper hand, here."

Abruptly, a burst of gunfire interrupted the relative silence. Carl ducked down, but then heard a thump on the floor from upstairs.

Another voice yelled down, "No one is surrendering! You hear me down there? You want me, come and get us."

Carl looked down at the gleaming marble floor, the flecks of gray amidst the white prompting thoughts of the blood that would soon be splattered—probably on both sides of the fight. Well, he had tried. Time for Plan B. He glanced to his left, to his right, nodded each time, then took a small cylinder out of his side cargo pocket. He pulled a pin on his while holding the spoon down. With his other hand, he counted to three with fingers held above him, and then threw his cylinder up to the upper landing, and two more landed on either side of his. He closed his eyes and covered his ears.

Bang! The flash-bang grenades went off, nearly deafening and blindingly bright despite his precautions. The other two lobbed up were smoke grenades. Carl wasted no time—he bolted up the left stairs and kept his rifle aimed at the right-hand landing. Those on the other stairs did the same, a mirror image. If anyone came out of those rooms, they'd get tagged.

At the top, the smoke grew thicker, and he could no longer see to the far side of the upper landing, nor its open doors. He only saw the closest one. All around him, people paired up at the doors on the landing as planned.

In the movies, people peeked around doorways, considered the surroundings, and then bolted inside with guns blazing, taking out five or ten guys by themselves. In reality, that first peek was fatal. Carl's training—and how he had briefly trained this team in the time available—was simpler. Take a deep breath, rush through the doorway, and step aside, shoot at anything that moved, but find some damn cover. The doorway was a kill zone, a choke point. To survive, you had to not be in it when the shooting started.

Carl led the charge through the doorway, saw one man standing with a rifle, and fired. His target went down screaming. The room was large, set up as an office and library. There was a counter to his right that housed a wet bar, and he slid behind it for concealment. To the other side of the doorway was a chair, and one of Sunshine's people crouched behind it. The rest hadn't made it inside. On the far side of the room was a huge mahogany desk, a couch, and a loveseat.

Carl barked, "Now!"

A second later, two more of the flash-bang grenades sailed into the room just as two men with rifles popped up. Carl crouched as low as he could, eyes shut, hands over his ears again. From this distance, as the grenades went off, the noise was deafening. He stood from behind the counter and through the smoke he saw the two armed men had dropped their rifles, and had their hands to their eyes. It was reflex, and it was fatal—Carl and his other man inside opened up, dropping both. Carl bolted for one end of the couch, his partner for the other, and still more of his team burst through the open doorway.

Once around the couch he could see behind the heavy wooden desk, and his jaw dropped, though his rifle barrel didn't. The Interim Speaker lay curled in a ball, someone dressed unlike any Liz Towner crouched down, hands over his ears, a pistol on the floor beside him... and Pamela, who lay on the floor with her hands behind her head.

He had never wanted to kill anyone so badly as at this moment. He trusted the others to cover the guards, and he had stopped hearing gunfire from elsewhere on the landing, so he focused like a laser on the three behind the desk. "Hands up, or die," Carl said, and half hoped one of them would make a move for a weapon.

They didn't, however. Hands slowly went up, and Carl barked, "Get up. Face the wall. Hands on the wall. Do it now."

Pamela, the Diamondback leader, and the unknown man all moved slowly to comply after a glance to the menacing barrel of Carl's rifle. Two other infiltrators also took aim on the three of them. One said, "Their guards are dead, Carl. Want me to smoke these three?"

"No. I'd love to, but if they comply, they can take their chances with Liz Town justice."

Pamela's face screwed up into a knot, and her bottom lip trembled. "Carl—"

"Shut up, Pam. You have nothing to say that I want to hear."

"I only did what's best for Liz Town," she cried out, her voice cracking.

Maybe she even believed it, but Carl learned long ago not to trust her tearful displays. Even if she was being honest, it didn't matter. Carl said, "I have an election decree. Your friend the Diamondback is going to sign it, or die." He took a sheet of paper from his pocket where it had been folded. With one hand, he unfolded it and set it on the desk. "Alright, you wannabe Speaker, turn around and sign the paper. If you don't, I'm going to kill you here and now. Move slowly..."

The Interim Speaker turned around. Carl didn't

recognize him, but that wasn't unusual in a town the size of Liz Town, especially with their division into Bands. The Speaker read the paper and turned pale. "You can't do this," he said. "It'll be the death of us all."

Carl aimed at the man's belly. "Sign now or die a slow, painful death."

The man didn't flinch or say anything.

"Ten. Nine..."

Finally, the Speaker slowly reached for the pen that laid idly on the desk. "Fine," he said. He signed the paper with a quick, shaky scratch. "But you've just killed Liz Town."

Carl ignored him as he folded the signed document and stuffed it in his pocket. "Tie them up, all three. Parade them through the damn streets. This third guy..." Carl pointed at him, stepping closer. "You're not one of us."

Before the man could answer, Sunshine walked up from her spot to the rear, smiling. "That would be the Empire guy. I've seen him coming and going in the night. There's an Empire troop camped in the northwest wildlands, too."

After the three had been tied up, Carl patted them down, then checked the desk drawers. In the upper left drawer he found a manila envelope. When he tossed it onto the desk, he realized it was heavier than it looked, and when it landed, it clinked. That got his attention. He carefully opened the envelope and poured the contents onto the desk to find a two-page document and a dozen of the Empire's gold coins. He picked up the document and read the heading—"Alliance and Peace Treaty Letter of Understanding."

Carl growled. "You assholes were really going to do it, weren't you? And all for some crappy bits of gold? You can't eat gold, you stupid sonsofbitches."

"Now can I kill them?" one of his fighters asked, but his tight voice and clenched jaw told Carl he wasn't joking around, this time.

"No. Get them to Kodiak headquarters. Mary Ann calls the shots from here on out. But if they resist or try to run? Kill them. And we'll send a war party after that troop Sunshine mentioned."

Carl's unit, all of them wildlanders other than him, roughly grabbed the prisoners and forced them downstairs. Diamondback might declare war against Kodiak or Timber Wolf over this, but with Carl's entire force made up of wildlanders it would be hard to get any sympathy from the other Bands. Diamondback would be fighting on their own—even Wolverine and Puma would join Kodiak against Diamondback if civil war came now. It was checkmate against the coup attempt, the Empire would be in for a nasty surprise, and Pamela was done. Finished.

* * *

During breakfast, two of Taggart's on-loan soldiers approached Michael at another table, and Cassy let out a long breath. To disturb Michael mid-breakfast meant something major was going on and they would no doubt head over to Cassy's table shortly. She scarfed her food as quickly as she could while waiting for the other shoe to drop.

Sure enough, a couple minutes later, Michael got up and then he and the soldiers walked over to her table. Michael sat across from her, frowning.

Cassy finished chewing her delicious eggs and cheese—the cows were giving milk again, having birthed recently—and said, "Hey Michael. What's up?"

"I have some bad news. It seems a couple of the raiders we slaughtered outside Liz Town had kept in hiding and were just spotted linking up with a dozen or so Empire bike troops. They waited an hour, then headed west."

Cassy pursed her lips. It wasn't unexpected that some

had escaped, but the other group meeting up with them was news. "Analysis?"

Michael shrugged. "Hard to say. My guess is that the riders weren't there for the survivors, but for some other reason. Nothing else makes much sense. Whatever they were waiting for, it didn't happen or didn't come back, so the group left and took the battle survivors with them because they were available."

"So, the Empire will find out their raiders got slaughtered, and I'd guess that something is going on in Liz Town involving the Empire."

Michael nodded. "Whatever it was, it must not have gone according to plan. The locals outside the wall said two of the Empire groups entered Liz Town but never came out. They're fans of ours right now, so they were happy to share what they had seen. Liz Town ought to bring them in, make another Band."

"Not that I don't agree, but that's their business. Let's get some scouts over to Liz Town itself. They're off the rails lately and I don't want any nasty surprises."

"I'd planned to, as soon as I briefed you. I'm going to set up a few scouts in a picket line east of Liz Town, as well, with orders not to engage, but to report any movement."

Cassy bit her lip, worrying the flesh with her teeth, then said, "Yeah, okay. Just make sure we have something between us and Liz Town itself, too."

"Yes, ma'am," Michael said with all seriousness. He often got formal in front of the troops, which irritated her, but he said it was necessary to firmly set the chain of command in the troops' minds. "I'll get units moving A.S.A.P."

Cassy nodded. After Michael left with the soldiers, she finished her last couple bites of eggs. They had turned cold during her conversation with Michael. Appropriate, she thought, given that the Empire was likely to move up their timetable for invasion, now. She had hoped beyond hope that none of the raiders had escaped, but knew that was unlikely. It just sucked that she had been right.

* * *

Ethan powered up the short-range hand radio from his perch atop the hill just outside the livestock fencing, and as he waited, his mind wandered. The way Cassy did things on the farm hadn't made any sense to him when he had arrived at her farm, but over time he had begun to see the reasons behind many of the little weird ways she did things and why it worked so well.

The idea of putting all the livestock *uphill*, for example, seemed dumb at first. Food had to be trekked uphill to them, for one. Milking, birthing, feeding, cleaning—all of it required a trip up the hill, then back down. And what about health risks to the humans, below?

But then he had seen how lush her crops were at the end of the last grow season. Now, in spring, he saw that the crops recently seeded downhill from the livestock began growing before anything else and were growing faster than the rest. The manure and urine, it turned out, turned to compost and nitrogen as they slowly seeped their way downhill. No fertilizer was needed, and yet the crops were already growing splendidly without having to plow, to weed, to add fertilizers, pesticides, liming, or other soil amendments... And the food that grew there tasted better than anything he had ever found at the neighborhood supermarket before the EMPs.

Most of the weird things Cassy insisted on were like that, and just as interconnected with everything else. It really was a web of life, not a chain, and—

The radio crackled, interrupting his daydreaming. He sat up suddenly and grabbed the radio.

"Romeo One to Charlie Two, come in," the radio said.

Ethan recognized Michael's voice, so skipped the passwords. "Romeo One, go ahead for Charlie Two." Ethan adjusted the satellite map picture he had downloaded of the Op Area.

As Michael gave his location, half a mile from the target coordinates, Ethan made notes on the map. "Change bearing two degrees north," he told Michael. "You're eight-zero-zero meters from target, with thirty-two mikes approximate. How copy?"

Michael confirmed. Ten minutes later they repeated the process. After that, Ethan settled down to wait—there would be radio silence from here out, until the operation was finished one way or the other. It gave him plenty of time to think, which he welcomed. It was nice being out in the open air on this first really warm day of the year and enjoying the late-morning sunlight, rather than hiding in his cave. When had he started to think of the bunker as a cave? It had been his "safe place," his retreat, for so long... his preferred habitat, even... but lately he had been finding excuses to have someone else man the radios. He was actually volunteering to help with planting and birthing and anything else that needed doing. It felt strange, but good.

"Whatcha thinking," came Amber's voice from behind him.

He turned toward her voice, and she looked stunning. Her hair was down and wrapped over her left shoulder to hang in front. She wore a black tank top and deep-blue sarong, and a pair of sandals, the straps snaking up to her mid-calves. He couldn't look away.

"What?" he asked, blinking, and still didn't hear her response.

Amber laughed, eyes sparkling. For the third time she asked, "I said, what are you thinking about?" She twirled, her sarong flowing outward and up like a flower blooming. "You like it?"

Ethan smiled and adjusted his shirt collar melodramatically. "Very much so. Hi. Surprised to see you up here."

"I just saw you go up here and it seemed unusual for you to be out of your bunker voluntarily, so I thought I'd come up and see what weirdness you're up to." She sat next to him in the grass and nudged him with her elbow.

Ethan leaned back onto his elbows and looked up at the sky, eyes closed for a moment, then replied, "Well, you remember I told you about a weird message from the 20s, saying they were sending supplies to Taggart in New Jersey?"

Amber's features shifted from relaxed happiness to unease almost instantly. "Yeah..."

"We decided that doesn't make sense. I contacted Taggart through the back channel and he confirmed it—he hasn't received any message about it. So, we're curious as to what it is General Houle is sending and where it's going. Just wanted to verify, so I ran the coordinates for the supply run's route, and there's a spot that's natural for ambush."

"Yeah, but what if it's legit, and it's real supplies for Taggart?" Amber raised one eyebrow at Ethan.

"Then we deliver it to him ourselves. Even if it's not legit, we may end up doing that anyway, depending on what it is."

"I don't know, Ethan. This sounds risky. The 20s are mysterious and all, but they've helped us, they've helped Taggart... Hell, they basically kept Taggart alive a few times, early in the war. Why shouldn't you trust them?"

"There's been some really bad discrepancies. Like when they sent orders to Taggart in a way that seemed like it was from me. Luckily, I found out about it, but there were probably others I didn't catch."

"So? We pretty much know they work for General Houle

in Colorado. He's the C-in-C, right?"

"He says he is. Taggart disagrees and so do I. There are other little things, too, that lead me to think they might be..." He paused.

"Go ahead, Ethan. You can tell me."

"I think they might be gaming both sides, Taggart and us against Ree. That doesn't make sense under any honorable scenario I can think of."

"So you think they want to keep Ree and Taggart weak, and keep groups like ours distracted? But why?" Amber looked concerned, finally.

"So he can take over everything. I think that's his endgame. Keep the 'vaders here, but not too strong, so you have an enemy to point to as you roll out a dictatorship for everyone's safety. It's an old game. Everyone is so busy looking at our foreign enemy that they don't see the domestic one until it's too late."

"You're kinda scaring me," Amber said.

Ethan closed his eyes and breathed deeply, feeling the breeze cascade through his hair. Looking away from Amber, he said, "I was recruited by the 20s without realizing who they were, shortly before the first EMPs. Someone—the 20s—had used my ego, before the war, to trick me into solving bits of programming problems that, when taken together with what some other hackers were working on, could be the source of some of the software used later to hack me. The same software I later used to hack... some government servers," he said. He had promised himself never to speak about his central role in the American counter-EMPs that sent the whole world into darkness, in retaliation for the attack on America.

"Meanwhile, if Houle is legit, then what you're doing really is treason. What do you have, really? Some orders they didn't send through you, and some code you wrote before the war? That's hardly damning evidence of Houle's treason, Ethan."

"No, it's not. But I'm not letting Houle run a caravan of supplies through Confed territory without knowing what the supplies really are, or who they're really going to. I see a connection running through all of this since even before the EMPs came. And if I'm right, then Houle knew they were coming and did nothing to stop the attack. Perhaps he even helped it to succeed, though we'll never know for sure."

They sat in silence together for a while, neither feeling much like talking anymore, until the radio chirped. The signal wasn't as strong as he would have liked, but it would do.

After the usual radio preliminaries, Michael said, "I doubt this was going to Taggart. Will brief you on return. Have Sturm ready with her field surgery kit for a couple of wounded, when we arrive. Michael out."

Ethan said to Amber, "Hanging out up here was nice while it lasted. Will you go find Sturm while I pack up this stuff?"

Amber nodded and said, "Alright. See you down there. And Ethan? Be careful with this stuff. Houle knows where we live." She rose, bent to give him a brief kiss, and headed down the hill to find Sturm.

Ethan watched her go, his dark and somber thoughts a contrast to the warm, sunny day, and then he headed toward the old driveway to meet the returning Clan raiders with their loot. He could have gone to the bunker for a couple hours first, but he didn't feel like sitting in the dim light surrounded by walls and maps and often-grim reminders of the war.

So he fiddled around topside, helping people with their laundry. It wasn't quite the easy process nowadays that it had been before the war, though it had become much easier since Dean had engineered pedal-powered washing machines using an odd, u-shaped gear to get the oscillating action. It still took a lot of effort, though it was faster than using old-fashioned washboards.

He was pretty well exhausted by the time his radio crackled again, Michael advising him he'd arrive in ten minutes. He made his way to the nearby driveway to wait, and found Lance Corporal Sturm and a couple helpers already waiting there. They exchanged nods, but she kept pacing back and forth, arms and legs tense and stiff, which Ethan took as a strong sign that she was wound tight and not in the mood to chat.

A short while later, the sounds of hooves and wagon wheels could be heard crunching down the driveway. The lead horses came into view from around the bend, followed by wagons, and then more horses. Ethan saw that several wounded had been loaded into the wagons, and he stepped aside to let Sturm take care of them.

The scene became chaos as Sturm quickly examined each of the wounded—there were four—and shouted directions to her helpers. Michael barked separate orders at the others milling around, and once they had off-loaded the wounded onto blankets, they quickly covered the wagons with tarps and camouflage netting. The surface chaos had obscured very purposeful orderly actions, Ethan realized.

He watched as Michael made certain his wounded were being taken care of and the wagons were hidden as well as they could be for now.

Then Michael made a beeline for Ethan. "It went well," Michael said as he dusted road dirt off his clothes. He had a blood stain of his own on one arm, Ethan saw.

"You hurt?" Ethan asked.

"No, that's from one of our wounded. Walk with me."

Ethan fell into step beside Michael, who walked toward

Cassy's house at a pace Ethan realized was slow enough to give them time to talk before she debriefed him. "So, what did you find?"

"Well, there are indeed supplies in the wagons."

That was no surprise. Ethan replied, "Yeah. You said you didn't think they were bound for Taggart?"

Michael shook his head and pursed his lips, then said, "There's a radio and a laptop."

"Taggart already has those things," Ethan replied.

"Yeah, from us, right? So that's not the big deal. What is a problem, though, is that the laptop boots up in Korean, or Chinese. One of those Asian symbol alphabets."

Ethan's jaw clenched. "You didn't log in, did you?"

Michael shook his head. "No way to. I don't read Korean. I wish Choony were around."

"Good. If you had, I can almost guarantee the 20s would have known, and probably got the location. I can only hope the GPS they installed only activates with login, not simply by powering it on."

"I thought of that, too, but one of the troops opened it before I knew about it. I saw the login screen and closed the damn thing, then removed the battery."

"Good. Let's hope that worked. I can open it safely in the bunker if I power off the router down there. What else was there?"

"Two of the wagons we retrieved contain a kind of drone I haven't seen before. They're smaller than the drones we recovered from the wacko cult compound, but they look just about as capable and much more maneuverable. They also have something I've never seen before."

"What was it?"

"The drones each have something that looks like a tiny gatling gun. Belted ammo fits into a bottom compartment. The ammunition is also new to me."

That got Ethan's attention. If there were a type of ammo that Michael, a Major in the Marines and in Force Recon, had never seen... it must be something special.

Michael continued, "The rounds look like they're about half the size of a twenty-two. Like BBs, but actual bullets. I think they're subsonic rounds, too, making them nearly silent at any real distance. The drone controllers have integrated screens, and a small red trigger built in, like those video game controllers of yours, down in the bunker."

"Wow. I think the dots are easy to connect, here, but why would the Mountain tell us where this supply convoy would be, and what path it would take?"

Michael frowned. "I thought about that. If I were General Houle, I'd have sent two or even three convoys, and only told you about one. If that one goes missing, then the odds go way up that they've discovered you're a traitor."

Ethan turned pale, and reached up to brush the hair from his eyes with a wobbly hand. "Michael, we can't use these drones, man. The 20s, and therefore General Houle, know where Clanholme is. A couple of Predators armed with air-to-ground missiles could turn this whole place to rubble!"

Michael's lip curled into a snarl. Calming himself, he said, "If the Predators aren't on their way already, we can never risk using these damn things. Not here. But they may already be en route to eliminate us—and you."

Ethan shook his head emphatically, eyes wide. "No, no, that's not true. If they were going to shove a Hellfire missile up our asses—they would have gotten here already. You've been back a little while, and they would have struck as soon as they had confirmation of your destination with the wagons."

"True. So either Houle knows and doesn't care, or doesn't know and mustn't find out."

Ethan took a deep breath and let it out slowly, feeling the

tension drain away. "So we must operate under the assumption that they don't know we seized their shipment. Using the drones could reveal both their location and the Clan's involvement in their theft."

Michael clenched his jaw, but nodded. "Fine. Please put the drones somewhere safe. I don't want some kid, or yahoo, turning one of them on and giving us away."

"We have plenty of room in the bunker's storage wing to put these things since we've gone through most of Cassy's original cache of food items over the winter. Why not just burn the drones, though?"

Michael shrugged and raised his hands out from his sides, palms facing up. "Just because we can't use them now doesn't mean we won't wish we had them down the road if things turn ugly with the Mountain. Or with Ree."

That was a good point. If the Confederation ever came to blows with General Houle and his troops from their mountain base, those drones could prove useful. "Hope for the best, plan for the worst," he muttered, nodding.

"Exactly," Michael said. "And since it appears, at least, that General Houle was sending these to the invaders in New Jersey and New York, it seems he's the traitor. Good to know that for sure. We'll probably end up at war with him, too."

"Especially after we kick in his Empire lackeys' teeth."

"If..." said Michael sternly. "If we kick their teeth in. It's far from guaranteed."

Ethan furrowed his brow. "Damn. You know how to rain on a parade."

- 21 -

0915 HOURS - ZERO DAY +254

CARL STARED OUT the front windows. They were huge, stretching almost from floor to ceiling, and had a great view of both the mansion's ornate front yard and the overgrown alleyway next to it. His mind wandered back to thoughts of his old Alpha. He remembered crawling through that very patch of brambles in the alley to come here, climbing to the Alpha's bedroom on the second floor in a vain attempt to warn him about Pamela's plot. Now Carl was effectively the Alpha, and it was his mansion since the Timber Wolves had overwhelmingly named him Alpha in the same election that would soon make Mary Ann the Liz Town speaker. How odd were the twists and turns that life put before him...

"Well," said his new bodyguard, "You sure did luck out. If the raid on the Interim Speaker and your ex-wife hadn't turned up so much dirt on them both, you might not have been elected Alpha of the Timber Wolves Band."

Carl shook his head faintly. The man had it all wrong, but Carl couldn't blame him. Things had been so chaotic for the last few days that all sorts of rumors had spread. "No, the truth is, we knew they were dirty. That's why we did the raid.

Without it—without putting the Diamondback leader and Pamela in shackles and making him sign the papers—they never would have allowed an election until it was too late to organize resistance."

"They wanted us to join the Empire, I heard," the man said.

Carl had forgotten his name already. He'd have to fix that. "That part's correct, unfortunately. The way they played on old pack rivalries to keep the packs at each other's throats..." He shook his head. "What's your name again? I'm sorry, but I'm having a hard time remembering everyone. It's been chaos trying to get things back in order."

His guard nodded. "My name's—"

He was cut off by the sound of air horns. First one, then another and another, raising the alarm all down the line on the north wall. A chill ran down his spine like a bullet. That many horns... They only blew when the watch saw an enemy. Then it was all hands to the walls. More raiders? Again?

"Let's go," Carl said. He jumped from his chair and grabbed his leather jacket—now the proper Timber Wolf red—and his M16.

He didn't wait for his guard, instead running outside to hop onto his mountain bike. It was a tool he had been slowly acquiring for all his warriors and their leaders, and he noted many others rushing out to their assigned positions as he rode hard for the wall. He reached the closest tower and hopped off his bike, letting it fall carelessly to the pavement, and climbed up the ladder as fast as he could. When he reached the top, one of the sentries reached down for his hand and helped him up to the ledge. He crouched to avoid exposing himself to anyone outside the wall.

Carl snapped, "Status report, sentry."

"Alpha," the man exclaimed, surprised. "You shouldn't be on the wall. It's danger—"

"Status report now dammit." If this guy didn't start to talk in three frikking seconds, Carl was going to throw him off the wall himself.

"Yes, sir. We have well over a company of bike-mounted people armed with rifles, some two hundred yards out. They're dispersed behind cover throughout the wildlands and appear to be waiting for something."

"Waiting?" Carl thought a moment. "It's a parley. They wouldn't have exposed themselves before an attack like this, unless they were here to talk first."

"They've made no move yet, sir."

Carl rose up enough to peer over the wall's protective ridge, formed much like a battlement but without the crenellations. Outside, he saw the wildlanders huddled behind cover near the wall, their backs to the Liz Town defenders, facing the new threat together not as pack mates but as welcome allies. Beyond them he saw the long stretch of empty space maintained by Liz Town for defense, and his eyes paused there briefly but he didn't see movement. Farther out, he saw a long line of armed men and women, mostly behind cover and definitely facing the town. Behind them lay their bikes and their packs, ready for a quick advance or retreat, as needed. Empire. Damn.

"Nothing to do but wait, I guess," Carl said to his bodyguard, who had finally caught up.

"Yes, sir."

Carl looked to the wall sentry he had spoken to before. "Any word on our new client Band?"

"What, the wildlanders you brought in?"

Carl frowned. "Do you know of another new client Band?"

"The Sewer Rats are on the wall a bit east, toward the Diamondback barrier. The new Interim Speaker said it would be best to keep Timber Wolves and Diamondbacks from getting too close for a while."

"Good idea."

Two figures on bikes separated from the line of trespassing fighters deep in the wildlands and slowly made their way toward the Liz Town wall.

"Parley it is, then," Carl muttered. "Go tell the speaker that she shouldn't risk herself. As her aide, I'll go talk."

The sentry nodded and left, going as fast as he could without falling off the catwalk. Carl set his rifle down and said to the wall defenders near him, "Keep aim on them while I'm out there. If anything goes wrong, make sure they die, got it?"

"Yes, Alpha," several said in unison, and then they propped their rifles on the wall for stability, taking aim.

Carl climbed back down, walked to the small gate nearby, and waited while the half-inch steel plate was slid out of the way. He walked through the gate and heard the gate slide closed behind him. Okay, then. Squaring his shoulders, he walked away from the wall, toward the two oncoming bike riders. They came together about fifty yards from the wall—easy sniping distance for his Timber Wolves. When the two cyclists stopped, Carl stopped as well, and stood silently facing them.

Finally, one said, "I am Captain Samuel Pease of the Midwest Republic. I ought to kill you all for letting the Clan ambush us the last time I came through here, but thankfully, two troopers were volunteered to get shot while I escaped." He pointed to the man beside him and said, "This is my senior NCO, here as a witness to what we say. And you are?"

The man had an aura that Carl didn't like. Creepy. Evil, even. But the man beside him, his NCO, was worse. Carl felt a chill down his spine when he looked at the two. If this is who the Empire sent to negotiate, Liz Town was in for rough days ahead. "I'm the Alpha of the Timber Wolves Band, Liz

Town. You can call me Carl. Now then—why are you on our land?"

Samuel grinned, but Carl felt it only hid the fangs of a viper about to strike. There was no friendliness in him. He replied, "Actually, the land belongs to certain individuals in accordance with deeds on record. Until next-of-kin can be worked out, they are administered by the prevailing governmental jurisdiction..."

"What government?"

"...which, in accordance with the terms of the declaration of Martial Law..."

"Declared by whom?"

"...is for the moment the United States federal government..."

"Show me a government."

"...as administered by the Commander-in-Chief..."

"Under what authority?"

"...who has allocated authority to the Midwest Republic..."

"Who? Show me Constitutional authority for that."

"...and we're here to enforce his lawful orders."

"Who says they're lawful?" Carl struggled to keep his temper under control and to appear calm. "Sounds like an asshole's power-grab to me."

Samuel shrugged, and a clearly mocking, pained expression crossed his face. "I'm so sorry there is some confusion on your end, but it's really quite simple. We're under Martial Law, and you must comply."

Carl clenched his jaw, then said, "And if we don't recognize your banana republic false authority?"

"Then, as much as it pains me and my commanding officer," Samuel said as a more vicious grin spread over his face, "we'd have to respond under the rules of Martial Law as pertains to high treason during time of war."

Carl froze. This bastard just threatened to kill everyone who resisted. It wasn't a subtle threat, either. "Interesting. However, I don't think a self-elected Commander-in-Chief qualifies as one who can issue lawful orders on any level, much less federal."

Samuel looked up into the sky for a moment, and for all the world he appeared to just be relishing the sunshine for a moment. Still looking up, he said, "Actually, all verified surviving members of the House of Representatives, who are enjoying the hospitality and protection of General Houle in Colorado, voted to make him the C-in-C for the duration of this crisis. It's legit. And your C-in-C demands you surrender all your horses and provide other material assistance, however much our commanding officer deems necessary for the success of our mission of peace."

"Huh. You got two-thirds of Congress and Senate out alive, did you? Because if you didn't, then it's not legit. The Constitution is clear on that. So it's a banana republic coup."

Samuel shrugged. "Not me, and I don't know the numbers. The U.S. Army under Houle got the authorizing members of Congress out alive, however many were left anyway. He has assured the Republic that it's legitimate. So I say, open your gates and submit or be treated as traitors. With all that entails, of course."

Carl forced his shoulders to relax, stood tall, and tried to look confident. It was hard, given that he didn't know what forces the Empire had brought with them. "From what you say, a coup has occurred. That makes Houle and you the traitors. I think we'll stick with protecting the Constitution from all enemies, foreign and domestic. That would be you, by the way. But I will bring your message and threats to the other Bands. Fair warning, though—our Bands weeded out the cowards a long time ago. I doubt our warriors will submit easily."

"Please recognize that I have legal orders to obtain your assistance and access to your resources by any necessary means," Samuel delivered as an obviously memorized speech. "In a violent confrontation, I will not have close control over my troops, nor would I try to rein them in should it become a clear case of treason. I urge you to become our peaceful allies and enjoy the full protection of the Midwest Republic, the duly authorized regional body of the United States Government-in-exile." He paused, winked salaciously and added, "I hope you have some attractive women left, because my troops will need R-and-R after the battle."

Carl bared his teeth in a wolf-like grin. "I will enjoy killing you myself, when you return, Captain Samuel Pease. See you later, then. And best of luck getting into Liz Town uninvited. You'll need it." He spun on his heels and strode back toward the gate into Liz Town.

From behind him, he heard the enemy captain shout, "Maybe not today, Alpha Carl, but I look forward to seeing you again real soon. If you're married, make sure she wears makeup, okay? I like my toys kept in good condition."

Carl reached the gate and couldn't get inside fast enough. Son of a bitch... He swore to himself that if he could, he'd be the one to kill that Empire captain when they came back for a fight. And of course they would attack, eventually. Thank God he had stopped Pamela's coup in time—she'd have thrown the gates wide open for those monsters.

Carl climbed back up on the wall and walked along it toward Kodiak territory. He soon found Mary Ann, leaning against one of the defensive towers spotted all along Kodiak territory. Carl disagreed with the Kodiaks' love of towers for active defense in addition to posting watches. He couldn't know for sure, but he suspected towers couldn't stop an RPG or a satchel full of dynamite, and making so many of them must have cost a ton of man-hours.

"Good morning, Speaker," Carl said, and tipped his ballcap to her.

"Interim Speaker, please. At least until it's official."

Carl gave a quick nod. "As you wish."

"So, what have you found out, Carl?"

Carl ignored her informality and said, "I need the Liz Town cavalry. We need to strike the Empire as their troops move out. I don't know where they're going, but they'll be stretched out and their supplies vulnerable. We want them damaged when they come back in force."

Mary Ann shook her head. "No can do. Sorry, Carl. I'm not going to basically declare war on the Midwest Republic before our last votes are tallied and I'm no longer merely the *Interim* Speaker. We need to be stable when this hits."

Carl kept his expression carefully neutral, but his irritation rang clear in his voice when he replied, "Dammit, Mary Ann, we have the perfect chance to hurt them. Right now, in the beginning of this war. We can't ignore this opportunity."

"Carl, if we don't follow our own damn laws, what would we even be fighting for? That'd make me a dictator, and even if the people approved of going to war, and of me, it would still be the end of a free Liz Town. What if the next speaker isn't as dedicated as I am? I'd have set a precedent for abuse of power. I won't do that."

"But—"

"No," Mary Ann repeated. "Have you already forgotten the abuses of our own government before the EMPs? Not again! We do it right, or there's no point to doing it at all—we might as well surrender and save a ton of lives, because what's the difference between one dictator and another? We don't strike until I'm officially the Speaker of Liz Town and can bring all of our Bands into the decision. I'll start that process as soon as we can stand down from the wall. Only then will we go to war."

Carl clenched his fists to his sides, and looked away from Mary Ann's gaze. "Okay. I only hope that, by tomorrow, there's still a Confederation to fight for. Where do you think this rump battalion is headed, the mall?"

He turned and strode away. At least he could spend this time getting his own warriors primed for taking the leash off tomorrow. The Timber Wolves would waste no time, once that leash was off. He hoped Mary Ann would include Sunshine's group in the vote.

* * *

The old air raid siren in the guard tower blared, startling Cassy badly enough to drop her fork. Then Ethan's frantic voice blared from the PA system they had rigged up. "Code three! To arms! All units to defensive positions. This is not a drill! Charlie One to position."

Cassy leapt from her seat and darted toward her house to get her rifle and get into position, dodging dozens of other Clanners who were doing the same. As she ran through the front door, she sprinted to the loft, with its excellent views and command station.

While taking the stairs two at a time, she pulled out her handheld radio and clicked on. She didn't bother with passwords, and shouted, "Ethan, it's Cassy. Code three! What you got for us?"

She almost slid into the wall as she crossed her loft and made it to the north-facing window, and raised her rifle to peer through the scope. She scanned past the tower to the horizon, but saw nothing yet.

Her handheld crackled, and Ethan said, "Scouts reporting in... Enemy sighted near Mastersonville, confirmed

Empire. Approx one-two-zero enemy, mixed foot and bikes. Armed with rifles, mostly civilian. I've alerted Michael, and he's gathering our forces at the north food forest."

Cassy cursed under her breath. A company of troops, probably one platoon on bikes—those would be their elites—and two afoot. Mastersonville was maybe two-and-a-half hours away. "What's their bearing, and are they on the move?" she asked.

"Bearing west northwest, but not moving. Not encamped, either."

They'd miss Taj Mahal. "Alert the Confeds, 9-1-1."

"Copy." There was a brief silence, then Ethan said, "Done. Scouts are being scrambled. Also, I... Standby."

Cassy looked through her scope again, but couldn't see Michael and the troops gathering yet. She probably wouldn't for another few minutes.

Ethan clicked on. "We just heard from Liz Town. They're reporting a large force of Empire troops, two companies on bikes, who initiated a parley. Their leader told the Lizzies to join or die. Liz Town says they wanted the Confederation to be aware of the OpFor's location, but no word yet on the Lizzie response to the Empire's demand. They did say they had major developments going on and would advise us of the details later. I'll ask what they're going to do, when there's time. The Empire unit then moved on, heading northeast. That bearing will take them to the company we found. They're headed toward us."

Cassy had to stop herself from punching the wall. Damn Liz Town and their politics. Why would the Empire send two companies there? Liz Town could have chewed up that many enemies and spit them out. Sending so few showed that the Empire had no immediate plans to attack Liz Town, and also that they weren't concerned about the Lizzies riding out to attack them. It would be nice if the Clan's supposed allies would at least fill her in on what they were doing. If they were joining the Empire, she needed to know. Though, the fact that the Empire's troops moved on was maybe a hopeful sign.

She clicked her radio and said, "Copy that. Send one scout team to Liz Town. Stay out of sight of any Empire troops but find out what's going on, whether Liz opens its gates to the Empire or fights, anything that might give us a heads up on whether we need to worry about Liz Town becoming a threat."

"Copy that. So what do we do about our own little Empire visitors?"

That was a great question. The Empire company bearing down on Clanholme and the two chatting up Liz Town were probably from the same battalion. "Ethan, get Michael to delegate rallying our defenses and send him to Charlie One." She needed to talk to Michael before deciding anything, and time was short.

Before Ethan acknowledged the order, she added, "And have Lititz send their company of Taggart's troops to Manheim, and ask Manheim to send their own guys to meet up with Michael en route. Those Empire troops coming from Liz Town might hit Manheim on the way, so leapfrogging the units like that gives us more troops without leaving Manheim defenseless."

"Copy that."

Two minutes later, Michael came bursting through the door and scrambled up the stairs. Cassy watched as he came up, his head appearing in the opening, followed quickly by the rest of him. "I'm here," he said simply. Wartime Michael was a very different person than peacetime Michael.

"There's a company of Empire troops coming fast. If we engage them, how long until the two bike companies sitting at Liz Town could get here to reinforce them?"

Michael's eyebrows went up. He hadn't heard about the Liz Town visitors, it seemed, but he didn't waste time with needless questions. "An hour and a half from Liz Town on bikes, with a two-hundred-foot rise at the end. They'd get here tired."

"What are the odds the two companies at Liz Town aren't tied to this company, or that there are more units nearby?"

Michael shrugged. "I can almost guarantee they aren't attacking us with a single company. Either they'll probe us for weaknesses before the main body arrives, without fully engaging us, or maybe parley to make demands. Or they're waiting for the other two companies to catch up. We have to plan for the latter and hope for the former."

"Alright. Get our scouts out there, so we aren't blindsided by another unit. Now, should we meet the Empire in the middle, or defend Clanholme?"

Michael didn't miss a beat. "Ideally, we could meet them out there so we aren't fighting them in here. We have elderly. We have kids. Fighting here endangers them all. But we can't intercept the Empire troops, so we need to set up here."

"Why can't we intercept them out there?" Cassy rubbed her jaw. Her mind ran through different scenarios, but she lacked Michael's training and experience, dammit.

"If our scouts report other Empire units inbound, we'd be far away engaging the first enemy we noticed. Clanholme could fall to the new Empire units without much of a fight. There's another option, though."

"Spit it out. The clock is ticking."

"We hit the company with our light armor—the battlecars—and some supporting cavalry. That leaves most of our strength here and gives us tactical flexibility."

Cassy shook her head. "No. If we use our battlecars now, they'll know we have them, and they'll copy them. This is just the opening salvo, so we shouldn't show all our cards yet.

Ethan has all the allies sending out scouts, so we're covered north, east, and south against being blindsided."

Michael nodded once, curtly. "What are our orders, then?"

"Ready the troops. We march out to meet the Empire, despite the risk. That creek just north and east of the abandoned equipment plant out that way is heavily wooded on both sides of the road. Station them there, spread out for ambush—we'll have cover, but the enemy won't. I'm coming, too, but this is your show once we're in the field."

Cassy then moved quickly to the stairs, closely followed by Michael. Her decision was risky, no doubt about it, but if she could spare their homes and children the risks of a battle in their front yard, she would. She hadn't seen Frank yet, but she didn't relish the idea of handing the responsibility for this decision off to anyone else, anyway. Some things were just the actual leader's responsibility. She'd lead, and from the front like a proper leader should, even if command in the field went to Michael.

* * *

Frank hobbled up to the assembled Clan force and spotted Cassy. He handed his horse's reins to someone and hobbled as fast as he could up to her, and grabbed her by the elbow. All around them, the Clan's warriors prepared for battle. Yet another battle, and yet another time this reckless woman wanted to rush into the fighting. "Dammit, Cassy. Didn't you learn from your last brush with death? The quarry battle wasn't that long ago. You're going to get yourself killed. We need you alive!"

Cassy glared at him, lips tight. Then she said, "I don't lead from the rear, and I don't ask people to take chances I won't." She turned to the assembled fighters, two hundred of them including Taggart's soldiers, and shouted, "Mount up."

"Fine," Frank said, loosening his grip, "then I'm going, too."

"With one foot? I don't have time to argue, Frank. Stay here." She yanked her arm free from him and stomped to her horse, vaulting into the saddle.

"My wife is going with you, but I can't? Sorry, Cassy, but you'll have to tie me up to keep me from coming. Someone has to try to see that you don't get yourself killed."

"I don't need anyone holding my hand, Frank. If you want to come, then come. Whatever happens to you out there is on your hands, but either lead, follow, or stay out of my way. Riders, move out." Cassy nudged her horse into a trot, through the north food forest toward the open lands beyond, the Clan's army trailing behind her.

Frank hobbled back to his horse, thanked the woman holding his reins, and mounted carefully. He slid his leg stump into the custom-made stirrup and tightened the strap that kept his leg in place even when the horse was at full gallop. So long as he didn't fall off his horse, it worked great. If he fell, he'd have to reach the quick-release that Dean had rigged for the stirrup or he'd be dragged. When seated securely, he nudged his mount into the line, trotting perhaps a quarter of the way back from Cassy at the column head.

They wound through the northern food forest, Cassy leading them around the many traps they had placed in the forest for invaders. Frank quickly lost himself in admiring the woods, a forest-by-design.

A nudge to his elbow snapped him out of his musings just as he exited the food forest into the grasslands beyond. He turned to look and saw his wife, Mary. "Hey, sweetie," he said, smiling broadly.

Mary didn't smile back, but gave him a wink. "I caught up to you by accident," she said, "while I was zoned out thinking about that food forest."

Frank nodded and his smile widened to an open grin. He had been doing the same, of course. "I feel like I could spend a lifetime watching every plant, every bug, every critter, and still not understand everything going on in there. It feels like looking at a miracle."

Mary looked up into the sky and closed her eyes, the warm sun bathing her in its brilliance. "I know what you mean. Everything in Clanholme is like that, you know? So much going on that we don't see, but can almost perceive. Sensed more than known. *Felt*, almost. And now it goes out beyond, too, into these fields all around us. Soon wheat or rice or quinoa, flowers or clover or tubers—they'll all start coming up, from the cuttings and seed bombs we threw out. And not just here. I heard other settlements are starting to copy us."

Frank smiled, and she opened her eyes in time to see him gazing at her. She grinned back at him.

He said, "After we start harvesting all that, we'll be able to feed three times as many people as we have now. Plant another forest. Build another Clanholme, maybe on the very ground we're crossing now. Self-sufficient little miracle farms spreading out over all these hills. It's like we're standing on the edge of something really important, watching it unfold in front of us. It's wonderful."

"That's why we're riding out to fight. Don't forget it, okay? We're doing this for Hunter. And the rest of the Clanners and their kids, and hundreds of other people, thousands, who survived that first terrible winter, they're all the reason we fight."

Frank thought of the many children back at Clanholme and nodded. They were worth the losses the Clan was about to suffer. "I know. I just can't wait till this is over," he said. "I want to get back to being a real dad. Between my duties and the craziness of spring sowing..."

"Frank, I know you don't spend as much time with him as you'd like to, but you're a great father to him. I know he looks up to you. A lot of the kids do."

"Yeah," Frank said. He cleared his throat and gazed off into the distance. "Who would have thought, a year ago, that we'd be riding horses to go fight a battle on American soil against Americans?"

Mary took a deep breath and let it out slowly. Then she replied, "Ethan and Cassy. They both did. And thank goodness for that, or we'd all be dead now, probably. Cassy wanted a place to get away from the world, and Ethan thought alien lizards were taking over the government. We lucked out, meeting up with those crazies."

Frank smiled. "Don't forget Michael—he just wanted to forget the violence, go out in the woods whenever he could and travel on his Marine woodcraft. Crazy isn't all bad."

She nodded and they spent the next few minutes in small talk. For a moment, it was nice to forget the terrible purpose for which they rode out and the danger they'd soon face.

Along the way, the Clan and Army forces were joined by two dozen more fighters from Taj Mahal. That was most of the smaller settlement's able-bodied adults, Frank knew, and he rode out to greet them as they approached the line, filled them in on what was going on, and directed them to take up the rear in the column to stay together, or meld in as they found open spots if they wished. They moved to the rear of the column as a cohesive group.

It was reassuring to know they had such willing allies, even if they couldn't contribute as many troops as some others. They were good friends of Clanholme, these displaced first and second-generation immigrants from India, who had settled here by Clan invitation and were rapidly mastering Cassy's methods.

Shortly after the Taj Mahal contingent joined them, Taggart's company from Manheim showed up. Right after that, a couple dozen bike-mounted troops from Renfar joined, most armed with civilian hunting rifles. Half of Renfar's group were paramedics, nurses, and doctors. They brought a lot of corpsman gear and field surgery equipment, along with a small two-wheeled wagon loaded with the kind of cheap ten-by-ten pavilions Frank used to buy for summer barbeques. Now they would serve as field hospitals for the Confederation forces. The Renfar troops also brought a second wagon, covered with a tarp. Frank assumed those were more medical supplies.

He made a mental note to set up an ongoing paramedics-level training program for the Clan and her allies. Those paramedics were damn valuable, and there weren't enough of them. Clanholme itself had only a couple, including Lance Corporal Sturm, one of Michael's Marine Corps fighters, but at least she was a qualified field medic. Renfar was about to become a medical school for the rest of them, if Frank could arrange it.

The column lead stopped on the crest of a low hill, and word came down the line to spread out to either side. Showtime was approaching.

As Frank reached the crest to join Michael and Cassy, he saw a broad, low valley full of brushes, scattered about with trees. On the other side, perhaps a quarter mile away, stood another low hill. On that hill were more troops than he could easily count, sitting atop bicycles. They made no effort to run, dammit. So, this valley would be the host for this Clan-versus-Empire party, it seemed. They hadn't time to deploy for ambush, unfortunately.

"Come on," Frank said to Mary as he dismounted, "let's go get good seats for the show."

Instead of answering, Mary got off her horse, grabbed

him, and wrapped her arms around him. She rested her face in the crook of his neck. Startled, Frank gently stroked her hair and rested his face on the top of her head. He could smell the comforting, welcome smell of his wife, and suddenly wrapped his arms around her, too, squeezing tightly.

"Stay safe, my love," he muttered into her hair, and on his cheek, he felt her lightly nod. Every time they were in battle together, Frank's insides twisted in knots. What would he do without her? It was a question he didn't want to think about, so he shoved it deep inside, into that little box of fear and doubt where he stuffed everything he didn't have the leisure or the desire to deal with.

"I love you always," Mary said into his neck.

Frank caught a teary note in her voice, and squeezed her tighter for a moment before replying, "All the days, baby... I love you all the days."

- 22 -

1145 HOURS - ZERO DAY +254

CASSY TURNED TO Michael amidst the clamor of people staking their mounts on the back side of the hill, spreading out to her left and right, and generally getting ready. "How many do we have?"

"We number about four-hundred troops, plus the medic team from Renfar," Michael said.

"Was the scouts' report on their unit size accurate?"

"I believe the Empire only has the one company there, for now. But if the OpFor's other two companies are en route to rally with this company, they'll be here in about half an hour, maybe forty-five minutes at most. We have to move fast."

She knew when they got there they'd be evenly matched. Damn, that truly sucked.

"Maybe I should have brought the battlecars," Cassy said. "What's done is done, though. I'm open to suggestions from our resident military genius."

Michael smiled briefly. "I'm no genius. But for what it's worth, my advice is to overwhelm this OpFor before they're reinforced. If we can render them combat-ineffective, we can then turn to face the other two companies, hopefully with a numerical advantage."

Cassy looked out over the valley for a brief moment, contemplating Michael's advice. It made sense. "Yes, let's do that," she said with a nod.

"Alright," he said. "I'll gather up a hundred good riders, starting with Taggart's troops, and ride north using the hills for cover. I want to circle them, and then hit them in the rear while the rest of you have their undivided attention." Michael frowned at Cassy. "You will, of course, stay on this hill so you can maintain line-of-sight to all our engaging units, right?"

Cassy shook her head. "No. I'll be with the troops crossing that terrain down there. I want to be with our boys and girls when they begin to scale that hill under fire. I will not send them where I'm afraid to go."

Michael's eyebrows furrowed. "Cassy, why don't you lead the riders, and I'll coordinate the battle? I can probably do it better, I can do it best from up here. That is my job, right? Leading our troops in battle?"

"No, not right now. I don't know how to lead an ambush, Michael. You will ride with the cavalry, and use your best judgment on when and how to engage them, once we have their attention. I'm the Clan leader—I can't stay in back where it's safe, and I can't leave the battlefield to launch an ambush during our end-game play."

A voice behind her made her spin, recognizing Frank's deep voice, saying, "Cassy, that's a very bad idea. I think you should let me and Michael lead here. We'll each take a flank, and you can go with the cavalry. Michael can assign some qualified Marine to stay up here and keep us all in touch with the big picture or approaching threats, using our short-range radios."

Damn Frank... Cassy didn't like being ganged up on, and it wasn't like Frank knew more about combat than she did.

They were both civilians before all this, for Pete's sake. "This isn't up for debate. I'm staying with the main Clan troops. Frank, you're better on horseback than on foot, so you and Michael decide who takes the cavalry and who takes our left flank. One of Michael's military people can stay here to observe and report, but I got our right flank."

Frank opened his mouth to say something but was cut off by Cassy almost immediately. "Dismissed, dammit!"

Cassy spun on her heels and strode away toward the "right" side of the hill, barking orders. At least the rest of her troops could listen to freaking orders! They moved quickly and efficiently to line up, get into position, check ammo... Whatever her orders as she walked her line, they obeyed quickly and well. That was a damn good thing, because they had precisely zero time to spare if they were going to mop up this company before their bigger, badder friends arrived.

* * *

As Cassy strode away, Frank looked to Michael, dumbfounded. "What the hell?"

Michael shrugged. Quietly, he replied, "She has a point, Frank. She's the leader. It has to be she who leads. You want the cavalry, or the frontal assault?"

Frank felt his face flush red, his palms sweating. "Dammit, Michael, I know you don't believe that. If we lose her, we lose more than just another Clanner. Do you think the Confederation is strong enough to survive without her leadership?"

Michael frowned, and grabbed Franks arm. He leaned in to whisper through clenched teeth, "Frank, shut the fuck up. Don't you get it? She's going to do this, right or wrong, and we can't stop her. Stop fucking with the troops' heads by being insubordinate. They have to trust her leadership to survive this, and they have to take that trust back home with them to their settlements to keep the Confederation strong. Get on board or get on your horse and go home."

Then, patting Frank's shoulder and smiling, he said loudly enough to be overheard, "Yes, she knows what she's doing. Damn straight, Frank. So you want the assault or the ambush?"

Frank, agape, stared at Michael. How could he agree with Cassy on this? It was so wrong... Or was it? If Cassy wasn't going to change her mind, then maybe throwing a hissy fit about it in front of the troops, minutes before they went into battle, wasn't the best thing for morale. "My wife is here. My people are here. You take the soldiers, and go—"

"Excuse me," said a dark-haired young man, maybe nineteen or twenty years old, approaching. He wore blue jeans, combat boots, and a denim jacket, with a John Deer cap on his head. "Is this where we should set up the mortars?"

Frank blinked. "The what?" The words made sense individually, but strung together, Frank was drawing a blank.

"The mortars, sir. We brought three mortars and twenty shells for each, from Renfar."

Frank turned to look at Michael, and saw he had done the same. They stared at each other for a second. Then Michael broke into a huge grin.

"How do you have mortars, kid?" Michael asked, his grin still going ear to ear.

The young man said, "Oh, we make them. The Renaissance Fairgrounds have all sorts of stuff for fabrication. Even welding. We got one of those wood-powered generators from Falconry to power a bunch of tools, a compressor... Anyway, one of our guys was a survival nut before the war, and made us a bunch of these."

Michael made a weird barking noise, then shouted,

"Oorah!" He pointed down the back of the hill, and said to the Renfar man, "Don't just stand there, son. Get them set up just downhill, there, where snipers can't get you."

Frank watched, still trying to figure out what that barking noise had been. It was kind of intimidating. And it made him look to Michael for orders, by reflex. Wow. How'd he do that?

Michael turned back to Frank and said, "My friend, this changes everything. You'll have to take command of our left wing because I won't be able to. I'll put the cavalry mission to flank the Empire troops in the hands of Taggart's ranking officer, Captain Willard if I remember right. I have to stay here and..." he paused, then continued, "and tell the mortar operators where to fire. I'm the only one I know for sure who's well-trained as a forward observer and spotter."

Frank grinned. For once, Michael had used regular English instead of Marine lingo Frank couldn't understand as readily. "Hot damn. You get them set up and run the artillery. I'll take left wing. You got your radio?"

Michael nodded, pointing at his hip.

Frank turned to hobble toward his part of the line, leaving Michael to do whatever it was he did as a "forward observer." He, Michael, and Cassy all had short-range handheld radios, with a couple spares extra. Frank assumed one would go to the cavalry detachment and the other to the field hospital. Already, down the hill, the medical pavilions were going up even as Michael's artillery troops got themselves into position. Frank glanced up and down his own line of people, and nodded. They knew what to do without him telling them—get in line, hurry up, and wait for orders. Standard operating procedure, SOP.

"Story of my life," he grunted, and pulled his M4 off his back, checked his magazines, and got back on his horse. He'd be the only one to ride into battle, the rest of his troops having staked their horses behind the hill's cover, just as Cassy's troops to the right had done.

* * *

Cassy keyed up her radio and, after it beeped to indicate it was transmitting, she said, "Charlie One to Delta One, status?" She was, of course, Charlie One. Delta One was the cavalry detachment and Delta Two was the mortar team. Frank was Lincoln One, a not-so-clever reference to the fact that he led the left flank.

"Delta One. We are mobile. Good to go," replied the cavalry detachment. Whoever was on radio duty for them had a familiar voice, so probably one of the Clanners who had gone with them, or maybe one of Michael's familiar Marines.

Frank's voice then came on, saying, "Lincoln is in position, Lincoln One standing by for orders."

Cassy handed the radio to a young Clanner who would act as her radio operator, and looked out over the small valley between her people and the Empire's invasion force. No doubt this valley would soon turn red with blood. Those bastards on the valley's other end were still in the same position, only now prone for the most part. They would wait for the Clan—no, the Confederation, she reminded herself—to come to them. Cassy's people would be assaulting people who were prone, using the hill crest as cover, and defending the high ground. They showed no interest in going on the offensive against Cassy's larger force. That would have been too much to hope for.

Her heart raced, and she felt like she couldn't catch her breath. In her mind, she heard Choony's calm, nearly monotone voice telling her how to slow her heartbeat and her breathing. She took a moment to slip into the memory, following his instructions, and felt her heart slow. Breathing came easier, too. The adrenaline subsided. It was only pre-battle jitters... During the actual fighting, she never seemed to freeze or panic. She shook like a leaf afterward, but never during. Michael had once told her she was naturally wired for battle, and it was far from common. He also said it wasn't always a good thing, and meant that she had to remember that most of her own troops wouldn't be wired that way.

Cassy nodded to her radio operator. "Get ready." Then she turned to face the enemy. She'd have to cross this valley with her troops, but there was plenty of cover. Only at the last rush up the hill would the Confed forces be completely exposed, but she'd worry about that after she crossed the four hundred yards between her forces and their prey.

Over the radio, Michael advised everyone that Delta One was on the way and to get their troops across as fast as they could without being reckless—the cavalry detachment would hit the enemy in the rear after they were fully engaged.

"Charge!" she yelled. "Keep covered for as long as you can but don't stop until you're close enough to shoot the bastards!"

Then she was running. The sun was warm and welcoming, the breeze was slight and refreshing. Above and around them, birds still chirped. Such a gorgeous day... She reached the first cover, a lengthy section of bush, and stopped, crouching down. In a few seconds, the rest of her unit had caught up, and she waved them on. "Go, go, go!"

After a few had passed her, the unit flowing around the bush, she bolted forward again. Three-hundred-fifty yards to go. Three hundred yards. Two-hundred-fifty yards, moving from cover to cover. They had heard some random potshots early on, until whoever was in charge up there put a stop to it. She guessed that the enemy would hold fire until the Confeds were within easier range, to conserve ammunition.

When they had gone another fifty yards, Cassy could feel tension building in the air, like she could actually read the minds of both the enemy and her units. The real fight was about to begin. She was wound up tight and ready.

* * *

Frank had organized his people into five thirty-person platoons, figuring that five unit commanders might be harder to coordinate, but would also be more flexible and require less attention from him. He had no idea if it was the right decision, but now, riding his horse alongside his running platoon-mates, it was too late to change it. He glanced to his right from time to time to make sure he kept more or less in line with Cassy's units. Ahead, the meters between him and his enemy slowly shrank.

When he had gotten about fifty yards out, the Empire troops opened fire, but it had only been a scattering and had quickly abated. No one in his platoon had been hit, and a glance left and right didn't reveal anyone else obviously hit, so he had kept going.

At one-hundred yards out, his units had reached the first sporadic cover. Cassy's side of the valley had more cover, or at least it had begun further back. "Two by two!" he yelled, and heard the call repeated all down his line. He nodded in approval when he saw that half remained in cover while half advanced; when they reached cover, the first half then moved out. It was a deadly game of leapfrog.

Another twenty-five yards, followed by another—and then all hell broke loose. The air filled with the deep echoes of rifle fire and hundreds of high-pitched buzzing sounds as the bullets streaked by. A scream to his left, and he saw a man fall, clutching his leg; two men rushed to him and dragged him to cover, one grabbing the man's rifle. Then from cover, all three popped up to return fire. The roar of shooting was all around him, then, as both his troops and Cassy's returned fire. A deafening *whizz* went by his ear, a bullet narrowly missing Frank's head, but he paid it no heed. It hadn't had his name on it.

"Advance, advance," he screamed to his left. A third of those men and women scurried out from cover and sprinted to the next cover in line, most sliding the last few feet. Then a hundred Confed fighters returned fire on the Empire's ridgeline, and Frank heard a couple of screams. The rest ducked down for a moment, hiding from the swarm of death that poured into their ranks, and Frank's troops in the rear took advantage. They sprinted forward, passing their companions who fired up at the ridge to keep the enemy down. This once, the enemy's elevated position worked to Frank's advantage as his troops continued suppressive fire even after they had been passed by their companions. The sprinting troops found cover and hid. Frank heard the sounds of dozens and dozens of rifles being reloaded.

Frank heard cheering from up on the hill. He put his binoculars to his eyes and looked up to find that a stretch of hilltop nearly one-hundred feet long had a low, two-tier sandbag wall. The top sandbags were positioned so that the prone men and women behind it could rest their rifle barrels between them and on the solid bottom layer. There was no way his people could effectively counter that no matter how much fire they hit it with. And with them being uphill, there was little chance of a grenade making it that far. Hell, they'd probably roll halfway back down the hill toward the thrower before detonating.

"Fuck this," Frank muttered as he plucked the radio from his belt. He keyed it and, shouting above the din of battle, said, "Lincoln One requesting fire support. Michael, I got a sandbagged emplacement. They got us stopped cold."

"Lincoln One, this is Delta Two. What are their

coordinates?" Michael's steady voice came out from the radio's speaker.

"On the ridge, maybe fifty yards east of the central hilltop," Frank shouted back.

His radio crackled, but there was a deafening roar and he couldn't hear whatever Michael had said. Frank looked over by reflex and saw two—no, three!—geysers of dirt and flame rising from the ground, swallowing some of his leading troops. The Empire bastards were throwing grenades. Frank cursed himself for not realizing that just because his troops couldn't throw grenades up there, that didn't mean the enemy couldn't. Gravity and descending terrain combined to give them a much farther range than they would on level ground.

As dirt rained down on him and the troops around him, Frank raised his radio to his mouth, but before he could click the button, he felt a deep rumble in his bones, and his ears were assaulted by the most menacing sound he had ever heard. He looked toward the source—the hastily sandbagged enemy position—and if grenades had raised geysers of dirt, then whatever had hit them raised monsoons, with almost blindingly bright flashes of light. The mortars! Michael must have been an expert with them, because his first three rounds all hit hostile targets. Those were followed several heartbeats later by three more of the huge, murderous blossoms of light.

Frank screamed—charge, and move it, and now-now-now. The entire line of Confed troops rose from cover and sprinted forward, first only a couple and then a tsunami, all rushing uphill screaming their war cries. Frank, atop his horse, rode back and forth along his line shouting encouragement. Twice he called for medics, but he knew there were more down, and there would be more still to come.

He spotted Mary, crouched behind a bush under heavy fire from a cluster of Empire troops, but those vanished in a flash of fire, noise, dirt, and gore as a mortar shell landed on them. Mary spotted him and waved, then rushed up the hill as well. He rode toward her, and together they made their way up the hill. Many of his unit were already at the crest, pouring fire onto the Empire troops. This was going to work!

And then Frank saw movement toward the base of the hill on the back side, and froze. Dozens, no, hundreds of Empire troops pedaled furiously at the base of the hill, and then dismounted, throwing their bikes down and rushing up the hill. Time seemed to both slow down and speed up as tiny details became crystal clear while the mass of battle around him seemed to occur in a haze. He clicked his radio on and screamed that the other two companies were coming up the hill, but didn't have time to listen to the response.

A hail of bullets flew up hill at him. Abruptly, he felt the wind knocked out of him and found himself looking up at the clear blue sky, and his mind reeled trying to make sense of it.

Mary's face came into view, red and screaming, but Frank couldn't hear the words. What was she saying? Get up?

The noise of battle crashed through to him once again, shattering the confused silence, and his mind caught up. His horse had been shot out from under him. Mary was screaming for him to get up. He looked down the hill and saw the enemy swarming like locusts as they rushed toward him.

Mary helped him up and they hobbled down the hill back the way they had come. He saw dozens and dozens of his troops rushing past him going the other way, up the hill. Screams of agony came from all around him, friend and enemy alike.

Frank took one last glance over his shoulder and down

the hillside behind him and saw doom approaching, for behind the wave of Empire people who were now halfway up the hill came another wave of them.

The Clan had misjudged the enemy. There were more than Cassy had thought. This was going to be a disaster, barring a miracle. Frank heard words coming out of his mouth. “Mary, there’s more! Run, *run* dammit!”

He couldn’t hear her response well over the din of battle and the din in his mind, but she didn’t run. She gripped him tighter and half pulled, half dragged him down the hill. Behind him, a cheer arose even as, all around him and Mary, Confed fighters ran past. Fleeing the enemy, as he was. He clicked the radio again. “Cassy, Lincoln falling back. Fall back!”

There was no reply. Frank felt desperation creep over him—something had happened. The fool must have charged into battle. Damn her!

As the Confed troops thinned out, fewer now running past him, Frank heard the cries of triumph on the hillside turn to screams. Frantic gunfire. Horse hoof-beats. Abruptly, people appeared all around him, running—Empire people. Half didn’t carry weapons, he noted, mind not making sense of what he was seeing.

Frank felt a bone-crushing impact on his back. Mary screamed in pain and fear as the ground rushed up at him.

* * *

Samuel pedaled hard toward the sound of battle. Ahead of him, he saw his troops rushing up the hill, killing the damned Confed troops up there. Around him, the fleeing Republic troops were rallying, joining his own people and heading back up that deadly hill. What Confederation troops didn’t die, fled.

Beside him, Brett panted but didn't slow down, the gentle slope tiring him but not stopping him, and Samuel was determined to keep up. Together, they reached the crest of the hill. They dodged corpses—Empire and Confederation alike—and almost pulled air as they kept pedaling. Ahead, he saw a knot of six people surrounding a seventh, who was barely keeping to his feet as a woman struggled to keep him upright and fleeing.

Samuel gathered some of his nearby troops, his voice carrying over the riotous noise, and they chased after that knot of Confed troops. An easy target, and in striking distance. He grinned, and felt like the cobra must feel right before it strikes.

One of his own men easily outpaced the rest of them, even Samuel himself, despite being on foot. Of course it would be a black. Dammit, there was no way he was going to let some darkie with a knife get this kill. Samuel pulled out his carbine, aimed, and fired at his trooper. The man fell headlong, right into the staggering Confed man and the woman, and all three landed in a tangle of limbs. Well, that's what you get when you try to upstage Samuel Pease, he thought, and grinned as he closed the distance to the group. They had stopped, five of the Confed turning around to fire on Samuel and his oncoming Republic troops while the woman tried to get the man back to his feet. Samuel and his men fired once, the volley dropping the brave Confed idiots like flies.

Only the hobbled man and the woman remained. Despite the hopelessness of their situation, the two struggled to flee, leaving their rifles behind in the mad rush to escape. He and his men had them quickly surrounded.

Samuel got off his bike and sauntered toward the encircled two, while his troops finished off the five downed Confeds. When Brett stooped at one of the bodies and took an ear for a trophy, Samuel grinned, then looked up at his next victims. The man... He looked family. Samuel cocked his head for a moment, and then it came to him. The ambush at Elizabethtown. He'd been one of them. Clearly someone in charge, if his people were willing to protect him, to die for him.

"So," Samuel began, trying to sound nonchalant, "I do believe I know you, mister."

Brett interrupted, the dumbass, and shouted, "Hey, he was at the ambush!"

"Shut up, Brett. You're fucking with my mojo. Now then—"

"Sam, I'm telling you, he was at Elizabeth—"

"Shut the fuck up, Brett. And don't call me Sam. Now then. As my moronic friend here points out, I recognize you. I bet you figured you were pretty clever with that ambush. How's being clever working out for you now?"

The man spat at the ground. "The Clan will never bow to you. Let us go and I might not kill you."

Samuel grinned again. The woman had that deer-in-headlights expression that just looked so damn hot on bitches. She probably knew that guy, too, or she'd have taken off. Women never stuck around when the going got tough, as far as Samuel was concerned. "Bow, kneel, lay down—it's all the same to me. I just like killing people, when it's called for. Not just random, mind you. No, people like you who deserve it. And when my orders call for me to get my hands bloody, that's a bonus. Who's your piece of ass?" Samuel wiggled his eyebrows at the chick. She was going to be his loot for the night. Plunder. Ha! Plunder that booty! Sometimes life was grand.

"She's nobody," he said, but Samuel noticed the man's jaw tighten, his body stiffen. "Let her go, and I'll go with you peacefully. I know the Clan's layout, where the traps are, all their secrets."

The woman wrapped her arms around him and cried, "Frank, no! You can't do that!"

That sure got Samuel's attention. But such a trade didn't seem like much fun. "How about I just kill her, and then cut your skin off your face an inch at a time until you tell me all those juicy little secrets?"

The man, Frank, put his cheek on the woman's head and squeezed her. Samuel grinned... He had been right about the two.

Brett said, "Screw that, boss. Let's kill him and take the chica for questioning? I bet she knows stuff too. I'll get her to talk. She'll beg."

Samuel laughed out loud. "Brett, bitches will say *anything* to get away from your limp-dicked stupid ass. That's no challenge. Hey, Frank, right? Who do you think she'd enjoy more, me or this slack-jaw?"

The man kept his expression rigidly neutral and said, "I wonder how all your troops feel about working for a monster like you? Some of them have to still have a conscience. Maybe one of them will put a knife in your back and do the world a favor."

Brett stepped forward and backhanded the man, closed-fisted, and Frank staggered. Only the woman's grip kept him upright. That's when Samuel noticed he had no left foot. "Goddamn, Brett. Can't you see the man's a cripple? Poor guy is only half a man. You know, beating up cripples is really low-rent. You should look into some etiquette lessons, my friend."

The woman finally spoke to Samuel directly, and shouted, "He's more of a man than you'll ever be, you monster! I bet two of your stupid coins that your own men frag you tonight."

Samuel frowned. "Firstly, Miss Sexdoll, their conscience will be just fine once I make 'em all take turns on you. Shared guilt, shared laughs. But you're wrong, you know, none of them will knife me. See, in the Midwest Republic we have this thing called 'discipline.' We make the trains run on time, and all that jazz. They get food, they get power, they get loot. It comes on time, every time. You—"

Frank turned and whispered into the woman's ear. Motherfucker. Samuel shouted, "You interrupt me again, half-man, I'll cut your damn dick off and choke your bitch with it. See if I'm joking."

Frank stopped, looked down at the ground. The muscles in his jaw flexed repeatedly, but he didn't say anything more.

"Good, our developmentally-disabled friend here knows how to follow instructions," Samuel said.

Brett said, "Sam, we shouldn't waste any more time with these two. Let's kill them and get on with the slaughter. I'm bored as shit."

Samuel grinned. Leave it to Brett to keep his eye on the big picture. "You have a point. Well, gimpy here will only slow us down. He doesn't look like cycling's his best sport, right?" He paused while his troops laughed awkwardly, dutifully. Then he said, "Brett. Shoot him and take the bitch, so we can go get to looting."

Brett took a step back without wasting a second, raised his rifle one-handed, elbow at his hip, and fired. He had a huge grin on his face.

But as he raised his rifle, the woman stepped in the way at the same time she yanked the man to the side—Brett's shot struck the woman in the middle of her back, and she collapsed without a sound. The man, Frank, tried to keep her from falling, but with only one foot he instead fell too, landing almost on top of her.

As Frank screamed the rage-filled primal scream of one losing a child or a wife, he draped himself over the dying woman, who lay on the ground gasping. Blood bubbled up from her mouth, and her jaw opened and closed like a fish out of water.

"Goddammit, Brett. What a shitty waste of hot ass. Hey Frank, sorry about that. We weren't trying to kill our fuckdoll, man. Brett just can't shoot for shit."

Brett laughed, and said, "That's what she said."

Samuel rolled his eyes. "Damn, Brett. You are so stupid. That joke doesn't work here."

His sidekick replied, "Sure it does! They do say that."

Samuel chuckled. "Whatever. So what do you want to do with the cripple?" Samuel looked at the man, who cradled the woman's head, stroking her hair, oblivious to anything going on around him. He kept making a weird, annoying, grief-filled noise. "This pathetic shit is like fingernails on a chalkboard."

Brett shrugged. "Fuck him. You want the honors this time around, boss?"

All eyes turned to Samuel. As long as he had their attention, he might as well have fun with it. "Sure. Let's water the grass," he said as he pulled out his Bowie-style knife, the heft feeling good in his hand.

A blur of movement in the corner of his eye made Samuel turn, only to find the gimp lunging toward him with a knife of his own. Stupid, but hilarious the way the man limped. Frank had murder in his eyes, which only made it funnier.

Samuel turned to face Frank, and readied himself. This sucked, because even a gimp with a knife could kill someone. Knife fights were never, ever a sure bet. But with everyone watching him, he had to do this to keep them in line. If he chickened out, they'd turn on him. Well, if you gotta do something, you might as well have fun with it. "Let's get this over with, cripple."

The sound of many rifles being fired behind him, some

on automatic, abruptly pierced the air. All around him, Samuel saw his men falling, then he heard hoofbeats behind him, a growing thunder. But with the cripple coming at him, he couldn't turn to face it. "Fuck! What's going on?"

Frank finally got within striking distance, and swung his knife. Samuel took two steps backward, but saw that Frank kept the blade moving as he shuffled forward. The knife whooshed in front of Samuel's face and he stepped back again. Now he felt a chill down his spine. Brett hadn't answered him, but worse, this Frank guy had some training —he slashed from left to right, but without slowing down, that strike shifted to a diagonal upward swing, then turned around for a diagonal downward swing. That was training—keep striking, hitting the compass points each time.

Samuel waited until the man swept his blade again, then jabbed his knife at the man's exposed left shoulder. Frank used his offhand to swat at the blade, and though it left a terrible gash in his forearm, it kept Samuel from thrusting his blade into Frank's shoulder.

Meanwhile, Frank's own blade never stopped its buzzsaw attack, and Samuel felt it slice into his left arm with an impact that told him the knife had cut him down to the bone. Samuel staggered back and locked eyes with Frank. This sonofabitch had cut him. Him, Samuel Pease, the fucking predator, had been stung by his prey. Samuel's blood boiled and a rage overtook him. He saw Frank's blade sweep right-to-left, and then he lunged, his left foot moving forward, bending at the knee, giving Samuel a bit of extra range and power while he thrust the blade. Samuel saw Frank take another cut to his left arm to block the thrust—and then he saw the ground rushing up at him.

What the fuck? His left leg, which he had lunged with, didn't hold him. It was like jello. Samuel landed in a heap, sputtering curses. He brought his knife up in front of himself defensively, but his enemy Frank wore a wicked grin, and stepped backward instead of coming in to try to finish Samuel off. That didn't make any sense...

The thunder of hoofbeats suddenly overwhelmed every other noise. Samuel risked a glance around but quickly wished he hadn't, for all around him horses thundered by, sped by gravity as they charged down the hill, dozens of them. And then they were gone, moving on. He wondered where the fuck they came from, but then snapped his attention back to Frank. His enemy had taken a couple more steps back and now stood still, hands at his side, one hand holding a bloody knife and the other dripping blood from the wounds Samuel had given him.

Samuel tried to get up, but that left leg gave out again. Reflexively, he looked at his leg with bewilderment, and then saw why it didn't hold him up. He bled profusely, and his mind registered that he had been shot, the bullet passing through his femur and smashing it in half. His weight had slid the jagged end through his muscle and skin, and it now protruded from the front of his thigh. He became suddenly aware of pain. Agony like he hadn't ever felt before. Part of him wondered why he hadn't felt himself get shot. He looked up at Frank.

Frank said, "Your friend is already dead. He died quickly, you know, just like that. And you're dying too, you disgusting little troll."

Samuel hated him. Standing there, looking smug. Motherfucker. "You didn't win, you didn't beat Samuel Fucking Pease. You arrogant little prick, I'm not on the ground because you won. Someone sucker-punched me with a fucking bullet."

Frank didn't smile, but only nodded. "Possibly. But that's kind of irrelevant, don't you think? My wife died in my arms while you were patting yourselves on the back."

Samuel grunted, his lips curling up into a grimace.

Frank's eyes narrowed as he continued, "You have no idea the mistake you just made. This was a battle for our survival, but now? Now I won't rest until you and everyone in this world like you are gone. I swear I will kill you all. Everyone you know, everyone you love, will die because of you. If it takes the rest of my life, no one in your psychotic fucking Empire will ever know what it's like to sleep soundly again. They'll never be safe from me. And *that* will be your only legacy."

Samuel's teeth were tightly clenched as he struggled not to scream from the fiery agony in his thigh. This verbose motherfucker... "Nice speech, cripple. Why don't you go gimp your ass over to your dead fucking wife and tell her all this shit, because I don't care. Idiot, I don't have any loved ones in the Republic for you to kill, and I don't give two shits about the Republic, either."

Samuel watched as Frank first nodded, then hobbled over to Brett's corpse—poor Brett, Samuel's only real friend, now staring open-eyed at the sky with one eye, the other eye a gaping hole from where the bullet that killed him had exited. Frank leaned over and picked up Brett's rifle.

"Go ahead and kill me," Samuel said, trying to keep his voice steady but coming out instead sounding whiny and panicked, even to his own ears. "It won't stop the Republic, and it won't bring your cockholster back to life." Soon enough, the Republic would be back with a vengeance. Then this snot-nosed punk would get *extra special* treatment before he died. The thought brought a smile to Samuel's face.

Frank stared at him for a long moment. "You talk about my wife like that, and then *smile?* What kind of a pervert are you?"

Samuel decided he wasn't talking his way out of this one. Sometimes the prey gets lucky, that's all. "I'm no monster.

I'm just a realist, and I figure the weak deserve to get used up by their betters. Go ahead and gloat, you fucking waste of oxygen. This new world has no room for useless meatbags like you—and you didn't beat me, you got lucky."

The other man watched Samuel as he spoke, but didn't interrupt, and didn't reply. He just looked at Samuel with his lip curled down, like he just stepped in dog shit. Women looked at Brett that way sometimes. Samuel bared his teeth at Frank. The little bitch probably didn't have the balls to do it right, anyway. "What are you waiting for? Trying to grow some balls? It doesn't work that way, cocksmoker. I bet you don't have the cojones to—"

Bang! The sonofabitch fired his rifle.

The last thing Samuel saw was Frank mutter, "There's some reality for you," before he turned to lower himself to the ground, crawled to the woman, and then just sat there. The bastard's eyes were dry. Then there was only blackness.

* * *

1400 HOURS - ZERO DAY +254

It was warm and bright, perfect for the afternoon nap Jaz had needed. She opened her eyes and saw the blue sky above, and Choony nearby cooking pemmican for lunch.

"Good morning," Choony said. "That was the shortest nap yet. How do you feel?"

Jaz slowly flexed her shoulder. It was tender, but no shooting pains like daggers. The fish antibiotics Choony had scrounged up actually worked, much to her amazement, and she had avoided infection. These days, infections had become once again a greedy killer. "Tender, but not as bad as it was. I think I might be able to ride in the wagon, actually."

Choony stood from the fire and brought an aluminum

camping plate to her. Full of totally gross-looking fried pemmican with a dash of flour. Biscuits and gravy without the biscuits—just flatbread to dip in the gruel. Ugh. “Thanks,” she said, but couldn’t bring herself to sound enthusiastic.

“I don’t think moving you is a good idea, Jaz. It hasn’t even been a week.”

“I think I know how long it’s been. I felt every minute. Thanks for your concern, though.”

Choony frowned. “Don’t be like that,” he said. “I’m not trying to say you can’t do something, only that I don’t think it’s a good idea.”

Jaz let out a long breath, and nodded. “I know you aren’t being insulting and stuff. I just don’t want to sit here anymore. We need to get back home. We’re running low on supplies, for one, and I don’t think you’re the one to hunt us up fresh grub.”

“We have enough for three more days,” Choony said. “I did inventory while you slept.”

Of course he had. Leave it to Choony to know how many fat-and-powdered-meat bars they had left. “Feed for the horses?” she asked.

“Lots of grass right here. It’s springtime. They can browse as much grass as they want.”

“Graze. They can graze on grass.”

“That, too,” Choony said.

“Look. It’s not like I got hit somewhere bad, like the shoulder.”

Choony frowned. “You did get hit in the shoulder. With an AK rifle. You should be dead.”

“It wasn’t the rifle that hit me, Choon. And I have a ton of damage, but no veins got hit, no arteries, it didn’t hit bone, and the ligament thingy didn’t get severed. I’m good to go.”

“It’ll take you months to get to mostly-normal. Years to

fully recover. You may never fully recover, in fact." Choony sounded so sure of himself. It was seriously irritating.

"You wrapped my left shoulder and arm, right? It's immobile. All good. I can ride a wagon, just maybe not a horse. I can fire a rifle, if I absolutely have to, because I shoot right-handed. And I want you to listen to me here, Choony—I can heal better at Clanholme with fresh vegetables and real medical care than I can out here. I'm well enough to travel."

"It's a bad idea, Jaz." He looked at her intently. The concern was etched on his face.

Jaz sighed. It was hard to be mad at him for being totally overprotective when he was all, like, trying to take care of her as best he could.

That was a new thing, a guy who actually cared for her. She felt her face smile and she reached her good arm up to cup his cheek in her hand. Oh, for fuck's sake—when did she get so gooey? Ugh. But she was still smiling.

Nothing for it so she plowed on. "We'll compromise. In the morning, we head back to Clanholme. You don't have to come, but I'm going, and I'm taking the wagon. But that gives me another most of a day to rest. You know that sitting still out here for too long a time is a sucker's game. Gotta keep moving."

Choony didn't reply at first, just stared at her intently. Well, he was probably trying to figure out how serious she was. She put on her most stern face and stared right back. Ha! Deal with that, Choon Choon.

Finally, he said, "Fine. We'll leave in the morning. I will do the packing, though, understand? You need to relax on the trip and try to stay as comfortable as you're able. How does that sound?"

Jaz grinned. "Deal. No take-backs. My diabolical plan worked—I got shot so that you'd have to pack the wagon."

Choony finally laughed then, and dug out some salt and

pepper for her meat-goo slop. Pemmican. Whatever, but she nodded a thanks as he handed them to her. Tomorrow—home again. Home... She liked having one, and she felt a smile cross her face again.

- 23 -

0800 HOURS - ZERO DAY +255

CARL RUSHED THROUGH the doorway grinning and saw Mary Ann burst from her chair in surprise, knocking it over.

"Horace Wattleberger is *not* the new official Speaker of Liz Town," he said, trying to look nonchalant. "The new Speaker is Ford Fairlane of the Puma Band."

Mary Ann snorted, then looked embarrassed for it. "Baloney. I didn't see 'Ford' on the ballot."

"I guess you got me. The final vote was about as lopsided as any I've ever seen, too. Horace Wattleberger got less than ten percent... not even all of the Diamondbacks voted for him. What a Band they are, eh?"

"They finished the tally, finally? Are those the results?"

"Yep, late last night, they told me. I went to check on them this morning and got the news. The actual numbers are: Horace, eight percent; Mary Ann, ninety percent; and two percent were people who voted for themselves or Donald Duck..."

"How cool is that?" Mary Ann asked.

Carl figured it was probably a rhetorical question, but so what? "Very cool," he answered. Then he took a deep breath.

"I have the results, plus three General Orders sheets for you to sign."

"Should I read them first?" Mary Ann picked up a pen.

Was she kidding? Carl wasn't certain. Either way, it was up to her. As her assistant, he'd never take advantage of the trust she had put in him since they met. "If you want, sure. The first is an official statement to place Horace and Pamela under arrest for trial on charges of Treason, plus other lesser charges. They're already detained, but this makes it official."

"No problem there," she said. Carl handed her the first sheet, and she scribbled her name at the bottom. "Second?"

"The second is to arrange for a gala celebration for your victory. Rub elbows with people, let them know you are still one of them, not moving into an ivory tower. Two days from now is good timing, according to your calendar."

Mary Ann took the sheet, frowned, and signed without reading it. "I thought you used some weird notebook thing to keep everything straight, not a calendar."

Carl nodded, taking the signed sheets back from her. "Yes, it's called a bullet journal. Best thing since sliced bread for keeping notes, schedules, and so on. Simple, and clear, too. I use it as a calendar so if I say it's a calendar, that's what it is, dammit," he huffed in mock indignation.

"I see," she replied with wide eyes and an innocent look, all in for Carl's little game, "and all this time I was sure it was a duck." More sincerely, she added, "I'm glad you take care of that part. I wouldn't know what time to eat breakfast if I didn't have someone telling me. What's the third General Order?"

Carl's smile faded, then morphed into a frown. He saw Mary Ann tense up when she saw it. He said, "Liz Town officially renounces ties to the Midwest Republic and reaffirms our commitment to the Confederation. It ends with a statement that any incursion by Republic troops into territory the Confederation claims will result in an immediate declaration of war."

Mary Ann nodded slowly, and looked to her feet. She was silent for a moment, then looked back up to Carl and said, "You know the Empire just sent a battalion of troops to attack Clanholme, right?"

Carl let out a long, deep breath and looked at the ceiling for a moment. Mary Ann had caught the implications immediately, of course. "Yes," he replied, and met her gaze again. "I sent two of my people to follow them, and I got word late last night that the Confederation met them head on, and pretty much handed them their ass. If your point is that the order would put us at war as soon as it's signed, then you're right—it will. You're not shrinking from a fight, are you?" Carl grinned to show that his words were meant in jest. "Not very Liz Town-ish if you ask me," he added, shaking his head sorrowfully.

Mary Ann threw her pen at Carl, but he ducked and the pen clattered into the kitchen cabinets behind him. "Shut up," she said, drawing each word out, her voice rising high on the first word and plummeting on the second. She continued, "I'm the Speaker. Whatever I do is Liz Town-ish, by definition."

"Good point," Carl said. "The order also officially announces Sunshine's new Band, by way of naming them in the list of Bands bound by the order. That way we avoid any need to discuss it with anyone. Like a president's executive order, in a way."

"No problem there. What were they called, again?"

"The Sewer Rats Band is what people have been calling them."

"That little ambush they put on, helping the Clan demolish the Empire unit right outside our front door, really turned the tide for us in getting the other Bands to support

Kodiak's agenda."

"Yes. Sunshine's a natural leader. She and the 'Rats' are going to be an asset."

"And now here you are, Alpha of the Timber Wolves and my right-hand man. That's a position that you turned down under the last Speaker, if I remember right. Pamela's job..."

"Yeah. Don't remind me. I learned my lesson about trying to avoid responsibility. When decent folks try to avoid the hassle and drama of leadership, it only leaves a void that people who want the position for the power will scramble to fill."

"You don't like the power?" Mary Ann asked, raising one eyebrow. It looked intentionally dramatic.

Carl said, "No, I don't. I like being able to protect my people and help others where we can, but I don't enjoy the position. I'd hand it over if I wasn't gun-shy after Pamela's power-grab. We'd all be slaves or dead as soon as she opened our gates to the Empire, and people are realizing it."

"Fine, I'll sign the order. And, Carl? Make sure we find out how many Confed people died fighting the Empire yesterday. We need to send tokens of our appreciation for their families. The Clan has some medal they came up with—maybe we could do the same. Start a real tradition. Call it a Medal of Valor or something."

"Yes, ma'am. I suppose you intend to let the Clan know about everything that's gone on here lately, and the outcome?"

"Ouch. I hate sharing Lizzie business with outsiders, but you're right—they need an explanation. There will be a lot of people angry at us for not joining in the battle, and rightfully so."

Carl nodded. Mary Ann was a damn good leader. He had always thought so, and this confirmed it. In the old world, authority never apologized for its actions, but these days people seemed to care more about integrity and justice than they did when it was all about zero-sum political games, brinkmanship, money, and revenge. Or maybe it was just that the cowards and scumbags were dying off faster than others. Most of the survivors did seem like ones other people trusted. People needed to rely on one another. Self-serving liars like Pamela were still getting tossed off the island, most places.

He shook his head to clear his thoughts. "If you want, I can tell Cassy and the Clan as well—they know me and that might be important right now." She nodded and he went on. "Now we have to plan the trial and go over the re-distribution plan for the food and other stockpiles that Pamela and her stooge Wattleberger illegally hoarded only for themselves. They won't need it after this trial, I bet."

"Let's get that trial going right away," Mary Ann said thoughtfully. "Start this evening, if you can arrange it that quickly. It's important. We need to close this out."

"You got it."

Now he had a little fun coming for a change—he got to go find Sunshine and tell her the good news about her Sewer Rats...

* * *

Driving off the Empire had been expensive and exhausting—but they had won. Now people were licking their wounds and mourning their dead. So what now, Cassy wondered as she and the rest of the Clan, together with representatives of most of their allies, made the somber journey to the northern food forest. They all had too much to do and never enough hours in the day, but Cassy had made sure everything in Clanholme came to a full stop this morning. The coming rites were too important not to.

Cassy led the procession. As they walked, she rolled her right shoulder, feeling the stabbing pain of her injury. She had dislocated her shoulder and pulled some ligaments, courtesy of yesterday's battle. As always, she had been in the forefront of the fighting. She refused to wear a sling until after she finished this unpleasant but crucial duty.

Behind her, Michael carried Mary's sapling for Frank. It was a Nanking Cherry that had rooted into dirt and compost over the winter. Normally, Frank would have carried it himself, but as a courtesy to his rank and in recognition of his injury, Michael had volunteered to help him with that part. Behind Michael, Frank hobbled on crutches with his son, Hunter, by his side.

The rest of the Clan came after. The dozen families of the Clan's fallen led them, carrying sacked saplings of their own, followed by all the rest and then the allied guests. Last up were thirteen new people, admitted from nearby isolated homesteads who now wished to join the Clan. They attended to see and learn the value of the Clan spots they had been given, and hopefully be inspired to earn those spots through hard work.

First the procession passed through the Jungle, with the column of Clanners weaving back and forth dodging boobytraps. The visitors and new members had been warned not to deviate from the path set by the Clan. Then came the open area between Jungle and forest. When they reached the very edge of the north food forest, Cassy stopped, trying to hide her relief and gratitude at having reached the walk's end. As usual, both Frank and Michael seemed to notice her physical distress—both had been watching her intently—but they didn't remark on it. She was grateful for that, too. The truth was, every step had jolted her injury painfully.

The procession leaders now waited for the rest of the procession to gather around Cassy. As they gathered, they formed a semicircle facing Cassy and the forest.

While they waited, Cassy put her good hand on Frank's arm and wished she could do something, anything, to take some of the pain for him. Except for a few hushed whispers to Hunter, Frank hadn't spoken a word since the battle ended an hour or so after Mary had been killed dodging in front to take the bullet intended for him. It had taken that full hour to mop up knots of survivors. And when she put her hand on him now, Frank didn't react at all. He was, simply, crushed. She figured he had withdrawn into his own inner hell, and she hoped he came back to them soon. Her heart ached for this good man.

Behind her, she heard Michael ask Ethan, "Why not put them in the south food forest?" Ethan quietly answered, "Because we walk through that more, and because everything flows downhill. Until they become fully part of nature again, we can't have them right above our water supply."

A chill ran down Cassy's spine. It was cold, logical, and true. She wanted to scream, but what good would that do? And anyway, what had they said that was actually wrong? She knew both men too well to think either of them was remotely cold. She pretended not to hear so she wouldn't have to say anything about it.

As the procession finished assembling, Cassy stared into the forest. They were near a recently cleared segment—they had broken the small forest up into chunks, each at its own level of maturity ranging from the freshly cleared, like this one, to almost fully mature forest. That patchwork quilt design gave the forest its maximum possible "edge effect"—and the edges had the most productive growth, whether of forest, mixed ground cover, or any other growing zone.

Within the cleared section where they were gathered, volunteers had dug thirteen graves, leaving the removed soil piled nearby. They would put the bodies of their fallen to rest there, planting trees over each both in commemoration and as a way for them to continue to give to the Clan. The trees would serve as gravestones for the families they had left behind. Mary's grave was front and center, with the others arrayed in a rough semi-circle facing south to catch plenty of sunlight. This would help the trees capture more heat, and improve the soil as much as the nutrients in the bodies would.

As always, Cassy and the more agricultural Clanners worked anything done at Clanholme into the warp and woof of the farm's complex, fascinating and thriving web of life. Most Clanners found it somehow comforting that the bodies of loved ones would stay a part of that web even after death.

When all had gathered and the crowd had quieted themselves—which didn't take long on this somber occasion—Cassy spoke to them all from the heart. She talked about the sacrifice they had made to save the Clan, their way of life, their freedom. She spoke of the Empire that had done this to them, and for what? More land? The Empire had enough land. They wanted more only because they were power-mad, pawns of a traitor general who was trying to take over America. The Clanners and allies had responded to that attempt as she hoped Americans always would, defeating it with determination, courage, and willing sacrifice.

She paused to look around the solemn group, then presented the Clan's Medal of Generator, first created by two of the Clan's children in honor of an act of extreme courage, posthumously to the five who had died trying to save Frank, a Clan leader and member of the Council. Their sacrifice had indeed saved him and, by that act, had saved his son from growing up with both his parents dead.

Next, Cassy honored the rest—living and dead—for their bravery and sacrifice. Only a free people like the Clan and their allies could stop the Empire from winning, she told them, and it would always take the kind of bravery the survivors and the fallen both had shown yesterday.

As she spoke, each of the fallen's families, except Frank, walked to their loved one's grave, said their goodbyes, and then began backfilling their loved one's grave with shovels. At the end, each placed their commemorative sapling atop the grave. The trees would live on and, in a very ancient way, so would their loved ones as parts of their trees, enriching the web of life at Clanholme.

By the time she was done, only Mary remained unburied. Frank had stayed by Cassy's side during her speech, still and silent. Past Frank, she saw Hunter, an expressionless look cast upon the boy's face as he stared past the crowd and into the forest. Then Cassy turned to face Frank. She wanted to reach out and take his hands in hers, to send him and his boy comfort somehow, but she didn't know how he'd react. He was behaving so differently, so bruised, that she was afraid anything was possible.

Instead, she bowed formally to him. It felt right to honor the man and his sacrifice that way, in solemn ritual. Of all the fallen, he was the only family member who had witnessed a loved one's death in battle, and what an awful, spectacularly messed-up death this one had been.

"Lastly," Cassy said for the crowd, though still facing away toward Frank, "we honor the sacrifice of Mary Conzet. She was a Clan Original, a founding member, wife to our leader Frank Conzet, mother to their son Hunter, and in many ways a mother for us all. When we try to console her son and her husband for the loss they feel—as do the families of all our fallen—we can only sympathize but not fully understand their grief."

She realized she had tears on her cheeks, and her breath caught unexpectedly in what she was sure onlookers would take as a sob, something she had not been able to experience since that awful, final fight with the insane Peter and his invading group last winter. She could say no more, her throat too tight for words.

Frank stepped forward then, Michael at his side, and spoke for the first time since the battle. He spoke loud and clear, and Cassy thought his voice must have easily carried to the back row of the crowd. "Yesterday," he said, then paused before continuing. "Yesterday, I lost my wife, and our son, Hunter, lost his mother. We are not the only family to have lost someone. Their sacrifice made it possible to fight off the Empire this time, but that fight isn't over. We'll need more courage, more sacrifice, and to suffer more grief before it's all over. But the Clan stands and will stand. The Clan remains. As a Clan we are all family, it really is true, and in that way we *all* have lost people here. I've been stunned, lost in my own grief, and in this, I'm sure I am not alone."

Frank paused and looked into the air for a long moment, as though steeling himself to continue. Finally, he continued, "I am a leader in the Clan. My wife was a leader as well, but she and I are not more important than any of you. My loss is not greater than yours." He looked around again, then continued, "But because we aren't any more important, my rush into battle was foolish. My ego and my pride made me risk myself so that I could fight alongside all of you. The difference between us is in our responsibilities. I'm responsible—as is Cassy—for making sure the Clan runs smoothly, that all of us can meet our needs, and that we can secure our future here against the Empire, against raiders, against hunger, and against the unexpected."

Again he paused, and he seemed to shake himself before saying, "I should not have risked myself so rashly, out of my own foolish pride. I knew how easily a life may be snuffed out in battle but I pushed that knowledge back. I ignored that reality. Yet it's true no matter how important a person may be to the Clan as a whole. If I hadn't gone, those Clan fighters could have likely fled, and lived. I won't make that mistake again, and I have not the words for the sorrow I feel. All I can do is apologize to all of you for my irresponsible recklessness. I won't make that mistake again, I can at least make that promise to all of you. I only pray that Cassy, our true leader, learns the same lesson, because her loss could spell the doom of the Clan. Those of us who, in some sense, hold the future of Clanholme in our hands must learn that our responsibilities are more important than our pride. Thank you. All of you."

Cassy had remained silent, first out of respect, and then out of speechlessness. She stood with jaw dropped, staring at him as he limped to Mary's grave and, with Michael's help, began to backfill her grave while Grandma Mandy escorted Hunter toward the other children.

* * *

Taggart stood on the roof and grinned while Eagan raised the American flag over the large fortress they had taken.

The complex had obviously been General Ree's headquarters while he had been cut off from the City, but it was almost vacant when Taggart had launched his surprise offensive at the northern boundary of Ree's badly shrunken, remaining territory. All morning long, riders had been coming in to give the same reports—few or no enemy troops encountered anywhere. Slaves left bound but unguarded. Supplies gone or burned.

Why had Ree not killed the slaves before Taggart's arrival, as he had so often done in the past? Was it possible he and Ree had launched offensives at about the same time and had managed to miss one another? Did that kind of thing even happen? Taggart had been mulling that over since his own troops had entered the first nearly empty compound. The puzzle deepened as each successive rider from other attack prongs reported finding no one but slaves and a couple of guards left behind.

They had freed the slaves, many of whom had joined his army as usual, and a deep feeling was growing in his bones that something truly strange and dangerous had occurred, was still occurring. The feeling left an itch in his mind that needed scratching, so he had ordered even more scouts sent out. Those would soon return, and then he hoped he'd have a clearer picture of what the heck was going on. All he knew for sure at this point was that they had damned well better get ahead of this... whatever it was that Ree had pulled.

When he finished raising the flag, Eagan came up behind Taggart and said, "General, you want to know what I think?"

"Not really, but you'll tell me anyway," Taggart replied.

"I think we just played Musical Chairs with Ree, and we both had enough chairs at the end. He's down in Hackensack and we're stuck with all this crappy wasteland. Looks like he got the better chair."

Taggart looked up and took a deep breath. Shitbird's words reflected his own line of thought, sadly. "If that's the case, it explains why he left all his civilians behind with so few guards and so few supplies. He intended to supply his entire army for an all-or-nothing offensive."

"So... now he has all our land that we worked, and most of our civilians to run it. And we got his worn out, half-starved slaves and a half-assed attempt at farming the "modern" corporate farming way, but without the modern machines to pull it off."

Taggart nodded. That about summed it up. "Let's not jump to conclusions until our scouts come back, but we do need to spread the word to settle in at least for a few days.

Tell our agriculture heads to start thinking about how to salvage this land, Clan style. We can't wait, if we're stuck here now."

"If Ree's down in Hackensack, boss, we got one blessing out of this SNAFU," Eagan said.

"Besides slaughtering the few troops he left behind, and occupying this admin complex-turned-fortress? The concrete construction is lovely this time of year, sure, but..."

"Yeah. We got all his civilians, while he didn't get all of ours, since a huge number were with us carrying rifles and so on for the offensive."

"The offensive that never happened."

"Yeah. But we save who we can, arm them, get cracking on getting some permaculture going. There's still time to get things growing so we'll have enough food for next winter. And with all these new civvies and plenty of weapons for them all, we probably now have as many troops as Ree does. Plus, he's the invader and we're home-grown. Any people still living around here are going to support us, not him."

Taggart frowned. "Yes, but now we have to re-do everything we already worked hard to set up if Ree's back in Hackensack. How is that a win for us?"

Eagan bit his lip for a moment before saying, "Boss, we just liberated almost all the enslaved Americans. If Ree has re-occupied the territory we were operating out of, he has some new slaves now, but not nearly enough. If he's down there, we just need to pounce. Hungry tigers on the hunt."

That did make sense. It was hard not to be disappointed about all that lost effort setting up Clan-style farming. Still, he agreed with his aide that it wasn't all bad. "Yes. Even if you're right and he's grabbed our Hackensack area farmlands, which we don't know yet for sure... even if he did, we have the farms his slaves already planted, and we have the people to care for it and harvest it when the time comes.

We have everything he set up and enough time to convert a lot of it to high-yield permaculture methods. Plus, he doesn't know a thing about how to use Cassy's permaculture methods. He has to be struggling."

Then Eagan grinned. "Even better. Maybe we can't really dig Ree out now, but we have him bottled up in New York City and the Jersey area right across the river from there. You get that? Bottled up. We won. He's neutralized so long as we're here to keep him contained."

Taggart forced himself to grin. Eagan was right, and he didn't deserve to have to carry Taggart's own doubts. That was the leader's burden, not the troops'. "Good perspective. Alright, set up people to meet the scouts coming back. Send a team straight to Hackensack to get the status there and see if your feeling is right about Ree being bottled up. Start recruiting any freed slaves we can use, and cut the rest loose. And let's see if we can't send another battalion to the Clan, now that we have more people than we know what to do with. They're fighting off both the Empire traitors and whatever troops Ree sent out to harass them. We owe the Clan, so let's help 'em out if we can."

Eagan stood bolt upright at that, heels snapping together crisply, and saluted. Taggart returned a proper salute because it felt appropriate for the moment and, as Eagan left, turned back toward the land that stretched out before him. Eagan was right. This wasn't the worst thing ever to happen.

And now, with so many new troops, he could start harassing the invaders to his north and east in Pennsylvania under the other North Korean commander, General Park if his intel was right. That would relieve a lot of the pressure on survivor groups up there in northern Pennsylvania. And though the Clan had kicked General Park's ass and sent his troops fleeing, according to Dark Ryder's back-channel reports, those troops were still out there, operating like bandits. If they could put pressure on Park, it would help the Clan, too, at least in the sense of reducing a potential future threat. A win for everyone but the invaders.

All in all, Taggart decided, the loss he now expected—everything from Hackensack to Hoboken—was a small price to pay for the results, when he looked at the big picture. Sometimes it took a friend like Eagan to point out the silver linings in life, even when he didn't want to see them.

He chuckled at a sudden thought. Being disappointed about not "winning it all" in this offensive was like the man in an old joke who thought he won a free Rolls Royce. When they instead sent him a free top-of-the-line Mercedes Benz limousine and a free pristine Porsche 918 Spyder, he screamed, "I was robbed!"

Still chuckling at himself, Taggart turned back toward his work.

- 24 -

1225 HOURS - ZERO DAY +255

THE FUNERAL COMPLETED shortly after noon. It seemed everyone wanted to share what they remembered about each of the fallen, and they had taken to calling it "Testimony."

Cassy suspected that memorial Testimony and burial in the forest would now be forever part of Clan culture, along with a tree planted over the fallen. Fine and good. People needed traditions, culture, ritual, heritage. The Clan, like every other group of survivors, had already created more of these than she probably even realized. And more would come. It was how humans connected the past with the future. It defined their place in existence as time moved them inexorably forward.

She reflected on her sudden turn toward philosophy for a moment and then turned her head to look at Corporal Sturm as the latter, acting as Clan medic, worked on her arm brace. "Thanks," Cassy said. "I didn't want to do this until after the ceremony, and then other things came up."

"What, like lunch?" Sturm asked. "You and I both know you wouldn't wear this thing at all if you could get away with it."

"I hate being seen as weak," Cassy muttered.

"No one would think that of you," Sturm said finishing up.

Cassy moved her arm, felt pain. She let her arm relax and the pain faded back quite a bit. "Thanks, I think this will do."

From the front door came Frank's deep voice, startling them both. "Sturm, can I speak to Cassy a moment?" He stood tall facing Cassy head-on as if Sturm were invisible as he spoke. His arms folded over his chest.

"Sure," Sturm said as she gathered herself and walked through the doorway leaving Cassy and Frank alone. There was a moment of deafening silence before he spoke again.

"Quite a wound you got there."

"Yeah, but people heal from their wounds and I will too."

"Yeah, it'll buff out," he said. "Just like last time. And the time before that."

Cassy almost did a double take. "I—"

"You're the Confederation leader." It wasn't a question, but he waited for her to reply.

She raised her eyebrows, a bit stunned by his assertiveness. She breathed in through her nose, a way to lift herself up. "Yes."

"And you're the Secretary of Agriculture for all of New America, right?" His arms stretched out as if to display the whole world.

Cassy tilted her head and nodded slowly. "Yes... but New America is pretty much—"

"And if you fail them, possibly hundreds of thousands of people could die?"

She said nothing.

"Passing along your knowledge of the permaculture is crucial to survivors."

She felt her temper begin to rise. "That's why I spend priceless hours teaching the so-called Agricultural Deputies how we do things here."

Frank glared at her but she had enough. She had no time for this. "I am the leader, Frank—"

"You're no leader! You're on the front lines fighting and hot dogging until your time is up. Then what? You want to leave your people to fend for themselves because you were too hotheaded, too late to realize you made a mistake?"

"I'm on the front lines as an example."

"An example of what?"

"Of leadership and courage."

"That courage almost got you killed and you go off and do it again?"

"Yes, I do it again. I didn't gain the trust of my people by hiding or leading from the rear."

Frank limped across her living room to stand only a couple feet from her, his finger hovering in front of her face like a challenging wasp.

"You want to know what your 'leading' is? It's a distraction. Our people can't concentrate on the battle because they are too busy trying to keep their leader alive. Step off the field and do your job so we can do ours." Frank's voice boomed. "For once, Cassy, stop trying to be a goddamn hero." And with that he turned his back and was gone.

Cassy was frozen. She took a deep breath and looked down at her arm. She had never seen Frank like this before.

The door opened again causing Cassy to jump. It was only Ethan. "Got some news," he said, shifting from one foot to the other. He put one hand on the other elbow, then dropped his hand down again.

Sometimes, Cassy thought Ethan was like a hyperactive ferret on crack. She said, "Spit it out."

"The Empire isn't wasting any time. They're on the move again."

"God, what now?" This couldn't be good, of course, so

she braced herself for bad news.

"At least two regiments. Well over two-thousand troops, mostly on foot, some on bicycles or horses. They're followed by extensive supply caravans. They could be here as early as tomorrow, though Michael thinks they'll slow once they get near us and therefore, not hit until the next day."

Cassy knew this was going to happen, a one-two punch of sorts, but hearing the words didn't make it any easier. The Empire's follow-up attack was looming over them, but their arrival so soon still was a shock. "That's still not enough time to get ready," she said. "There's never enough time."

"There's more," Ethan said. "Liz Town's Interim Speaker and that replacement envoy, apparently, got caught doing something treasonous and were just hanged."

"The woman envoy that was here?" Cassy asked.

"Yeah, and Carl, the envoy she replaced, is now a leader of one of their groups."

"Okay, so why do I care?"

"The new Speaker has ratified our alliance treaty," Ethan said.

Cassy felt her spirit soar. "That's fantastic news," she said. Liz Town's alliance could mean the difference between freedom or slavery, life or death.

Cassy began to pace. "Maybe we should send out more scouts, a lot more, so they can relay messages. We'd know where they'll hit, and where they're thin and vulnerable. And then we'll know where to send people."

She stopped and turned to Ethan. "Let everyone we can contact by radio know, and ask them to relay troop movements so we can act quickly next time. Let Taggart know about the reported Empire movement too. If the 20s give you an update, I don't care if it's real or an attempt to mislead us, report back immediately. We need to stay alert. Got it?"

Ethan nodded. "You got it, Cassy. Right away." He turned and disappeared out the door.

Cassy rubbed her chin. She had an idea.

* * *

The sun was well past its zenith as the wagon jostled and bounced toward the hill just south of Clanholme, and Jaz's spirits rose despite the shooting pains that hit with every bump and dip. As they traveled—more slowly than she'd have liked—Choony hovered over her like a worried mama hummingbird. Are you okay, are you doing okay, are you still okay...

"Yes, dammit, I'm fine. Stop asking," she snapped for the thousandth time after his millionth such question. Again. And again. And again. She doubted he'd listen now any more than the last three hundred times she had said it.

"I know it bothers you, but you're wounded," he said this time, sounding like her wound was torturing him. She looked at him out of the corner of her eyes, trying to dream up a suitable wisecrack about that, but he continued before she could put one together. "Your condition could change in an instant for all we know. You look pale and sweaty, and those are signs of either shock or infection. I'm worried."

"It wasn't infected when you finally let us set out this morning."

"Then perhaps you're in shock."

"I'm only shocked that you keep asking if I'm okay," Jaz replied. He was annoying, yes, but only because he cared. And in truth, she didn't feel great. Light-headed from some of the worst pain she had ever felt. Her stomach churned more than the wagon did.

"There's the south hill up ahead," Choony said. "We'll be home in half an hour at the most." He paused for a moment, then continued, “I’m sure they saw us long ago. I wonder why they didn’t ride out to meet us this time.”

Jaz had no answer, so she stayed quiet. She shut her eyes and focused on fighting the pain and on not throwing up. Soon they had ridden around the south hill and were approaching the south food forest. Jaz peeled one eye open and saw two riders coming out of the woods toward them, each bearing a pack. “Took ’em long enough,” she said between pain-clenched teeth.

The guards greeted Choony, recognizing him and Jaz, and handed over the packs. They contained fresh bottles of water, and—glorious!—tupperware with fresh salad. Miracles! Too bad her stomach was churning too badly to risk food. In her mind, Jaz added the emoji for frowning to the end of her thought.

They were led through the woods toward the Complex. Jaz noticed they weren’t very talkative, though, and slowly her concern grew as they rode on in silence. She leaned over to Choony and whispered, “They’re awful quiet, don’t you think?”

He only nodded. She saw the tension building in his shoulders, though his face remained neutral. She had come to learn that it happened when he was trying to get all Buddha-Zen, or whatever, trying to accept something, calm himself down, prepare for bad news... That made her even more concerned. Something seemed, like, really wrong.

When they reached the Complex, Jaz saw that very few people were out in the fields. No one was up with the animals, which was unusual at this hour of the day. People waved and smiled as the wagon went by, but to Jaz they looked sad. Like shell-shocked or something.

The wagon halted, and Choony hopped down, came around the back of the wagon, and scrambled up to Jaz. He offered his arm to help her down and she reached out to take it, but Choony was politely elbowed aside (can you be politely elbowed?) by Sturm and another paramedic, a guy whose name Jaz forgot.

While helping her down, Sturm said, "How bad is it?"

Jaz said, "I don't think I'll be able to play the piano again."

Choony said, "You play piano?" and Jaz rolled her eyes.

Sturm led her toward the chow pavilion, sat her down on a bench, and told her to take off her shirt. The other paramedic and Choony turned away and stayed at the entrance flap to keep people out.

Jaz pulled off her unzipped hoodie, and then took off the purple tank-top she wore beneath it. Sturm let out a low whistle. "Nice stitching. Choony's work?"

"Yeah. How'd you know I was hurt?"

"One of the guys who rode out to meet you came and found me. Said you looked really sick, but I saw right away it was shock. How long ago you get shot?"

"Days ago. Three days? I can't remember. But it's just a flesh wound."

Sturm shook her head emphatically. "No, no, no. Bullets don't leave flesh wounds, they leave wounds. Shoulders are among the worst."

Jaz raised an eyebrow. "It just grazed my armpit."

"Let me take a look," Sturm said. "Oh, you're right—I see where it passed through, just under the skin. Missed that big tendon in your armpit, too. What you got here is a 'one-in-a-million' shot. A quarter inch to either side and you'd either be dead or permanently crippled. Did it get cleaned out?"

"As best we could," Choony said over his shoulder. "Everclear and antibiotic ointment."

Sturm nodded, but didn't look satisfied. "It's hard to tell how bad the infection is," she said. "It's inflamed a little, but puncture wounds don't always present infection clearly until gangrene sets in and then it's too late. Have you checked your temperature?"

Jaz shook her head. "You got a mercury thermometer?"

"No, but I have a regular one from down in the bunker." Sturm fidgeted around inside her medical bag, then brought out an electronic thermometer. She rubbed it with an antiseptic wipe, and practically shoved it into Jaz's mouth. "Under the tongue, please."

When it beeped, Sturm said, "It came out one degree high. That could be bad, or it could be nothing. Just to be safe, I'll get you a bottle of antibiotics."

Jaz groaned and said, "Not that fish stuff, c'mon..."

"Nope, not from the feed store. Real human pills for you, Jaz. I'll go let Cassy know you're here and wounded. She'll want to debrief you, and I'll find you later with the antibiotics."

"She can't have my briefs," Jaz told her, sticking her nose in the air.

Sturm looked Jaz in the eyes, smiled, and said, "I'm glad you're back alive, both of you."

Before Jaz could ask what she meant, Sturm and her sidekick bounced out. "Well, deuces..." She put her shirt back on, then said, "It's safe to turn around again, Choony. Your virgin eyes won't be damaged by seeing my upper girl parts."

Choony turned around and sat beside her. Maybe ten minutes later, the flap rustled and Jaz looked up as Frank and Cassy came inside. Frank looked terrible—sunken red eyes with huge dark bags, as though he hadn't slept, or maybe he had been crying. Or both. Cassy sported a new injury, it seemed, with her arm in a blue sling with white straps, the velcro type. Totally not a good look on her. Too many scars already. She really needed to take better care of herself.

Choony bowed to them, and Jaz waved with her good

arm, wiggling her fingers.

Frank only nodded, while Cassy spared an obviously forced smile. Something bad had happened, Jaz sensed.

Then Cassy said, "The Empire came. Then came again. And they're on their way again now, with more troops than we've ever seen in one place. We had... some bad losses."

Jaz felt a shiver run down her spine and her pulse sped up. It was suddenly quite hot in the chow hall, despite wearing only her tank top and jeans. "Who... who did we lose?" she said, her voice cracking. She felt her throat tighten up. She realized she was getting scared.

Cassy closed her eyes and lowered her head. Frank looked up, his eyes blinking rapidly. Neither replied right away.

Jaz didn't want to ask. If she did, it might be true and that would make it real. But she had to know who it was. Obviously it was someone close. "Who did we lose, Cassy?" she said, sounding more like a demand than a question. Please, God, don't let it be her...

Cassy looked up again and gazed into Jaz's eyes. Cassy's eyes were suddenly red-rimmed. "We lost ten Clanners. And," Cassy croaked, "we lost Mary."

Frank had teary eyes, one fat drop crawling down his left cheek, leaving a trail of despair that stretched up to his eye.

A helpless feeling crashed into Jaz and ran through her. She felt a physical pain in her stomach. Unable to look Frank in the eyes, she looked down and fixed her eyes on her shoes. It was the only safe place to look. It had been a while since she felt this familiar old feeling.

"I'm so sorry, Frank," Jaz said. Her voice cracked into silence at the end, and she only got half of his name out. The tears began to flow freely, then.

Beside her, Choony bowed low to Frank. "I feel deeply for your loss, Frank. She had a beautiful Chi. A great, vast

Karma. Surely she has reached Heaven, if anyone has."

Jaz understood what a compliment that was from Choony, who had his own deep beliefs. She caught his last three words, as well, which prevented it from being dishonest. Even now, Choony cared for other people's feelings as much as for his honesty.

"Thank you, Choony," Frank said. Jaz thought he just looked lost and hopeless, but she said nothing as Frank straightened himself and cleared his throat. "The Empire will be here and soon. At least two regiments, over two thousand of them at minimum. We have scouts reporting continually, and the number inches upward as new companies are seen."

Jaz's jaw dropped. "Seriously? How... how many Confeds do we have to face them?" She heard the note of urgency in her own voice.

Cassy shrugged and said, "Four hundred of Taggart's soldiers, roughly. A hundred Clan. Thirty Taj Mahal. Fifty Manheim. Three hundred Lititz. Five hundred Ephrata. Five hundred Lebanon. A hundred Brickerville. One-hundred-fifty from the Gap."

Jaz nodded slowly. That was something, at least. "What about Liz Town?"

"Who knows? They don't advertise. Maybe six or seven hundred, but that's a guess."

Choony muttered, "Figure roughly twenty-one hundred total, though not including Liz Town, and of the rest, not every person can go. Of course they'll have to leave enough behind to keep order back home. I would guess we can actually field eighteen-hundred at most, when you take away the ones who have to be left behind to guard their homes and even that is only if they give all they can to the effort."

Cassy said, "We have some equalizers, though."

"That's good," Jaz replied.

Cassy tugged at her shirt sleeve and her eyes darted back

and forth between Frank and Jaz. She shifted from her left foot to her right, and as she spoke, her words came out just a touch too fast, a bit too loud. "We have eight cars that are armed and armored—Ethan calls them 'battlecars.' " Then she leaned forward and in a suddenly hushed voice, she said, "We have working airplanes. Propeller-driven, really old. One's a biplane that Dean named Betsy. They were crop dusters, and now they're the Confed Air Force. Only a few of us know about them and we have to keep it that way. We want them to be a surprise."

Jaz looked at Frank. His jaw was still clenched, though he had uncoiled his fingers from the balled-up fists he had before. He looked like he had aged several years in the weeks since she last came back to Clanholme. If Frank was taking it that bad, how messed up would his and Mary's kid be? Totally bent. She had seen it before, street kids raised in hate. It twisted them. She had to help, she had to do something. She didn't want to see that lost, hating, poisoned look ever again, the one that such kids got.

Then Jaz looked back to Cassy, because it was awkward and heartbreaking to look at Frank. Tanks and fighter planes... "How the hell did planes that still fly even happen?" She tried not to feel insulted that no one had told her, though she understood that she couldn't narc about what she didn't know, after all. They probably hadn't told more than a couple people even inside the Clan. It still irritated her though.

Cassy replied, "Just something we've been working on for quite a while now. As far as we know, none of our allies have them nor do they or the Empire know about these."

"When is the battle?" Jaz asked.

"Tomorrow, or more likely the next day," Cassy said.

Jaz thought for a moment, then said, "You know, we still have a really big silo full of grain that hasn't been used for food or planting. And we know where there are hundreds of survivors scattered all over the place."

Frank tilted his head as he looked at her, pondering. "Where are you going with this?"

"I'm not sure, but it seems to me—and this is just an idea —we could gather a bunch of them up, arm them, and tell them if they fight for the Confederation they'll get guns, food, and land to farm, with the Clan helping and teaching them how to do it without farm machinery."

Frank slowly nodded. "Yeah... Well, we have maybe one-hundred-fifty spare rifles. That's another company's worth of cannon fodder."

Cassy bit her lower lip and Jaz could see her wheels turning, thinking hard. Then Cassy said, "Actually, if we include sidearms we have over two hundred. And if we include our own personal sidearms, we have almost four hundred. That's a light battalion, I think."

Frank said, "After the war, there'll be plenty of guns for everyone. We can trade them rifles to get our pistols back, then organize them into new Clanholme-style settlements on the abandoned farms around here. Slowly bring them into the Clan itself. Or let them make their own clans. More allies."

Jaz said, "This is totally fascinating and all, but for right now, I'm just worrying about living that long."

"Of course," Choony said, "you'll have lots of time for that, Jaz. Assuming the Confederation wins. If they lose we'll leave quickly, before the Empire gets here. Head south with whoever else wants to come."

Jaz shook her head. "I'll worry about that if I survive the battle, Choon."

Choony's jaw clenched once, then he looked calm again. He said, "You can't go to the battle. You're wounded."

He had said it like that was some sort of final answer. Like hell it was. No one was keeping her from that battle. She had a bone to pick with those bastards. “I’m going. Try and stop me. I want to be there to see us win or lose firsthand. Besides, I’m a good enough shot that I’ll do a lot of good. Instead of an M4, I’ll take one of those hunting rifles and play sniper with... what does Michael call them? Targets of opportunity.” Jaz put on her best war-face, head tilted down so she was looking at Choony fiercely through her eyebrows, and in her deepest, rumbling voice said, “Sniiiperrr!”

Choony’s expression became more somber. He stood from where he had been sitting near her, looked down at her and said, “Well then, I’m coming with you. I’ll carry your pack and your ammo.”

“I don’t need you to—”

“You can’t carry all that alone, and I doubt you’ll get more than one or two shots off before you have to discontinue this really bad idea—it’ll hurt too bad to keep shooting.”

“Choony, you really shouldn’t come. The pacifist thing.”

“It’s not a ‘thing,’ and that’s up to me to decide what is good and bad Karma for me. I won’t harm anyone, but since I can’t stop the misery that is coming for everyone involved, I can at least help reduce yours by carrying things you’ll need.”

Jaz felt a nagging doubt about the idea. He was great at running ammo to the foxholes and so on, but to accompany her into battle? Despite the fact that as a sniper she’d be far from the battle lines, coming with her as she killed people... That was another issue. And with her shoulder hurting so bad, would he nag at her the entire time to head back to safety?

Finally, Jaz replied, “Fine, you can come. But I don’t want to hear anything about heading back. Not one word, understand? If you can decide your Karma stuff, I can decide when it hurts too bad for me to keep taking those bastards down.”

Cassy cleared her throat, and Jaz turned to look at her. So did the others. Cassy said, “I don’t suppose I get a say in this, and you’re a grown woman. But I’m in charge of this operation, Jaz. If I say it’s time to go, I expect you to follow my orders. If you agree to that, then I won’t have to go through the hassle of keeping you behind, or trying to find you when you slip away and head to the fighting.”

Jaz felt a knot of fear in her belly, twisting and turning like like she had swallowed a snake, but there was no way she’d let others take her risk for her. She hadn’t backed out of her job as envoy and that was at least as dangerous as this battle would be.

But Cassy had said yes! It was official. She was going to be part of the biggest battle for independence in America since that war in eighteen-something-something.

Jaz nodded, looking Cassy right in her eyes. “Deal.”

- 25 -

0800 HOURS - ZERO DAY +256

JOE ELLINGS LOOKED at the shabby buildings of Elizabethtown, many partially collapsed already. He hadn't thought it could happen so fast—it had not yet even been a year since the EMPs took away all them fancy toys people liked so much, along with their cars and trucks, their power, everything. Apparently, without people inside them, buildings rotted faster than he had reckoned possible.

"Well," said Carl, walking next to him, "I'm glad we could help each other out like this."

Joe kicked a tin can and watched it bounce and clatter down the road. "You ain't half bad for bein' a king and all," he said with a grin.

The woman, Sunshine, who had come out with Carl, said, "He's no king. He's the Timber Wolves Band's Alpha. It's like your Clan leader. And I think it's great what the Clan is doing here."

Joe nodded, his head bouncing from side to side with his lips pursed. "Yeah. One of them win-win things. Carl gets rid of a mess o' refugees, you get to help your people get settled, and the Clan gets fighters and settlers."

Carl said, “Beautiful day for the march. We got what, three hundred for you now, waiting by the Liz Town gate?”

Sunshine nodded. “Yeah, plus children—what few are still alive after all this time. But like I said, you needn’t worry about the kids. The Sewer Rat Band will take care of them until this battle is over. If you get slaughtered, we’ll try to foster them, but we can’t guarantee anything.”

“That’s a tragedy, Lord knows, but I figure it for a square deal,” Joe said. “We all just do as we can, now. But if we win, they all get new homes and new lives as Clanners. Them kids and their parents, what’s left of them after we whup the Empire and send them packing.”

Carl said, “It’s just too bad you don’t have more trucks, Joe. Drive them all back to Clanholme. It’s about ten miles otherwise, right?”

“Ten as the crow flies, maybe. More’n likely it’s gonna take most’a the daylight we got left to get there. We’re all just hoping the Empire don’t come around before then. If they do, we got guns for all these here people, though, so’s they can at least protect themselves. That’s why the truck. I’m a big guy, but I don’t reckon I could carry four hundred guns all the way here.”

“So you don’t have more trucks?” Carl looked at Joe with one eyebrow raised, a corner of his lip turned up. It was what them educated folks called a ‘knowing smile,’ and it made Joe feel uneasy and maybe just a little bit guilty. Not that it was an outright lie... He shook his head, annoyed at himself.

“You know darn well we ain’t got enough trucks for all these folks. Nope, they gotta hoof it if they want to join us. If they want it bad enough, they’ll make the trip. It ain’t far enough to kill no one, though. And we got a little room left in the back with the guns if someone gets hurt on the way.”

A low, distant noise first bothered his subconscious, making Joe look around uneasily, and then his mind suddenly grasped what it was as the noise grew louder and entered his conscious mind.

"The alarms," shouted Carl. "Quickly! We have to get back to Liz Town. *Run, dammit!*"

The three of them turned on their heels and ran, then broke into full-on sprinting. Joe kept his head down and focused on running. His lungs began to ache. The muscles in his legs first tingled, then burned. Just running... And then the end was in sight, and his heart leapt for joy—the gate! And inside that, safety. And his truck... Just run. The gate slowly swung open as they approached. Behind him, Joe heard the sound of a rifle going off. Then another, and then a dozen. Tufts of dirt scattered around him. Just run.

Then they were through the gate, and Joe let out a whoop. He heard it *clang* behind him as it shut. Only then did he lean over, resting his hands on his knees and sucking air for dear life. It felt like he'd never have enough air again, after that half-mile sprint. He turned his head and saw that both Carl and Sunshine were inside as well, both doing the same darn thing he was. Yup, a body needed air, more than it needed whiskey, even. Just breathe...

A Lizzie, dressed in the same colors as Carl, ran up and saluted him. Carl waved the salute away and said, "Get on with it."

"Alpha, our scouts returned just before you did. It's the Empire, and they came in force."

Carl looked up at the sky as he said, "And you say there's a lot of them?"

"Yes, sir. We counted at least twenty of their banners—they got one for each company—and maybe a third of them are on bikes and horses. The rest on foot."

Damn and double-damn. Joe looked at the gate he had just come through. At least all his recruits had been let inside even before he came running back. "I reckon we'll have to man the wall with you then, Carl. I don't figure we can get out in time to run."

The guard ignored the interruption, not even looking at Joe, and said, "Also, they're moving in two groups, and not in the same direction. They split up just before the scouts came rushing back to report. It seems one is heading for us, and the other headed on to the east."

"Crap," Joe said, and then spat onto the pavement. "They'll run over Manheim like a frog on the highway."

Carl pointed to the south. "There's a gate that way. It's big enough to get your truck through. You can't help Manheim—the Empire will have a head start—but you can hightail it toward Clanholme. Once you get in range with your radio, you can alert them and they can give Manheim a warning."

"Pardon, but first I reckon I better give the guns to these here people we turned up, then I can drive my butt back east right quick till the radio works. Then come back and get the people. Would you set 'em on what way to go and pass out my weapons while I get that other stuff done?"

Carl nodded and said, "I will, I promise." He set his hand on Joe's shoulder, then said, "Good luck, and keep your head down."

They shook hands, then Carl had Joe follow the messenger toward where they had stowed his truck. Joe turned back once and waved. It was a crapshoot whether he'd lay eyes on any of these here folks again after the battle, but he sure did hope so. Carl was good people, as his mamma used to say. These folks already done for some bad players just recent and that shoulda been enough trouble for one winter, he figured. Well, we all do what we gotta do.

"Alright," Joe said to his escort as the truck came into view, "let's get my guns passed out so's I can get the hell out of here and let the Clan know what's up."

* * *

Cassy cursed, then shot her mother an apologetic look. "Sorry. But dammit, this is happening too soon. We needed more time!"

Grandma Mandy said, "Don't you worry. But whatever you would have liked, you don't have more time. So what will you do now?"

Cassy looked toward Michael, who stood next to Frank. "Alright, Michael. Just like we talked about. Get everyone out to the hills leading to Clanholme. The units in front get the horses so they can get there in time and get out alive."

Michael said, "Yes, ma'am. Our allies are on the way, and hopefully this will slow the OpFor enough for our friends to get here well before the big showdown at the end. We'll let the enemy roll us back, one hill at a time."

Frank smiled, but it was a grim expression. "The battlecars will be on standby, ready to move in when Michael says the time is right. The planes will be on standby as well. We finished moving them east of our position last night so the Empire won't see them until it's too late."

Cassy took a deep breath, put her fists on her hips, and let the air out slowly, then said, "Okay. Joe Ellings got put in a plane, and I told Jaz that if she wanted to do any fighting, we needed her and Choony to lead the Lizzie refugees to Clanholme. We'll decide where they're most needed after they arrive. In the meantime, I'll be on lockdown with Ethan in the bunker."

Michael said, "Mueller and our Marines will stay in Clanholme until I get back. I want them fresh for our counter-attack with the allied reinforcements. Taggart's battalion will be in the front, getting rolled back from hill to hill to buy the rest of us time. A lot depends on timing."

"I guess I should be off to the battlecars," Frank said. "Be safe, Michael."

"You too, my brother," Michael replied.

Cassy knew it was the oldest of ceremonies for embattled humans—declaring blood loyalty, making them brothers in spirit—and she could almost feel the power of the ancient oath. She stood stone-still for a moment and then, hesitancy cast aside, she practically leapt forward into Frank's arms, hugging him hard, and then did the same to Michael.

"We'll all be safe," she said into Michael's chest, "and I'll see you all back here in time for dinner, okay?" The emphasis on the last word made her sound like she was almost begging them to be okay, to survive the day, but she didn't care how she sounded. In a way, she was.

Mandy wiped her eyes with the heel of her hand, saying, "I know some of you aren't believers, but would you all humor an old woman and let me lead you in a prayer?"

Cassy nodded, as did Michael. Frank said, "I'm a believer, Grandma Mandy. I'd be grateful for it."

Mandy made her prayer short and sweet, but Cassy got the impression her mother intended the prayer as much to boost the courage of the people with her as to please the Lord.

In her head, Cassy said her own longer prayer for them. She half believed, half didn't know, but at least it couldn't hurt. Then she turned away and walked back toward her house and its hidden bunker entrance without another word. She wouldn't let them see her cry before they went to war.

* * *

The trip out to the Liz Town refugees would take very little time using the truck, especially the way Choony drove the beast. It was a Ford F350 with dualies in back, and when it revved Jaz thought it sounded like a dragon. It was awesome. Cassy had said time was of the essence, so it was probably okay for him to drive all reckless like that. Sure hurt like a bitch, though—her shoulder throbbed with every bump.

In the bed, in addition to the gasifier and a quarter-cord of wood, were supplies that had been thrown on before it was clear the truck had to go back out again. There hadn't been time to remove them. Food, blankets, cooksets from sporting goods stores that were, in a post-civilization world, very far away. Ammo. Med kits. Not a lot of each, other than the mounds of food, but enough that Jaz figured they'd be totally useful if she had to fight before getting back to Clanholme.

To their right, far in the distance, they had caught a brief glimpse of the Empire column, snaking half a mile along the highway, and had veered left, southward, to get out of sight before being spotted. Ten minutes later, they saw the mob of Lizzie peeps trudging through the grass that grew for miles, recovering from last winter and from the brown goop that had left the countryside bare for miles after the initial 'vader attacks. Grass and self-selected weeds were thriving again. As Choony pulled the truck up to the mob, they looked concerned, but with three hundred of them, they weren't terribly fearful. A good sign, really.

Choony jumped out of the truck and circled around to help Jaz down. She didn't have her sling on, of course. It would be in the way if it came to a fight, she had told Choony, and when he said they were supposed to avoid battle till they got home, she had just laughed and asked him what they were doing out there, if not going to a fight. He had left it alone after that. Still, she babied it, especially with it throbbing still from the drive.

As she reached the ground, soft and springy from rains a few days ago, she waved to the mob. "Yo, peeps," she called out, and they started to gather around. "I'm Jaz, and this is Choony. We'll be guiding you back to Clanholme today."

Someone shouted out, "How far is it?"

"It's like, ten miles from here. We'll get there just after lunch time. I figure you peeps don't have, like, tons of food, so we brought some—you get it when we're half way there, okay?"

Choony shouted, "Follow the truck, please. We don't have time for a ton of questions, but I'm told you know the program from our guy, Joe Ellings, when he found you?"

Heads nodded all around. Choony continued, "We're going to drive ahead and then stop, to conserve fuel. If you can't see us waiting, you should follow our tracks or just stay on the road. You'll reach us every twenty minutes or so. We'll stop when we need to turn onto a new road, as well."

"Alright. Let's go guys!" Jaz said.

Choony headed around the back of the truck toward the driver's side and Jaz climbed up the passenger side without help. She had told Choony before they got there to avoid helping her in front of the troops. Choony threw the truck in gear, and they drove slowly ahead. Soon after they got completely out of view, Choony pulled to the side of the road and turned it off to conserve wood—though it wouldn't save much, since the fire that created the woodgas fuel had to be kept going. It wasn't practical to put it out and relight it every time they stopped and wanted to get going again. Supposedly, Dean was working on a way to store that heat up or something, but she hadn't really been listening.

Jaz yawned dramatically and, peering at Choony from the corner of her eye, said, "Thanks for coming. I know you didn't have to, but I think I'm braver with you around."

"You're brave all the time," he said. "And strong of heart. Few people would do what you do every day or do what you did back when you first met the people who would become the Clan."

"What, set them up to get killed by wandering murder-hobos?"

Choony laughed, a deep, barking noise that was his totally cute version of a belly laugh, then he replied, "No, not that. Just the part where you risked your life for complete strangers to warn them about the 'murder-hobos.' The fact that you did that, knowing you'd be killed too if Frank and them lost that fight, that was brave. After the way they'd treated you?" Choony shuddered, horrified at the thought.

Yeah, she had told him the story once. Now she wished she hadn't, because it was really uncomfortable to be reminded of it. Those men had treated her no worse than lots of other dudes in the old world, but they were the *last* to ever treat her that way. They stood out in her mind, just as they clearly did in Choony's even though he hadn't been on the scene yet himself.

"Frank and his people had kids. I was used to being treated a certain way, you know? It was *normal* to me. It's just how things were on the streets. But I'd be damned if I was gonna let them do that to the kids in that camp. Frank's camp. They were all about family, and I never had one... Oh hey, there's our peeps."

Jaz looked out the window, off to the horizon. It would be grand to just drive off into that horizon and put all this crap behind them... But of course, wherever she went there would only be more of this. Maybe worse. Still staring off into the distance, she said, "Okay. Manheim is like, two miles from here. If we're lucky, we can swing through there and gather up more volunteers. Cassy said they could only send fifty, but I bet I can get half the dudes still there to join us, too."

Choony grinned and said, "Maybe, but they only get paid with food, got it? No favors."

* * *

Cassy sat staring at the monitor, watching the timer count down. The radio beside her had an earbud plugged into it so she could listen in on the chatter while Ethan handled communications. He had shown her last night how the two computers could easily share a screen. He had a simple, open-source program called VASSAL on both computers. Originally intended to create a virtual tabletop for what he called miniature wargaming—moving little army guys around a table and rolling dice for combat—he was using it now for the real thing.

"How did you get this map onto the VASSAL?" she asked.

Ethan replied, "It's a satellite map image. VASSAL—not 'the VASSAL'—lets you use fake maps you draw yourself, on paper or with another program, so I just load in my sat-maps."

"What would we do if you hadn't hacked into satellites?" Cassy was only half-listening to him, between paying attention to the screen and considering how to proceed.

"Before the lights went out, a magazine kept a website that let you download geographical maps. You know the one, it always had cover pictures of topless women from Africa carrying water, or Indians on elephants."

Cassy watched the map update, with labeled squares and rectangles of different colors representing both sides' units. Ethan was correcting the unit positions as reports came in, and it was interesting to watch from a bird's-eye view as the battle unfolded. Occasionally she'd give orders to a unit to turn this way or that, and Ethan then relayed those orders. The enemy wasn't close enough to engage yet, which meant Clanholme had enough time to set up their defense-in-depth, as Michael had called it, before the fighting started.

Ethan said, "The radio in Jaz's truck is in range. They just sent confirmation of their location and heading. They're on their way to Manheim, en route to Clanholme. Three hundred refugees, armed, accompanying them just like you planned."

Cassy grunted acknowledgement, but went back to listening on the radio. Every radio the Clan had, including a couple dozen Ethan had put together with his treasure trove of Raspberry Pi modules, was out in the field now and set to go from platoon leader to company leader, from them to battalion leader, and so on. Cassy and Ethan, the HQ, couldn't talk directly to the platoon leaders, but could go directly as far down as the company level or even broadcast to all channels as situations changed.

Once the reinforcements arrived, of course, many of their already-distributed radios would have to go to them. HQ would probably only be in direct comms with battalion-level leaders, then, and maybe a few key company leaders.

The red and blue rectangles drew closer and closer to one another. There'd be blood soon, she knew, and the waiting wore on her. Was that what Michael felt before battle? She hoped not. The feeling sucked.

* * *

Carl ducked as three rounds ricocheted off the rubble wall's edge, sending a sprinkle of gravel down onto his head. "This is getting out of hand—there are so many of them, it seems like every Empire goon I take down gets replaced by two more."

Sunshine fired a round from her Remington 700 hunting rifle—powerful, but slow to fire—and said, "If it hadn't been for the wall, Liz Town would have been overrun by now." The Empire's commanders had already tried to breach the wall once, using a pair of propane tanks tied together. Two "goons," as almost everyone had taken to calling Empire troops, had died getting the improvised device to the wall.

"Yeah, probably so," Carl said. "The bomb that cost them two goons would've been real trouble if our guys didn't know how to build a solid barrier."

Sunshine shook her head, smiling wolfishly. "Yeah, that was something to see, when those tanks exploded." The rubble wall had just collapsed in on itself while gravel from left and right of the hole poured in, sealing it. This had been followed by the sound of Lizzies laughing and jeering from the ramparts.

Carl scanned for any more goons sticking their heads up. Seeing none at that moment, he dropped back down behind cover. "I don't fool myself into thinking the Empire has been stopped. They'll try something else, soon enough."

For now, though, this fight had turned into a siege. Liz Town could hold out against a siege for at least a couple weeks, and by then the rest of the Confederation would either be conquered or have defeated the forces the Empire had thrown at them. If the Confederation won elsewhere, Carl was certain they'd come to Liz Town's rescue.

He reminded himself that the damn regiment outside his walls would be fighting the Clan if it wasn't fighting Liz Town, so it was vital to hold out as long as possible to give the other Confed forces the best possible chance of winning. Hell, the Empire probably attacked Liz Town just to keep her from striking the Empire's own troops from behind again, or messing with their supply lines through guerrilla actions.

If that was the case, then Liz Town's attackers wouldn't try very hard to push an assault through, now that they had figured out it wouldn't be easy. They'd just wait until victory over the Confederation freed up those troops to assist, and then the mayhem would begin in earnest for Liz Town. But knowing Cassy, they'd have some surprises waiting.

"C'mon, Sunshine. Our troops got this, for now. Let's go

find the nearest officer and tell them to sound the horn if a hard attack comes in."

"Cool. Trying to get it in before we die?"

Carl wiggled his eyebrows at her, but said, "No, as amazing as I'm sure that would be. I was thinking more like getting something to eat and then check out Mary Ann's war room."

Sunshine feigned disappointment—or maybe it was genuine, Carl could never tell for sure—and then said, "Sounds great. Maybe she has one of those maps with the wood blocks on them, like in the old movies."

Carl, climbing down the wall ladder, laughed. "No way. In this day and age?" But then he thought about it. Maybe Mary Ann would use a map and blocks... After all, this day and age wasn't really "this day and age anymore," was it...

* * *

"I can't stand being cooped up in here, Ethan. I'm not even useful here. I should be out there, fighting with my people." Cassy stared at the monitor as red blocks closely followed blue ones, all heading east toward another line of blue blocks.

Ethan continued typing as he replied, "The forward elements of the Confed forces have been forced back now and are fleeing toward the next line of troops. Once they arrive they'll join that line, and both elements will fire at the oncoming enemy troops."

"So at each line, the defense will stiffen?"

"Yeah. Meanwhile, the Empire's troops become less organized, less concentrated and will lose more troops to mounting casualties as they push forward."

"Our wounded will probably be murdered by the Empire as the bastards pass over wherever they're laying. Dammit, I don't know how you can stand to be inside this tiny little box while people are up there fighting for their lives."

Ethan stopped typing, and looked at Cassy with a frown. Cassy saw that his cheeks were flushing red. He said, "Cassy, I'll ask you never to question my courage like that again. Remember when Jed died, before we ever arrived at Clanholme? That wasn't you rushing the 'vader position, that was me and Jed." He turned away, looking back to his computer.

Cassy could see how stiff his shoulders were. Crap... She hadn't meant to insult him, but that's how it came out, and she couldn't blame him for being upset. The way she had said it was wrong and insulting. "Look, Ethan, I know you can't read minds or know what I was thinking, only what I actually said. I'm sorry, but it just came out different from what I meant."

"Forget about it," Ethan said, but he still looked tensed up.

"No, I'm serious. I'm sorry for what I said. What I meant was that I don't know how you can do this all the time without going nuts. Being down here while they're fighting? That's hard. I'm having trouble with it but you just keep going. I don't think I could."

The muscles in his shoulders eased up a bit, and he sat taller and less closed off. That was a damn fine start as far as Cassy was concerned. "Someone has to do this, and I'm pretty sure I'm the best person for the job. I never get tired of the bunker, either. When there's a battle raging, I do sometimes wish I were there fighting alongside Michael and the rest. Amber's out there, too, you know, and here I am, dug into a spider hole. But I know they have a better chance to live if I'm here doing this job. So, I do it. My biggest fear is that I'll fail and cost us lives."

Cassy thought about that for a moment. Did his words

have a hint of judgment, that insolent little... But had he meant it as a judgment of her, or had she only taken it that way because it was what she felt in her heart? Inconveniently, that thought carried a ring of truth to it.

She took a deep breath before replying. "You have a point. And I forgot Amber's out there with the rest of them. But I'm still convinced that out in the field I'm more..." She suddenly went silent.

"More what?"

"Hold on," Cassy said, almost snappish. "Trying to listen. Did you hear that? A faint signal on pre-programmed channel two?"

"No, I—Oh, there it is. Let me clear it up, boost the signal."

Ethan fiddled with some program on his computer, and the signal strength indicator leapt upward. Through her earbud, she heard Jaz's voice. "... going in. Looks like we'll be late to your party, Charlie One."

Ethan clicked his mic and said, "Ten-nine? Say again, please, you're coming in faint."

"I'm ... Manheim is getting hit ... at least a company. No, it's ... companies. We're going to ... and help them out. Wish us ... Jazoony out."

The signal went flat. "Damn that girl," Cassy said. "I have no idea how many she's attacking. How can I give her orders if she turns off her radio? We won't even know if she's alive unless she checks in afterward."

Ethan wrinkled his nose at Cassy, almost like he smelled something foul. "With all due respect, Jaz is a big girl. She and Choony survived out there in the wilds on their own for weeks and months, and they did just fine without you holding their hands."

"Yeah, but—"

"Cassy, we're friends, right?" Ethan asked, cutting her

off. "So as a friend, let me just say, you're pissing me off. You can't be everywhere at once, and we have a job to do right now. So let's do that job and worry about 'Jazoony' later."

Cassy felt a faint blush rise as a smile grew on her face. He was right, of course. There was nothing at all she could do about Jaz and Choony at the moment, and she still had a job to do that, mathematically speaking, mattered more for the Confed's fighters than Jaz and Choony did. Even if they were friends, and Choony was something of a head-shrink for Cassy, there was another bigger battle going on. It was time to concentrate on her own damn job.

She looked down at the VASSAL map again, getting her mind back on task. Worry about the rest later... "Ethan, notify Lincoln One to adjust his Third Squad to face heading two-four-zero to respond to unit designation alpha-two-three, or they'll be flanked."

"I copy," Ethan said, and then sent out her message to Michael, who would pass it on or not, depending on his strategy on the field.

Cassy watched as, on her map, the unit labeled "L1-3" swung around in a wide arc, pivoting on the leftmost edge until it faced west-southwest, and then moved forward. Michael must have approved of the idea. She would have liked to be able to issue orders directly, but out there in the field, Michael was in charge. There could only be one commander, after all, and warfare was a task for which Michael was frighteningly well qualified, and Cassy wasn't.

Watching the VASSAL map update, with impersonal blocks moving around on her monitor, Cassy had to remind herself that this wasn't a video game. Those blocks were real people out there getting shot up. She swore she'd keep that firmly in mind with every decision she made. She had to stop flailing around.

- 26 -

1000 HOURS - ZERO DAY +256

JAZ LED HER "Army of 300," as she thought of them, northeast along High Street, straight through the center of Manheim. To either side were buildings that had been mostly abandoned or burned down. The cars were gone, but she could see knocked-over hydrants and poles, houses with holes, all the signs of moving vehicles that had suddenly turned off. Where those cars had gone—along with the ones that should have been parked everywhere at four a.m., when the first EMPs had gone off—Jaz didn't know, but the effect was creepy. The papers and other debris that lay strewn across every street and lawn didn't help either.

"Is this wise?" Choony asked. "We can still go around and get three hundred people safely to Clanholme."

Jaz shook her head, her eyes squinted to see farther ahead. "This is the only choice. Manheim is our ally, a member of the Confederation. They're under attack by at least a battalion of Empire dweebs. If we leave, Manheim falls and then that battalion just moseys on up to Clanholme to join the party there."

"That may be true." Choony's voice was flat, and Jaz

didn't hear any sign of judgment.

"And also, these people won't be safe at Clanholme either. It's under attack, too. But our 'Three Hundred' have guns and most of them know how to shoot. Better to squash these goons here, so Manheim and our recruits can *both* head north and relieve some pressure up there."

"Either way, we all fight," said Choony. "Only the part of town east of Chiques Creek is inhabited, except for a few odd survivors. We're coming from the west just as the Empire must have done. There's a creek blocking the west edge, though, and a bridge to the north."

Jaz nodded, and saw where he was going with that line of thinking. "So the fighting is on the north end. We'll be hitting them from behind." She grinned. "I always did favor fighting dirty if I had to fight." Choony gave her his tolerant, slightly disbelieving smile. If he only knew.

They continued on, and then on the left, she saw the tennis club. Only a few hundred feet further, the bridge over the creek. It was fully sandbagged into a strong defensive position, but there were no guards. Eerie. But in the distance now, far to the north, she could hear the popcorn sound of battle.

Jaz called out to her column of refugees-turned-soldiers, "We cross that bridge and take the next left, leaving the truck behind. That's White Oak Road. It takes us north toward the fighting. Anyone who doesn't want to join us, that's fine—turn in your gun and best of luck to you. No hard feelings. In three minutes, we move out. The rest of you, if you're willing to fight, check your weapons and ammo. But do not fire until I tell you to. They'll be looking forward and we don't want them to know we're coming up to flank them. As soon as I fire the first shot, go to town on them. We're the 'Army of 300' and we'll take 'em all down! Questions?"

She saw little patches of discussion but, of the three

hundred or so armed Elizabethtown refugees, only five turned in their weapons and headed west, probably expecting to go back home. One was helping another who walked with a crippled-looking limp. Very good—she only wanted the brave ones and those who were physically able to fight.

When the clicks and clacks of rifles being checked quieted down, she and Choony led the column on, then turned left and headed north. As the sounds of battle grew louder, Jaz's heart sped up, adrenaline pumping in anticipation of what lay ahead. Her face gradually assumed a predator's intentness. Yes. She was ready.

* * *

Cassy cursed and threw a stapler against the bunker wall. Their defense-in-depth had worked in part, slowing down the enemy advance and buying the Confederation time. Time for what, she didn't really know. The three hundred refugees would be a huge help, but she doubted they could make the difference between victory and defeat in the end. Her mother's voice in her mind said God would provide the miracle they needed if they kept hope in their hearts, but Cassy found it hard to put trust in that. Still, some circumstance might arise that the Confederation could take advantage of, and anyway, where would they go if they ran? It was win or die, and running would only delay, not change that.

"I guess we'd better win," she muttered, completing her thought aloud, then looked at the VASSAL map again. Still nothing leapt out at her, nothing obvious to give them a chance at victory. And she was stuck down here in the bunker. If the Confederation lost, she could well be one of the last Clanners alive—stuck in a bunker, stuck with her guilt. The thought terrified her.

The map was clear, though. Defeat was imminent. Of the six advanced defensive positions the Confederation held in the beginning, only one remained. It was heavily defended now but when the tactical situation became untenable, Michael was sure to order them to fall back to Clanholme itself. The enemy had taken heavy losses, but they had the advantage of numbers and could afford to press on, and on until, threatened with being overrun, the Confed troops fell back. Then fell back again. And again...

Michael's command radioman's voice came through the radio with the dreaded news, "Cassy, we're falling back. Mortars are out of shells." All pretense of formality was gone, and in the background she could hear the overwhelming sound of heavy gunfire and people shouting in the chaos of battle.

Ethan confirmed receipt of the information. His other radios squawked and he continued typing in his data. Always his damn data...

Cassy noticed the VASSAL map refresh. At map's top edge, a gray box appeared. And another, then another. "Ethan, what the hell are you doing over there?"

Ethan, totally focused on his task, didn't answer right away, but Cassy felt like she would burst with the need to know. How many enemies were showing up? Where had they come from? "Dammit, Ethan. What the hell are you typing in? Who are those new people?"

Ethan snapped back, frustration in his voice, "Unknown. Units appearing north. Organized, in formation, advancing quickly on foot. Armed with rifles, looks like. I can't tell what kind but they all seem the same. They're wearing cammies."

Cassy felt her heart drop into her stomach, and then her stomach rolled. She grabbed her radio and clicked to programmed channel one, the regimental radio. "Charlie One to Lincoln One Actual, come in."

A pause, then Michael's voice came through. "Go ahead for Lincoln One."

"Multiple inbound units from heading zero-one-five. Estimate at least two battalions, in formations. All with rifles, wearing BDUs. Intent unknown, source unknown. Neg radio contact."

"Copy. We'll pull back to position Zulu. Keep me advised. Over."

"Wilco," Cassy replied. Michael's voice had been rock solid and carried that tone of authority even through the radio. His voice was simultaneously comforting and frightening, and she'd had no problem hearing him clearly even over the noise of battle.

Ethan said, "Still neg contact with the unknowns." He began typing furiously, and Cassy glanced over. His screen was all text, but then the view switched to a satellite image. It was their general area, and Ethan zoomed in repeatedly until he found what he wanted, the unknown force, and zoomed in further.

Cassy saw they were split into four distinct groups. One was maybe a dozen squads, while the rest were five times larger. When Ethan zoomed in still further, she could see that they did indeed all have rifles but, unlike the initial report, they didn't all carry the same rifle. Most looked like hunting rifles, though it was hard to tell for sure.

Her heart soared with hope, leaving her stomach alone and lodged firmly in her throat. The alliance! Could they be Confed forces? Of course they could. Lititz, Lebanon, and others were sending troops, and these could well be them, despite the lack of radio contact.

"Any bicycles?" Cassy asked, her throat feeling dry and sounding raw with mixed dread and anticipation.

"No!" Ethan's face grew a smile, and he let out a sharp "Whoop!"

Cassy understood the feeling, and leapt to her feet. She couldn't bear to sit any longer, feeling way too excited for that. "Reinforcements! It's the Confed troops. Quickly, tell Lincoln One."

On her monitor, the VASSAL map showed Michael's defenders on their way toward the rolls of defensive concertina wire, which had a few gaps intentionally left for them. When the enemy got there, they'd be forced to either get through the wire, slowing them down, or go through the channels, which would slow them less but would send them into a kill zone of overlapping lanes of fire from Clan defenders—Mueller and the dozen Clan Marines, manning automatic weapons from hastily built earthbag defensive positions.

That same wire would slow Lincoln One's forces if they broke and routed toward Clanholme, but she doubted that would happen—not with Michael at the helm.

Sure enough, she saw the blue blocks of Michael's forces stop, then reverse direction and line up along the last low ridge between the enemy and Clanholme. The red blocks of Empire troops halted suddenly. Cassy could imagine their confusion when their prey, on the run, had turned around and started fighting back with gusto. Ha! Eat that, Empire bitches...

"Radio contact with new units, confirmed Confed. Orders?"

Cassy looked at the screen and said, "Tell them to change heading to one-seven-zero and engage the Empire. Hit them in the flank!" Then she clicked her radio again. She had a hard time keeping her voice from shaking when she said, "Charlie One to Lincoln One Actual."

"Go for Lincoln One Actual," Michael replied, his voice still rock solid.

"Let's deploy Delta One and Two," she said. It was time

to bring the battlecars and planes into this. "Request instructions." That hurt, but Michael would know how best to deploy them.

"Roger. Send Delta One to flank them and strike their line from the south. Delta Two focus on the north end of the OpFor, repeat, north end. Soften them up before new arrivals engage these Empire sonsabitches. Over."

"Copy. Wilco. Charlie One out." Cassy grinned at Ethan and added, off-radio, "Roger Wilco and hot damn!" because it felt so good and she felt like it. Ethan was grinning back.

She looked back to her monitor and watched the blocks move around. Blocks made of real people, out there. Other blue blocks appeared far to the south, Frank and the battlecars moving into position. Thin blue lines appeared with a white circle in the center, showing the rough location and heading of their planes. At this scale, she could barely tell that they headed north, taking off, then shifted as the planes banked. She knew it was largely Ethan's guesswork and his computer algorithms showing estimates of their location and direction, but deep inside, she felt the thrill of a hunter about to leap to a kill. The planes would be deadly...

Abruptly the leading red blocks began moving west, a reversal of direction. Those behind stopped at the crest of hills. Dammit, the enemy was disengaging, regrouping. Right now, the red blocks were pretty scattered, but she was certain they meant to regroup just out of range of the Clan's current position. "I think they've seen the planes or something."

Ethan grunted then said, "I doubt it. They probably saw the concertina wire behind our lines. They know they've got our backs to the wall now—we have nowhere left to retreat, after that. They're just regrouping to hit us harder." The smile on his face looked vicious.

Cassy saw Michael's blue blocks stop. He was smart

enough not to leave his hasty defensive line to chase the larger enemy up a hill right into the teeth of the other red blocks in defensive positions there, of course.

Crap… The new Confed units were set to engage, but would do so without support from Michael's troops. "Ethan, designate the new regiment as Lincoln Two. Contact them fast and tell them to hold position. They're rushing in alone. It's too soon, dammit."

Ethan got busy on the radio, and moments later, she saw the new blue blocks halt. Ethan said over his shoulder, "I told Frank and Joe to hold off, too. I got Michael on the horn, figuring out what to do."

Cassy frowned. This sucked, having all their allies and weapons of war poised to fall on the Empire's goons yet having to delay while everyone figured out what to do. It was hard to imagine that, only one hundred years earlier, this was how the superpowers fought.

The screen now showed red blocks overlapping each other in a long, thin line stretching north to south. Blue blocks, perhaps a third as many, were similarly arrayed at Clanholme's western edge, east of the red blocks. North of both of them the cluster of new Confed units were bunched up rather than in a line. South stood the battlecars, now motionless. The planes circled low, well east of Clanholme. Everything was completely on hold. So this was what it meant in books when she had read about "a lull in the fighting."

Ethan grinned and said, "And so the stage was well-set for a true ballet of death…"

Cassy rolled her eyes. "Okay, dungeon master, but let's hope it's more like a mosh pit than a ballet, and those Empire bastards do all the dying. Let me know the instant Michael tells us what to do."

Oh God, the tension of that moment was enough to make

a person crack. Sitting in a dim bunker in front of a monitor, she decided, was turning out to be at least as stressful as being shot at.

* * *

Frank sat in the lead battlecar, an old pickup truck with a specially rigged clutch pedal holstering his stump of a leg. He may be missing a foot, but in his armed and armored truck he felt more useful than ever. It was liberating... except that he and the other cars were sitting idle while the battle raged to his north. The thrill of anticipation was overwhelming when they received orders to flank and attack, but then came the order to halt and the feeling of letdown was soul-crushing. The only reason he wasn't screaming in frustration was that he knew they'd be called in soon. And then he and his other cars would stride across the battlefield slaying the enemy by the hundred, like medieval lancers descending upon a line of pikemen. That's what these cars were. Modern knights. Rulers of the battlefield. But they'd only be useful once the enemy was fully engaged with the Confed troops, and that hadn't happened yet.

As he waited, his mind drifted to thoughts of his wife. Mary had died bravely, which made it easier to live with for him, but it hadn't made it any easier to tell their son, Hunter, that his mommy was dead. If only he'd had time to console the boy, guide him out of the depression that fell on him like a soaking-wet stage curtain. The news of his mother's death had sucked the light right out of Hunter.

Between the loss of his wife, whom he had been in love with as much as the day they had said "I do," and his son's loss of innocence, hope, and light, Frank wanted payback. Revenge. And today, he meant to have it. Whether the Confederation won or lost this battle, Frank intended to even the score before he died.

The new radio chatter gave him mixed feelings. On the one hand, it was clear the Confederation was being pushed back on two fronts, north and west, despite the arrival of new troops. They had evened the odds, made the enemy fight harder for every foot they advanced, yet still the enemy came. But on the other hand, now that everyone was back to fighting, it meant he'd be out there slaughtering Empire troops any moment now. His heart began to beat a little faster in anticipation.

Frank glanced up and to his rear, and gave a smile and nod to his gunner. His truck didn't just have a cowcatcher on the front—which Frank thought of affectionately as his "eviscerator"—and armor all over. It also had a light machine gun mounted on a swivel on the roof and a trooper behind a curved bullet shield, in the truck bed to fire it. That was in addition to his hood-mounted AK-47s with triggers mounted on the back of the steering wheel. The only thing missing was rockets, he thought with glee. Maybe Dean, redneck engineer without peer, could invent some for him.

Looking around, Frank saw seven more battlecars arrayed to either side of him. As with his own, smoke billowed from them as the crews kept the gasifiers ready to go on the attack at a moment's notice. He had ordered them kept lit, and now the fires were being stoked and fed to get the woodgas they produced back up to pressure.

"Charlie One to Delta One, engage on heading zero-one-five," Ethan's voice said through his radio. Yes!

Frank snarled confirmation into the radio and pressed the gas pedal. These battlecars were armored and heavy, so they wouldn't win any races, but once they got up to speed they had amazing momentum. He watched as his speedometer crept up toward twenty-five miles per hour, about as fast as he could safely go across the terrain. It was pretty even, having once been plowed, but it wasn't a road. Breaking a strut now would waste a perfectly good killing machine, right when it was most needed. This was all part of the briefing the battlecar drivers had received, and he kept it in mind. A quick check showed the rest of his group keeping pace, not trying to leap ahead.

Ahead, the western front came into view. The Confed troops were stretched out in a long line, firing from cover at the onrushing Empire troops heading for a rough line of cover from boulders, scattered trees, and hedges. Getting there would put the enemy in range to exchange fire—and they vastly outnumbered the Confed forces. Frank could easily see Michael's was a losing position, but what else was the Confederation to do but try to hold the line? Oh yeah—drive makeshift tanks straight up the Empire's ass...

Into his team radio, Frank said, "Delta One form on me, wedge formation. We're a fastball coming right down the middle. Once we're through, turn to bearing zero-seven-zero and keep pressing that attack from the north side."

As the other drivers acknowledged the orders, Frank shifted a little to the right as he had instructed the rest. After the first pass, it'd be impossible to give his unit beat-by-beat orders. They'd be mostly on their own. His plan was to drive *through* the east front's enemy soldiers, then do the same for the goons hitting Clanholme's north side. That might take pressure off the allies who had shown up, and let them shift some pressure back to the east lines.

Frank drove fast over the crest of a low rise and felt his stomach tingle, the truck's suspension extending as gravity reached to hold them down. Not quite "pulling air," it still felt nice and dramatic. A great entrance. He aimed for the first enemy unit on a bearing to plow right through the whole length of it. He tapped his hood guns, and heard his top gunner firing bursts one after the other. People screamed and fell, hit point-blank, but he was past them before they had hit the ground...

...And plowed into a squad clustered behind a lone chunk of stone wall. The rest of that wall was who-knows-where, since long ago. The result was the most gratifying kills of Empire goons he had ever made. Bodies went flying left and right, some directly into the cowcatcher of the next car in line. Blood sprayed. Screams echoed as they flew away, scattered like seeds in the wind to land in bloody heaps. His truck bounced and swayed violently as he ran over several bodies.

Through his team radio, Frank heard one of his men shouting for joy before saying, "Hooah! Are we having fun yet?"

Frank let the drivers chatter, congratulating each other on spectacular kills or a headshot with someone's hood guns. Let them have their emotional high—he understood the joy they felt, the primal satisfaction of utterly smashing an enemy into pulp. He felt it too, but in his heart he knew that no amount of killing would fill the hole left in his soul by his wife's death, but he'd give it his best. "Die, motherfuckers," he muttered as he sent another Empire goon flying, blood spraying across the truck's hood. Still, it was a start.

* * *

Joe watched the conflict below, banking left to get a clearer view. Michael had been right—the biplane could go slower than molasses and stay in the air. He and the other five crop dusters had been prowling the battlefield, dropping dynamite wherever they found the sonsabitches clustered together.

A glimmer caught his eye and he banked toward it, his wingman pulling up, breaking off a bombing run to keep on Joe's wing. On the radio, he said, "Delta Two Actual. Y'all keep doing what you're doing. Heading one-three-zero to check something. Over and out."

As Joe and his wingman flew on, the source of the glimmer grew clearer—a wagon. No, a dozen wagons. Cut-off truck beds harnessed to two-horse teams. In back of the trucks, he saw a mess of boxes all stacked and ready. Joe grinned and clicked his radio. "Delta Two Actual to Delta Two. All units head one-three-zero and get ready to drop some presents. We done found their supply train, sittin' all nice and pretty for us."

As the other pilots replied, confirming, Joe slid into a descent that would take him about a hundred feet above the wagons. He looked through the contraption Dean had put in, a metal circle with crosshairs, which extended horizontally from a PVC tube. The idea was that at two-hundred feet, flying at a snail's pace of eighty miles-per-hour, the dynamite "bombs" would hit whatever was under the crosshairs when he dropped them down the tube. The other planes had to fly at one-twenty, and their crosshairs were set up a mite different, but the idea was the same. As far as Joe figured, the whole contraption needed to be re-jiggered, because they surely didn't work too good. Though, it was better than hucking them over the side, he reckoned, but not by much.

He watched as the rearmost wagon appeared to creep toward his crosshairs, bomb at the ready. On the mark, he let the girl loose and she spiraled down, down toward the wagon. He saw her falling, and had that gut feeling she was gonna fly true. And damn if that bomb didn't fall square onto that trailer! Joe grinned despite the wind buffeting him, and below, the explosion—a whole stick of dynamite—was pretty impressive. But then he felt a huge blast, and a fireball rose right up like God's own hand reaching up to swat him! Joe rolled right and shoved the throttle forward, and the fireball missed him by only a few meters. It looked like a fireworks finale, flaming chunks rising into beautiful, deadly arcs and colliding into the ground in their own individual brilliance.

He got on the radio and shouted, "Holy crap! Did y'all see that?"

"Must've been their ammo supply," said one of the other pilots.

Then Joe and the others passed back and forth, bombing the crap out of them boys and their wagons. Only one other wagon went up like that first one, so the rest had to be vittles and such. Their poor horses didn't deserve to go out like that, but there was nothing for it. This was war, and he cared more about his own people than about his enemy's horses. The Clan was kin. They'd rescue any surviving horses later.

After the last wagon blew up, Joe banked back toward the front lines. Sure, the battle could have used them bombs, but the Empire couldn't fight with "no bullets and no bacon," as his pawpaw would have said it.

The radio crackled, Ethan's voice coming through. He said, "Charlie One to Bravo Two, our troops are pulling back. They have to go through the wire and it's slowing them down. The north corner, by the edge of the forest, is about to be overrun. Focus heavy fire on the enemy there. Strafe them as you go by! Make it count, you only get one of those."

Joe acknowledged, and went to full throttle. It was slower than the other planes wanted to go, but that was just too bad. He had all five other planes form up on his wings. They'd fly in, skimming the tops of them trees by a whisker's length, and drop all at once, all along the enemy line. With twelve bombs and over seven hundred rounds going out within seconds, they were sure to chew them bastards up, and good!

Three... Two... One... "Let 'em have it," he shouted into the radio. He dropped two bombs right after each other even as he pulled the trigger with his other hand. The plane shook a little from the recoil, but nothing to get riled up about.

Joe banked left to watch the bombs fall, but it only took two or three seconds at that height. Just before impact, as he was at a descent, he drew closer to the action on the ground. Then his heart froze. Them troops down there weren't just Empire—it was both sides, fighting hand to hand, shooting at point blank as the Empire had come up on the defender's ridge! He heard a strange noise and then realized it was himself, cryin' out for them bombs to miss, but he knew they wouldn't. They was gonna hit right on target...

Yellow and red blossoms sprouted along the ridgeline, over one hundred meters, a snake of fire and death. That strange noise wouldn't stop coming out of his mouth, neither. He didn't know what to do, and froze up. Someone was yelling on the radio, but he didn't pay it any mind. He stared down at the ground, willing it to be different, praying he had been wrong, but knew he wasn't.

Then the air was full of bullets. A dozen punched through his left wings, canvas flapping where the bullets ripped it. Then he realized the people left on the ground, easily hundreds of 'em, maybe a thousand even, was shooting up at the planes. That snapped him out of his fog, and he throttled up again. "Break zero-nine-zero," he shouted at his radio, but in his haste he forgot to click the transmit button. He banked, however, and the others followed him. Joe circled toward the east and flew low over Clanholme.

The others then broke off, banking away from him, but Joe kept flying straight. The next hill was under a minute away. Maybe he'd just plow that plane right into it... How could he ever face the Clan again? Who had he killed? Hellfire, it didn't matter who he had killed. They was Clan, and his brothers and sisters. No, he never could go home, he reckoned.

Then the voice on the radio penetrated his fog. It was Cassy's voice, shouting, "Joe, Joe, you there? You're a flippin' hero! You crazy, suicidal sonofagun, you broke the charge."

The two didn't compute. Hero and friendly fire. Who the hell done named it that, anyhow? Weren't nothing friendly about no "friendly fire," as far as he could tell.

"No ma'am. I just killed a bunch of our own boys and girls. Ain't you got eyes? When this is over, you ain't gotta worry. I'll turn myself in."

"What are you talking about, Joe? You just saved an entire company of Taggart's troops, holding the rear while we got everyone through the wire."

"Cassy, I done killed our own troops! What don't you get about that?"

"We were falling back, Joe. Those troops knew they were going to die. You made it worth the sacrifice."

"Ain't nothing they did, ma'am. They didn't sacrifice themselves. I gave the order, and I sacrificed them. I swear I didn't know they was there!"

"Joe... You broke the enemy's back. They're pulling back to regroup. Now we can re-deploy and get our wounded out, get our troops resupplied. We can get through the wire safely and shore up our lines. We would have fallen without that strike. You think on that, okay? Now get back out there and start dropping dynamite!"

Joe lifted his goggles and wiped tears away. He took a quick, deep breath and then replied, "Yes, ma'am. I'm on it."

"Just stay focused, Joe. You're doing great."

It didn't feel great.

- 27 -

1300 HOURS - ZERO DAY +256

CHOONY HANDED JAZ a reloaded rifle and took her empty one in return. Load, exchange, load, exchange. The hardest part was keeping the satchel of ammo and magazines from sliding down the roof on which he and Jaz had positioned themselves. Bullet holes here and there all around him taught him very clearly the difference between cover and concealment, and that he and Jaz only had the latter. If the few people who shot at them struck the roof, the bullet passed right through, barely slowing down.

Given how much ammunition Jaz had fired off, and her pretty impressive hit rate, her Karma must be deeply negative. Once this war was over, he'd have to work hard motivating her to do good works to bring herself into balance again. She was a jaded cynic, so that would take some work, but she also had an inner light that was practically blinding to one such as him. A wonderful, beautiful spirit. She could do it, no doubt about it, if he could only motivate her.

"Choony, more ammo!" Jaz's voice was strained, tighter than the strings on a fiddle.

He handed her the loaded rifle in another round of rinse-

and-repeat. She didn't normally sound so strained, but then again, she must be in terrible pain from her recent wound and so much shooting. Or maybe it was something else... He finished loading the rifle she had handed him, then peeked above the roof ridge.

He immediately wished he hadn't. There had to be at least a platoon down there in the city some fifty yards away. Not far enough. And they were all looking around frantically. They'd spot Jaz in moments if she kept firing.

"Jaz, we have to fire and move. We can't stay in one place." Choony struggled to keep his heart rate down and his voice even. He failed.

"The last thing I need is the stress of you freaking out." Jaz had ducked down for a moment. Too many people looking in their direction, perhaps.

"My fear is for your life, not my own. If we die, I will go to the Pure Land, while you remain stuck in the cycle of death and rebirth."

Jaz glanced at him, then nodded once. One of the many things he loved about her was her acceptance of his beliefs, even if they weren't her own. "One more shot, then we relocate. Where to, boss?"

"Two roofs over that way." He pointed west. Here, the buildings were close enough together to jump from one roof to the next. "Then fire until they start shooting too close, and move again."

"Fine." Jaz slid her rifle up over the roof's ridge, aimed, fired, ducked back down. It was all done in one fluid motion. "So, we should like, go now... I think they spotted me." Jaz let herself slide halfway down the roof.

Choony, unable to resist his curiosity, peeked up over the ridge. "The Buddha, the Dharma, and the Sangha protect us..." He scurried down from the ridgeline too and with satchel in hand, sprinted after Jaz. There had been well over a squad of Empire troops rushing toward them. Down below, he saw half a dozen Manheim fighters burst out the back door of that same house, scattering toward other nearby buildings.

This was getting ridiculous. As the Empire's forces drove deeper into Manheim, they'd have to relocate more frequently. The end was closing in on them, the fighting more frantic as both sides inched toward their breaking point. Manheim was still going strong, but as the intensity of the fighting grew, so did their casualties. At least the Empire's troops were being cut down, too. What a waste of life, and over what? Buildings, empty ones. Needless suffering. But such was the way of the world.

Choony jumped the last chasm and then scrambled to Jaz. She was already aiming to fire. One shot. Then another. Soon, she had emptied the rifle's five-round magazine.

"Shit, *run,*" she said, voice frantic. They tossed their rifles to one another, then scrambled toward the roof's far edge with Jaz in the lead—she didn't have to carry the burdensome satchel of ammo and supplies, and quickly outpaced him.

As he sprinted toward the edge, Jaz leapt into the air. Just then came the three bellowing roars of an AK rifle burst. Midair, Jaz cried out in pain. She hit the roof on the other side like a bag of wet rice and, seemingly in slow motion, slid down the steeply-angled roof toward the edge. Choony didn't turn around to look at who had fired, but landed in a crouch on the far side. Pulse racing, panic took over. He let his feet slide out from under him, and when he reached the edge, he dangled off it. He had to get as low as he could for the drop...

Choony glanced up at movement to his right and saw two Empire troops had come out that back door, and now aimed their rifles at him. One was an AK. His options were limited. Choony let go and felt his stomach lurch as the ground, twenty feet below, rushed up at him. The impact was painful despite his tuck-and-roll turning much of his momentum into a forward roll. He scrambled to his feet and part of him wondered if he had been injured or shot. He didn't feel anything, but that could be adrenaline, some clinical part of his mind told him.

The two soldiers took aim at Choony as he reached Jaz's limp form. Choony looked at Jaz's rifle lying next to her, then back up at the soldiers. One of them grinned.

Then multiple shots rang out from seemingly all around him, and the soldiers dropped to the ground, one clearly dead and the other crying out in pain. As another Empire trooper came out the door, he too was cut down. It was the Manheim troops! They were covering him.

Choony wasted no time. He slung both rifles over his back and the satchel over his shoulder. He sat Jaz up, resting her torso on his knees. Reaching under both of her arms, he laced his fingers together over her chest and pulled himself to his feet. An inch at a time, he dragged Jaz out of that bloody courtyard to the nearest door. It opened when he got close, and a young man darted out to help. Together, they got Jaz inside and then closed the door. For a few seconds at least, they were safe.

"Thank you so much," Choony said. "Our lives are yours. But once enough goons get together, they'll clear that courtyard and come in here. Is there a back door?"

"Window," the man said. He picked up an AR-15 that leaned against the doorway. "I'll cover you. Be quick."

Choony nodded and rushed to kneel by Jaz. She was unconscious, but still breathing. He looked her over, checking for wounds, and found it immediately—a round had passed through her thigh. There wasn't much blood, not as much as he expected to find. Buddha bless her, they had missed her main artery there, just as they had missed the one in her shoulder. Once again, her luck had held. He breathed a sigh of relief, took out his med kit and got to work applying pressure to stop what bleeding there was while the young man rapid-fired single shots through the window into the courtyard, occasionally ducking back to reload. The noise in the house from his rifle was deafening.

Then Choony noticed Jaz was oozing blood from a nasty gash on the left side of her head, her hair slick with crimson. That explained her unconsciousness. She surely had a nasty concussion. All he could do was bandage it.

That done, he bolted to the back of the house to check on the window the Manheim fighter had mentioned. It was small. Even if he broke it out, he wasn't sure he could get Jaz through it, especially with the glass that might remain in the frame. Even worse, outside he saw lots of movement. Empire movement. He dropped to all fours and crawled out of the room, closing the door behind him.

When he got back to the living room, the fighter was firing frantically. He glanced at Choony, but no more than a moment before he was firing again. "They're overwhelming us. Too many. Can you get her through the window?"

Choony shook his head. "Window's too small, and there's a lot of movement outside it."

"Shit..." He fired three times in rapid succession. "I'll cover you. You've got to drag her out of here if you want her to live. We'll be overrun in minutes."

Choony nodded and spent the next minute getting his rifles slung onto Jaz. Then, with a moment's help from the Good Samaritan, he got Jaz onto his back in a Fireman's Carry. He was already sweating by the time he reached the door.

The fighter said, "Good luck, mister. Now... *Run!*"

Choony heard the man's rifle, unloading half a magazine in the time it took Choony to get out the door and swing right. He trotted as fast as he could, headed southeast. Anywhere but here.

A cry behind him almost made him turn, but he caught himself in time. He didn't have the time or physical energy to waste checking it out. Besides, he recognized the voice. The young man had been brave, and noble. But things were what they were. He would pray to Buddha for the young man, but knew that was more to assuage his own remorse than for the young man's soul.

Then another cry, but of alarm rather than pain. Choony was halfway to the alley he intended to escape through when he heard a loud explosion. Someone had a grenade back there. Then he heard the sounds of boots pounding pavement, several people running toward him. He turned enough to see who was coming, but saw only three Manheim troops, two men and a woman. They all had U.S. flag shoulder patches, their simple statement of defiance to the Empire, someone had told him.

"Fucking run," one of the men shouted. Choony turned back around and did his best. Whatever they were running from, he knew he had better avoid it too.

As they ran even with the overburdened Choony, the men pulled Jaz off his back and wrapped one of her arms around each of their shoulders. They moved as quickly as they could holding Jaz up between them. Choony had been there once himself, back in college after his first and only experiment with getting far too intoxicated.

Choony, Jaz, and the three fighters made a lot faster time after that. They reached the end of the alley and turned right, then doglegged left into another alley. At the end of that was a chainlink fence, but the woman said, "Don't worry, Clanner. Follow me."

She lifted the edge of the fence where it overlapped another section of chain link, and it came up easily. She held the flap for the two men and then for Choony. "Come on. There's a safehouse around the corner."

Just as she said that, a shot rang out from behind them. Choony, looking at the female fighter, saw from the corner of his eye one man's head explode. The other man, pulled by the weight of Jaz and his fallen teammate, collapsed on top of her in a heap of arms and legs.

The Empire trooper pulled the trigger again, but nothing happened—Choony heard the *click, click* of him trying, then he fumbled with the charging handle to clear the jam.

Rather than return fire at the helpless Empire man, the woman beside Choony said, "Sorry, man. You're on your own." She grabbed her fallen Manheim fighter and half-pulled him to his feet. The two were gone in a second.

Just as Choony was going to rush to Jaz's side, the Empire soldier behind him racked his charging handle. Choony heard the once-jammed round tink off a wall and then skitter along the pavement. Choony stiffened, waiting for the shot that would end his life rather than try to run. He wouldn't leave Jaz behind.

"You don't got a rifle, bud," said the man behind him. "Turn around. Look at me."

Choony turned stiffly. He didn't mind the idea of being dead, but the process of dying? It was hard to maintain his detachment. His mind was fine with it, but his adrenal glands disagreed. And there was Jaz... Why didn't she move?

"Why don't you got a rifle?" asked the enemy fighter, keeping his own rifle aimed at Choony.

Looking down the barrel of that rifle, Choony slowly regulated his breathing and managed to get his heart rate down to something that didn't thunder in his ears like a woodpecker. "We Buddhists don't practice violence against our fellow man."

"Then you keep strange company," the man said, tossing

his head toward Jaz's limp form without letting his aim slip from Choony. "Oh ho, she's got two rifles on her. One of them yours, right?"

"No, sir. I don't fight. I help reload or I retrieve wounded, but I won't do anything to harm a person directly."

"Seems to me that reloading for her helps kill my people. You can't say you won't do anything to harm someone."

Choony nodded slowly. That was a topic he struggled with, actually, but he had reconciled it long ago. "Perhaps. But if I help those who oppose the Empire, the bandits, and other evil people, then in a way I am reducing suffering in this world."

"You killing someone like a raider would do the same." He took a step toward them, briefly eyeing Jaz. "Surrendering and not fighting at all would do the same. I mean, there's always gonna be evil in this world. Give in, suffer less." He took another step toward them.

"Are we really debating philosophy in an alley with a battle all around us? Why haven't you killed me yet?" Choony, his head cocked, was clearly interested in the answer, and by now had come to grips with the notion that he was about to die. Then Jaz would, too. Things were what they were. Why suffer by fretting things out of his control?

"Mostly because I don't like the idea of shooting an unarmed pacifist civilian. I'm a soldier of the Republic, not a damn raider."

"I notice very little difference. Please kill me first, okay?" Getting back to accepting his fate, rather than fighting it, had calmed him and restored his harmony. He just didn't want to see Jaz die. Seeing her light snuffed out would destroy his harmony, he knew, putting him back into the curse of life, death, rebirth.

"I told you. I don't kill unarmed civilians. Especially a pacifist. Run along. I have a job to do here." The man approached to within about six feet from both Jaz and Choony, then swung his rifle to point toward Jaz.

She lay unconscious still, and unknowing. Choony's heart sped up, his harmony gone in an instant. "No," he cried out, and took one step toward the man without thinking.

The fighter looked to Choony, eyes narrowing. "Stay back, fucker, or I'll shoot the bitch in the knee first."

Choony froze. What could he do? But that was Jaz lying there. She was vulnerable. She was hurt. She would only be a victim. She had told him about her life before the Clan, at least bits and pieces of it. He wouldn't allow her to die as she had lived, a victim right to the end. "You mustn't. Please, for your own harmony, your energy. Killing me first would be merciful. Mister... have mercy. Please, you must."

Still looking at Choony, the man spat on the ground, the wad of spittle and phlegm landing next to Choony's boot. "I don't kill civilians. But the Confed bitch dies," he said. His voice was steady, calm.

As the Empire fighter turned his head back toward Jaz, time seemed to slow down and little details leapt out at Choony. The beads of sweat on the fighter's forehead, the mole on his right cheek. The sounds of gunfire in the distance. His own heart beating like a drum. And then Jaz let out a whimper and rolled her head to the other side just as the man was raising his rifle to his shoulder again.

If Jaz died in front of him, he would find his harmony so disrupted that he'd spend the rest of his life—whether five minutes or five decades—unbalanced. He'd be in the torment that those who were without Buddha's guidance lived in, a world without color or joy. But if he attacked, then the fighter would be forced to kill Choony first. The entire complex chain of thought ran through him in an instant, like a bolt of lightning. He didn't have to actually harm the soldier, only make him *think* he was going to do so.

Choony exploded in a burst of movement, sprinting at his enemy. The man turned his head, eyes widening so far that Choony could see whites both above and below his dun-colored irises. Choony came in low, crossing the six feet in a blink, and at the last instant he leapt forward. His shoulder struck the fighter below the arm holding the rifle.

The trooper's feet came out from under him. As he and Choony flew through the air, the rifle went off, clattering away as they both landed on the pavement. Choony had knocked it out of his hands, but had the shot struck Jaz? No time to check yet. The fighter was scrambling to get free.

Panic flooded through Choony—if the enemy got that gun back, he'd definitely kill Jaz first, if only out of spite. As his opponent rose to his feet, Choony kicked the back of his knee. It buckled, and the trooper fell face-first into the pavement.

The man was trying again to rise up, hands under him and pushing. Choony got to his feet before his enemy. He ran over the man to get the rifle, his right foot landing squarely on the other's back and knocking him violently to the pavement again.

Choony picked up the rifle and pointed it in his enemy's general direction, shouting, "Get back or I'll shoot you."

The fighter smiled a toothy blood-stained grin, and a bit of crimson dribbled down from one corner of his mouth, thin lips swelling into fat lips already. "You're in a world of hurt now, mister. I know you won't use that."

Choony clenched his jaw. "You going to bet your life on it?"

The fighter pushed hard with his hands on the pavement, palm down, and jerked his knees in a kip-up so that he landed on his feet in a deep crouch. As he rose to his full height, he said, "Sorry, mister. Now you both are gonna die." He drew a large fixed-blade knife from its sheath at his waist, and turned toward Jaz.

Choony realized the fighter would kill Jaz first, more certain of Choony's pacifism when it was someone else getting killed. The fighter would test that pacifism in a moment, after Jaz was dead. Killing another was wrong, even in self-defense. But what of killing in defense of another? He had never done so, but that didn't prove it was wrong. What would bring more joy in the world, alleviate more suffering—killing the soldier or allowing Jaz to die? How many more would this soldier kill if left alive? And how was Choony, a man only in his early twenties, supposed to know the answer?

Buddha help him... Choony pulled the trigger. The report was loud enough to half-deafen him. The fighter fell, clutching his ribs, but when he landed, his eyes were open and vacant. The bullet had certainly gone through a lung into the heart.

Choony's heart beat like the wings of a hummingbird, deafening him as much as the shot had, and sweat poured down into his eyes. He looked at the horror he had wrought. He had done it... stained his soul...tainted his own Karma. He felt lost, bewildered, his mind reeled.

He dropped the dead man's rifle... and threw up, splattering his shoes.

* * *

Cassy listened, thanked the Manheim officer on the other end, then turned to Ethan. He stared at her with one eyebrow raised, leaning forward in his chair.

"So that sounded interesting." Ethan waited expectantly.

Cassy sighed. He was right, of course. "Very interesting. It seems just by showing up for the fight, Jaz was able to re-energize Manheim into a rally from almost being routed.

They circled around using their knowledge of the town's layout and struck the Empire's command platoon. Once El Jeffe was dead, the rest mostly fled. The ones that remained were defeated."

"That sounds like Jaz." Ethan's knee bounced and he flipped a pen around one finger. "But you don't look thrilled."

Cassy would normally find his hyperactivity amusing, but right now it only irritated her. "That's because the ones who fled headed north. They're heading right toward the bigger battle up here. Tell Michael the Empire has some reinforcements coming within the next half hour."

Ethan took a deep breath and closed his eyes. "We're barely hanging on, even with our planes and battlecars. Telling him will only stress him out, without changing the situation for the better."

"If we don't tell him," Cassy said, voice rising, "he will be blindsided. He can handle stress. So please, do what I fucking asked, and tell him!"

Ethan turned back to his radio, grumbling under his breath. She didn't have time for Ethan to question every order she gave him. Surely Michael would handle the stress of this information better than she had. Though, maybe Ethan didn't really deserve to be snapped at either, but there was no time to think about that now. Her radio squawked again, and it was back to work.

* * *

Frank felt his face turning red. He could hardly deal with Cassy right now as he drove through the thick of an enemy concentration while his gunner and cowcatcher laid waste to them. "Cassy, I know they're coming from the south. You said that already. But we can't strip our north defenders just because the enemy is light up there right now. There's an entire missing goon battalion, or what's left of it, and we don't know where they are yet."

"I get what you're saying," Cassy replied, her voice sounding strained, "but we do know what's left of another battalion is headed your way from the south. We have to deal with the enemy we know is there, first. Head south. Coordinate with Michael to detach those north food forest troops."

Frank fumed. She made a certain sense, but the upside to her plan left them vulnerable, and the downside was possibly losing Clanholme through an enemy end run. "Negative. We have to leave those troops there. Let me bring my battlecars and Joe's planes south. We can intercept the new forces while they're strung out and on the move, rather than waiting for them to attack us en masse when they're ready."

"Dammit, Frank! Why won't you listen? Do I have to pull rank on you? I know your idea is what you think is the most practical, but this is it. This is the endgame. If we screw it up now, we lose it all. We have to move to face this new threat, not string our forces out even more. We're on the ropes right now, and those north troops aren't doing much. *Move them into place*. Let them do some good."

"Cassy, you may lead us, but this is war. Right now, Michael leads us, not you. I'm not doing what you ask. I'm gathering my team and Joe's, and we're going south." Damn, that woman was stubborn. And she wasn't the only one who knew the gravity of the situation, not the only one who realized this was the make-or-break part of the battle.

Cassy's voice crackled through again, and this time she sounded tightly wound. He could almost picture her in the bunker, face red, sitting on the chair and leaning over the table, shoulders back and tense. "Frank, as leader of the Confederation and Clan Leader, I command you to follow my instructions. Head north, relieve the troops there, and scout for that missing battalion while the troops head south to stop a new one."

Frank was not yet ready to give up this important fight just because Cassy pulled rank. Damn, here she was, once again, using her title to get her way. Normally that wouldn't be an issue, but here and now it was life or death. He was about to reply, when a new voice came over the radio.

Michael said, "Break, break. This is Lincoln One to Charlie One. I'm in the middle of a battle and don't have time to mediate this. You may be in charge every other day, but today I am in charge, and next time you want to shift battle plans, you'd better run it by me first—"

"Michael, don't you dare—"

"I'll deal with the blowback later," Michael counter-interrupted, cutting off Cassy's transmission with his own. "Bravo One, head south with Bravo Two. Flank the approaching column and strike at the same time. Over and out."

Frank ignored Cassy after that, given that Michael was in charge right now as far as he and everyone else was concerned. He contacted Joe directly and coordinated their attack. Joe would locate them from the air, then get out of sight. Hopefully he wouldn't be seen. Then Frank would hit the enemy mid-column from the east, and Joe would hit at the same time or just after, hitting the enemy's forward elements. Between the two, the hope was that the troops in the middle and rear would flee from the main battle.

It didn't take long for the planes to find them, or for Frank to close in with his deadly Road Warrior battlecars. He gave the command, and all eight vehicles fanned out into a line and gunned it. Over the rough terrain they went, and only two cars had been damaged enough to have a hard time keeping up. They'd be right behind him, though.

The enemy troops rose into view. At the sound of engines, they turned to look. Such sounds stood out like a powder-blue tuxedo at a funeral, these days. Once they saw the onrushing battlecars, curiosity quickly turned to panic. The troops, having already been routed once that day, weren't up for a fight. Rather than get set and concentrate fire, they scattered as best they could. On foot, against cars, it wasn't good enough. Thud. Thud. Thud. Soon the entire front of his car glistened with a fresh coat of blood, contrasting with the dried brown gore already on the cars. The vehicles swept through the enemy ranks, firing, then split in half to circle back.

Just then, Frank caught sight of Joe and the other planes. Betsy began a crazy, slow spiral to its left, throwing bombs out at any group of Empire sonsabitches that managed to cluster up to defend against the battlecars.

Drive through. Turn around. Drive through. Pass ammo to the gunner. Drive through. This cycle repeated for what seemed an eternity, but a glance at the sun showed it couldn't have been even half an hour. The lead units crumbled, and Frank was merciless about grinding them under his solid tires. Die, you bastards...

As he swept around once again, Joe came over the radio. "Hey, Frank. Look south. You see what I see? Yeehaw! Tell me it ain't no mirage!"

Frank glanced and the sight made his heart soar—the middle goons had stopped piling into the fray and were running away. They headed south through their own oncoming troops, and from what Frank could tell, it had been enough to make the followers flee as well. Getting routed once had probably shaken them, but seeing their people flee yet again broke their spirit. Or so Frank figured from watching them.

Frank shifted back up into third gear, gaining

momentum and streaking toward the crumbling lead units again. On the radio he said, "Nope, that's no mirage. Ha ha! Boy, look at them go!"

Cassy's voice came through again. "Bravo One, status?" She sounded tired, even defeated. She was mentally strong, sure, but she was emotionally fragile, and Frank figured the mutiny—which was really only following the chain of command in the middle of a damn battle—might have cracked her spirit. He hoped not.

Sounding as upbeat as he could, he replied, "Charlie One, this is Bravo One Actual. I'm happy to report the OpFor is routing. I say again, enemy forces are retreating to the southeast. We're about to slam the door behind them."

"Negative, Bravo One Actual."

There was a pause, and Frank steeled himself for another round of verbal jousting. No way she had forgotten about the last conversation they'd had, after all.

"Charlie One to Bravo One, be advised that Lincoln One reports the north flank is being hit hard. The missing Empire battalion did show up, and hit the north food forest. He instructs that all available forces disengage if possible and reinforce forest north. How do you copy?"

Shit, no wonder Cassy sounded so dejected... Michael had been proven right, and on top of that, Clanholme itself was in imminent danger. "Bravo One Actual. Roger that, and Wilco. Cavalry coming. Out."

Joe came through on the radio then, telling Frank he had heard it and was disengaging. Then Frank radioed his team, telling them the news. He turned to look southeast, and as he saw the backs of the enemy, fleeing, his eyes narrowed with a fire in them. It took everything in him not to chase after the wounded, fleeing prey.

Only the thought of Mary's disappointment with him if he disobeyed and left his Clanmates in danger kept him steering back northward. He swore that the next units he fought wouldn't be so lucky.

* * *

Cassy watched the blocks, red and blue, moving about on her monitor. A red block crashed into a blue one half its size. The blue block first backed up, then turned around as it fell back and then routed. Thankfully, it routed around another blue block behind it, this one much larger. The bigger blue block then moved quickly into the oncoming red one, and both halted. Up in the real world, she knew, those weren't abstract blocks, but real flesh-and-blood people. Watching them took her mind off the white-hot coal in her brain that burned so hot she could practically feel it. Anger. Betrayal. Fear. Frustration. All feelings that were completely unwelcome, and completely out of her control.

Of course, she knew she shouldn't be feeling that way. Frank ultimately had followed orders. What burned was that they hadn't been her own orders... and that she had been wrong. Intellectually, she knew she was out of line. Michael was the warlord, the military commander, and far more qualified than she was.

Perhaps it was just pride... She had never thought of herself as being especially prideful, but one doesn't always see one's own faults, she reminded herself. Her mind was so fuzzy with fatigue, adrenaline, anger, and doubt that she couldn't be sure she was even rational. She felt jacked up, confused, and terrified she was about to lose it completely.

In the background, the radio barked away endlessly. Calls for help, orders to retreat—those outnumbered the ones to advance, to charge, to flank. The Confederation was losing this battle, despite the spectacular advantages of having airplanes and battlecars. Those were more or less unstoppable killing machines, the tanks of this post-civilization era, but they weren't enough. Nothing seemed to be enough. There were just so many goons. The Empire was huge, and they had thrown so many people into this war that it had to be virtually everyone they could spare across their entire pseudo-nation.

No goddamn wonder General Houle, sitting safe in his mountain fortress in Colorado, hadn't just zapped the Clan with Predator drones and Hellfire missiles, or whatever they used these days. He could probably have done that, but drones and missiles were irreplaceable right now. Priceless.

Cassy felt her rage boil over as every detail cascaded through her mind. The doubts about her motive. Her sanity. It was a crappy, vicious circle of thought she was stuck in, and in a flare of rage, she lunged upward, hearing her rolling office chair skitter back as she rose. She leaned over the desk and swiped both arms to her right, bulldozing a mass of papers, pencils, and a couple books that fell to the floor with a thud. She heard Ethan get up behind her, probably surprised by her outburst, but she ignored him. Gritting her teeth, she slammed her palms down onto the desk, and the sound of sweaty flesh on wood drowned out the incessant radio chatter. Her heart pounded in her temple, and when she gazed down at the desk once again, she saw it—the lone blue pencil eraser, sitting there in mocking stubbornness. She grabbed the stupid pencil eraser and flung it to her left toward the stupid monitors that watched the stupid battle and the stupid cows and—

What the hell was that in Camera Three? She went through her mental list of cameras, and decided Three was the camera that pointed east, mounted maybe five hundred yards east of the guard tower. She walked slowly toward the monitors, then leaned in closely to try to figure out what was going on. Something was moving, that was certain, but what?

It was big, stretching hundreds of yards across. Cows, maybe?

They got a bit closer and the picture grew clearer. Then it struck her like a hammer blow to the head... it wasn't something huge. It was *people*. Armed people. There had to be hundreds and hundreds of them. Had Liz Town fallen and their attackers come east? No, these were coming from the east. Had Ephrata fallen? That made no sense either—the Empire would approach from the north or from the west. What lay east of the Confederation that could have swept through Ephrata so quickly they didn't have time to warn Clanholme?

The invaders. Those two words danced around and twisted in her mind like a tornado, blowing all her other petty, stupid personal concerns aside like so much loose hay in a storm. "Shit..."

Ethan said, "What?"

"Camera Three," she replied, tilting her head toward the screen.

"Three? What the hell are you—Oh. Fuck..."

Cassy only stared at the monitor. What else was there to do? "The invaders must have heard about the chaos going on and are taking advantage of it to try another attack."

Ethan squared his shoulders, the fabric of his *Game On!* tee-shirt wrinkling in the middle. "We'll be safe from the 'vaders down here, and I know Mandy and the kids are already set up in the Kidz Kastle—I gave them the order hours ago. But what of the..."

Cassy caught the crack in his voice on the last word, and didn't expect him to finish that sentence anyway. Instead, she just reached her hand out and rested it on his forearm. "If we get overrun, the others up there know the drill."

Ethan nodded, but remained silent.

Cassy said, "I'm not the blind faith one. That would be

my mom. But I think praying couldn't hurt."

Ethan turned to face her, and extended his hands. She took them lightly in her own, then bowed her head. "Lord, I haven't prayed much, but—"

"Holy shit," Ethan said as he looked away from her and leaned in toward the monitor.

Cassy followed suit and leaned in as well. What was he all wound up about? So, they were now clearly visible, much closer. "What?"

Ethan pointed at the screen, practically bouncing. "Look at their guns!"

Cassy did and was underwhelmed. All the rifles she could see were AK-47s. She expected that from the invaders. "Korean AKs..."

Ethan huffed in frustration. "Yeah. But the soldiers sure as hell aren't Korean. Who has Korean AKs but isn't Korean, back east?"

She stared into the screen. Could it really be?

The people showing on the monitor were men and women. They were white, and black, and Hispanic. They were Americans. "My god, Ethan. They're from Taggart? Is that possible?"

She threw her arms around Ethan and they both jumped up and down. "Ethan... *We're saved!*"

- 28 -

0445 HOURS - ZERO DAY +257

JAZ SAT AT the folding card table the Manheimers had set up outside of town, a makeshift command post closer to the action than their actual HQ in town. That was Choony's idea, smart as always. After sitting for a few minutes, her arms and legs had grown lead weights somehow. That was the only explanation for how heavy her limbs felt. She was totally wiped out. The concussion probably didn't help.

With what felt like superhuman effort, she was able to once again slide the bandage up and out of her eyes. Choony had bandaged it like, a thousand times, but it kept coming loose. Her scalp wound was just in an awkward location on her head. She didn't mind it being loose, though, since it hurt her skull when it was tight.

"You Clanners and your recruits were vital to this victory. You know that, right? We almost collapsed even with you guys here, but when you went on the counterattack—on your own, no less—it motivated our troops. We shouldn't have won this battle." His name was like, Charlie or Carl, or maybe Dan. Jaz couldn't remember. Her eyelids felt like they had weights on.

"Thanks, Lieutenant," she managed to get out. "I'm glad we could help. Truth is, Choony and I were just, like, at the right place at the right time. It's not like we fought them alone—we had our Army of 300 running around in squads—and your people saved us a few times."

Choony sat down, finally—his pacing had become annoying—and said, "In fact, from what we learned on the radio, our distracting all these Empire goons here at Manheim probably saved the day at Clanholme."

The lieutenant said, "How did Clanholme hold out? I know they had reinforcements from all over the Confederation, but still, fighting at least two regiments..."

Jaz tilted her head back to look at the still mostly dark sky, but that made her dizzy so she leaned forward again. "The Clan had some secret weapons that helped. But from what they told us, it almost wasn't enough. It was still a close call, just like here."

In the distance, sporadic gunfire still played out as Manheim finished mopping up Empire stragglers. The battle was over, but a few enemy survivors hadn't yet got the memo. Plus, Manheim was hunting down survivors as best they could, keeping as many as they could from heading home to fight again. Mercy was in short supply these days.

"What sort of secret weapons?" His voice pitched upward at the end. He sounded surprised and maybe envious. Or paranoid.

"We got cars working," Jaz said. "Armored them up, put on turrets and hood guns. Like something out of a cheesy '80s road warrior-type flick. And we got some really old planes working. Not much in the way of guns, but they gave good info for troop movements, and they dropped a lot of little dynamite bombs."

"Wow. Impressive. And what is the Clan planning on doing with those after this war ends, may I ask?" He had leaned forward, probably without realizing it, and Jaz saw his jaw clench.

Damn. Not another paranoid soldier-type looking for enemies... "I dunno. Cassy said we'd be sharing the technology, or whatever, so everyone in the Confederation gets them. Maybe through advisors or something."

"Why not just tell us so we can make our own?" His eyebrows furrowed together.

"You're a lieutenant, not a president, and I'm not even on the Clan's leader council. What the hell do I know? I only just found out we had them."

"Maybe you should tell us what you really know, since you're such good friends."

"Maybe you shouldn't make enemies out of friends, mister. In case you forgot, we just fought alongside you. Shut the hell up or I'm going to go find your C.O. and let them know about your sudden interest in shit that's over your pay-grade." Jaz felt a kick to her calf under the table, cutting off the awesome trash talk she was about to spit at this jackass wannabe.

Choony coughed, a deliberate sound, and said, "Lieutenant, you'll have to forgive her. As exhausted as you are, she traveled far even before this battle began, and she's injured."

The Manheim officer clenched his teeth, but instead of snapping back, he shut up. Good for him. Too bad the little spaz hadn't figured out how to shut up before he did his best to cause a flipping diplomatic incident. Jaz let out a huff. Time to change the subject. She turned to Choony and said, "We should get going. I want to get back to Clanholme to eat and, like, sleep for a year."

Choony stood and offered his hand to the lieutenant, who paused but then shook. "You and your people fought well today," Choony said.

"Thanks. Yours did, too." The lieutenant stood and made his way out.

"I don't like that guy," Jaz said when he disappeared. "Let's go. If you don't drive like Grandma Mandy, we could be there in time for breakfast."

Choony laughed. He raised both eyebrows and said, "Have you seen how she drives? The wagon's airborne half the time. She's dangerous behind the reins, I tell you."

* * *

An hour until breakfast, the computer chirped its distinctive alert for incoming messages. It was the theme song from the most popular multiplayer online role-playing game. Damn, that alert was reserved for the annoying popup box the 20s had hacked onto his system long ago. He had moved it to a protective "sandbox," of course, so they couldn't see his real system information. A small gesture of defiance on his part. He trudged to the computer, ran the suite of programs he used to protect his computer and decipher their transmission, then waited for it to decode. It didn't take long. Then the green, monochrome chat box opened up as usual.

Watcher1 >> *Good morning, sunshine*

D.Ryder >> *It was. I was dreaming of the best fast-food on th planet. So what's up*

Watcher1 >> *Happened 2 b a bird over u yesterday. Quite a show !*

D.Ryder >> *Meh. It was alright. The middle sucked but th end wuz uber kewl.*

Watcher1 >> *Ya, so anyways, what did u think of the supplies we sent Taggart?*

D.Ryder >> *Can u b more specific?*

Watcher1 >> *The drones and computers we sent. Seems a bird got a pic of them coming into your area but it never came out.*

D.Ryder >> *Huh. Well, u know there was raiders all over the area so maybe they got it.*

Watcher1 >> *Yeah maybe. But the King Under the Mountain doesn't think so.*

D.Ryder >> *Yeah? Why's that? It could happen.*

Watcher1 >> *I thought so 2. But I hear he doesn't agree. Says he made arrangements the whole way for it 2 go thru without problms.*

D.Ryder >> *Any chance General Whosit, in Penn, or General Ree in New Jersey, got them 1st? Seems like a long way 2 go these days*

Watcher1 >> [Watcher1 has changed his name to BcarefulNwatchUrAss]

BcarefulNwatchUrAss >> [BcarefulNwatchUrAss has changed his name to Watcher1]

Watcher1 >> *I think the General may be doubting your loyalty to his cause. U shud b on xtra-good behavior 4 a while if u want 2 stay on the winning team*

D.Ryder *>> I assure you that I'm on board Team Houle. I don't know what happened to the supplies, but I will have our peeps keep their eyes open to see if there's evidence in other towns. One of them maybe? They wouldn't have known it was for Taggart. What was in them, so that we can be alert for anyone trying to offload or use it?*

Watcher1 *>> It doesn't matter. See what you can find out, but the contents are Need-to-Know, and I don't need to know so they didn't tell me.*

D.Ryder *>> OK, well I will keep eyes out for anything, whatever I can without knowing the contents. If I find out anything I will let u know*

Watcher1 *>> 10-4. I hope you r right becuz if Houle suspects u stole Army property in wartime, then u and ur Clan r in for a ruf time. I'll let the 20s know u don't have it but r looking. Watcher1 out.*

<<Session terminated>>

Ethan didn't bother to shut down the sandbox or the "virtual machine" he ran it in for security's sake. He leaned back and stared at the ceiling for a long while, mind racing. An uneasy feeling had lodged in his gut, and he tried to rationalize it away but couldn't. He was fearful of the 20s, and Houle, for good reason.

If Houle was catching on to him... He knew too much for them to let him walk away, that was certain. Ethan was probably the only other person on Earth who knew the details of how and why America had detonated bombs to create many large-scale EMPs, darkening the rest of the planet just as America had been darkened. Houle wouldn't want that loose end left uncut, running around spreading rumors, even if they were true. Especially since they were true.

Ethan picked up his notebook, a 5" by 7" journal that he used as both day-planner and to scribble notes and ideas, and began brainstorming just how he might reassure the General of his loyalty. Turning in Nestor should have done the trick, even though Ethan had only done it after becoming convinced—wrongly—that Nestor's Night Ghosts had turned to banditry. The only way for Ethan to really prove his worth was to find out what the General wanted. He'd have to try to drag that info out of Watcher One, as he didn't know anyone else in Houle's circle, but he didn't know how to put leverage on the guy to get the information he needed. Ethan would have to think of something, though.

For the sake of Amber, Kaitlyn, and the rest of the Clan, he needed to succeed.

* * *

It was an hour before lunch when Ree finished compiling the data from a hundred or more field reports sent in by his unit commanders. What he saw was like having a drunken nobleman for an ancestor—good to have a noble, bad to have a drunkard. Good and bad mixed together like rice and weevils.

On the bad side, he had lost half his forces and most of his People's Worker Army. He lacked the strength to be a clear and present danger to Taggart unless his nemesis made a terrible mistake at some point. Expansion and re-conquest was out of the question. There was, after all, only so much he could accomplish when the majority of his forces were those filthy, undisciplined, sandy ISNA animals. Without his slaves, he'd even be hard-pressed to complete the plantings he would need to grow enough food for next winter, or even just to handle the day-to-day farming tasks a soldier shouldn't be burdened with. He lacked the slaves to plow Central Park.

But a worthy commander sees opportunity where others see only hurdles. The smaller People's Worker Army meant his food stores were enough to last at least until harvest time. And the island's existing population was still high enough that he could press as many people into service as he needed to restock the Worker Army. Also, while he lacked the troop strength to project force into Taggart's territory, he still posed a big enough threat that Taggart would also be constrained. He had to defend his territory against Ree's raids, or against any strikes against targets of opportunity that Ree may launch. Taggart would be unable to strike hard against Ree, too, because the island's access points were few and small—perfect choke points, easy to defend.

Kim sat in a chair across from him in Ree's fortress north of the City, gazing out a window that overlooked the water. "You told me at breakfast, sir, that you had two things weighing on your mind. But you were occupied with other business as well, so I did not want to distract you from that with my ignorant questions. Do you have time now to enlighten me?"

Ree favored him with a friendly smile. "I do. Perhaps in your ignorance you will have ideas that have not yet occurred to me." When Major Kim smiled at that, Ree knew he had played that just right. Ree rarely offered praise, much less suggested a subordinate might have ideas he didn't come up with. It was important to keep Kim loyal after the recent setbacks. "First, the odd farming that Taggart had been doing in what are now our holdings, in New Jersey. Second, the notion of pulling railroad cars with horses had been successful out there, but how can we achieve the same efficiency here in the City?"

Kim nodded but didn't reply for a couple minutes. It was a comfortable silence, and Ree had no issue working on paperwork and issuing orders until Kim was done turning the two things around in his mind.

At last, Kim cleared his throat. When Ree looked up from his writing and nodded, Kim said, "The easy question is how to use the trains idea here in the City. The answer is the subways. They travel all about the city, underground. If we guard the stations and blockade any we don't wish to use, our goods will be safer underground. And we don't need many horses. Not when we have all the people we need in the Worker Army. I can experiment to find the most efficient number to use for pulling cars of different weights and lengths."

Ree puckered his lips and raised his eyebrows, expressing surprise. "Indeed. You have a good point. Very well, begin immediately. Once we know how many, then you will need to compile a report on which stations will be most useful and which we will want to blockade. Now then, what of the first problem?"

Kim looked solidly pleased with himself. Ree may not have admired or appreciated the lack of discipline that occasionally showed, but keeping Kim loyal and working hard required the *very occasional* 'pat on the back,' as the Americans liked to say.

"The farming methods Taggart used. Yes... We've interrogated people just as you instructed, General. They were uncooperative at first, but we found alternative means of questioning that worked better. By comparing their statements, we have the core of the truth despite the inadequacies of that method of questioning, I believe."

"Adequately done, little brother. And what truth have you uncovered?"

"It is a way of farming that uses no plows, no fertilizer, no heavy machinery—only compost and dead plant matter. This is made possible by connecting all aspects of the crop's life and health, and the various things that aid it. It is a philosophy of using, rather than conquering, nature. I have made copious notes and will complete my report soon."

Ree looked into the fireplace, comforting though it was unlit. It reminded him of the burn piles on his family's farm when he was a child. Even his grandfather would have found Taggart's farming ideas eccentric at best. "The only thing I like about it is that it does not require fertilizer. Those chemicals are hard to acquire now, at least here. But farming without a plow? Impossible. The ground must be broken up to remove the weeds, and to allow the water to seep down to the roots."

"According to the answers we received, those issues are dealt with in new ways. They consistently said that 'healthy soil,' whatever that means, absorbs water far more readily when unplowed, and grows stronger roots for healthier plants that provide more nutrients."

"I don't believe such nonsense. It breaks rules of farming that have stood for centuries. Perhaps you didn't question hard enough." Ree stared at Kim. Was the man being honest? Why would he lie?

"The method for accomplishing it is complicated, with many steps and huge numbers of related tasks that need to be coordinated, but against all reason, it does appear to work. They spoke truth, as we easily confirmed by observation. I was stunned and required much more than the usual confirming evidence before bringing you this information, but I am sure my general will accept the verdict of evidence and farmers alike. In your wisdom, you may accept this evidence far more rapidly than I did. I am stubborn in my ways, older brother, where you bend gracefully before the wind, and therefore always know the direction in which it blows."

Ree stifled a frown. Kim had an annoying habit of stating the obvious. Of course all that was true—it was the reason Ree was a General and Kim had only the rank of Major. "If Taggart would risk the lives of many thousands to starvation should the techniques fail, he must have some knowledge others did not."

"It would seem so," Kim said. "He hasn't shown himself to be foolish or reckless."

"So it is settled. We must learn more and emulate these methods. Other than defense and keeping order, our highest priority must become farming Central Park—half of it normally, half this new way, and we will soon see how well it works. Promise double rations to those who know about this technique and help us implement it. Provided it works as well as they claim, of course."

"Yes, my leader. Anything else?"

"Just one other thing. We are on the defensive now. Yet we still control a large territory—and we will probably be here for a long time. Administering a large territory is a problem with no technology to help us. I want to encourage our soldiers to settle down, marry the natives, start families —and have their children learn our ways, not their parent's. Unfortunately, most of the soldiers are ISNA and shouldn't even raise donkeys, much less children."

"You have a plan, sir?" Kim leaned forward, and Ree saw his eyes glimmer. Ree knew rumors had been flying for days about some mysterious new system.

Well, they were about to learn. Given the technology, the barbarism and violence everywhere, the disparate cultures and the low population densities that were still falling... Only one historical model worked for long, so far as Ree knew.

"Yes," Ree said, and allowed a faint smile to show. "I call

it the Program for People's Defense and Social Advancement, but I'll forego the rhetoric and explain it in plain and simple terms. First, inform all our forces that their spouses back home are probably dead, and in any case, they'll not likely return home in this lifetime. Then, divide the western half of our territory among our four colonels. Tell them to do the same with their majors, and for them to do the same with their captains. Divide our total troop strength to correspond with the land allotments."

Kim rose to his feet and bowed deep respect. "You are the Great Leader now, my general. A return to our feudal past. Genius..."

Ree permitted himself to smile. "Yes, a return to our past, in many ways. Tell them also that any landholder who marries an American and has offspring will pass their assigned territory to their eldest son, along with their rank."

Kim nodded slowly, obviously considering the ramifications. Then he said, "So, if they are all widows and widowers, they are free to remarry and you've given them a reason to do so. I suspect that, with the offer of hereditary holdings, they will be eager to start."

"Indeed. Lastly, for their children to be eligible to inherit landholdings, they must attend schooling and training in my territory, under instructors of my choosing, until they reach adulthood."

Ree knew this would ensure their loyalty by hostaging their children—and by knocking the ridiculous culture of the ISNA troops out of the offspring. The ISNA troops' barbarism would die with them. And the children, having been in his instructors' care for most of their lives, would grow into loyal adults, properly educated in their culture and ways.

Ree continued, "Now, as far as the Central Park project goes, each of my colonels will be responsible for sending workers, however they choose to select them, but in return will get an equal share of the harvest to keep or pass on to their underlings."

"Further tethering their loyalty up the chain of command. Wise, sir. But what of conquest? With you on the island, any new land we liberate will be taken by others. What if one such member of our nobility grows large enough to challenge you?"

Ree bared his teeth, upper lip curled back, and his eyes narrowed. "Easy. All land taken, beyond their original landholding boundaries, belongs to me. This lets me someday assign a new colonel, and in the short term, it curbs their desire to conquer by removing any reward for doing so. I want us on the defensive for now. We must be the strong turtle if we are to defeat Taggart the Fox."

The lunch bells rang, interrupting their conversation. Ree's grumbling stomach reminded him that he skipped breakfast to work. "Come, Kim. Let us go eat and discuss the details together. And let us also discuss how to divide the landholdings... Colonel."

Kim's eyes widened, and he stood again to bow, this time so low that Ree thought he might fall over if he went any lower. Yes, a truly loyal servant among his colonels would ensure Ree's primacy, no matter where his other colonels' loyalties might lay in the future.

"You're welcome, little brother. And Kim? Find me the most beautiful American girls so that they can come live in luxury as my wives. I will take four to wed out of the ones you gather, so choose well."

Ree knew Kim would "cast the net wide" looking for possible wives, but Ree only wanted women of beauty and grace who came to him willingly. For food, security, and power, there would surely be some who came willingly. "I think maybe fifty to choose from should be enough. You have one month to gather them."

And the ones who didn't come willingly to him would be given to his subordinate officers, beautiful gifts from their Great Leader. Yes... 'Great Leader Ree' had a nice ring to it.

* * *

Work around Clanholme had slowed to a crawl that afternoon, in the wake of their difficult victory. Most of the necessary chores were done for the day, other than evening animal feeding and the milking of cows and goats after dinner, so it made this the perfect time for Cassy to gather the Clan together. The refugees and other visitors were invited as well, and many attended, standing like spectators in the back. Cassy wanted them to take accounts of this speech back to their home towns, together with word of the victory, which would spread quickly in any case.

This, Cassy mused, was the beginning of a legend—the Confederation's invincibility, luck, determination and sheer tenacity. The Clan's support for its allies, its courage under fire, its willingness to help other settlements despite losses, its aggressive program to save what refugees it can... The list just went on and on. And it would all look great for the Confederation and Clanholme.

Part of her wondered whether Grandma Mandy might be right when she said God had blessed the Clan because of the way it treated strangers and allies, and the way the homestead operated—as close to being "a good custodian of the earth" as it was possible to be on this side of Heaven, she had said. Well, sometimes she felt God in her life, and other times she was just as certain there was no such thing. She kept that to herself, of course, out of respect for her mom.

But enough musing. It was time to address her people, both Clan and Confederation allies. She walked up her patio's three outside steps, and once on the patio she turned around to face the crowd. There were hundreds there, which was a bit intimidating.

"Good morning, Confederation," she said, voice carrying over the din of hundreds of conversations. A few people cheered, and many clapped. She continued, "I know we're all exhausted. The Confederation and our new friends just fought the largest battle we've ever seen. Somehow, against all probability, we won. It was a close-fought battle, but in the end, the Confederation was the one still standing. You did that, people. But we didn't do it alone. Let us not forget the steep sacrifice paid by our newest Clan members, who fought alongside Manheim's sons and daughters without hesitation despite the odds. They have certainly earned a place at the Clan's table. Of the three hundred who volunteered to help at Manheim, only two hundred survived to eat breakfast with us as free Americans. Manheim paid a price just as high.

"And what of Liz Town? They fought against an enemy much larger than themselves and in so doing, they kept a vast number of Empire raiders from joining the battles for Clanholme or Manheim. And then, when Clanholme was in dire peril, far-away New America lent its might to our cause. Arriving trail-worn and exhausted, they nonetheless jumped in to help other Americans stay free. We stood together, and in doing so, we prevailed."

Cassy looked down at the ground, lowering her head, and said nothing for a moment, letting the tension mount as they waited for her to finish. When she heard the first hints of murmured conversations and restlessness from the crowd, she raised her voice even louder and said, "Today, our Confederation has proven both its strength and its worth. Though we lost many, their sacrifice has allowed the rest of us—standing strong, free and proud, together as one—to defeat the growing evil of the Empire. The enemies of peace and rebuilding have failed to enslave us. Our Confederation sent them back to their masters with their tails between their legs, and they left their best and strongest lying dead on our land to water our crops with their blood!"

With that, Cassy waved and then turned around as more cheers rose. She opened her front door and walked inside without looking back. Behind her, she heard ranking members of the various allies coming up to the patio, each to make their own brief speeches. Inside, Cassy saw Grandma Mandy, Michael, Jaz, and Choony and allowed herself to slump a little.

Michael raised his hand in greeting. His left arm was in a bandage and he wore a splint on his right ankle, though Sturm had assured them it was only a sprain. He said, "Poor Frank... He'll have to stay out there as the Clan's representative. I imagine they'll all chant until he, too, has to give a speech. Why do we need speeches when we all want nothing more than sleep and a snack?"

Of course, Cassy thought she knew the answer to that. "Speeches have the power to glue a community together—or tear it apart," she said. "We learned that when politicians used that power to destroy us during the last few years before the EMPs, all to stay on top, keep power, and feed their own greed."

Grandma Mandy clucked at Michael and added, "Speeches distribute *ideas* faster than word of mouth. Those ideas sort of 'program' a crowd to feel and believe a certain way. They can certainly immunize people against destructive ideas, which are often more appealing to angry people than messages of hope or love. Satan coats his poison in sugar."

Cassy took a deep breath, shoulders rising, and then let it out in one big gust as her shoulders fell again. "Of course you're right, Mom. I guess that's why I felt the need to give a little speech instead of entering a blissful coma in my comfy bed for the next decade." She smiled at her mom and was pleased to see her smile back. Good, she had taken it in the spirit Cassy intended instead of getting all prickly about it.

When no one said anything further, Cassy said, "I've been thinking of some sort of memorial for our fallen. Jaz and Choony's volunteers lost a full third of their numbers and all of us suffered terrible losses. I want to put something up at the battle site itself. Maybe an earthbag building. We could build it atop a single, mass burial site for all of our dead. Inside we can have etched clay tablets with quotes from the families of the fallen. What do you think?"

Michael nodded, even looking pretty darn enthusiastic. He said, "Maybe outside we could have a plaque to commemorate the battle but also remind people that those who are buried at the site came from all the Confederation allies, demonstrating the unity they had forged in life, and so on."

"Michael, that's brilliant. I was just thinking urns for the ones with family who insist on cremation. Most will probably want their fallen loved ones buried, to become an integral, unified part of the memorial. We can certainly encourage that."

"I'll make the rounds to the allied leadership and see if they'll let us bury their fallen with ours on that battlefield, then. At least the ones who died in the Battle of Clanholme during the Empire War."

Cassy was a bit surprised. The "Empire War" seemed a good title, short and memorable.

Mandy added, "Let's all pray the name never gets changed to be 'the First Empire War,' shall we?"

On that, Cassy definitely agreed with her mom. And the memorial would serve another important function, too—it would surely help cement the alliance, and it'd become part of the culture of the Confederation. People needed examples of heroes to identify with and emulate, demonstrations of honor, loyalty, and bravery so they could aspire to greatness, too.

But it also put the dot at the end of the sentence, as far as the Empire War was concerned, so that they could get a clean break from it. That was important, because life went on and there would always be more sentences in their history—she wanted them to be positive ones. The future was, for the first time, looking fairly bright. Sure, there were enemies still to fight or defend against, and other survivors to bring into the fold. But all in all, she felt hope again, and that was mighty nice. It had been a while.

Michael interrupted her thoughts. "So what's this idea you mentioned about Clan expansion?"

"Simple. We're the Clan. What if there were others? We found new enclaves, support them, train them in our ways. All these settlements, individually only bands, could be part of the Clan. The Taj Mahal Band, the Clanholme Band, and so on, just like Liz Town does it. All ultimately part of the Clan."

"Well," said Mandy, smiling at her daughter, "it's a solid way to build for the future. And thank God we'll actually have one, now."

As they chattered about brighter days ahead, a Clanner brought in lunch from the outdoor kitchen. Fresh salad, sandwiches, Clanholme's own apple cider... And not a drop of constant stew, thank goodness.

- 29 -

1800 HOURS - ZERO DAY +257

CHOONY SMILED AT the man serving evening chow as he ladled sautéed venison over rice onto his tray. He disliked the constant stew after half a year or more of eating little else, but venison wasn't his favorite either. He'd rather eat grains and vegetables, but getting visibly upset about that would accomplish nothing, except perhaps to make the server unhappy. So, like most other hardships in life, Choony accepted it for what it was and tried not to judge it. And now, with spring arrived, the constant stew had some fresh vegetables and herbs in it, improving it over the bland gruel it had been for most of the winter. The Clan had greatly expanded their cold frame gardening program, so there were more of the basic garden veggies than he'd have expected, given the time of year.

After grabbing a few slices of bread and a pat of butter—real, fresh butter!—he turned to face the massive Army-surplus pavilion the Clan used as a chow hall. The thought of going in there, seeing so many people, having to smile at his many friends and well-wishers... it was too much. He turned right instead, and headed toward the Jungle. It was a huge area full of raised planters, sunken planters, barrel planters, and self-selected ground cover. Its charm now lay in the fact that it was green again after a long and hungry winter. Bugs buzzed around within that maze, lizards scrambled about and birds flittered around as well. It was full of life, and that was just what he needed right now.

Choony followed the Jungle's internal maze, taking random turns, until he found himself at a spot hidden from the mass of humanity nearby. The raised bed had a large flat rock to one side that made a perfect seat, though its real purpose was to catch the sunshine and warm up. This extended the growing season for nearby planters. He settled down, got comfortable, and set down his tray. The hot stew still bubbled. It would be a few minutes before it was cool enough to eat. That gave him some time to think.

And Choony needed it. His inner balance was now far from harmonious. He had killed another human being.

He caught sight of someone else coming around the corner, through the Jungle's maze. Jaz. She wasn't carrying a tray, so she hadn't eaten yet. Choony felt a simultaneous thrill at the sight of her and disappointment that his solitude was being interrupted. He tried to focus on the former. "Hey, Jaz. Have you eaten yet?" Of course, he knew the answer to that, but wanted to find out why she hadn't.

Jaz smiled as she approached, then she sat down beside him on the large stone. "Just not hungry. I thought I'd come kick it with you—if that's alright with you, of course."

"Always." Choony would never turn her away, of course, but he sensed a tension in her bearing and thought perhaps she needed to talk, as much as he needed solitude. "You're welcome to join me. Want a bite of my stew?"

Jaz wrinkled her nose at his tray. She really did hate that stuff... "No thanks. I just, you know, wanted to talk." She looked over at him, frustration clear on her face. Choony turned to look her square in the eyes, giving her his undivided attention. Something was clearly bothering her.

"What did you want to talk about?" Choony asked.

Jaz looked down at the mulch that lay thick on the soil all through the Jungle. She kept silent for a long while, and Choony was content to let her speak when she decided to.

Finally, she said, "Choony, you haven't been the same since the battle. And not just a little off. You're really different." Her voice faded.

So, she had felt the change in him as well, though he hadn't wished to cast a pall over anyone else. She always could see into him. He looked away, uncomfortable, and focused on a bird circling above as it looked for some prey to eat. Birds killed. Wolves, too. All of nature, in fact, killed in defense or out of hunger. But they didn't have the spirit of a human, so how could they understand that killing was wrong? With no soul to darken, they had no reason not to kill when hungry or afraid. Moralizing was the burden of mankind, and in Choony's opinion, it was too high a price to pay for intelligence and self-awareness. He was aware that Jaz was waiting for something, but his mind was too jumbled to think his way through it. Or maybe it was simpler than that.

"Jaz, do you hate me for killing that man?" He kept his face carefully neutral.

"What? Don't be silly. How could I hate you? I'm grateful."

Choony sensed there was more to it than that, however, and decided this would be their moment of truth. He couldn't put it off any longer—it was too disruptive of his Chi, his harmony, to let it rest there. "You're grateful. But?"

He cringed, afraid of her answer. She would lie or she'd tell him the truth. Either way, he was afraid her answer would destroy him.

After a pause, she replied. "Choony... In your heart of hearts, will you ever forgive me for being the reason you took someone's life? Did I survive that battle only to lose you?" She still looked away, now worrying at her lower lip with her teeth. She had tensed, her shoulders hunching forward, a picture of torment and misery. And the worst part for him was that he couldn't blame her for wondering that.

"You know that my philosophy carries the weight of religion in it. Killing another stains one's soul. No amount of chanting Amitabha Buddha's name will impart enough blessing to wash that stain away. I won't see the Pure Land, and must again suffer the pain of birth, the eight torments, and the suffering of death. Perhaps my Karma will achieve the Pure Land on that next cycle, but it won't be this me who benefits."

Jaz peered into Choony's eyes for a long, quiet moment. Her eyebrows made it a sad look. Or anxious, perhaps. Then she added, "Choony, do you regret your choice?"

It was as though a heavy weight had struck him in the gut. How could she think that? Well, perhaps it was a reasonable question. How could she know his thoughts unless he told them to her? "No, of course not. Jaz, I made a choice, and I don't regret it. How could I have chosen to watch him kill you? It has nothing to do with the fact that regrets accomplish nothing but to cause needless pain and suffering. He forced me to choose and I surprised myself at how quickly that decision came to me. I do wish the choice hadn't been put on me, but I regret only that we were forced to fight this war. I would make the same decision again, with no more hesitation than last time."

Jaz smiled, bright as sunshine, and she darted forward to wrap her arms around Choony, almost knocking him over. She laughed, and it was contagious—Choony found himself laughing too, even while trying to keep his precarious physical balance. He failed, and both toppled over, Jaz on top of him still laughing.

Choony grinned at her open joy, and then realized the somewhat compromising position they were in. His eyes locked with hers by reflex, mind frozen with the wonder of what she would do.

Jaz, too, froze for a moment, and her cheeks flushed a bit, her skin showing a slight tint that in a lighter-skinned person would have been a bright, self-conscious pink. Then without warning, Jaz closed her eyes and leaned in until her tender lips touched his. At first he was stunned but then, as he unwound, he closed his eyes and felt her passion stream through him as he became lost in the kiss. It was everything he'd imagined, and more. A revelation.

* * *

The living room was in more disarray than Carl would have liked, with maps and papers everywhere. Battle maps, strategic maps, handwritten orders, proclamations. All the residue of a new Band leader consolidating power, and doing it in time of war no less.

On the couch, Mary Ann sat with her feet up on the overcrowded coffee table, leaning back with hands behind her head. "Thanks for taking time to meet with me, Carl. I know you're busy."

Carl nodded as he collated the pages of some new general orders from the Speaker to the Bands—a task Carl, as her right-hand man, got saddled with—and replied, "Of course. I appreciate you coming here. Funny thing, now that I have people to do just about everything I used to do by myself, I have less free time than ever before. Part of me misses my time in exile."

Mary Ann smiled wryly. "You needn't explain that to me. Leading a Band—or a town, in my case—is a 24/7 thing in the best of times. Add a war to that..."

"How are the Sewer Rats getting along?" Carl asked. There was a lot more he wished to ask, but preferred to play those cards close to his vest.

"You mean, why hasn't Sunshine come by to see you in your new pad?" Mary Ann was a perceptive person, it seemed. Her grin matched her teasing tone.

Carl huffed. Oh brother, why even try? "Fine, yeah. Keep it to yourself, please. I've found myself getting rather attached to Sunshine. We've always flirted a bit, but when we were fighting on the wall, I found myself as worried about her as anything else. She's rough around the edges, but she's had to be to survive so long without a settlement to protect her... Hell, on her it just looks honest, not crude."

"My lips are sealed. Hers aren't, though. My informants tell me she speaks of you often, and seems as excited about your release from exile and your promotion as she is about her people being accepted as a Band, with all those protections and comforts."

Carl felt his cheeks grow warm and his pulse quicken. He told himself he was being silly. He was a grown man, not a school kid. But he couldn't help feeling excited to hear that. "I've been waiting for her to come by, but haven't heard a word from her."

"Jeez, Carl. It's only been a day. She's looking for the best vacant part of Liz Town to settle in. There are strategic, political, and logistical considerations, and she's responsible for hundreds of people."

Carl nodded. "Yeah, I guess you're right."

"Hell, her Band was by far the smallest until yesterday, now with all the little knots of wildlands survivors that she knew joining her. She's already bigger than Diamondback."

"That would make those bastards the smallest Band again," Carl said.

"Yes, I realized that." Mary Ann scratched at the scabbed-over cut on her forehead, a memento of the siege even if it wasn't a terribly impressive wound. "Like the Sewer Rats, all of us in Liz Town have some new things to think about. The future is coming whether we're prepared or not."

Carl put together the last of the handwritten copies of various orders from the Speaker to this Band or that, and set the stacks aside. He took a deep breath, snapping out of the half-daze he had been in from the monotonous task. "I wish I didn't have to be the one to put all these stacks together for you. No offense," he said.

Mary Ann shrugged and nodded. "Yeah. It won't be long, though. Soon I'll have an assistant with the right security clearance to handle this and you can go back to doing more important stuff like advising me. We have much to consider, you know."

"Well, spring planting is going well," Carl said. "At first, some of Cassy's methods were a bit jarring and didn't make much sense to a traditional small farmer, but the classes are helping a lot and our people are eager to learn more."

"I can read status reports too, Carl." Mary Ann took her hands from behind her head, her feet from off the table to set them on the floor, and leaned forward, her elbows on her knees. "I meant rearmament, and the whole ugly political situation."

Carl stopped messing with papers. He really didn't want to have this talk but, as the right hand of the Speaker, it was his job. It also helped the Timber Wolves immensely to know what was coming before it actually happened. "Rearmament. Politics." He repeated her words and waited for Mary Ann to elaborate. He had an inkling of what was coming, from their prior conversations in passing.

"Yeah. We're running low on ammo after that monster battle. And the region's politics are unstable. The future isn't written yet, nor is our role in that future clear yet."

Carl frowned, and shook his head. She was right, of course, that they'd need more ammo soon. "We have some plans in place for ammo. First, we are already setting up reloading stations. Components are limited, though. Primer and so on. But there's a National Guard station within striking distance. I intend to raid the hell out of it."

"Timber Wolves, or Liz Town?"

It was a pointed question, and a loaded one at that. "Well, we'd obviously pay our scavenge tax. And what we don't need ourselves out of our plunder, we'll trade out honestly, first to other Lizzies, then to the Confed, and lastly to the Falconry."

Mary Ann nodded, satisfied. "Yes, it has proven handy having a neutral trading hub nearby. We're getting very good prices on finished goods from that 'vader general's warehouses. Not Ree—that other one, in northern Pennsylvania."

"We aren't at war with the Falconry, so why not trade for what we need?" Carl was pragmatic. The threat of war was far away, and not likely to press into Confed turf again after the 'vader losses the one time they had tried. "The refugees sitting on the armory don't even know it's there, so I expect to get in and out without violence, if we're lucky. If not? They aren't Confederation, so it doesn't really matter."

"You've become hard, Carl."

"Practical. There are still a lot more people than resources, and some of them will want what we have. We—the whole Confederation—must be able to protect ourselves. Better that we get the armory than someone else. But what of politics? That situation seems pretty self-explanatory. Not all that unstable, at least not locally."

Mary Ann smiled wanly. "Self-explanatory? Perhaps. Certainly within the Confederation, I'm happy with our situation. Only the Clan ranks higher than us now, since Ephrata wasn't much involved in the Empire War."

"What else is there, then? Seems like we're set. Future looks good. A solid foundation for our children's children and so on."

"Carl, you don't think far enough ahead. That's not healthy for a Band leader, especially not for the largest Band in Liz Town. The King Under the Mountain is still out there, still dreaming of taking over the world, or at least the corpse of the United States. General Houle in Colorado Springs isn't going to give up just because we demolished their puppet, the Midwest Republic. And he's still posing as a loyal American, which has fooled some people before and will again if he pushes the lie. The pols were using that strategy even before the EMPs."

"When Houle comes, it's simple. We resist. We fight. We hold what's ours, whatever it takes."

Mary Ann let out a sigh. "It's that simple and that complicated, at the same time. He's in NORAD, safe and sound. He can keep throwing challenges our way at his convenience. If he wins one out of ten of those challenges, he still wins the game. We have to win every challenge or we lose."

Carl frowned, his eyebrows scrunching up together.

Mary Ann continued, "Sorry, but we have to look at that. The only long term solutions I see are to either neutralize Houle... or join him."

"And be a slave? Mary Ann, we will *never* join Houle. Timber Wolves will resist any such plan if it is made, and we'll burn the joint down around our ears rather than let that bastard take over."

Mary Ann laughed, then, which was pretty confusing. It was a good-natured laugh, sounding relieved. The tension had broken, it seemed. She said, "Good! The mighty tiger baring its claws. But I agree, we will never join Houle. But there will be those who want to, because he still has a veneer of legitimacy, though we both know how flimsy his claims are. He's not even a real General now, just a slaver and a warlord."

Carl felt the heat flow out of him, his heartbeat beginning to slow. Thank goodness.

"But I have a solution," Mary Ann continued. "We take the fight to him. He can't fight us here if we're fighting him there."

Carl frowned. "Sounds um... risky. And that's not really true—ask Hannibal of Carthage. Or the enemy I assume brought a nuke into the U.S. to launch the first EMP." He paused. "Or ask the Soviets, who broke their own back trying to conquer Afghanistan. And a Chinese officer sent to hold onto Tibet was being punished, not rewarded. Some places are simply impossible to invade successfully, and there are more like it. We should make ourselves into one of those places, not go out and invade others."

"Hannibal didn't go for the kill, didn't use politics to his advantage. We won't make that mistake," Mary Ann declared. "We can take that bastard down."

"I won't hesitate to go for the kill when the time comes," Carl replied, making his own declaration, "especially if we can find a way to decimate them without a face-to-face battle."

"You'd kill the women and children inside NORAD just to avoid a fight?" Mary Ann raised her eyebrows, but her gaze was direct and unwavering. He wasn't sure of the answer she was looking for, but he wouldn't have lied even if he knew she wouldn't like it.

"Yes. I'd kill them all to end that threat. They've proven they are our enemies. America's enemies. I hope I don't have to, believe me, but if the chance came to end this? Yes, I would."

"Good. I'll fill you in later. For now, just know that we have to solidify and expand the Confederation. We have to strengthen the alliance with New America or maybe formally join, and we need to find new allies. Maybe even the Empire itself, if we get a chance to make a deal with a leader we could trust without holding a knife to his throat."

"You're thinking of the intelligence reports we got from questioning Empire survivors and defectors." It was a statement. Carl already knew the answer.

"Yes, and there were many. We've discovered that northern Michigan kicked the Empire's ass like we did. So did some group west of the Empire, though details are more sketchy there. If we can get the Empire to join the Confederation, as partners or as a member nation under New America's authority, then we can put the pressure on the Mountain that we need. Sooner or later we'll spot a chance to kill them all, and then it'll be over. We have to find out what that is when the time comes, but that's for the future. Right now we have to think about spring planting."

Carl nodded. "Nice dreams. For now, for tomorrow, for this week, the future looks pretty bright. Maybe I'll schedule an appointment with the Sewer Rats' Alpha. See what she thinks."

Mary Ann's eyes glinted mischievously. "Maybe you should. After all, you Alphas have to stay in touch. Besides, rank has its privileges..."

* * *

Cassy sat in her recliner, which had been pushed back practically into her small kitchen to make room for everyone. Her house was tiny, and fitting the whole Council in it was always a hassle. Choony had volunteered to act as server rather than have more people bumping elbows in her tiny kitchen, and he handed her a glass of fine, sparkling hard apple cider. It had aged well and tasted like nothing she had ever had before.

"Everyone set?" she asked, and the others nodded. Cassy moved her wireless mouse and the laptop, connected by HDMI cable to a projector, threw the image of her desktop onto the bare wall for all to see. She clicked the button to call Taggart.

Eagan answered, and smiled. Cassy really liked that guy —insubordinate and stubborn, but good-hearted and extremely loyal, all qualities Cassy admired. He wore a Sergeant Major's insignia lately, according to Michael, but she had noticed Taggart went back and forth between calling him Private and Sergeant Major. Or 'shitbird,' when he forgot to turn off the call before barking at his sidekick-slash-subordinate.

A few seconds later, Taggart came into view and sat down facing his laptop, the one they had managed to send him. "Good evening, Chancellor," he said to Cassy, using her official Confederation title rather than calling her his Secretary of Agriculture. That little cue let her know the nature of tonight's conference call. "I was pleased to learn of the timely arrival of my reinforcements."

"Yes, Mr. President," Cassy replied, using the title he officially wore and hated to no end. The game amused them both. "They arrived at a key moment, and turned the tide rather spectacularly. We had many losses before they arrived, but we held out. Just long enough, as it turns out."

"Excellent. So, Cassy, I thought I'd share my own bit of happy news. General Ree, who controlled New York City, New Jersey, and southeast Pennsylvania, has been defeated as well. He still has the City and much of New Jersey, but he's hemmed in. I have to guard against raids and the like, but in terms of offensive capacity, he's been rendered ineffective."

"You were in New Jersey. And now?"

"Now we're in northern Jersey. His chunk of the state is where we had started implementing your permaculture program, so we're back to square one here, but it will go much faster this second time around, I think. So what's the status of the Midwest Republic threat?"

Cassy glanced to Michael, who stepped into view. "If I may, Mr. President, we're happy to report that their offensive capacity is greatly reduced. Our rough estimate is that they must have sent about a quarter of their entire force, up to as high as one half. The remaining enemy strength must only be adequate to hold on to what they already have, given the growing threats to their northern and western borders. The few details we have on those threats were in the briefings we've sent."

"Yes, thank you, General," Taggart replied. He had taken to calling Michael that even before the Empire War, given that he was ultimately in charge of all Confederation forces. "Good, so that takes pressure off of all of you, too."

"Yes, sir."

"Hooah. For the remainder of spring," Taggart said, "my plan is to clear a path for trade between the Confederation and New America." Cassy knew he disliked that name too, but New America was what everyone seemed to want to call it, so he had decided to run with it. "We are also reaching out to other nearby survivor groups and trying to integrate them into New America."

Cassy nodded. It only made sense, now that they had all seemed to weather the storm of chaos more or less intact. "We're doing likewise. Expanding both the Clan and the Confederation to the east and south. West is blocked by Hershey, and we can't go much further north without hitting the Pennsylvania invader cantonment. We're also scrambling to find more ammunition."

Taggart pursed his lips, paused a moment, then said, "My advice is to go in and systematically loot Lancaster. It was gassed, and so there must be a ton of civilian weapons and ammunition in there. Also, I am sending Ethan my intel report on a supply depot within a reasonable distance of you guys, so you can re-arm and resupply. It was a supply point for FEMA and it isn't on any maps, so other than squatters you shouldn't have much to deal with in terms of opposition."

Cassy blew out through pursed lips, relieved. "Impressive. And good timing. We burned through ninety percent of our ammunition during the Empire War."

"Yes, well. You'll need to stock up for the next war, then."

Cassy was suddenly paying much closer attention to Taggart, to his facial features, the inflection of his voice. "Excuse me, next war?"

"That's affirmative. General Houle controls Colorado and a whole lot more. We don't know the extent of his holdings, but we do know he can't expand westward—the whole of the southwest U.S. must certainly be depopulated by now. It's a vast desert, and only had so many people in it because it was possible to ship in apples from Washington, artichokes from California, oranges from Florida. And the water tables hadn't been drained yet for cities and golf courses and lawns."

"Oh. Yes. Without infrastructure, they didn't have the food resources to survive. And all that piped-in water they used." She frowned, reflecting on what must certainly have been grim reality in the deserts states after the EMPs hit. "If they didn't die in the first weeks from dehydration, they probably starved when the food ran out." Cassy hadn't really thought about much beyond the Clan and the Confederation for quite a while. Considering all those deaths... it was sobering.

Taggart said, "Yes. The net effect now is that Houle must

expand east and north, but I doubt he could do much going north. Utah apparently split into Mormon and non-Mormon areas, and they fight each other more than anyone else. The only thing that unifies them is to resist outsiders. And, from what I understand, they don't much like Houle."

"The land up there isn't rich enough land to bother fighting over," Cassy commented.

Michael added, "And beyond Utah there's Montana, Idaho and Eastern Washington. An old song called 'em 'nothing but a reason to keep riding.' And plus, that whole region was half-paramilitary even before the EMPs. And they know the country."

Cassy nodded. "Yes, he'd probably figure we'd be an easier prize to take."

Taggart said, "We all know that the eastern state ranchers and survivalists took over and have stood against the invasion force occupying western Washington the way you just did in Pennsylvania. Before the war, the preppers called everything from Eastern Washington through Montana 'the Redoubt.' Houle will want their resources, but he won't want that fight."

"He won't want to weaken the Redoubt anyway, at least not to the point where the invaders can break through and hold the passes," Cassy added, nodding as she grasped some of the implications. "They're his buffer against the invaders and desperate people along the coast."

Ethan said, "Northeast, Houle has his Empire lackeys, so he expanded southeast, but those little settlements are more like colonies than conquests."

The corner of Taggart's lips turned up. "It's a strategy I'm planning to use myself, going down the East Coast through the Carolinas. Provide protection, but make them pay to cover costs. Houle demands tribute for leaving them alone, like the Romans did. I don't hold with that kind of extortion.

The towns we protect from raiders and such can pay their own way, though, with food or volunteers or whatever, kind of how your Confederation handles it. Protection and affiliation as a trade good."

He paused to look over his shoulder and nodded at someone, then held up a finger in the universal *give me a minute* sign before turning back. "But all that's for next year at the earliest. For now, I believe we'll be set before winter. Recruits are pouring in faster than we can arm and integrate them, so I need something to do with them anyway. They're prepping small farms using your permaculture methods, and it's going well."

Cassy smiled. "Mr. President, I must say, your problems are the right kind to have."

Taggart chuckled, nodding. "I get your point. So what are your 'right problems' these days?" Behind him, Cassy saw Eagan briefly throw up "bunny ears" behind Taggart's head, and she resisted the urge to laugh. Behind her, she heard Joe Ellings *snrrk*, stifling his own laughter.

Cassy said, "Oh, wow, that list is endless. So much land to plant, so many seeds to spread around. I have more mulch than I know what to do with—I may have to let local independents come get wagonfuls in return for a live bullet, unless I want tons of unused woody compost. And I'm only one person, Taggart—I don't have enough hours in the day to officiate for everyone who wants me to do their wedding this spring. It's like a wedding flu is sweeping through the Confederation. When the Empire left, I think they all went into heat."

Taggart laughed, his eyes sparkling. He rarely showed it, but Cassy long ago realized he had a wicked-sharp sense of humor. "So, just like me, your spring and summer is booked up. So much for that trip to Disney World."

Cassy took a deep breath and nodded, feeling satisfied

and happy. Sure there would be more problems to deal with in the future, but here and now, for today at least, her problems were the everyday ones. The ones that let her know she was alive and that there was a future for her and her family.

"Maybe I'll meet up with you in Orlando next year, then," Cassy told Taggart. "There's always next year."

"It's a deal," Taggart replied. "Next year, Orlando."

# # #

To be continued in
EMP Retaliation (Dark New World, Book 6)

About the authors:

JJ Holden lives in a small cabin in the middle of nowhere. He spends his days studying the past, enjoying the present, and pondering the future.

Henry Gene Foster resides far away from the general population, waiting for the day his prepper skills will prove invaluable. In the meantime, he focuses on helping others discover that history does indeed repeat itself and that it's never too soon to prepare for the worst.

For updates, new release notifications, and more, please visit:

www.jjholdenbooks.com

Made in the USA
San Bernardino, CA
17 April 2019